THE LAST WARRIOR

SHIFTERS UNBOUND BOOK 13

JENNIFER ASHLEY

JA / AG PUBLISHING

CHAPTER ONE

*C*an't *a guy just drink a beer in peace?*

Ben took a determined sip, pretending to ignore the seven men who'd gathered around him in the bar on the outskirts of New Orleans, a place where he'd always been able to blend in and have a quiet drink. Not tonight, it looked like.

The men who'd decided to be a pain in his ass were human, but their body language screamed as loudly as any Shifter's that they were protecting their territory.

Ben had settled himself on a barstool at the far end of the counter, a long way from anyone. He'd returned to New Orleans to check on the haunted house and take a load off for ten minutes before he went back to work. Unfortunately, while he'd been in Faerie these last however many months, this bar had been taken over by a group of buttholes.

The leader, a guy with a beer belly, stubbly whiskers, and flyaway brown hair, leaned his elbow near Ben's arm. "We don't like your kind in here."

Such an original opening. Ben guessed that when the man said *your kind*, he didn't mean *goblin*.

"Short people?" Ben offered. In his human form, he stood a

few inches below the average human male, which meant a lot less than Shifters. And weren't Shifters smug about that?

The man frowned. "You know what I mean."

Ben could have toyed with him, asking, *Do I? Do you?* but he didn't have the patience tonight.

"Listen, boys." Ben carefully set down his bottle. "I'm not here for trouble. I'm just taking a break. My boss—" *A badass* dokk alfar *who'd make you guys wet your pants when he looked at you*— "has me working my rear off"—*recreating a magic iron doohickey that will keep* hoch alfar *from invading whenever they feel itchy*—"a long way from home—" *in the dank lands of Faerie.* "This is the first night out I've had in months."

"Not our problem," the leader said. "Go drink somewhere else."

"Delighted to." Ben dropped another five on the bar for a tip and slid off the stool.

As he'd suspected, these ignoramuses had no intention of letting him leave that easily. They were half-drunk, belligerent, bored, and ready for any scrap they could find.

Ben hid a sigh. Really, he'd returned to this world only to find a relaxing beer and then go to bed. No Shifter insurgents, no *dokk* alfar breathing down his neck to hurry it up with the magic already, no Fae lords being their arrogant selves, no Dylan Morrissey on his phone saying, "Ben, I need you to ..."

A little peace and quiet with a sentient house keeping everyone away by being terrifying. That was all Ben wanted. He'd also returned to reassure the house that he was all right and hadn't abandoned it. It was always good to be kind to an abode that could eat you.

"How about we take this outside?" Ben suggested. If tables and chairs got broken the manager might add it to Ben's tab.

"Sure thing." Leader smiled. He had the straight, white teeth everyone in this country seemed to have, whether they were corporate execs or biker dudes.

Ben made for the door, and the men herded him along like wolves circling their prey.

Outside, the warmth of the September night was pleasant after the chill of Faerie. Ben never remembered it being so stupidly cold in Faerie, but after a thousand years in the human world, it was the little things that he'd forgotten.

The parking lot was deserted this late, and several of the lot's lights were out, making the place inky dark. The guys flanking Ben moved him beyond the floodlights at the door and into deep shadows.

Ben could cast a glam on them, distract them while he slipped away, but while a glam rendered him almost invisible to human eyes, it didn't render him intangible. He'd have to push past the wall of guys surrounding him, and once they focused on him, they'd see him. Better to face them down and be done with it.

"Are you sure you want to do this?" Ben asked. "How about I buy you whatever you're drinking, and we call it a night?"

"Not taking shit from you." A man with sandy-blond hair glowered at him.

Ben heaved a sigh. "All right. I'll make it quick."

They had no idea. The men stared at him, slightly puzzled, then they went for him.

Ben feinted back, encouraging the pack to attack him en masse, then he came out of his half-crouch and spun like a whirlwind, roundhouse kicks catching three of his attackers in the head.

He felt the beast he truly was coming out, the beast he held tightly inside because he had no choice. Ben's inner self wasn't a cute furry animal like a Shifter, but an ancient warrior who'd been forced into exile in this crazy human world.

His body thickened and grew, and his hands became powerful things as his true form struggled to emerge.

Ben reminded himself that these assholes weren't *hoch alfar* coming to massacre his family, just lazy booze-heads looking for something to do on a Saturday night.

He stopped himself from becoming a destructive force of nature, only changing form far enough for what he needed. Ben kicked and punched, pummeled and whirled, the men's drunkenness and the darkness not letting them see exactly what they battled.

Three went down, groaning, but the other four, not understanding their odds, wouldn't give up.

Ben didn't wait for them to regroup but simply launched into them. The legs of one went out from under him at the same time another doubled over with an *oof!* as Ben slammed a heavy fist to his abdomen.

Chime.

The cell phone-like sound distracted the remaining two men for a second, but only a second. One of them drew a knife.

Chime!

"Is that you or me?" Ben resettled into his human guise. "Maybe you should get that."

The men hesitated, glancing at each other. Ben lunged at them, ripping the knife from the first one's hand and throwing it across the parking lot. Then he knocked the two men together with inhuman strength. They fell, insensible, to the uneven pavement.

CHIME!

"All right, all right." Ben jammed his hand into his pocket and pulled out not a cell phone but a small round crystal about an inch in diameter. Its white glow heated his fingers, its insistent peal ringing in his ears.

"What?" he yelled into it.

"Ben, dear, I need you." The faint but musical tones of a woman called Lady Aisling came to him across the void from Faerie. The scary woman had powerful enough magic to do that. "Now, please."

She said *please*, but she meant the *now* part. No arguments.

Ben glanced at the seven moaning men at his feet, none about to rise anytime soon.

"Yeah, I guess I'm done here. I'll be there as soon as I can."

"See that you do. It is very important."

Which meant, *Get your ass back to Faerie in the next five minutes or deal with me.* The men Ben had just fought wouldn't stand a chance against Lady Aisling, who could wipe them out with her pinky. Ben stood in awe of her, admired and respected her, but damn, the woman could frighten a hundred years out of a goblin.

Ben walked to the motorcycle he'd left near the building, mounted, and started it. The men were barely twitching, so he thumbed 9-1-1 on his cell phone and sent first responders to them before he strapped on his helmet and rode out of the parking lot.

He sped the few miles to the haunted house, patted its wall as he went inside, and then had to talk to it for thirty minutes before it finally opened the way to Faerie for him.

Ben went through, leaving the house to creak in his wake, emitting a sound suspiciously like a mournful sigh.

———

"I don't think you understand." Rhianne mac Aodha shook the chains that stretched from her wrists above her head to the stone wall. "*No* means *no*. And ladies don't *really* like being locked up in dungeons."

She spoke the words in the language of the *hoch alfar* so that Walther le Madhug, the idiot who'd put her down here, would understand. He'd never bothered to learn Rhianne's language, that of the Tuil Erdannan, but for some reason expected Rhianne to marry him.

When Rhianne had politely declined, Walther had

signaled his thugs to grab her and drag her to his castle in the middle of ice-cold nowhere, locking her in this cell until she changed her answer.

"I shall count to three ..."

Silence. Darkness. Walther wasn't listening. He hadn't bothered to put guards on the cell door, which wasn't even a door, but a grating in the low ceiling she sat beneath.

"One ..."

This always worked so well for her mother. When Lady Aisling started the count, the faint of heart fell all over themselves to do whatever she wanted.

"Two ..."

The silence and darkness unnerved Rhianne more than she wanted to admit. She had magic, not anywhere near what her mother had, but enough to conjure a pinpoint of light to keep her company. She'd extinguished it after about two seconds because the filth of the grisly dungeon, not to mention the skeletal remains chained up opposite her, had been truly horrifying.

"*Three.* All right, I warned you."

No response.

Rhianne growled in exasperation. This was going to hurt, but she couldn't stay in this dungeon any longer. She had things to do, papers to write, celestial charts to draw.

She closed her eyes—not that it wasn't already pitch dark—and honed her concentration on a spot about a foot in front of her head. A glow began within her, giving her a modicum of comfort. Sometimes the glow didn't appear when she called for it, which meant she needed to recharge, preferably in her mountain observatory or taking walks along cliff paths above the sea, which she'd been doing when Walther and his men had captured her.

The chains needed to go first. Rhianne's arms had been pinned over her head, just enough to make them ache. That soreness would gradually grow into deep pain, which had been Walther's plan, the prick.

Rhianne whispered a word of power, infusing it with all her strength. The cold metal of the chains warmed, as though touched by sunshine. Then they became hotter, the cuffs around her wrists heating with them.

Rhianne gritted her teeth, bearing the pain the best she could. Shutting down her power because it hurt would leave her sitting here like a lump, still bound, when Walther finally came to fetch and then seduce her.

Yuck. He'd send a lackey to fetch her, because Walther wouldn't soil his boots in this place. Rhianne wondered if he'd have the lackey do the seducing too. She wouldn't put it past him.

The metal began to sear, and Rhianne sucked in a sharp breath. The chains had been spelled—Walther wasn't foolish enough to put anyone from Faerie down here without magic infusing the bonds—but they were ordinary *hoch alfar* spells. To wield against a Tuil Erdannan, one needed much stronger stuff, which Walther did not have.

Or did he? That thought had bothered Rhianne since she'd woken up here. Walther's men shouldn't have been able to capture her at all. Not with even the small amount of magic Rhianne had inside her, which should have bested *hoch alfar* magic any day.

Tears wet Rhianne's cheeks as the metal scorched her skin. The cuffs became hotter and hotter, as though she plunged her wrists into fire. She had to stop—she couldn't take it anymore.

Just as Rhianne opened her mouth to shut off the magic, the chains disintegrated in a flash of fire, and her cuffs fell away.

In relief, Rhianne rolled to her hands and knees, her aching arms and burned wrists bringing a groan. The stone beneath her was damp, even squishy. She didn't want to think about what she knelt in, which motivated her to climb to her feet.

The cell's absurdly low ceiling ensured she couldn't stand all the way up. The grate, the only entrance, loomed above her, designed to make it easier for guards to drop in food and water, or whatever noxious substance they wished, without having to enter the cell.

Rhianne examined the lock above her. She'd have to open it with a lock pick because her word of power had been spent on the chains and had to renew itself. Walther's guards had taken everything from her but her clothes, including the pins that held up her long hair, which now dragged in the filth. She had the feeling these locks wouldn't be that easy to pick anyway.

She put her hands on the lock, closed her eyes, and tried to call up her fleeting magic.

Boom!

The walls shuddered. What the hell? A shower of rubble rained down on Rhianne, and she coughed.

Brilliant light suddenly filled the tunnel above her, and another *boom* sounded. The light cut out immediately, but Rhianne's pulse leapt in hope and excitement. Had her mother found her? Walther would pay dearly if so. Rhianne hoped she could watch.

"Hey!" she shouted. "I'm down here!" Rhianne yelled in her own language, then switched to *hoch alfar*, then, more shakily, to a human language. Who knew what rescuer her mother would send?

The shouts of *hoch alfar* filled the distance. Guards bellowed orders, cursing at each other, the words *who the hell let them in?* streaming down to her.

The next flash showed a pair of giant hands gripping the grate of her cell, hands belonging to a bizarre-shaped creature of impossible size. Rhianne cried out, then pitch darkness made the creature invisible.

A screeching sound burned her ears as the grate tore away. More rubble poured down, and Rhianne threw up her arms to protect her face from the cutting stones.

Another flash burned its way past her closed eyes as Rhianne was hauled upward by a pair of large and immensely strong hands.

Whatever pulled her out was massive, its strength unreal, but it set Rhianne gently on her feet, the grip easing away.

One more flash of light. Rhianne gingerly opened her eyes, expecting to find a colossus hunching over her.

Instead, she saw a man about her own height with dark skin and hair and the blackest eyes she'd ever seen. They sucked her in, those eyes, and that in only one instant of dazzling light.

The light vanished, and the man gripped her hand.

"Hey there," a rumbling voice said in perfect Tuil Erdannan. "I'm Ben. I'm here to rescue you."

CHAPTER TWO

B en couldn't see much of his rescuee in the dark, but her hand in his was soft and sweetly warm. And strong. She clung to him without squeamishness.

Another flash from where Cian was enjoying himself blowing up pieces of castle showed Ben a mass of very red hair and a chiseled face that wasn't like Lady Aisling's at all. The face was grimy and bloody, as were the young woman's loose trousers and shirt, which made Ben's fury boil.

Then blackness. Their only connection was the firm clasp of their hands.

The ceilings on the dungeon level were low, built to stymie the tall *hoch alfar* and *dokk alfar,* but they were perfect for Ben's height. His lady's too. Rhianne mac Aodha appeared to be only an inch, if that, taller than Ben. Unusual for a Tuil Erdannan, but Ben wasn't complaining.

His night-sight took them unerringly to the stairs at the end of the corridor. The door that had barricaded it leaned raggedly against a wall, torn from its bronze hinges. Ben had been too impatient to pick the lock.

Ben started up a flight of stairs, pulling Rhianne behind

him. Flashes and rumbles sounded from above, the walls shaking in a manner that alarmed him.

"What *is* that?" Rhianne asked in Tuil Erdannan, probably figuring Ben was fluent in it.

Ben wasn't. He'd learned a little during his sojourn in Faerie so he could speak to Lady Aisling when needed. Not that Lady Aisling didn't know many other languages, including several human ones. Today when she'd met Ben at an ancient sundial in the woods and marched him to her house, she'd told him his task in perfect English.

My daughter's been taken by that wretched Walther le Madhug, she'd said in rage, but Ben had felt her great fear behind the anger. *He's a high lord among the* hoch alfar *and far too full of himself, but he has grown dangerous. He wants to force Rhianne into marriage, believing it will help his bid to become emperor. Ha! You are to rescue her and then keep her safe for me.*

Sure, your ladyship, Ben had thought. Easy-peasy.

Ben said to Rhianne now in careful Tuil Erdannan, "Don't speak your language much."

"*Parles français?*" Rhianne went off into a string of French, until Ben squeezed her hand.

"English?" he suggested. "Or one of twenty Native American languages? Some don't exist anymore. Up to you."

"I don't know English as well as French." Rhianne answered in English without a falter. "Mother goes to Paris so often that she likes to speak French."

"Well, it's that or *hoch alfar*, and I'm not sullying my mouth with that." Ben gummed at his tongue, reflecting he was seriously thirsty. He hadn't been able to finish his beer. "Since I'm thinking you don't know my language, English it will have to be."

"Agreed," Rhianne said.

Another flash rolled down from above, and the entire castle

shuddered, dust showering them. Over the loud rumbles came the sound of maniacal laughter.

"That's Cian," Ben explained. Cian could dig his fingers straight into walls, handy for carving niches for incendiaries. "I hope he leaves enough of the castle standing for us to escape."

"I hope the entire place explodes into dust," Rhianne growled. "We should run."

"Word." Ben leapt up the last step of the staircase from the dungeon, Rhianne directly behind him.

Light filmed the corridor on the next level, courtesy of the holes Cian had blasted in the walls, plus the glowing stones the *hoch alfar* used so they wouldn't stumble in the dark and bruise their little toesies.

The place was a maze, but Ben had marked the walls as he'd made his way to the cells below. Of course, when they reached the door through which he'd entered the castle, rubble blocked it. Cian was having too much fun.

"What's he using?" Rhianne asked, sounding merely curious. "I didn't think *dokk alfar* had that kind of magic."

"He doesn't. He has explosives." Ben scanned the corridor and chose a side hall, hoping it would take them to another exit. "How do you know he's *dokk alfar*?"

"You said his name is Cian. That's a *dokk alfar* name."

"Fair enough." Ben pulled Rhianne around another corner to an even darker corridor.

"Do you know the way out?" Rhianne asked.

"When I came in, yes I did. Now, no."

"I don't know the way either. I wasn't awake for most of the journey."

"Nice way to woo a girl."

Rhianne's laughter was shaky but held a hint of richness. "That's what I said."

"This way, I think. Or ... Okay, maybe not."

Three *hoch alfar* stopped abruptly in front of them.

They obviously hadn't expected to see Ben and Rhianne, because they hesitated a hair too long before they shouted and attacked. Ben was already engaged in the fight by the time they sorted themselves out.

Hoch alfar were much harder to brawl with than drunk guys in a Louisiana roadhouse. Fae had nasty pointed weapons for one thing, usually loaded with spells, plus these guards were trained from childhood to do battle.

Ben wasn't any kind of *alfar*, which worked to his advantage. The *hoch alfar* were honed fighters who occasionally faced *dokk alfar* but mostly they battled other *hoch alfar* from rival clans. These guards didn't know what to do with a pissed-off goblin who hated them on principle.

Ben's fight with the barflies had been a warmup. This was the real thing. He kicked and spun, punched and jabbed, dodging knives headed for his gut, breaking a hand that wielded one.

The guards also didn't know what to do with the yelling whirlwind of red hair who sprang at them instead of waiting on the sidelines like a good damsel in distress. Rhianne had found a piece of bronze pipe in the rubble, and now she whacked left and right.

The wall next to Ben exploded. Shards of dust and metal sprayed into the corridor, and the guards began to scream.

Rhianne stepped back in bewilderment, her bronze bar held like a sword as the guards writhed and clawed at their faces.

Ben grabbed Rhianne's hand and pulled her through the newly made hole. "Cian packs iron into the explosives."

"That's mean." *Hoch alfar* hated the touch of iron. It burned them, crippled them, killed them if they were hit with a big enough dose. Rhianne shuddered. "On the other hand, Walther let half a dozen of his guards grope me when he tracked me down, so they can eat it."

Ben's body tightened. He debated wading back into the castle and breaking necks and crushing bones, but it was more important right now that he whisk Rhianne to safety.

The hole led to a space between the castle's inner and outer walls. Another opening had been blasted in the curtain wall, through which fresh wind blew. The outside world. Or, at least, Faerie.

Ben climbed through, pulling Rhianne behind him. She scrambled over the broken stones, her hair snagging on the jagged opening. She impatiently jerked it free, never letting go of Ben's hand.

Ben slid a few feet down the steep hill the castle perched upon before he planted himself to help Rhianne to firmer ground. At least the hole in the wall hadn't opened to a sheer part of the cliff.

The only road to the castle was a precarious one from a river valley, the better for defense. All other ways involved clambering around densely packed trees and scrub on a near-vertical slope.

Cian leapt out over the pile of rubble, landing with the grace of a cat. He wore close-fitting black clothes and soft shoes, which made him look much like the popular movie image of a ninja in the human world.

Cian's usually grim face split into a broad smile. "Head's up," he said in *dokk alfar*.

Ben grabbed Rhianne and yanked her to the earth. Cian removed a small object from his pocket and tossed it through the hole he'd just emerged from then slammed himself face-down in the dirt.

A final *boom* rang out and a cloud of dust burst from the opening. Screams, curses, and shouts rose over the rumble of falling stones. The hole that had been their escape route vanished as the wall became a pile of debris.

"Time to go," Ben said.

He helped Rhianne to her feet. She clung to him and dragged her hair from a black-streaked face, her breath ragged.

Cian sprang up. "This way, my friends."

Ben did not know if Rhianne understood *dokk alfar*, but she caught the gist and started off after him.

Cian led the way down the hill, Rhianne and Ben behind him, Ben steadying her. Somehow, they'd never released hands.

No one pursued the three fugitives. *Hoch alfar* were renowned archers, but the land behind this side of the castle was thick with trees. No arrow stood a chance.

Cian led them with confidence, though the woods looked the same in all directions to Ben. He'd grown up in Faerie, but that had been a long time ago, nowhere near here, and everything he'd ever known had changed. A thousand years did that to a place.

Rhianne kept pace easily, without hysterics or terror. She was outwardly composed, but her grip on Ben's hand was tight, as though she remained calm only through the lifeline of their touch.

The hill smoothed out the more they descended until they came out of the trees to a fairly flat space beside a rushing river. Cian turned and led them upstream.

Rhianne hung back. "Not that way."

She spoke in English. Ben called softly to Cian, who glanced behind him with impatience.

"We need to hurry," Cian said in *dokk alfar*. "Once Madhug regroups, he'll be on us."

Rhianne didn't move. "We're going the wrong direction. My mother's house is downstream from here. That's the safest place. We can seek refuge with her."

Ben cleared his throat, his face growing warm. "We're not going to Lady Aisling's."

Rhianne's angry stare pinned him. Her eyes were dark brown, not the black that most Fae and Tuil Erdannan possessed, but a rich chocolate. If Ben had glanced quickly at her and away, he might have decided her eyes were black, but closer observation showed him that this was untrue.

"No?" Rhianne pulled from Ben's grasp. A chill touched his palm, his hand emptier without hers in it. "I thought my mother sent you. Who are you?"

Ben saw her fear rise as she assumed she'd gone from frying pan to fire. Cian, glaring, didn't help.

"Lady Aisling did send us," Ben said quickly. "But her house isn't safe for you, according to her."

Rhianne took a step back, fear changing to outrage. It was not a good idea to enrage a Tuil Erdannan, even a beautiful and vulnerable one in tattered clothing daringly rescued from a *hoch alfar* stronghold.

"How could her house not be safe?" Rhianne demanded. "Where else could be better? No one would dare harm me there."

"Not even your father?" Ben asked gently.

Ben hadn't wanted to explain until he had her in the haunted house on the other side of the gate exactly why Lady Aisling had told Ben to take Rhianne to safety. The middle of *hoch alfar* territory, exposed to whoever decided to hunt them, was not the place for revelations or loud arguments.

Rhianne's mouth dropped open. "*My—*" Her arms went rigid, ending in tight fists. She clamped her lips shut, but the flash in her eyes bode no good. "Fine then," she said tersely. "Let us go to wherever you think you can hide me from Walther le Madhug and my not so very dear father."

She pushed past Ben and marched after Cian, who'd already strode on. She did not reach again for Ben's hand. Chin lifted, back straight, she followed Cian along the river path, the queenly Tuil Erdannan in her making her beautiful and untouchable, but Ben saw her back tremble.

My father. Rhianne fumed as she followed the *dokk alfar*. Her rescuer, Ben, whatever sort of creature he was, tramped heavily behind her.

She had heard her mother mention Ben's name, but she'd never met him. Rhianne hadn't been home in a long, long time, pursuing her own life and trying to find peace far from here, on the coast, where the stars shone in abundance in clear skies.

She hadn't set eyes on her elusive father in many years. He and her mother had separated when Rhianne had been a child, both she and Lady Aisling happy to see the back of the evil man. Ivor de Erkkonen had made it clear he had no interest in his daughter.

Until now, it seemed. If *he'd* convinced Walther to kidnap her, and even helped him do it, then Lady Aisling was right. Rhianne wasn't safe. Ivor was a powerful Tuil Erdannan, even more so than Lady Aisling. If he wanted Rhianne, he'd find her.

But where could she go to escape him? The *dokk alfar* and the ... Ben ... seemed to believe they had a place. The *dokk alfar* lands would be marginally safer, but not if Ivor truly wanted to find her. Even a fortress surrounded by iron and spells wouldn't keep him out. Rhianne's father was a dangerous man, not to be trusted.

The *dokk alfar* moved quickly. He left the river instead of crossing it, winding his way down a narrow side gully until he halted before the sheer face of a cliff.

He gestured to it, saying a word in *dokk alfar*. Rhianne did not know much of that language, but it wasn't hard to understand what he meant. *Here?*

Ben nodded. "Should be." He reached into his pocket and pulled out something that flashed in the dim light. Silver? Metallic anyway.

He tugged one side of the silver box, and it unfolded on a

hinge. Inside, tiny buttons with markings on them filled one side, and a blank space filled the other.

Ah. Cell phone. A communication device. Her mother had brought one home from the human world once. It didn't do anything in Faerie, but Rhianne had enjoyed herself taking it apart. The tiny pieces had fascinated her.

Ben pushed a few buttons. "You there? Let me in."

Cian watched him skeptically. He didn't believe in this human magic either, Rhianne could see.

No, not magic. Technology. Technology had driven magic out of the human world almost entirely. A few pockets of old magic existed there, her mother had said, along ley lines, but they were difficult to find.

"I told you I was sorry," Ben said into the cell phone. "I'll be staying home a while this time, promise."

Nothing answered. Rhianne heard wind in the trees, a pebble moving under her boot, the cry of an eagle in the distance, which tugged at her heart.

Ben rolled his eyes. "I mean, I'll stay as long as you want."

The cliff face shimmered. Cian stepped quickly away from it, his soft shoes making no noise on the ground.

Ben took Rhianne's hand again. She'd liked the surety of his grip on hers as they'd escaped the fortress—strong and warm, an anchor that told her she'd be all right.

"Do *not* let go of me, no matter what," Ben said. "Understand?" He regarded her sternly until Rhianne gave him a quick nod.

With a word of farewell and thanks to Cian, Ben braced himself and then sprinted directly at the cliff, pulling Rhianne behind him. She tried to resist at first, but she realized the tingle she felt was the forceful magic of a gate, and knew they'd not run into the sheer rock—at least, she hoped not.

She gave Cian a wave, wishing she could reward him for his

part in springing her from Walther's dungeon, then she closed her eyes, holding tight to Ben's hand as she raced behind him.

Cold touched her, and then an emptiness that sucked at her soul. A void, horrible, clammy, and desperate, like fog with a determination to siphon off her life force.

Rhianne wanted to gasp for breath, but feared to breathe at all, not wanting to draw the chill denseness into her body. Her chest burned, and she prayed to the Goddess it would be over soon.

Her lungs were bursting. She had to breathe, had to, even though it might be her death.

The cold abruptly vanished. Rhianne landed on something warm that smelled of wool, and light touched her eyelids. She opened her eyes to find herself on her side on a carpet, Ben sprawled next to her.

The light—morning light—came from open windows, sunshine streaming into a large room with wooden panels and strange furniture. A small black chandelier hung from the white-painted ceiling, and it swayed slightly as she gazed up at it.

Ben rolled over. They lay face to face for a moment, Ben's eyes like the dark of an ancient night.

His face was hard, but not unpleasant, handsome even. One side of his strong neck bore an inked drawing of a spider's web, the ends of the web touching his cheeks. Rhianne had seen tattoos before—*dokk alfar* liked them. She'd never found them attractive, at least, not until now.

After a few heartbeats, Ben pushed himself away from Rhianne and climbed to his feet. He reached down to help her rise, the strength in his grip welcome.

"You all right?"

Rhianne, on her feet, brushed off her shirt and trousers, which were beyond saving. Her hair was also grimy, clumped with ooze and stinking of the dungeon.

"Where are we?" she asked. "Is this a *dokk alfar* house?"

"No." Ben wouldn't meet her eyes. "It's a human house. Kind of a weird one ... no offense." The last statement wasn't spoken to Rhianne, but to the walls.

"A human one." Rhianne stated the words slowly. "I'm in the human world?"

"Yep. Sorry."

Rhianne glanced around the room. It was a pleasant space if unfamiliar, the furnishings odd but comfortable-looking, the air warm. The breeze coming through the half-open window smelled humid, almost musty.

Rhianne's heart squeezed in fear and banged dully in her chest. She was alone, in the human world, far from anything she understood, at the mercy of this man. And she had to stay here because her own father presented so much danger that she couldn't go home.

"It's all right." Rhianne's throat closed up. "I'm fine."

She took a step and her legs buckled. Rhianne fell, but Ben's powerful arms caught her, holding her with his strength, his warmth the only comfort in this place.

CHAPTER THREE

B en didn't mind that his arms were full of soft woman, even one that smelled like a sewer. Her own fragrance was there somewhere, but overlaid with filth from her cell, sweat from the run through the woods, and fear.

He should be terrified of a daughter of the all-powerful Lady Aisling and the equally petrifying Ivor de Erkkonen, but Rhianne was shivering against him, her head on Ben's shoulder, her wrists bearing welts from the cuffs that had bound her. She'd been jerked out of her world and thrown to a place she didn't know, and this after being captured and locked up in a dark, disgusting cell.

"You're okay now." Ben tried to sound soothing as he stroked her back. "No one will harm you here."

The house would keep her safe—if it decided to. Ben glanced at the walls and ceiling, sending the house a silent admonition.

Rhianne relaxed for a brief moment, then stiffened. Ben started to carefully release her, but she hung on to him for another few seconds. One of the Tuil Erdannan, the most powerful beings in Faerie, clung to him, Ben, for support.

"How about you get cleaned up?" he suggested to Rhianne. "We have several nice bathrooms upstairs. Your choice. One has a whirlpool. Another a shower with four or five heads, so it's like standing in a rainstorm."

Rhianne wiped her eyes with the heel of her hand as he released her "You think I need a bath?" Her mouth shook in a watery smile. "What gave you that idea?"

The smile made Ben's heart stop. This woman was stunningly beautiful. Ben's breath had gone somewhere, and he choked as he tried to get it back.

Her smile vanished, brow puckering. "Are you well?"

Ben coughed. "Inhaled too much Faerie gunk. So, the bathrooms. Upstairs. I'll see if I can find you something to wear."

Closing his mouth so he wouldn't babble too much, Ben led the way out of the sitting room. The door to Faerie, which had been in the paneled wall behind them, had utterly vanished.

Rhianne followed, her mud-caked boots squeaking on the polished wooden floor. The house rustled softly, the wind chimes on the porch emitting a silvery sound.

"Is this your house?" Rhianne asked as they mounted the stairs. The crystals on the ponderous chandelier that hung between the turns of the staircase tinkled as the chandelier swayed ever so slightly.

"Nope. I'm its caretaker. The owner is a sweet young human woman who is a little bit witchy and mated with a Shifter. No accounting for taste, I guess."

"Shifter?"

"You know. Tall, crazy eyes, change into animals whenever they want. Some humans think they need a full moon or something, but no."

"I know what they are." Rhianne's touch of impatience made her sound like the Tuil Erdannan she was. "I've never met one. I hear they are very dangerous."

"Very. I mean, seriously, seriously dangerous. Make great

friends and drinking buddies, but I never forget how savage they can be."

"Why are you a caretaker? Where is your fortress?"

They'd reached the top of the stairs. Ben huffed a laugh. "Gone. I'm in exile here, have been for a long, long, long time. I can go back to Faerie now, thanks to your mum, but there's nothing for me there. I thought that once I could return I'd find some closure, but ..." A knot tightened in his chest. "Everything has changed, and my people are gone ..." Ben trailed off, realizing he'd said too much.

Rhianne gazed at him with her black-brown eyes, framed with thick black lashes. Red-haired Shifters or human women usually had light-colored eyelashes, but not Rhianne. But then, she was a super-all-magical Tuil Erdannan. Maybe they could have eyelashes whatever color they wanted.

"If you've lived in the human world for so much time, you could have built a fortress," Rhianne pointed out. "Or a house like this. Which is clearly not a fortress. Too many windows." She glanced through the one on the landing, which looked out onto the thick trees behind the house. Sunlight glistened on her hair, despite its dirty tangles.

Ben shrugged. "I like to move around, meet new people. Plus, humans in general live less than a hundred years. If I stay in one place longer than, say, fifty, they get suspicious. I remember when they burned people who were odd recluses, blaming perfectly innocent, magic-less souls for all kinds of troubles."

Rhianne's eyes widened. "Seriously? And you want me to hide out *here*?"

"Don't worry," Ben said cheerfully. "They stopped burning people a few hundred years ago. Mostly."

Rhianne shook her head. "Not reassuring."

"Anyway." Ben continued resolutely along the upstairs hall. "Bathroom." He opened a door to a large room with a full tub and a shower stall. "Lots of towels. Hot water. I'll show you how to work the taps."

Rhianne watched in cautious curiosity as Ben demonstrated hot and cold water in the tub and then the shower. He showed her the sink for good measure.

He tried to stop himself picturing her peeling off her clothes and stepping delicately into the tub, steam rising around her lithe body, but it was tough.

Ben hurriedly opened the cabinet beside the sink. "Hairbrushes and things in here. Towels, like I said. Lots of soap. Jasmine knows how to stock the place for guests."

"Jasmine." Rhianne smiled, and once again Ben's imagination went places it shouldn't. "Pretty name."

"Yeah, she's great. Her mate, Mason, is really into her."

Rhianne stood very close to Ben. As he'd observed, she topped him by about an inch. Interesting, because Tuil Erdannan were mostly tall. But again, maybe, like Ben, they could choose how they appeared.

Their similar height let him gaze into her eyes. Behind the dirt on her face was a beauty Ben wanted to touch.

Nope, no touching. Not the daughter of Lady Aisling mac Aodha. He wanted his guts to remain on the inside where they belonged. Ben was a powerful being on his own, more so than he usually let on, but Lady Aisling ... pinky ...

"I'll find clothes and leave them outside the door," Ben said rapidly. "I won't be anywhere near when you open it."

Rhianne's next smile held amusement. "Okay." Her nose wrinkled fetchingly. "I like that word."

"It's kind of universal. Nowadays, that is. Only been around for about the last sixty or so years."

Now he truly was babbling. Ben gave Rhianne a tight grin then forced himself to move past her and out the door.

She watched him go—Ben felt her gaze on him. He pretty

much ran the last few steps then shut the door firmly behind him, leaning against it to catch his breath.

The house whispered, and Ben heard faint laughter. He opened his eyes and pointed at the ceiling.

"That's enough from you."

Swallowing, he walked away from the door, telling himself to go hunt through Jasmine's closet for clothes. He tried to ignore the sound of water gushing into the tub, tried not to imagine the garments falling from Rhianne's limbs, and failed miserably.

———

RHIANNE LAY BACK IN THE HOT WATER AFTER SHE'D washed and rinsed her hair and body, and started to shiver. All the soap in the world—whichever one she was in—couldn't wash off the stink of Walther's cell or the touch of his lackey's hands. They hadn't found her bare flesh, fortunately, but the imprint of their palms on her made her sick.

Ben had burst into her cell in a flare of light like a god, but he hadn't looked like the solidly muscular man with the black hair and eyes he did now. She wasn't certain what she'd seen—a massive creature, a nightmare beast that had torn off the cell door like it was paper.

What was Ben? And why, by the Goddess, had her mother decided he should take her away to the human world?

Lady Aisling indulged herself with trips to this world, but she'd always emphasized that though she liked to visit, she wouldn't want to live there. *Too dirty*, she'd say, fastidiously brushing off whatever human clothing she'd returned in. *But I had the loveliest time.*

Why hadn't Lady Aisling simply taken Rhianne on a shopping trip to Paris? Letting Walther cool down and get over his disappointment?

Even if Rhianne's father was involved—terrifying thought—his powers would be limited in the human world ... Wouldn't they?

Rhianne shivered again. She had no idea and did not want to find out.

She grabbed the soap, which had a rich, floral scent, and rubbed it all over herself once more. Her wrists were already healing—burns from her own magical fire always faded quickly. Her stomach growled as she lathered her skin. She couldn't remember when she'd last eaten.

A bottle of bath oil stood on a shelf beside the tub. Rhianne was happy her mother had taught her English, so she could read the words on the label, though it was also in French. Rhianne opened the bottle and dribbled the oil into the water. More florals overlaid with spice, not too heavy, drifted to her. The lady of the house, Jasmine, had good taste.

Rhianne closed her eyes, but too many images flashed behind her eyelids, so she opened them again. More shivering, though the water was plenty warm.

She pressed her fingertips to her temples, massaging the skin. "Get over it, Rhianne," she said in her own language. "Shake it off. It's just Walther the slug. He can't help being slimy."

Soft whispers answered her words, or maybe it was the breeze outside the window. Warm air touched her, bringing with it the fragrance of roses.

She didn't remember opening the window. Or had it already been open when she'd come in? She couldn't recall.

Letting out a long breath, Rhianne hoisted herself out of the tub and reached for one of the large, soft towels on a nearby rod. She dried her skin, wrapped herself in the biggest towel, and made her careful way to the door. The oil made her feet slick on the tile floor.

She opened the door a crack. Ben was nowhere in sight, but

a pile of clothing lay outside on the carpet, folded neatly. Rhianne snatched up the garments and slammed the door.

The clothes were odd but fairly simple. Leggings, a tunic with printing on it, and a short coat of the same cloth as the leggings. The printing on the thin tunic said: *Ç'est chaud.* Rhianne understood the French words but had no idea why someone would print them on a piece of clothing.

There was also a smaller garment, pink and lacy, that was meant to go on under the leggings. Such a pretty thing to be hidden under the clothing, but she knew what lingerie was.

The shoes Ben had left were interesting. Three different pairs, presumably so she'd find a size that fit her. Rhianne chose ones made of cloth with highly cushioned soles. They had no lacings, only tabs that stuck to the shoe and made a tearing sound when she pulled them off.

Once Rhianne had dressed, she braided and tied her damp hair with a stretchy band she found in the cupboard. Her stomach rumbled again. She needed food.

She padded out of the bathroom to the long upstairs hall. The staircase lay to her right, but many other doors lined the hall to her left.

The cooking smells coming from the left clinched it. Rhianne followed her nose to an open doorway, beyond which was a large, sunny room. A dining table filled a niche in a bay window, with benches on the window side and chairs on the table's opposite end.

Ben stood at what she guessed was a stove. It had a flat surface and no fire she could see, but a pot on it bubbled, and something in a frying pan sizzled. The rest of the room was taken up with long rows of cabinets, counters equally as long, and a worktable filled with dishes and foodstuffs.

"Feeling better?" Ben asked. "At least cleaner?"

"Cleaner, yes. Please thank Mistress Jasmine for her hospitality."

Ben grunted something that sounded like a laugh. "Yeah, I'll do that. Hungry?"

"Yes. Very. Do you have golden bread?"

"I don't know what that is, but you're welcome to look around." Ben indicated the counter full of food and another tall cabinet with metal doors. The cabinet hummed.

Rhianne moved to the counter. "Golden bread has honey and seeds in it. Sometimes raisins if the chef has plump ones."

"Sounds good, but I guarantee we don't have anything like that."

Rhianne found a transparent bag with what appeared to be bread inside it, but it was pure white and smelled unpleasant. Also very squishy, she realized when she squeezed it too hard.

She shoved the bread behind a large jar of some substance with a bright label and approached the stove. "Perhaps I will have whatever you are cooking. Is that the flesh of a hunted beast?"

Ben poked at the bits of meat sizzling in the pan. "Sort of. It's bacon, anyway."

"Bacon?"

"Comes from pigs. From their stomachs."

Rhianne gazed at Ben in surprise. "You eat this?"

"It's good. Especially with eggs."

"Eggs. I can eat those."

"I scrambled up a mess." Ben moved his flat stirring implement to another frying pan on the back of the stove. Inside this lay yellow blobs flecked with black.

Rhianne eyed the concoction dubiously. "Well, I am hungry."

Ben's laugh echoed in the room. "Are you saying you don't like my cooking? You haven't even tasted it."

"I do not wish to be rude, but ..." Rhianne looked over the pans. The one with boiling water had sausages floating in it. "I can have those."

"Oh, you can, can you? Tell you what. I'll fix you up a plate. Check the refrigerator—might be something else in there you'd like."

He indicated the humming cabinet. Curious, Rhianne approached it. The door's handle was cool, and she had to yank at it several times before the ponderous door swung open.

A wave of very cold air wafted out, as though she'd walked into a deep root cellar. More surprising were the shelves filled with a curious array of food.

Peppers, carrots, and onions she knew from her mother's garden at home, as well as market stalls, but she'd never seen the variety of packages, all with the same colorful labels as the jar on the table. She didn't recognize the words—salsa, ketchup, tabasco, soy sauce—or if she did know the words, she didn't understand the food—hot sauce, curry paste, honey mustard.

Apples. Those she understood. She pulled one from a bowl, wiped it on her shirt, and took a big bite.

Crisp. The iciness of the cabinet made the apple pleasantly crunchy and cold. Rhianne wiped a droplet of apple juice from her chin.

Ben had filled two plates with all the things on the stove. He took browned slices of the squishy bread from a device with slots on the top and added them to the plates.

"Breakfast is up." He carried the plates to the dining table.

"How is that done?" Rhianne, apple in hand, approached the stove. Its top was smooth and black. No fire anywhere or any sign of smoke. "Magic?"

She touched the surface.

Ben slammed the plates to the table and was leaping back to her at the same time Rhianne shrieked and jumped. *"Shelarank!"*

Arm around her shoulders, Ben dragged her to a basin. He touched a tap similar to those in the bathroom and shoved her hand under a cold stream of water.

"Your mum should have given you a manual to the human world," he grumbled.

Rhianne wriggled her singed fingers, which felt better under the chilly stream. Ben's hand engulfed her wrist as he held her steady, but his touch was gentle on her healing skin. His other arm was still around her, his support solid.

Rhianne recalled the gargantuan creature that had ripped the bars from her cell, setting her free. The hands that held her now were much smaller, but she felt the same strength in them, saw battle scars on his skin that a change of form couldn't hide.

She peered at him as she let the cool water soothe her fingers. "What are you?" she whispered.

Ben's cheeks grew red, but he shrugged. "*Ghallareknoik-snlealous.* Don't try to say it. Goblin is fine."

Rhianne stared at him. "Goblin? But you're extinct."

A hardness flickered in his eyes. "That's me. Extinct." He released Rhianne's hand and tossed a towel at her, turning away for the table.

"That's not what I meant," she said quickly.

"I know. Come and eat before it's cold."

Rhianne somehow still had hold of the apple. She dried her hand and moved to the table. Ben dragged out a chair for her, and Rhianne sat.

"I didn't mean to offend you," she said. "Not after you rescued me so kindly."

Ben grunted. "Goblins are gone from your world. They were never very important to Tuil Erdannan anyway."

Rhianne realized his gruff tones masked a pain so deep she would never understand it. She suddenly wanted to. This creature had braved a *hoch alfar* lord's fortress, with only one companion, and had whisked her to safety. Relative safety, that is. Rhianne wasn't certain if she was out of danger here.

"You're important to *me.*" Rhianne set down the apple and picked up a fork—at least humans knew about eating implements—and scooped a hunk of what he'd called scramble. "You took me out of that shithole."

Ben's hardness remained as he nonchalantly crumbled his toast. "That place literally was one. So how the hell did you get *in*to that shithole? I can't believe a plain old *hoch alfar* took down a Tuil Erdannan."

Rhianne grimaced. "Well, he did."

"Give me the whole, sad story, sweetheart. I need to know what we're up against."

He said *we're* as though he were part of this fight.

Rhianne made herself take a mouthful of the eggs and paused in amazement. They were good, rich, and peppery, cooked to perfection. She revised her opinion of egg-scramble.

"I was taking a walk on a cliff path above the ocean," she said after she swallowed. "I live in a village on the coast—I'm a scholar. I research the heavens and write papers and books about it, and I also teach children about it, not just the Tuil Erdannan aristocrats, but the servant-class children as well. Some of them are quite bright, and I help them study to go to university and become scholars too. I take that walk during the evening before I set up to stargaze. It's beautiful. Soothing. I guess Walther knew I liked it too. He had his toadies surround me."

"You didn't see them coming?" Ben stared at her in amazement. "All that Tuil Erdannan magic couldn't let you get past a circle of dumbass *hoch alfar*?"

"It should have." Rhianne's forehead grew tight as she remembered. "I didn't realize my danger—I was ready to hurl them out of my way and continue my walk. Then one of them poked a tiny barb into my arm. It didn't hurt, but suddenly, I couldn't walk, and I fell unconscious. When I woke, I was in Walther's keep."

She'd been disoriented, afraid, confused. His men had

searched her, pulling out and taking away all her weapons down to her hairpins. Walther had watched, and smiled.

"This is bad." Ben's face darkened as he stabbed at his eggs. "What kind of tranq can take out a Tuil Erdannan?"

"Exactly my thoughts. There must have been powerful magic in it."

"If your dad's involved, then there probably was. Why would Ivor What'shisname want Walther le Madhug to capture you?"

"And marry me." Rhianne drew her fork across her plate. "Even if I did want to marry, Walther is not the one I'd choose."

Ben reached to her, turning her hand over to reveal her burned wrist. "Did Walther do that?" His voice rumbled menacingly.

"No, I did." Rhianne liked his touch, though she knew she should pull her hand away. "I used a spell to melt the chains, and it made the cuffs hot too. Do not worry—it will heal quickly."

"I'm sorry I didn't reach you sooner." Ben lightly traced her wrist just outside the burn. A warmth that rivaled what the cuffs had done wound its way up her arm.

Rhianne held herself still. "It was soon enough. For which I thank you. You and your *dokk alfar* friend were very courageous."

Ben's eyes flickered and he suddenly withdrew his fingers, as though he hadn't realized he'd touched her. "Yeah, well. When Lady Aisling says *do this*, you do it."

"I owe you my life. You saved mine, at risk to yours. I do not hold that lightly." Rhianne's face warmed. "And it's a little embarrassing."

"It's Cian you should be pleased with. He loves messing up a *hoch alfar's* day. He's one crazy dude."

"But he's very helpful."

"Yep, very helpful." Ben met her gaze again. His midnight

dark eyes held so much—the pain of an ancient being, the faint flicker of hope deep down that Rhianne suspected never went away.

"I am trying to say thank you." Rhianne gave him a shaky smile. "I'm not good at it."

"You're Tuil Erdannan. Everyone else is dust to you."

"You are not."

Ben's lips parted at her statement. He started to answer but his words died, and he simply looked at her.

Rhianne's heart thumped. Ben had beautiful eyes in a face that held her attention. She thought of his strong hands on hers, first pulling her to safety in the dungeon, then thrusting her fingers under the cold water when she'd burned them.

He helped people. That must be his purpose. Rhianne didn't know much about goblins, because they'd died out or disappeared before she'd been born. Ben had obviously found a way to survive in the human world.

She knew she had no business feeling safe around him. Ben claimed that Lady Aisling had sent him, but she had no way to communicate with her mother and find out if this was so. For all Rhianne knew, Ben was working with her father in this mad scheme to get her married to Walther. Ben might be softening her up so she'd trust him, before he delivered her back to the *hoch alfar*.

For some reason, Rhianne knew this wasn't the case. The rage in Ben's eyes when he spoke of the *hoch alfar* was real. That rage touched on an old wound, one he kept buried.

Rhianne likewise had no business finding beauty in his eyes. Ben wasn't Tuil Erdannan. Not for her.

But the thought of his powerful hands on her body, perhaps sliding over her soapy skin in the bathtub, warming her breasts while he pulled her to him to take her mouth ...

A shrill peal of a bell sliced sharply through her daydream.

Rhianne jumped. Her fork slipped from her fingers and clattered against her plate.

Ben raised a quick hand. "Just my phone. Don't worry." He pulled the cell phone he'd used before from his pocket, unfolded it as it pealed again, and put it to his ear. "Yeah?"

A voice sounded, tinny and far away. Ben's brows slammed together, and he glared out the window as he listened, as though he could see the speaker there.

"How the hell did he find out so fast? What? ... Yeah, yeah, I know. Thanks for the heads-up, Sean. Sure. See ya."

The device went dark when Ben pushed a button, then he folded it and set it gently on the table.

"Company's coming," he announced.

CHAPTER FOUR

Rhianne's sudden apprehension made Ben's anger surge. She'd been through trauma—she needed to heal, not be interrogated.

But that wasn't how things worked in the Shifter world. Shifters lived on the edge of danger all the time, and they investigated any new threat, or potential threat, immediately.

How Dylan had found out so quickly that Rhianne had been sent here, Ben had no idea. Dylan just seemed to know things.

"It's okay." Ben laid a hand on Rhianne's arm once more, trying to soothe her. Before today, he wouldn't have dreamed of touching a Tuil Erdannan, but Rhianne was scared, uprooted, alone. "It's only Shifters. You could blow them to dust if you wanted. They know that too."

"Can I?" Rhianne did not pull away from him. "I'm not as gifted as my mother. I've always understood that."

"Even a weak Tuil Erdannan is more powerful than Shifters. They'll be aware. Don't let them mess with your head. They like to do that."

"Mess with my head?" Rhianne touched her thick red hair, which fell down her back in a loose braid.

"Not on the outside." Ben tapped his temple. "On the inside. Dylan will look at you as though he knows everything that has happened, is happening, and will happen to you. He tries to make everyone go along with his picture of the world. To do whatever he wants. He's a serious alpha, which might not mean anything if you're not Shifter."

"Dylan Morrissey?" Rhianne's mouth quirked when Ben started in surprise. "My mother has mentioned him. She's met him, and she keeps abreast of the Shifters and their situations. She became interested in them when the leopard Shifter— Jaycee?—came to her for help. Mother talks to Jaycee quite often, apparently."

Ben felt a qualm. "Don't tell Dylan that. I don't want him up in Jaycee's face. Not that Jaycee would betray to your mum anything that would harm Shifters, but Dylan's touchy." He considered. "Of course, watching Dylan *try* to get into Jaycee's face might be fun. She's loyal to her mate and her leader and no one else, including Dylan. She'd probably tell him to go lick himself. Big cat Shifters do what the hell they want, and now that Jaycee has a cub, she's even more likely to tell everyone to back off."

"The Morrissey family are big cat Shifters too, aren't they?" Rhianne asked.

"Exactly. Not that wolves are much better, and don't get me started on the bears."

Rhianne's smile dimpled her cheeks. Damn, she was gorgeous when she did that. Ben kept reminding himself who she was, *what* she was, but the needs in him didn't care. Rhianne was a beautiful woman, alone with him, helpless ...

All right, maybe not *helpless*. She could probably kick his ass if she tried. But she didn't know the human world, or Shifters. He was her buffer against both.

Ben had never seen Rhianne at her mother's house, which could mean she'd left home to have her own life. Lady Aisling could be pretty intense. Or maybe Lady Aisling had kept Rhianne out of the way for a reason. Like her own father being a danger to her?

Puzzling. There was more going on here than met the eye, and Ben had pretty good eyesight.

"Let's finish breakfast," he said. "Before Dylan shows up and ruins our appetites."

"This is good." Rhianne resumed her fork and devoured more eggs. "I'm surprised."

"Now don't break my heart." Ben pressed his hand to his chest, feigning offense. "I worked damned hard on these eggs. And the toast. And the pig stomach."

Her nose wrinkled in a cute way. "Don't ruin it."

She continued eating, complimenting his cooking by finishing everything on her plate and sopping up the last of the eggs with her toast. She even ate most of the bacon. Between the two of them, they consumed everything Ben had made.

"I guess getting captured and rescued makes you hungry," Ben observed. "Rescuing is hungry work too."

"Do you do it a lot?" Rhianne rose with him and carried her dishes to the sink. "Rescue people?"

"Unfortunately." Ben took her plate and scrubbed it off under the running water. "I don't mean I dislike rescuing people. I hate that others put them into situations where I have to do it."

"I'm glad you came for me."

The words were soft, the light in her eyes sincere. Ben's chest felt tight, as though his heart was trying to climb into his throat. He whipped his attention back to the plates and scrubbed them as hard as he could.

"I'd like to see this place." Rhianne had turned away, surveying the room.

Ben rinsed the plates and started stacking them in the dishwasher. "I take tourists around the downstairs and the grounds twice a week. Or at least I did until the *dokk alfar* made me their bitch. Jazz hired a new guide who hauls tourists out here from New Orleans. But I don't mind showing you around. The house was built in the eighteenth century, beginning as a modest farmhouse, and growing to its present size by the turn of the nineteenth century."

"No, I mean ..."

Rhianne paced the middle of the big room, her gaze straying out the window to the trees and the glimpse of industrial lots beyond.

"This world," she finished. "If it's to be my prison, I want to know all about it."

"Not prison." Ben folded his arms and leaned against the counter. "You're not locked in. This house is a place of refuge— it's safe—but if you want to go somewhere else, you're free to do so." He'd have to go with her, though, because he didn't trust the *hoch alfar* or her father not to sneak through from Faerie and try to grab her.

"It's exile, then." Rhianne ceased pacing, her braid swinging. "If my mother thinks Faerie is too dangerous for me, she'll not let me back in."

The distress in Rhianne's eyes broke Ben's heart. He knew exactly what it meant to wake up on this side of the gate, knowing he could never go back home, that he had to figure out this bizarre world of humans and survive in it. When he'd crossed, it had been about the year 1000, as they'd counted years in Europe, and he'd found chaos.

"I'll show this world to you," Ben offered. "We'll go wherever you want. I have some places that are favorites. Favorites now, I mean. Things change."

They'd changed a hell of a lot in the last thousand years. He realized that in Rhianne, he might have met someone who'd seen as much change as he had. Tuil Erdannan lived a long time.

Couldn't really start off their relationship asking her age, though. Bad idea.

Ben made his tone light. "We'll listen to Dylan try to convince us to do whatever he has in mind, and then I'll take you out. How's that?"

He'd intended to make her smile, but Rhianne gazed mournfully at her sweatpants and jacket covering the T-shirt Jasmine had picked up in New Orleans.

"I'll need different clothes. This shirt seems to be telling everyone that it's hot outside."

Ben hid a grin. The heat level was rising in here, that was certain. "I'll find you anything you want. I'm here to take care of you, love. Promise."

———

IT WASN'T LONG BEFORE DYLAN SHOWED UP. EVEN though he in theory had to ride from Austin, which could be an eight-hour trip, Dylan seemed to cover distances in half the time as other mortals. True, he might have already been in Houston or thereabouts, making the rounds in his territory, but Ben swore he must have some Fae magic hidden up his sleeve.

Only an hour or so after Ben had cleaned up the kitchen and taken Rhianne on a tour of the house to distract her from her troubles, he heard a motorcycle roar to a stop outside. Not just one, but three. Dylan always brought backup.

Ben had been showing Rhianne the rear veranda, on which Jazz kept comfortable chairs, tables, and a small bookcase, and explaining to her about the ley lines that ran under the house. When Rhianne heard the engine noise, she swung around in alarm.

Ben took her hand. As she'd done when he'd pulled her

from the cell, she closed her fingers around his, not letting go as he led her through the house and to the front door.

The house whispered. Ben touched the wall by the door-frame. "I know Dylan's a pain in the ass, but we should probably talk to him. Put it this way, he'll camp out here until I either let him in or go outside and see what he wants. I think Rhianne will be okay."

He felt the weight of Rhianne's stare. "Who are you talking to?"

"The house." Ben gave the wall a pat. "If it doesn't want to let them in, it won't. It's very protective. I think we'll have to meet them on the porch."

"I thought you said they were only Shifters."

Ben bit back a laugh. "Yeah, but Dylan's special. He usually doesn't mess with me, so stick close."

Rhianne's puzzlement settled into caution. She kept hold of Ben's hand as he opened the door and led Rhianne out onto the porch.

Dylan had already climbed off his motorcycle and stood waiting for the other two Shifters to join him. One was the huge form of Tiger and the third ... Uh-oh. Liam.

Dylan had the smallest build of the three who approached the porch, though that wasn't saying much. Despite this, Dylan had more power even than Tiger, who, well ...

Tiger was big and bulky, with tiger-striped hair and a golden stare that could skewer you until you shriveled up and tried to find somewhere to run. But it didn't matter if you ran because Tiger would catch you. He always did.

Liam Morrissey was Dylan's oldest son. He resembled his father with his near-black hair and intensely blue eyes, tall body, and swagger. Dylan had honed his swagger into something subtly intimidating, but Liam, young, fairly newly mated, and father to a female cub who was his pride and joy—his arrogance had reached its height.

Liam now led the Shiftertown in Austin, having taken over from Dylan when Dylan had stepped down. Actually, Liam had kicked Dylan's butt in a fight while Liam was going through issues, though Ben always wondered whether Dylan had let his son win. Dylan had much more freedom now to roam over the Morrissey territory, which was vast, and more time to annoy everyone inside it.

Both Morrisseys wore Collars—the chain with the Celtic knot pendant containing a mix of magic and technology that in theory controlled Shifters' violent tendencies. Tiger wore a fake one—when he'd come to live in the Austin Shiftertown, Liam had tried to put a real one on him, and it had not gone well. They'd given Tiger a fake one to fool the humans, and life had been better for all concerned.

"Dylan, Liam." Ben nodded at them. "Tiger. How you doing, big guy?"

"My cub, Seth, is beginning to talk." Tiger's pride beamed from him. For a man in a leather jacket that stretched over a huge but tight body, with a face that terrified many, he looked almost sappy.

"Beginning to, he says." Liam Morrissey approached the porch. He spoke with an Irish accent that Ben suspected he exaggerated. "Seth said his first word a few weeks ago and hasn't ceased gabbing since. He's under the bad influence of my nephew, who hasn't stopped talking in twenty-three years."

"How is Connor?" Ben liked the kid, who would soon be as intimidating and terrifying as Liam and Dylan, if genetics ran true.

"Oh, he's getting by. He'll be approaching his Transition soon, I'm thinking. A bit early for a Shifter, but the lad has always been precocious. The shite will hit the fan then. Maybe we can all move in here, and leave Connor the bungalow." Liam ran a thoughtful gaze over the house.

Dylan hadn't spoken at all. It was Liam's way to chat and

put people at their ease before Dylan got down to business. Tiger ... well, Tiger always did his own thing.

"This is Rhianne," Ben said before Liam could wind down and let Dylan take over. "Rhianne mac Aodha. Daughter of Lady Aisling." *And don't you forget it.*

Liam chuckled. His handsome smile and blue eyes usually had ladies melting. Another reason, probably, that Dylan had brought him along.

Rhianne had stiffened, her hand clenching Ben's. Her first taste of Shifters likely wasn't what she'd expected. If she'd been told they were the *hoch alfar's* tamed beasts, she must be in for a shock. Shifters had never been that, no matter what the *hoch alfar* thought.

"We know who she is, lad." Liam put a hand to his chest. "I'm Liam Morrissey, my lady, at your service. The quiet one is me dad, Dylan, and the seriously quiet one is Tiger. We call him that because, you know, he's a tiger."

"My mother has mentioned him." Rhianne's voice was a bit hoarse, but she held her head high, determined not to be intimidated. "And Dylan Morrissey."

"May we speak?" Dylan indicated the porch. The three Shifters had halted at the bottom of the porch steps, being familiar with the house and its arbitrary obstructiveness.

"Come on up." Ben led Rhianne to the porch swing. "Let's see how far it lets you go."

Tiger, who never hesitated over anything, climbed the stairs without impediment. He gazed down at Rhianne for a time while she, brave lady, met his eyes. Her hand squeezed Ben's, and he squeezed back, there for her.

Tiger's brows came together. "You are troubled."

"You think?" Ben spoke before Rhianne could. "She's been abducted, held prisoner, threatened, yanked here without anyone asking if she's okay with it, and now being given the eyeball by you three."

Tiger sent Rhianne a slow nod, as though she'd answered herself. "The trouble is deeper. Dylan is not your leader."

With that pronouncement, he moved to the end of the porch and lounged against the railing, positioning himself to be the lookout.

Liam glanced uneasily at the porch ceiling as he mounted the steps. He carefully didn't touch the railings. When Dylan's foot brushed the bottom stair, the house trembled. The shutters banged and the rose vines rustled ominously.

"Maybe you should stay down there, Dad," Liam said quickly.

Dylan halted in irritation. "I've slept here many a night," he reminded the house. The shaking and banging ceased, but when Dylan put his boot back on the step, it began again.

Dylan growled, his eyes becoming the flat, slitted eyes of the wild cat. But he withdrew his foot and remained on the ground. The house settled down, emitting a creak that sounded a little bit smug.

Liam kept to the third step of the five, resting one arm on the railing. Ben made a show of settling Rhianne on the porch swing, plumping the pillows around her before taking a seat next to her. Not only did they sit hip to hip, but he'd be able to jump in front of her if one of the Shifters decided to try anything.

"So, what's this about?" Ben asked.

Dylan kept his lips firmly closed, his intimidation tactic. Tiger likewise stayed silent, but that was just Tiger.

Liam had ridden along to be the mouthpiece of Dylan, Ben decided. Though Liam was his own man—if he didn't agree with his father, he wouldn't back him.

"This is about a Tuil Erdannan coming through a Fae gate close to Dad's and my territory." Liam held up a quick hand. "Not to worry, lass. We don't see you as an enemy. But 'tis a strange thing."

Ben scowled. "Stop trying to sound like a leprechaun. What do you want, Liam?"

Tiger turned slightly, just enough to watch Ben. While Dylan might be in charge and a huge badass, it was Tiger Ben needed to worry about.

Liam grinned, ever affable. "Sorry." The accent faded somewhat. "You're welcome to stay with the Austin Shifters, Rhianne, who will defend you to the death. Or here, in the house with a big personality. Or ..." Liam rubbed his chin. "You could do us a massive favor."

Rhianne had edged closer to Ben, her warmth spreading over him. Ben started to answer, but Rhianne cut in, her imperious tones worthy of her mother.

"What sort of favor?"

Liam's blue eyes glinted in the September sunshine. "I hear a *hoch alfar* lord with the peculiar name of Walther le Madhug is trying to woo you. If you let him ... you could become our inside man, so to speak."

Ben was on his feet, rage lifting him. "Are you shitting me? That asshole stuck her in a dungeon, for fuck's sake."

Tiger straightened to his full height as Ben felt the thing inside him coming to life. Tiger's golden eyes fixed heavily on him, his rumble a warning.

"I know, I know," Liam said placatingly. "He's a shitbag of the highest level. But think about it. Le Madhug is one of the top *hoch alfar*, and we know they're planning hard to re-enslave the Shifters. It would be a temporary thing, lass. We'd extract you if it got too rough. You'd be in contact with us or Ben the whole time."

Rhianne rose beside Ben, and her hand sought his again.

"How do you know all this?" she asked Liam. "I mean about Walther kidnapping me and wanting to force a marriage? I've never met you people."

Ben liked the imperious lift of her chin, her natural arrogance rising as she beheld Liam and Dylan. *You go, sweetheart.*

Liam shrugged. "Your mum told Jaycee you were coming, asking her to inform those in power here. Jaycee told her fearless leader, Kendrick, and Kendrick called Dad. Shifter information network, best in the universe."

He waited for Rhianne and Ben to laugh, but both remained impassive. Liam sobered.

"Your mum also charged us to look out for you," Liam went on. "Her words about any hair on your head being harmed and what would happen to us if they were—" He broke off and flinched. "Let's just say I'm glad she didn't come with you."

Ben glared at him. "What did she say about you asking Rhianne to go *back* to that *hoch alfar* bastard?"

"We haven't exactly told her," Liam said. "Wanted to run it past you first."

Dylan, who'd taken root at the bottom of the steps, finally spoke. "As my son says, you'll be in constant contact with Shifters to pull you out as soon as we have what we need, or in case it grows too dangerous for you. Ben would be recruited, as well as a *dokk alfar* who lives in the Las Vegas Shiftertown. An Iron Master."

Ben knew full well which *dokk alfar* Dylan meant, a powerful one who made the *hoch alfar* shit themselves in fear.

True, between himself, Shifters like Tiger, and Reid the Iron Master, Rhianne would have more protection than a precious diamond in the most secure vault on the planet. But in return, she'd have to go to that scumbag who'd abducted her and pretend to suck up to him.

"No," Ben said firmly.

CHAPTER FIVE

R hianne regarded Ben in surprise, which was swiftly followed by gratitude. She had assumed, when the Shifters began their demands, that Ben would take their side. Goblins had always hated the Fae, and the Fae had killed them off. He'd have given his loyalty to the Shifters, wouldn't he?

The fact that Ben met Dylan's even stare with one of his own and gave him a solid *No*, made her heart warm.

The three Shifters were not at all what she'd expected. Rhianne had pictured rangy men with shaggy hair, like the lions they were, who spoke in guttural tones and possibly let off a roar every once in a while.

What she saw in the Morrisseys were two tall, solid-bodied, black-haired men with hard blue eyes. Dylan, the older, had some gray in his hair, but otherwise, he appeared almost as young as his son.

The third, Tiger, fascinated her the most. He was taller and larger than the other two, with variegated hair and the yellow-black eyes of a tiger. Rhianne had never seen a real tiger, but paintings of them graced books she'd grown up with.

Though Dylan and Liam had obviously brought Tiger as muscle, he was curiously detached, as though he'd come for his own reasons, nothing to do with them. Plus, he'd easily gained the porch, while the house had put off the two Morrisseys.

"What does the lass say for herself?" Liam asked pointedly.

Ben didn't back down. "What you are asking her is wrong on so many levels."

"Wouldn't do it if we didn't think we could keep her from harm," Liam said. "You'd be first on the scene, Ben, along with Tiger."

Ben glowered. "Seriously, Liam, take yourself and your requests out of here. This is exactly what you asked Reid to do, and it almost killed him, and his mate."

Liam's frown couldn't erase the appealing handsomeness of his face. "Now—"

"I'll think about it." Rhianne took a step in front of Ben, her chest tightening.

"Rhianne, you don't have to do anything they say," Ben said quickly. "I can have the house throw them off the property if you want."

"I said, I'd think about it." Rhianne kept her voice quiet. "I understand the request. They are correct that it would be an excellent opportunity." Not one she wanted to take, by any means, and she wasn't about to agree. Let the Shifters do their own dirty work.

"There you have it, my friends," Ben said in a firm tone. "She'll get back to you."

Liam chewed his upper lip then he spread his hands. "So be it. If your answer is no, then it's no. We'll not force you, lass."

"Damned right you won't," Ben rumbled.

Tiger straightened. He'd been still so long that his coming to life was startling. He left the porch railing and went straight to Rhianne. "You will take a walk with me."

Tiger moved past her and down the steps to the front drive, without waiting to see if Rhianne would follow. She started after him before realizing that she did so.

"You don't have to go." Ben's touch on her arm was gentle, comforting, his eyes concerned.

"It's all right. I am interested in what he has to say."

Ben released her and started to follow as she resumed her steps, but Tiger whipped around. "No. Only Rhianne."

Ben clearly didn't like that, and oddly, neither did Dylan or Liam. Had they not planned this? Or, Rhianne realized with sudden insight, they had no control at all over Tiger. He was here by his choice, not because they'd commanded him to attend, or even asked him politely.

Rhianne gave Ben a reassuring nod and walked sedately down the steps. The railing was warm from the sunshine, soothing somehow.

Tiger strode around the house, ending up at a path through the trees to what looked like a garden. Rhianne hurried to catch up with him, her cushioned shoes gripping the slightly damp path.

A break in branches led into a small clearing with a lawn, a few benches, a riot of rose vines climbing the trees, and flowerbeds dark with new earth. Someone cared for this patch of wild garden—Ben?

Tiger waited in front of a brick wall where rose vines greened over it. Blossoms covered it in spectacular color, reds, pinks, whites, even silvery purple.

A sudden bite of homesickness struck Rhianne. Her mother's rose garden, lovingly tended by Akseli, the gardener, was also a tranquil retreat.

Rhianne halted next to Tiger. "Why did you bring me here?"

Tiger's height was incontrovertible when she stood this

close to him. Well over six feet, with a bulk to match, the Shifter was terrifying.

Or should be. Rhianne sensed that Tiger was out of the ordinary. Special. When he'd spoken of his child saying his first words, he'd glowed with pride and love. Not frightening at all.

"I thought you would like the garden." Tiger's words were simple.

"I do like it. Beauty without overdoing it."

Tiger didn't answer. He studied the wall with the roses and green leaves as though it were the most fascinating piece of sculpture he'd ever seen.

Rhianne swung her arms. "Go ahead. Try to convince me to return to Walther's castle and spy on him."

"You should not go."

Rhianne blinked. "But the Morrisseys are adamant." Their urgency had touched her—much fear lurked beneath their request, likely with good reason. The *hoch alfar* took what they wanted and cared for no one outside their realms. Shifters to them were Battle Beasts and nothing more.

"The danger is too great," Tiger said. "Stay with Ben. Whenever you are with Ben, you will be safe."

Tiger closed his mouth, a breeze stirring the ends of his short tiger-striped hair.

"Who *is* Ben?" Rhianne asked on impulse. She shook her head, her braid bouncing across her back. "I know he's a goblin, but *who* is he?"

Tiger's gaze flicked to her. "Someone very important. Take care of him."

"Take care of *Ben?*" Rhianne regarded him in puzzlement. "My mother told him to look after me."

"Lady Aisling does not know. None of them do. Ben must stay alive. He is the last warrior."

Rhianne stared at him, getting lost in his golden eyes. "The last warrior? What does that mean?"

"When trouble comes, he is all." Tiger tapped the side of his head. "I do not know what it means. It is what I see when I look at him."

"Are you clairvoyant? I didn't think that existed in Shifters. It barely exists in the *hoch alfar*, no matter what they claim."

"I can see things in my mind. I was made, not born. I am different from other Shifters."

Rhianne understood that without asking. Liam and Dylan, as fearsome as they were, had a normality about them. They were Shifters, through and through. Tiger was an anomaly, though not lesser than the others.

Rhianne started to smile. "You must drive them spare."

Tiger's eyes flickered, then suddenly he grinned. The expression lit his face and made Rhianne understand that his mate was a lucky woman.

"Do not tell them I know," Tiger said.

Rhianne laughed softly. "Your secret is safe with me."

Tiger held up his hand, palm toward her. He left it there, while Rhianne studied it quizzically.

"You are supposed to slap it," Tiger said. "A high five, Connor calls it. My son can do it already."

Rhianne stared at his hand a moment longer then tentatively tapped his palm with hers. "Is this a Shifter greeting?"

"No, a human one. Shifters growl and sniff at each other."

Rhianne wrinkled her nose. "That's pleasant."

"It is not. I don't need to sniff. Scents pour into me. You smell like roses."

"Oh." Rhianne softened. "Are you always this nice?"

Tiger shrugged, his mountainous shoulders moving. "To people I like. My mate. My cubs. Connor. Liam's mate and cub. Sean's mate and cub. Olaf. You."

"I will treasure that. Thank you." Rhianne held up her hand in imitation of his high five. Tiger grinned and gently met it. "Should we go back?" she asked. "I imagine Dylan will come running out here to look for us if we don't."

"He trusts me." Tiger paused. "Sort of."

"I will consider what you have told me."

"Do not consider. Returning to the *hoch alfar* lord will be your death, and Ben's as well. We need him. We will also need you." Tiger's adamancy quieted. "And I do not want to see you hurt. Or Ben. I like him too."

Rhianne searched Tiger's eyes and found certainty there, coupled with worry that she'd ignore his warnings. She needed to do much thinking before she made any decisions, and also ask questions. Her mother probably knew more than she was telling.

But Lady Aisling was like that. Powerful, assured, and cryptic. Rhianne loved her mother but growing up in her house had sometimes been hell.

Hence, her relocation to the coast, where she could find purpose and steadiness. Her interest in astronomy helped. The heavens comforted her with their never-changing constellations. Well, they actually did change, but over vast amounts of time, and made the problems of the Tuil Erdannan and *hoch alfar* seem trivial. She felt a scholar's pull of curiosity about the constellations here.

"All right," Rhianne said to Tiger and smiled. "Now let us go back to the others before they fall over in apoplexy."

Tiger gave her a grave nod and led her from the garden.

Only when they rounded the house to where Ben, Dylan, and Liam waited anxiously, did Rhianne realize they'd conducted the entire conversation in the language of the Tuil Erdannan. Tiger's speech had been flawless.

———

BEN'S TENSION FLOWED OUT OF HIM AS RHIANNE returned. She strode easily, far more relaxed now than when she'd walked off with Tiger out of Ben's sight.

Tiger was like that. He scared the shit out of all males he came near, unless they were cubs, but women melted to him. Females of every species were like, *Tiger? He's a sweetie. How can you call him terrifying?*

Ben wasn't sure how he did that. Maybe Tiger should give a seminar.

"I've made up my mind, gentlemen." Rhianne spoke clearly, her faintly accented English making Ben's blood hot. "I will not be going back to Walther's castle. You will have to gain your knowledge another way."

Dylan didn't hide his disappointment, but Liam gave Rhianne a broad smile. "Ah, well. We had to try. Would you be willing to give us any information you have on the bastard, and what he is up to?"

"Certainly." Rhianne met his gaze. "Though I am rather tired today."

Ben put himself in front of Liam and Dylan. "Give her some space. We'll call you."

Dylan had the wisdom to know when not to push. Ben understood Dylan wasn't trying to be cruel but was seriously worried about the *hoch alfar*. The *hoch alfar* had repeatedly indicated their wish to bring all Shifters back under their control, reversing the outcome of the Shifter-Fae war that had freed the Shifters hundreds of years ago.

Dylan nodded at Rhianne with respect, lifted his hand to Ben, and turned away to his motorcycle.

Liam's face softened, and his right eyelid lowered in a wink. "Catch you later, kids. Coming, Tiger? I'm starving. I'll make Dad take us into New Orleans where we can sample some of its fabulous food."

Tiger gave a faint shake of his head. "I will return home to my mate and cubs."

"I don't blame you, big guy. Going home to Kim and my sweet Katriona sounds fine, now that I think about it. I'll take them all out when we get there. Austin has great food too."

He waved at Ben and Rhianne both and sauntered to his bike. No, swaggered to it. Liam had perfected the move.

Dylan had already started his motorcycle, straddling it easily as he waited for his son and Tiger. Liam mounted his bike and let it roar to life, revving it to be obnoxious.

Tiger and Rhianne exchanged a glance, then Tiger turned without a word and joined Dylan and Liam.

Not long later, the three swerved their motorcycles in graceful curves and glided down the drive toward the road. A warm breeze, scented with exhaust, brushed Ben and Rhianne in their wake.

Rhianne's hand was in Ben's again. How did that happen? *Never mind*, Ben told himself. He'd roll with it.

"Food sounds like a good idea." Ben kept his voice light, but his throat was dry for some reason. "How about I take you into New Orleans, and we have a night on the town?"

Rhianne scanned the bright blue sky. "We just had breakfast. Is it still morning? Or does time move differently here?"

"A day and a night make twenty-four hours as humans mark time. More or less. The days are a little shorter than in Faerie, but not much. You get used to it. In other words, it's morning and will be for another hour or so."

"Then how do we have a night on the town if it's morning?" Rhianne sounded genuinely confused. "How do you have a night *on* a town? Perhaps I am not translating correctly."

Ben squeezed her hand. "You heard right. In New Orleans, you do have a night *on* the town—on the streets, on the rooftops, on the tables. Partying is an art form there."

Rhianne's slight frown told him she took the words literally. "It sounds very interesting."

Ben grabbed her around the waist in a quick hug. "It is, sweetheart. Stick with me, kid. We'll have an awesome night."

———

RHIANNE FLICKED THROUGH THE SELECTION OF CLOTHES in the large closet of the bedroom Ben had ushered her to, contemplating the paradox of human clothing, which was both simple and complex. The Tuil Erdannan had all kinds of different garments to hang on bodies, but humans had it down to only a few shapes—leggings and tunics, skirts and one-piece dresses.

However, within those shapes, Rhianne discovered amazing choices. Fabric from thin stretchy material like that of the tunic she wore—Ben called it a *T-shirt*—to tissue-thin lamé to pliable soft leather to silky fabric that shimmered. All kinds of patterns seemed to be possible: flowers, stripes, abstract shapes with soft outlines. Humans had clothes in every color imaginable.

Rhianne found the leggings she already wore very comfortable, but Ben said she needed something fancier. He told her that the comfortable leggings and jacket were called *sweats,* because in theory, humans sweated in the clothing when they went running.

"Running from what?" Rhianne asked him.

Ben had laughed and waved her to the closet.

Lady Aisling sometimes brought home human clothes from her trips to Paris or Milan. She and Rhianne had fun trying them on and sometimes Lady Aisling would wear them to fancy-dress parties. The experiments helped Rhianne now to choose an outfit.

The ladies who stored their clothes in this large closet had diverse tastes. Ben had pointed out who owned what. The woman called Jasmine wore colorful shirts and subdued skirts that must fit her closely. The Shifter Jaycee liked black leather, leopard prints, and anything glittery.

Rhianne took her time and put together an ensemble she liked. She started with a flowing, silky tunic in a rich blue that skimmed over a tiny satin white camisole beneath it. On bottom she'd chosen leggings of blackest leather whose outside seams were trimmed with a bright pink satin stripe studded with glinting stones.

Ben had showed her stockings and the array of shoes Jaycee and Jasmine had collected. Rhianne decided on a flat pair of slippers from Jasmine's side—they fit the best, though a trifle small.

She moved to the bathroom to comb out and re-braid her hair. Peering at herself in the mirror, she supposed she didn't look too awful. The bath had helped, though she thought she'd never wash away the grime from Walther's horrible cell. At least her wrists had healed, only faint pink marks remaining.

Rhianne left the bathroom and found Ben in a room down the hall that had deep chairs for lounging and a large, upright box with moving pictures on it. Right now, the pictures were of men with very long legs in colorful clothing bouncing a ball or running, their shoes squeaking on the polished wooden floor.

Ben rose from a chair when he saw her, clicking something in his hand. The box went dark.

"Just catching up on highlights of last season. I missed a lot in Faerie. Oh …" He stopped, looking Rhianne up and down, then he nodded, a slow smile on his hard face. "Nice."

Rhianne warmed with pleasure, spreading her arms. "You like it? These raiments are strange but quite pleasing."

"Raiments?" Ben's smile broadened. "Aren't you sweet?"

"The slippers pinch a bit. Even the soft ones I had before did."

"No problem. We'll take you shopping for shoes." Ben started. "Wow, did I just say that?"

"One shops for shoes? Are there that many cobblers to choose from?"

Ben shook his head. "Cobblers are still around, but mostly you walk into a store full of shoes and pick out a pair. Or two. Or, if you're Jaycee, five."

"Oh." Rhianne's interest grew. "May we see these stores?"

"Sure thing, love. Like I said, I'm taking you on the town. A day *and* a night."

THE NEXT AMAZING EXPERIENCE BEN INTRODUCED Rhianne to was the noisy two-wheeled vehicle of the type the Shifters had ridden.

"Motorcycle," Ben explained while Rhianne gazed at it in apprehension. "*Cycle* for wheels that go around, *motor* for, well, the motor. Bike for short. From the word bicycle, which is not at all the same thing ... er, never mind." Ben swung his leg over, steadied the vehicle, then patted the seat behind him. "Hop on."

"Hop?" Rhianne's brow puckered. "Do I have to jump?"

"Figure of speech. Climb up however you can, rest your feet on those footholds there, and hang on to me."

Rhianne was dubious, but she placed her hands on Ben's shoulders and tried to swing her leg over the seat as he had. She didn't quite make it and then couldn't catch her balance to land on her feet again. Clinging to Ben's back, she slid and slithered until she straddled the seat, propping her feet on the bars he'd indicated.

A very intimate position, she realized as she settled in. Ben sat between her legs, his body even closer when she wrapped her arms around him as instructed.

Not such a bad thing. Ben was solid and warm. She felt his heart beating beneath her hands and against her chest.

Ben twisted around to give her a round thing with a hard, shiny surface. "Put that on. Just in case. Shifters can survive a crash, but not sure about Tuil Erdannan."

Ben had to show Rhianne which way was up, but soon she had the helmet, as he called it, on, a face shield in place. She must look like a strange kind of bug, she mused, with her legs akimbo and the large black bubble on her head.

Ben turned a key then pushed buttons or pulled levers—she couldn't see exactly—and the motorcycle let out a roar. Rhianne had been expecting it after hearing the Shifters ignite their machines, but she squeaked and held Ben a bit tighter.

The motorcycle throbbed beneath her, its vibrations strange yet exciting. "Hold on!" Ben yelled.

Rhianne was already clutching him tightly, but she increased her embrace as the world moved. No, it was the bike that moved, speeding in a long curve around the house and onto the front drive.

They were going so fast! Rhianne regularly rode horses and liked nothing better than a hard gallop, but this motorcycle surpassed even the fleetest steed in her mother's stable.

Ben guided the bike down the tree-lined lane, leaving the house behind. Rhianne glanced back at it. The rose vines on the house danced in the wind, almost as though they were waving. Rhianne waved back.

The bike slowed, disappointingly, but only because Ben had paused at a roadway. An impossibly large thing thundered at them, a vehicle of some kind, menacing and huge. It would strike them surely.

Ben waited without fear while the many-wheeled thing tore past them. A human, sitting in the small room at the front of this monstrosity, lifted a hand to Ben, and Ben returned the gesture.

After the thing had passed, splashing mud and stirring an unpleasant wind, the roadway was relatively empty. Ben moved the motorcycle forward, accelerating as they turned.

If she'd thought they'd moved swiftly before, their subsequent speed took Rhianne's breath away. Ben leaned forward, pulling her with him, and the motorcycle raced along. The trees to either side of the road were a blur, as were the giant buildings that smelled of metal, oil, and decay.

More vehicles came straight at them. Rhianne cringed against Ben, but the other conveyances whipped past them, the wind of their passing sharp. Rhianne realized that the continuously paved road had a stripe down its middle. The drivers kept their vehicles going one way on one side and the opposite direction on the other.

Still, only a painted stripe separated them from the gargantuan conveyances, which could easily come over the line and scatter her and Ben across the meadow beyond. The purpose of the helmet became clear.

They sped by open fields, some green, some fallow. Dampness and mud lay everywhere. The road wound over gullies and washes and passed lanes reaching from the fields, sometimes with vehicles in these lanes waiting to join them on the road.

More and more conveyances surrounded them as buildings crowded closer together, until they reached a large city, with many houses, vehicles, and people everywhere.

Ben slowed as they left the road, which had widened into many of the striped divisions, and went down a narrower lane. The sun had reached its zenith, the air hot and sticky.

The bike inched over a bump into a place where many vehicles sat silently. Ben slid the motorcycle to a halt and turned off its engine. The roar died, but Rhianne thought she'd have a ringing in her ears for a long time.

Ben gestured for Rhianne to climb off first, which Rhianne

attempted to do, hopping on her left foot that hit the ground until Ben grasped her ankle and helped her pull her right leg over the seat. The twinkle in his eyes told her she amused him.

Rhianne unfastened the helmet and pried it from her head. "Where are we?"

Ben swung off the bike and hung the helmet from the seat. He spread his arms. "New Orleans, baby. Welcome to The Big Easy."

CHAPTER SIX

R hianne wasn't certain why Ben assigned the phrase *The Big Easy* to the city, but she admitted he showed her a wonder.

They left the motorcycle behind and moved on foot through narrow streets teeming with people, far more than she'd see gathered in one place in Faerie. Rain began as they walked, but no one seemed to mind. It pattered down lightly then drifted off.

The number of shops amazed her. Ben took her first to find shoes—she walked into a room full of them in all shapes and colors. Rhianne rarely paid much attention to her footwear. She had boots made for comfortable walking and slippers for the occasional ball she attended, and those were enough. Now her eyes were opened to the possibilities.

Ben lounged on a chair with another man who had come in with his girlfriend. Soon Ben was conversing with him, coaxing laughs from the man.

The young woman with bright eyes and an eager smile who waited on Rhianne bubbled with enthusiasm that Rhianne soon caught. There was something refreshing about examining the shoes and trying on each pair, then surveying herself in the mirror the saleswoman ushered her toward.

Rhianne thought she looked very odd. The leather leggings hugged her calves, and the blue tunic flowed over her thighs. She had no cloak, hood, or fur-lined boots, and her single thick braid hung loose, when she usually pinned up her hair in a looped style. She felt open and exposed without her many layers of clothing. At the same time, she appeared to be ... cute. Fun. Playful. Everything Rhianne, the dignified Tuil Erdannan, was not.

"How about these?" The saleswoman returned with her hands full of hot pink straps. "They're adorable, but wanna know a secret? They're *so* comfortable."

She said it as though comfort was a shameful thing. Rhianne slid on the shoes with the young woman's help. The heels were higher than Rhianne was used to, but the straps formed a pleasing design on her foot and matched the glittery stripe on her pants. They were, as claimed, surprisingly comfortable.

"I have two pairs," the young woman whispered to Rhianne in confidence.

"Then I, too, will have two pairs," Rhianne announced.

"Sure thing, honey. Tell you what, you wear those out of here, and I'll bag up the boxes. I'll take you right over here."

The young woman led her to a long counter with small machines on it. "That's one seventy-five thirty-three for both. A bargain, right?"

Before Rhianne could ask, *one, seventy-five, and thirty-three what?* Ben was beside her. He handed the young woman a plastic rectangle, and the young woman snatched it from him, slanting Rhianne a knowing look.

"Lucky you," the young woman said admiringly. "Shoes *and* a good-looking guy to put them on his credit card." She laughed as she slid the card through a slot on the machine.

Ben flushed as the young woman returned the card, giving him a wink. Liam had made the same signal. People in this world liked to gesture with their eyelids.

"Here you go, honey." The young woman slid a bag across the counter, not to Rhianne, but to Ben. "Thank you, sweetie," she said to Rhianne. "Y'all come back anytime."

Rhianne nodded her appreciation and said good-bye. Ben led the way out of the store, he giving a wave to the man he'd been chatting with.

"I never thought the goblins were a servant race," Rhianne said in perplexity as she and Ben strode down the street past more stores with colorful and unusual wares in their windows.

In the human world, it seemed, the merchants made certain everyone passing knew exactly what was on offer inside their shops. In her part of Faerie, merchants kept their houses plain, with only a modest sign above a narrow door to indicate what they sold. One knocked and inquired if they had the thing one wanted.

"What?" Ben glanced at her. "Ah." He hefted the bag from the shoe store. "This is called being gallant. A lady shouldn't have to carry her own parcels or pay for her own shoes. You're my guest."

"Oh." Rhianne regarded him in confusion as pleasure crept through her.

She studied his solid body, lined with interesting tattoos, his hard face, his shorn black hair. People melted out of his way, but he was in no way gruff with them. He nodded at strangers as they passed, or said, "'Sup?" in a cheerful tone. Whatever that meant.

Ben did not possess the radiant handsomeness of the Tuil Erdannan nor the arrogant good looks of the *hoch alfar* or *dokk alfar*. Those of Faerie might even consider him ugly.

Rhianne had seen his other guise, only in a flash, when he'd rescued her. His human form was far more pleasant than that one, though she'd never find Ben ugly. He'd stormed into the fortress and taken her out, which would make him forever beautiful in her eyes.

Take care of him, Tiger had told her. *He is the last warrior.*

Last warrior for what?

Ben caught her hand and dragged her into the dim coolness of a building with a colorful façade and open doorway. "'Sup, Holly?" he said to the young woman at a podium, who had skin as dark as a *dokk alfar's* and beautiful brown eyes. This town seemed to be full of lovely young women.

"Ben." Holly stepped from behind the podium and hugged him. "Long time. Where've you been?"

"Oh, around. Busy. You have a table for two?"

"For you? Anytime." The woman peered with frank curiosity at Rhianne, grabbed two giant cards, and led them at a fast pace across a floor crowded with tables and people.

When they reached an empty table near a window, Ben held out a chair for Rhianne, to Holly's great interest. Ben settled Rhianne, as he had on the porch swing, before taking his own seat.

"They have the best shrimp gumbo here," Ben announced.

"We sure do," Holly said. "If you want authentic New Orleans food, this is the place. The menu is small, but that's because everything is just right." She laughed as she laid the cards in front of Rhianne and Ben, then sashayed away. Her tight dress emphasized her very curvy curves.

Rhianne leaned to him. "What is shrimp gumbo?" She paused. "What is shrimp?"

"Little critters that walk along the bottom of the sea. You put them in a kettle with sausage, bell peppers, and spices, and they sing to you."

Rhianne recoiled. "You eat them alive?"

Ben's laugh rumbled across the room. "My colorful way of talking. They're plenty dead when they go into the pot.

The gumbo sings." He kissed his fingers and popped them open.

"Little critters that walk along the bottom of the sea?" Rhianne repeated, still uncertain.

"Maybe you'd prefer jambalaya. That's rice with bell peppers and sausage, maybe some chicken. Oh, and shrimp."

"Do they have anything without this shrimp?"

"Possibly." Ben scanned the menu. "But don't knock them 'til you've tried them. Trust me, sweetheart. You'll love them."

Rhianne looked at the words printed before her but didn't understand any of them. She could read the English, but nothing made sense. "I must put myself in your hands."

Ben rubbed his together. "You won't regret it. I hope. Hey, Janie," he said to the next attractive young woman who stopped at the table. "Bring us one shrimp gumbo, one jambalaya, a mess of bread, and two blonde ales."

"Sure thing, Ben. How about a side of beans and rice?"

"Maybe later. We're starting small. This is Rhianne. She's new."

"Oh, hey." Janie turned a big smile to Rhianne. "Welcome to New Orleans."

She gave Rhianne the same interested once-over Holly had. They must believe her Ben's paramour. As Rhianne couldn't exactly explain how she'd met Ben and what she was doing here, she only smiled.

Janie took away the cards, and a young man sloshed two glasses of clear liquid to the table. Water, Rhianne guessed, though it smelled slightly metallic.

Two mugs of ale landed on the table only a few moments after that. Ben raised his once Janie had departed.

"Here's to freedom," he said.

Rhianne frowned in bafflement. "What are you doing?"

"It's called a toast. You raise your glass, say what you're drinking to, then we clink the glasses and drink."

Rhianne liked the idea. "To freedom," she echoed. "And the goblin who made it possible."

Ben's cheeks reddened. He moved his large glass to hers and gently tapped it. Then he drank.

Rhianne sipped the foamy liquid and found a drink she recognized. Ale, clear and tasty, with a zip of bubbles.

"It's good," she said in surprise.

"Yeah, humans can make decent beer. It's one reason I've stayed here all this time."

He tossed the words off casually, but Rhianne saw the flame of deep pain in him once more. What was Ben's story? He'd said he was exiled no longer, but the pain hadn't gone away.

Sadness and frustration tugged at her. "I can't stay forever. No matter how good the beer is."

Ben quickly set down his mug. "It's too dangerous for you to go back. Dylan can kiss his own ass."

"I will not return to be a spy, not that way." Rhianne shook her head. "If I were cold and calculating, I'd do it, but I'm not. No matter how much my mother tried to make me so."

Ben looked surprised. "I owe her. She's a great lady, Lady Aisling."

"Don't I know it." Rhianne's bitterness flowed out before she could stop it. "I love and admire her greatly. My mother kept my dangerous father away from me. But everyone expects me to be exactly like the imperious Lady Aisling. She can be ruthlessly brutal sometimes." Rhianne trailed off, rubbing the chilled beer glass with her fingers. "I don't want to be like that."

"She's Tuil Erdannan," Ben pointed out.

"So am I. But don't have the urge to create or destroy an entire race for the fun of it, or to devastate *hoch alfar* who are just trying to get through their days. The average *hoch alfar* are fine, trying to make a living and not draw attention to themselves."

"If you say so." Ben's rumble was dark.

Rhianne turned her mug on the table. "I know what they did to goblins. But that was the lords and princes, the same people who enslaved Shifters. The ordinary folk likely had no problem with goblins, and I know they don't want any pet Shifters."

Ben listened. Actually listened, meeting her gaze, his shoulders moving slightly. "You could be right. It's hard to have compassion when you watched your own people be slaughtered."

"I know." Rhianne swallowed. She couldn't imagine such a horror. "I'm sorry."

They fell silent, awkwardly so. Rhianne reflected that she and Ben might have had a nice day together if the whole history of Faerie and some of the bad people in it didn't lie between them.

"Here y'all go." Janie returned with a large tray, followed by the young man who'd delivered the water. The two of them laid steaming dishes in front of Ben and Rhianne. "I brought you a mess of silverware in case you want to share." In great delight, she set down the forks and spoons as though she bestowed an exciting gift.

"She's the best," Ben said, his affability returning. "Thanks, Janie."

"Y'all enjoy." Janie and the lad bustled off, leaving Ben and Rhianne with the savory smelling food.

"Dig in." Ben lifted a spoon and scooped up thick broth from his bowl. He stuck the spoon into his mouth, then an expression of great pleasure softened his face. "This is damn good gumbo. Here, try some."

He grabbed one of the extra spoons, filled it with broth and meat, and held it out to Rhianne.

The droplets would splatter all over the table. Rhianne leaned forward and quickly caught the spoonful in her mouth.

Incredible flavor poured over her tongue. A bite of spice, but not too much, savory sensations of herbs and sausage, and something pleasantly fishy.

"Oh, my," she said when she could speak.

"Didn't I tell you? There was shrimp in that. Here." He took up a fork and speared a curled pink thing on her plate of colorful rice.

Rhianne opened her mouth and Ben gently slid the bite into it. Their eyes met over the fork, and Rhianne felt suddenly hot.

Was the food too spicy? Not at all. It was the sensation of Ben's hand behind the fork, the smile on his lips, the enjoyment in his eyes.

Ben had been exiled, but he'd not forgotten how to live. He was now trying to show Rhianne how to live too.

She sat back, chewing and swallowing the mouthful. "I think I like shrimp," she announced.

"It's pretty awesome." Ben retreated to his side of the table. "Humans have come up with some wonderful stuff."

"How did they think to eat critters that crawl on the bottom of the sea?" Rhianne loaded her fork with the shrimp and rice and ate, closing her eyes to enjoy it.

"When you're hungry, anything's food. After a while, you figure out how to make it good. Very resourceful, are humans."

"You like them," Rhianne said with sudden insight.

Ben nodded. "They're not so bad. I've always had to try to fit in. When I first came to this world, I figured out fast that if humans didn't know what you were or where you came from, you were pretty much dead. I adapted. Try the beer with the jambalaya."

Rhianne took an obedient sip. He was wise—the flavors of the warm rice and the cool beer complemented each other well. He also was trying to distract her from prying into his hardships.

"I understand why Dylan wants me to spy on Walther," she said, returning to their earlier topic. "It's not only because he's worried about what a *hoch alfar* lord, even an ambitious one, is up to. He wants to know why my father is helping him."

"Probably." Ben ran his spoon through the gumbo. "If your dad's so dangerous, why did Lady Aisling marry the guy in the first place?"

Rhianne had wondered this most of her life. "She fell in love, she told me. My father is a very handsome and compelling man. Other ladies have fallen hard for him before, during, and since their marriage. Ivor de Erkkonen is powerful, smart, and extremely confident. When my mother was young, he was irresistible, so she says. She said she fell to the delusion many women have—that she could change him into something good." Rhianne let out a sad breath. "Maybe some women do transform other men, but my father was impossible. A man has to have some goodness in him, even if buried deep, for it to work."

"Yeah, some of us are true sweethearts." Ben assumed a mock modest expression, which evaporated. "Your dad, not so much?"

"I was very young when my mother sent him away, and I don't remember much about their marriage. He certainly never had any warm feelings for me. He regarded me more like a game piece he could use when he needed. My mother kept him away from me, which I didn't understand then, but for which I'm very grateful now. I grew up in innocence, thanks to her. She encouraged my studies, and for me to travel far from home once I'd finished university, to remove myself from his domains. He's mostly ignored me until now."

Again, Ben listened with his full attention, nodding along in sympathy.

"He'll have a harder time reaching you here," he declared. "The power of Faerie only extends so far into the human world.

Too much iron. Which, looking at you, doesn't bother you at all."

"I'm not *hoch alfar*." Rhianne took another sip of the beer. Still good. "Iron confounds *hoch alfar* magic, changes the very molecules in their bodies. They could have corrected that genetic flaw centuries ago, but they preferred to keep their magic as intact as possible. Becoming resistant to iron would have robbed them of some of their power. I've done research on the subject."

Ben's eyes crinkled in amusement. "Read a lot as a kid, did you?"

"Pretty much everything I could. I took a degree at the university. There's not a translation in English for that degree, I don't think, but in Tuil Erdannan, I am a master in astronomy and the science of the heavens."

"Ah, a learned woman as well as a beautiful one."

He was teasing, but Rhianne flushed in enjoyment. She had no business being flattered by him—her stay here was temporary, and they were from completely different worlds. Even in Faerie their paths never would have crossed.

Ben tucked into his gumbo, oblivious to her fluster. "If you like to read, the house has a huge library, including books on astronomy and astrophysics. It can find you what you're looking for...if you ask it nicely."

"A sentient house," Rhianne said thoughtfully. "How did that happen?"

"Who knows? It's on a ley line, but there's also a lot of woo-woo stuff around here. Maybe it taps into that."

Rhianne's brows went up. "Woo-woo?"

"Magical shit. Unexplained phenomenon. There isn't much in the human world, but you get pockets of magic here and there, and it's concentrated in this area. There are many popular vampire stories set in New Orleans."

"Are there vampires here?" Rhianne glanced about, but the

inhabitants of the restaurant were normal humans. She didn't have the gift for discerning auras, but she knew the telltale signs of magical creatures.

"Nah. They avoid the place. Had a run-in with a few vampire-like beings Dylan thought about using to help Shifters, but Dylan changed his mind. *After* I worked my ass off contacting them and setting up meets. Dylan decides they're too dangerous, and that's the last I saw of them. Fine by me. They gave me the creeps."

"This is a very interesting world." Rhianne finished the jambalaya, which was filling, but she could have eaten more.

Janie came by just then with a plate of doughy pastry covered with icing sugar. "Beignets. On the house." She grinned at Ben, swept away their dirty dishes and settled the sweets between them. The young man hurried out of nowhere with small, clean plates and set them in front of Rhianne and Ben.

"Janie's awesome." Ben offered the pastries to Rhianne.

Rhianne carefully lifted one of the small, delicate cushions and bit into it. She tasted warm, crackling layers of crust and the sweet brush of sugar.

"Women in the village near where I live make something like this," she said as she savored. "But I think not as good."

"Food is king here." Ben ate a beignet whole. "Not just the tourist food you're supposed to eat, but everything. French, Creole, Cajun, Caribbean, South and Central American, Southern ... everything."

"Have you lived in New Orleans long?"

"Not very. Spent a lot of time in North Carolina and in Las Vegas. Moved here when Jasmine needed someone to look after the house. I knew about haunted houses—I was a resident ghost in one in North Carolina for a while."

Rhianne narrowed her eyes as she took another bite of the wonderful beignet. "But you're alive."

"I know that, and you know that, but the owners of the inn and guests who came for the authentic ghost experience didn't." Ben chuckled. "Those were good times."

"I do not believe I will ever understand you." Rhianne finished her beignet and chose another. "Though I thank you for showing me your city. Or perhaps you think of it as your adopted city?"

"I do. But you ain't seen nothing yet, sweetheart. The sun's still up."

"And I barely understand your English."

"You'd understand my goblin less." Ben waved at Janie, who arrived with a slip of paper that she laid next to his plate. He pulled out his square rectangle again and handed it to her.

"Your coins are interesting." Rhianne rested her chin on her hand and nibbled the last beignet. "Not coins at all. And they give it back to you."

"Credit card." Ben tapped the slim leather pouch he kept the card in. "It's like keeping a running tally with a merchant and then paying everything at the end of the month. Except a separate company keeps the running tally and pays the merchants for you, and then you pay up to that separate company."

"Ah." Rhianne licked sugar from her fingers. "A few *hoch alfar* tried to set up a syndicate rather like that. Whenever a debtor could not pay them, they'd threaten to take their home or livestock or even their lives. It happened too many times, so a *hoch alfar* prince had the creditor syndicate put to death."

Ben's brows went up. "Well, that might make credit card companies think twice about raising their interest rates." Janie returned the card with more paper and a smile. "Thank you, Janie. You're the best."

"And you're a flatterer. I'd watch this one," Janie said to Rhianne.

Banter seemed to be common, and good-natured. "I will, I promise," Rhianne returned.

Janie laughed and danced off to another table.

"Come on." Ben reached for Rhianne's hand, and it felt natural to clasp his. "Time to show you the rest."

———

BEN'S WORLD WAS ONE RHIANNE NEVER KNEW EXISTED. New Orleans had shops filled with many delightful things—books, trinkets galore, colorful wraps and clothing, and more shoes, plus places that proclaimed their psychics could read your future or your past lives, whatever past lives were.

Rhianne lingered next to a clothing store, knowing she could not borrow from the two unknown women forever.

Ben led her inside, telling her to pick out whatever she wanted. They left with two shopping bags, one containing a T-shirt that read: *New Orleans, Where Partying is an Art Form.*

Rhianne expressed curiosity about the psychics, so Ben took her to a shop with books and crystals on its shelves, a waft of incense in the air. In a small, pleasantly sunny room in the back, a young woman with dark skin, wearing colorful wraps similar to what Rhianne had just bought for herself, instructed Rhianne to sit across from her at a table.

They were alone in the room, the young woman telling Ben that the reading was strictly private, but Ben lurked on the other side of the curtain.

"Let me look at your palm, honey," the young woman said. "I'll do your lines and then a set of cards. That's the basic package."

Rhianne wasn't certain what she meant about a package, but she laid her hand on the table, palm up. Ben had warned her that the psychics in many of these shops were charlatans, but Rhianne wanted to know what this one had to say. Perhaps she could give some hint as to how long Rhianne would be here, or what specific danger her father posed to her. Even if she were a charlatan, this venture was all in good fun.

The young woman brushed Rhianne's palm, her fingertips warm and relaxing. She peered at Rhianne's hand a moment before she gasped and jerked upright, her eyes widening to dark brown pools of fear.

"By the Goddess," the woman whispered. "What *are* you?"

CHAPTER SEVEN

B en heard the psychic's words loud and clear. By the time
Rhianne finished a quick intake of breath, he had shoved
aside the curtain and charged into the room.

The psychic was a young black woman with long, glossy
hair pulled into loops on the back of her head. She'd donned
the swirling scarves and necklaces of a stage psychic, but Ben
sensed the aura of no ordinary woman.

The psychic should have snapped at Ben to leave, but she
was too busy staring at Rhianne in shock.

"I'm no one special," Rhianne said faintly.

The woman seized Rhianne's hand. "No one special?
Sweetie, these lines are crazy. And your aura—" She waved at
the air in front of her. "Never saw anything like it. And you ..."
More shock as she beheld Ben. "Shit, should I call nine-one-
one?"

Ben leaned his fists on the table. "You should forget all
about us instead."

"How can I? Both your auras are screaming at me. No,
don't run away." The woman clamped her hand down on

Rhianne's to keep her seated at the table. "You're in trouble, honey. You need to hear what I have to say."

"Release her," Ben said in a hard voice. "*Now.*"

"No." Rhianne's quick word cut through Ben's order. "Let her speak."

For a moment, the room hung with silent tension. Then the psychic slowly uncurled her fingers from Rhianne's hand.

"I'd never hurt you," she said. "I'm Lily, by the way. And you are the most magical people who've ever come in here."

"Rhianne." Rhianne touched her chest then indicated Ben. "And Ben."

"Well, you make a nice couple."

"Oh, we are not ..."

Lily cut off Rhianne's protest with an imperious wave. "Yes, you are. I'm never wrong. But the danger I see for you both is huge." She brushed Rhianne's palm with a pink painted nail and glanced at Ben. "Let me get you a chair."

Ben waited as Lily exited through a door in the back of the tiny room and reappeared instantly with a straight-backed chair identical to the other two. Once Lily had Ben seated, she leaned on the table and gave them both a frank assessment.

"I don't know what you people are, or where you come from. It's not this world, I'm pretty sure. I don't think you mean me any harm, because believe me, when evil walks in this place, I know it." She tapped the table with a stiff finger. "But you're not exactly angels either. Though they can be pretty tough when they want."

"What kind of danger is she in?" Ben asked sharply, returning her to her point.

"Something pretty bad." Lily's brow wrinkled in worry. "I see much darkness, fear, and rage. Fury. Against you." She pointed at Ben, her finger a skewer.

"Fury from me?" Rhianne asked in concern.

"No, no. From outside forces. *Bad* outside forces." Lily turned to Ben. "Who the hell did you piss off?"

Ben grimaced. "A lot of people. I've gone through my whole life pissing off anyone who comes into contact with me."

"Hmm." Lily peered at him. "Recently, you've done some kind of damage, or it might be damage you're going to do, but the rage I'm detecting is serious. They want to kill you, whoever they are. Not only kill you, but erase you completely. And you." She switched her attention to Rhianne. "The trouble is, if you stay with him, you'll share the danger. The only way to avoid it is to be far from him. But like I said, you're a couple, so that choice might not be up to you."

"Can you be more specific?" Ben asked Lily. "I can prepare better if I know what I'm facing. What are they? Vampires? Shifters? Fae? *Zilithal* annoyed that we canceled the meeting on the winter solstice?"

Lily's eyes went wide. "*Zilithal?* You mean those evil, bloodsucking demons? You were going to *meet* with them?"

"Yeah, well, in retrospect it was probably better we called it off," Ben conceded. "So, who is it?"

Lily shook her head. "I'm sorry. I can see a general danger— it's like a blackness, hovering, waiting to crush you. But not who will cause it. When it gets closer, yes, I might be able to. Right now, you have a chance to avoid this danger if you go far, far from here."

"How far?" Ben asked. *Alaska? Russia? The Arctic? How about the Antarctic?*

Lily blew out a breath. "A hell of a long way. You might not be able to go far enough."

Every once in a while, Ben ran into someone who wasn't fooled by his glams or the tough magic he wove to keep himself appearing human. Lily impressed him.

"Can you dig into it?" Ben balled his hands. "I won't ask

you to if it's too dangerous for yourself, but I'd appreciate any intel. Will pay for it too."

"That's kind of you. I can look. Won't charge you unless I find anything specific. Now you." She switched back to Rhianne. "I *can* tell you not to go home. You'll find the most danger there. Stay away, and let things work themselves out."

Rhianne shot Ben a troubled glance. "I hope it doesn't take too long."

Lily shrugged. "I can't divine that. I can tell that you have a lot of power. It radiates from you. Like I said, though, it might not be enough to battle what waits for you at home."

"My power is not that great." Rhianne shook her head. "If you sense something, it's only because of my ancestry. The talents my parents have did not get passed down to me."

She stated it as a simple fact, one she'd come to accept long ago. Ben forbore to point out that a Tuil Erdannan with a tiny amount of magic was more powerful than the highest *hoch alfar* magician. He supposed it was a matter of perspective.

"If you say so, honey." Lily withdrew her hand. "But your aura is powerful—I bet you have more in you than you know. It's almost ..." She looked thoughtful, then shook her head. "Never mind. I'm not sure what other advice to give you. Either go so far away you're on the moon, or prepare yourself for battle."

Ben regarded her with disquiet. Lily might be overconfident in her abilities, or she might have the clairvoyance a few rare humans had.

He was acquainted with one other woman with similar talents. "Do you know Jasmine McNaughton?" Ben asked her on impulse.

"Sure I do." Lily's brows rose. "She's the real thing. You're friends of Jazz? Why didn't you say so? How is she?"

"Doing well. Expecting."

Lily's foreboding disappeared and she flashed a smile.

"That's awesome. Tell her congratulations. And to call me. She and I need to talk."

"I'll relay your message," Ben said.

"Now, I don't usually ask for details—don't need to—but who are you? *What* are you?"

Ben shrugged. "Let's just say we're not from around here."

"That's for sure. You liking New Orleans?" Lily turned her interest to Rhianne.

"So far. I have discovered I enjoy shrimp."

"Wish I could. I'm allergic. Can you imagine living in New Orleans and being allergic to shellfish? It sucks. But I know a great bakery just around the block—bread and pastry to die for. The guy who runs it is Honduran and one hell of a baker." Her dire predictions had vanished on the wind.

"If we're in so much danger, we'd better skip the bakery," Ben said.

Lily shook her head. "You're not in danger *today*. What I'm seeing is to come. Might as well enjoy yourself now. So much to do in New Orleans."

"This is what I mean about being specific," Ben said. "When will all this shit go down? I'd like to be prepared."

"I'd have to do more research. What I see for you today is ..." Her eyes lost focus, then her smile returned. "Fun stuff. Enjoy yourselves."

"Eat, drink, and be merry, for tomorrow we die?" Ben quoted.

"Something like that. Be home by midnight so you don't turn into a pumpkin." Lily faltered. "Wow, I hope that doesn't happen for real. Now, that's twenty-five dollars for the reading. I took five dollars off because we never got around to the cards." To Ben's frown, Lily shrugged. "If riches were in my near future, I wouldn't worry about it, but they're not. A psychic's got to make a living."

RHIANNE FOLLOWED BEN, WHO CARRIED THE BAGS OF THE things they purchased, into the sunny street. Her heart thumped in apprehension, and she couldn't help scanning the road for danger.

"Should we go back to the house?" she asked.

"You heard what Lily said," Ben answered easily. "Today is free and clear, and she sounds like she knows what she's talking about. I say we forget our problems for now and have some fun."

"But ..." Rhianne drew closer to him. "She's only a human. How can you be certain?"

"I can't. But hell, I've been facing danger for centuries. I know that when there's a window to party in, you do it."

Rhianne wondered how anyone partied in a window without falling out of it, but she hurried her steps to keep up with him.

"I have to tell you something." Rhianne's braid slapped her back as she jogged, her new shoes clicking on the pavement. "When Tiger took me aside to speak to me, he told me I should look after you. As though he also knows danger is coming."

Ben halted, bags swinging. Rhianne bounced into him then planted her feet to stay upright.

"Tiger said that? Shit." Ben gazed pensively across the street, studying a small park encircled by railings. "Tiger's another person who can't be specific. He senses things and gives you cryptic-ass warnings." Ben sighed. "But he's never wrong."

"What should we do?"

"Right now?" Ben flashed her a smile. "We keep on having a good time."

Rhianne wanted to protest, but Ben strode swiftly away, and Rhianne quickened her steps to join him.

She saw the wisdom in this approach of enjoying themselves while they had the chance once he'd swept her across the street, through the park, and to the bakery Lily had mentioned. The warm smell of baking bread, chocolate, and sugar floated out from the open door, inviting them inside.

The shop was narrow and tiny, with glass cases filled with cakes, sweet biscuits, and pastries, many of which Rhianne couldn't identify. She saw beignets similar to those they'd had at the restaurant and many loaves of round, crusty breads.

There was also a line of people, several of them chatting as though they were old friends, but as Rhianne listened to their conversations, she realized they didn't know each other at all. Strangers were laughing and talking, asking questions, answering without reserve. Such a contrast to the Tuil Erdannan society, where few trusted anyone else, and definitely no one spoke with casual friendliness to strangers.

When it was their turn, Ben ordered what he called cookies and some of the beignets, paying again with his plastic card. He led Rhianne out of the shop to a table on the sidewalk, plunking everything down before he sat.

"We need to eat these right away," he said, pulling out the beignets. "They'll get soggy if we wait."

He'd purchased a dozen. Rhianne ate two, still full from their luncheon, and Ben downed the rest, licking icing sugar from his fingers.

There was something in what he and Lily had said, to enjoy themselves for the moment. If there was no danger now, make the most of the time. Better than hiding behind walls and brooding.

Rhianne admitted to herself that it was simple to enjoy the day with Ben. He had mastered the art of relaxation. Soon she was conversing easily with him, the worry of the future forgotten for a while.

Yes, it was easy to be with Ben. Too easy. Rhianne let down

her guard and told him all kinds of things about herself before realizing it, including her regret that she had far less power than her mother. She didn't mind so much for herself, but she feared she disappointed Lady Aisling. She'd also worried that her lack of power might have begun the wedge between her father and mother.

"Nah," Ben said. "Lots of kids think their parents' breakup is their fault, but they're wrong. When a couple is that unhappy, it's about a hell of a lot more than what the children were doing."

"I know that intellectually." Rhianne tapped her temple, then touched her chest. "But in here, I'm still the child who saw their incredulity when I couldn't perform the smallest of magical tasks without effort."

"Again, not your fault. Magical ability is born into you. They should blame their own genetics, not you."

"I suppose that's true."

"It is true. Now, no more depressing talk. Cookie?" Ben held up a biscuit studded with bits of chocolate.

Rhianne smiled and accepted.

———

IT SEEMED AS THOUGH NO TIME HAD PASSED BEFORE twilight fell. Ben and Rhianne had walked everywhere, listening to street musicians, buying more trinkets, stopping for coffee and then a beer. After the ale, Ben took Rhianne to another restaurant, this one dark and elegant. He knew the person at the door here too, a man this time, and they were brought to a candle-lit table in the back.

After more incredible food, Ben led her to another shop, but instead of going inside, he took the stairs to the floor above it, balancing the bags.

"I rented a storage room up here." He pulled keys from his

front pocket. "I want to stash our stuff before we go dancing. We'll pick it up again after."

"Go dancing?"

"You know. At a club. Not a Shifter one, though. I can't imagine what would happen if I brought in a Tuil Erdannan. They'd scent Faerie on you before you got in the door and all hell would break loose. I mean, all *Shifters* would break loose. Best not to risk it."

Ben ushered her into a basic room with four walls and a high window. Shelves lined the walls, holding opaque boxes with colorful lids.

"What is all this?" Rhianne asked in curiosity.

Ben set the packages of things they'd bought in a vacant space and opened the nearest box to show her. "Things I've collected over the years. Should probably get rid of most of it."

He pulled out a smaller box and removed the lid. Inside lay a string of diamonds surrounding a glittering, blood-red stone that had to be a ruby.

Rhianne stared in astonishment and brushed the necklace with a shaking finger. The stones were cold, belying the fire they held.

"Where on earth did you find this?"

Ben shrugged. "Russia. The empress gave it to me, oh, two hundred fifty years ago? Catherine, her name was."

Rhianne had no idea where Russia was or who its empress had been, but she did know that this necklace must be worth much. "You keep this, in *here*, in a box?" She glanced at the worn room and the door that had only one small lock.

"Why not?" Ben tucked the necklace away and the room lost color. "Who would look for something like that in here? Besides, no one crosses the threshold that I don't want to."

"You've warded it?" Rhianne scanned the walls but saw no sign of magic sigils, visible or hidden.

"Not really. There's a ley line under the shop downstairs I

tap into to cast a glam. Humans ignore this place. So do Shifters, come to think of it. Not that they'd invade my privacy. Shifters respect other people's stuff."

Rhianne regarded the boxes with new respect as Ben opened another one.

"Here we go." He lifted out a string of tiny sapphires that flashed in the wan light. "Wear this tonight."

Rhianne blinked. The stones were a deep blue that would go perfectly with her tunic. "Are you sure?"

"Why not?" Ben turned her around and draped the necklace across her chest, his fingers warm as he fastened the catch. He turned her around again, studying her with flattering intensity. "Perfect."

Rhianne tried not to wilt in too much pleasure—at the gift, his touch, his admiring gaze. She kept her knees from bending and managed to thank him with dignity.

Ben waved her thanks aside and led her out. He snapped off the light and shut the door, locking it with a small key.

By the time they emerged it was fully dark, but the streets were bright, the city more alive than it had been during the day. Bands played on almost every corner, and flashing lights enticed attention. Rhianne glanced into one open door they passed to see a human woman in very little clothing dancing on a raised platform in the middle of the room. The patrons at tables were eating and drinking as though this was nothing extraordinary.

Ben caught her hand. "Not far now."

Rhianne pulled her attention from the dancer and hurried beside him. "Are all human cities like this?"

Ben laughed. "No, sweetheart. New Orleans is unique. Probably a good thing."

He guided her around a few more corners and halted before a brick building from which people spilled into the street. The large man at the door hailed them as they approached.

"Ben! How you doing? Thought you'd gone forever." He caught Ben's hand in a clasp and thumped his shoulder.

Ben returned the handgrip enthusiastically. "Work. You know how it is. Can you squeeze us in?"

"You? Of course. Come on in. Good evening, miss." He gave Rhianne a cordial nod, his gaze swiveling back to Ben, brows rising.

Another person who assumed she and Ben were in a relationship. That should bother Rhianne, but for some reason, she didn't mind.

Loud, thumping music met her ears as they stepped inside the building. The bass notes throbbed through her body, an entity of sound. She'd never heard the like.

Ben took her hand and steered her around tables to an empty one. A wave of his fingers brought a waitress to them, and a moments later, she cheerfully deliver two chilled bottles of ale.

"You want something else?" Ben asked Rhianne over the music. "Wine, whiskey, martini?"

Rhianne lifted the bottle. "Thank you, but no. I like the ale." They sipped, Rhianne appreciating the cool liquid after their walk.

The music was compelling. Men and women gyrated with each other, but young women also danced together, and young men danced by themselves, showing off like cocks in a barnyard. Rhianne laughed as she watched them, her feet tapping. She loved to dance.

"Want to?" Ben gestured at the floor.

"Indeed."

Rhianne rose eagerly, and soon they were in the midst of the bouncing, pulsating humans enjoying the hell out of the night.

Rhianne had no idea how humans danced. She had been trained in the stately art of grand pavanes and the brisker galliards, but she'd also learned folk dancing from the staff in her mother's house when she'd been a girl. She and the staff had kept this a secret from Lady Aisling.

The music seemed to suit the folk dancing. There was no room for high kicks, but the beat was fast enough for jumping footwork and twirls. Ben wouldn't know these dances, but in them, the man often acted as an anchor for the lady's antics.

Rhianne began the so-familiar movements: heel and toe, rapid switch to the other foot, heel and toe, jump, her feet flashing as they crossed back and forth. Ben started to laugh.

He swung her around in a circle, then he began footwork that was just as boisterous and complex. The music wrapped Rhianne, filling her with its vibrations and repetitive sounds. It urged her to make the folk dance's steps jerkier, integrating pauses and stops. The sapphire necklace bounced against her chest, glittering like stars under the club's lights.

A young woman near her jumped and gyrated in a crazed way, her arms going in and out, her rhythm perfect. Rhianne imitated her, weaving the moves into the Tuil Erdannan dance.

Ben ceased being the easygoing, laidback man who'd wandered the streets with her today and transformed into a dancer. He rolled arms and shoulders, spun in place, and undulated like a snake. His moves were charged with sensuality, smoldering the air.

Rhianne's heart beat faster, and not simply from the energetic dance. Ben kept his allure dampened, but all day Rhianne had felt a pull toward him. Had since he'd lifted her from the horrible cell.

Maybe she was becoming infatuated with him because he'd rescued her. And showed her his world, showering her with gifts and wonderful food, hovering protectively near her.

Could be.

At the moment, reasons didn't matter. She tossed off her usual caution and reticence to enjoy dancing with a gorgeous man who had the strength of a dozen.

Ben caught her gaze, his eyes warm, his hands in hers solid. The heat of him flowed all the way inside her, winding around her heart.

———

As Rhianne's body flowed and wove in the patterns of her impromptu dance, Ben was enchanted. The haughty Tuil Erdannan would never look twice at his kind, yet here and now, that didn't matter. They weren't goblin and Tuil Erdannan but Ben and Rhianne, far from anyplace that cared about such things.

Ben took her hand and spun her, space on the dance floor opening for them. She swung back into Ben's arms, where they swayed together, Rhianne naturally graceful.

Their otherworldly dancing attracted attention. Soon Ben and Rhianne were in the midst of an appreciative crowd who punched the air to indicate their approval. Some couples tried to imitate their moves, with mixed success.

Ben and Rhianne got separated, she cut off from him by the wild dancers. Before Ben could reach her, a curvy woman with hair a mixture of blond and brown with golden-brown eyes gyrated next to Rhianne.

"Hey, I have pants just like those." She pointed to Rhianne's leg-hugging leather with the pink rhinestone-studded seams. "Wait a minute. Those *are* my pants." Jaycee Bordeaux growled, her eyes slitting to those of her leopard. "What the hell are you doing in my clothes?" She sniffed, and rage changed her fingers to claws. "*Fae.*"

CHAPTER EIGHT

B en broke through the dancers between him and Rhianne, reaching for Jaycee's paw as it went for Rhianne's face. Before he could reach her, Rhianne gripped Jaycee's wrist with a swiftness that stunned him.

"Are you Jaycee?" Rhianne shouted to her.

Jaycee caught sight of Ben as he landed next to Rhianne. "*Shit.*" Ben watched her deliberately calm the leopard, her hands and eyes returning to human shape. "You're her?"

Rhianne carefully let her go. "I'm—"

Ben stopped her words with his fingers on her lips. Couldn't be too careful with info in here. Many humans worked for the *hoch alfar*, rogue Shifters, and who knew who else.

Jaycee's face was red under the dance floor's flashing lights. "Sorry," she said. "Sometimes I strike before I think."

Ben gently removed his fingers from Rhianne's soft, warm mouth, and Rhianne gave Jaycee a gracious nod.

"Quite all right," Rhianne said. "I'd be incensed if I saw an unknown woman in *my* clothing."

"Incensed?" Jaycee's smile flashed. "That's a good word."

"Where's your other half?" Ben asked her.

Jaycee rolled her eyes. "Charming people at the bar. Or he *thinks* he's charming them."

Rhianne's gaze went to Jaycee's throat, which did not bear the Collar that Dylan and Liam had worn, or even a fake one like Tiger's. Ben saw her curiosity, but this was not the place to discuss such things.

"Should we go somewhere quieter to talk?" he suggested to Jaycee.

Jaycee sent him an incredulous look. "Right now? When your dance moves are so hot? I say we party a little longer. You with me?" She transferred her attention to Rhianne, her instinctive fury forgotten.

Rhianne shot a quick glance at Ben, as though soliciting his opinion.

"Why not?" Ben said. The psychic Lily had told them they had nothing to fear tonight, and Ben believed her.

Rhianne nodded her acceptance, and Jaycee spun to put herself next to Rhianne.

"Sweet. Teach me some of that, will you?"

Rhianne began to dance again, hesitant at first. But Jaycee, though she could be a deadly enemy, was also a fast friend and protector. She was a tracker, which meant she guarded her Shiftertown leader and his family, doing whatever it took to defend their group. She could fight better than many male Shifters Ben knew, and her skills had only sharpened after she and Dimitri had their cub, a cute little guy called Lucas.

Jaycee studied Rhianne's flurried footwork and began to copy it. She was a great dancer—her leopard had swiftness and grace—and soon she was hopping from foot to foot in exact time with Rhianne.

Rhianne's face lit with laughter. She and Jaycee quickly became a well-honed team. Jaycee's outfit was similar to Rhianne's—leather pants and a silver lame shirt, though Jaycee wore motorcycle boots to Rhianne's strappy high-heeled sandals.

The crowd surrounded *them* now, clapping time, encouraging the two. Both women were beautiful, hot, and could dance up a storm. Every male in here, and some of the females, must be drooling for them.

A tall, red-haired man pushed through the crowd, his eyes lit with rage. Ben knew he sensed the testosterone flaring from the guys ogling Jaycee, and the wolf in him wanted to come out and play.

Ben intercepted the man. "Keep it cool," he yelled over the music.

Dimitri Kashnikov was a red wolf, tall and tough, a savage fighter. But this wasn't a Shifter bar—he couldn't go all Lupine and start slashing his claws around.

Dimitri growled, the sound rumbling to Ben through the music. Ben watched him force his eyes to flicker from the wolf's, then Dimitri waded through the crowd to Jaycee.

He got behind her, his mate, and began gyrating with her, arcing her body inside his. Jaycee didn't mind. She leaned back into him and caught his rhythm, the two becoming one in the dance. Their undulating was very sensual—no one dirty danced like Shifters.

Mate-bonded pairs. What could you do?

Ben made his way to Rhianne and caught both her hands in his to continue their groove. He wished he could fold himself around her as Dimitri did with Jaycee, to imbibe her warmth and her swaying body.

What the fuck was he thinking? Rhianne was Tuil Erdannan, the daughter of Lady Aisling, a woman who could raze this club and everyone in it by simply drawing a breath. If Ben touched her daughter, she'd crumble him to dust and feed what was left into a furnace.

But what a way to go.

Ben jerked his thoughts from their treacherous path. He had this dance, and he needed to enjoy it. His job was to protect Rhianne, that was all, and to return her home when it was safe. He didn't have time to fantasize about the beautiful woman.

Why did it always have to be this way? Something deep inside him mourned. Ben always did his job. Had for a thousand years. Did it so others could walk unharmed, live their lives, find happiness.

Everyone but Ben.

The endless song finally drew to a close. Not that this club ever let the music stop. One piece segued into the next, which was equally thumping and harsh.

Jaycee gave a final twirl and laced her arm through Dimitri's. "Okay," she yelled. "*Now* we go talk."

Dimitri had danced out his aggression and beamed his affable smile on Jaycee's and Rhianne's admirers. He could be smug—he was leaving with the hot Jaycee.

Jaycee led the way through the crowd and out into the street. It wasn't much quieter here, with the roads and sidewalks teeming as the New Orleans night ramped up.

Ben suggested they walk to Jackson Square. As they strolled along, tourists rode past in horse-drawn carriages and bicycle rickshaws, bands and street performers did their thing, food carts sent aromas into the air. Couples walked hand in hand, or danced near the bands, just generally kicking back to enjoy life.

People moved aside for the group without realizing why, though Ben and Dimitri greeted strangers with warmth. They smiled back, happy and unafraid.

Jaycee found a vacant bench near the middle of the park, the fragrance of grass and late flowers floating around them. Lovers ambled by or blatantly kissed on the lawn.

"I apologize again," Jaycee said to Rhianne as they settled

themselves, Dimitri and Ben bookending the two ladies on the bench. "I smelled Fae and my instincts kicked in. My bad. I owe you a debt."

Rhianne blinked. "Why should you owe me a debt? I stole your pants." She stretched out a leg to admire the black leather, stones glittering.

Jaycee laughed. "I like her," she said to Ben then returned her attention to Rhianne. "But I like your mom too, so I guess it's natural. And hey, you look great in those. Ooh, nice shoes."

Dimitri groaned. "Goddess, Jaycee, we didn't come out here to talk about shoes."

"Are you kidding? We should always talk about shoes. They're perfect with the outfit. You have good taste, Rhianne."

"I tried to find something worthy of your clothes," Rhianne said.

"And you did a fantastic job. Stop poking at me, Dimitri. I swear, ever since he mate claimed me, he's been all over my case about everything."

"Someone has to keep you in line," Dimitri rumbled. "Or try anyway."

Jaycee ignored him. "So, Ben, what's the deal? Did Dylan find you? I didn't want to involve him, but Lady Aisling told me to, so..." Jaycee opened her hands in a helpless gesture.

"Yeah, he found us," Ben said. "Wanted Rhianne to go back and be his pet spy. She said no. *I* said no. Hell, even Tiger said no."

"Good for you," Jaycee said approvingly. "Dylan is always eager to recruit people, whether they like it or not. Well, we're here for you, Rhianne. Whatever you need."

"You are very kind," Rhianne said sincerely. "And you've already lent me your clothes."

"I can find you much better things than that. There's a boutique on—"

Dimitri's groan turned into a growl. "And we didn't come here to go clothes shopping."

"Again, why not?" Jaycee turned on him. "You are such a shit."

"Yeah, but you love me, baby."

Dimitri used to stutter, badly, but after he'd mated with Jaycee, the stutter had faded until it was now almost nonexistent, unless he grew agitated.

Rhianne turned to Ben. "I have had a wonderful day, but perhaps we should go back to the house. We are safe there?"

"Yep. No one goes into the house that the house doesn't want there." Ben rubbed his upper lip. "Including me sometimes."

Rhianne's brow furrowed in worry. "Do you believe it might not let *me* in?"

Ben slid his arm around her, trying not to get lost in the curve of her waist, the warmth of her body. "I think it likes you. And when it likes you, it will defend you to the death."

Rhianne did not look reassured. "There is a way into the house from Faerie, though. We came through it. Can others?"

"No, sweetheart." Ben tightened his embrace, pleased when she didn't pull away. "It will keep them out."

"An uninvited Fae did get through once," Dimitri said. "The house took care of him. It wasn't p-pretty. But the dude had had me beaten and thrown into a dungeon, so he kind of had it coming."

He grimaced in memory, and Jaycee leaned closer to him. Dimitri calmed instantly, his face smoothing. Shifters could ease each other with a mere touch.

Ben realized he was watching the two in wistful envy and rose abruptly to his feet.

"Rhianne is right. We're starting to push our luck. Let's go back. You two coming with us?"

Dimitri leisurely stood and pulled Jaycee up with him.

"Yeah, we were going to ask if we could crash at the house. It's a long ride back to our compound. We're from Texas," Dimitri told Rhianne. "From the very flat, very dry, very empty part. Which is most of it."

"Crash?" Rhianne accepted Ben's hand to assist her to stand. "Why would you crash yourself into the house?"

Dimitri chortled. "It's an idiom. It means sleep, flop, snooze, get some kip."

Rhianne listened carefully. "I see."

"English is a hell of a language," Dimitri said. "I learned it when an American family adopted me. I was confused for the first few years I lived with them."

"That hasn't changed." Jaycee wove her arms around him as he feigned offense at her quip.

Dimitri leaned to her, and Jaycee rose on tiptoe and kissed him. The darkness gave them relative privacy, not that human couples weren't doing the same thing forty feet away.

Ben drew closer to Rhianne as Dimitri's and Jaycee's kiss went on. And on. Dimitri smoothed his hands over Jaycee's hips, and she flowed up to him.

"They share the mate bond," Ben said in Rhianne's ear. "Have you heard of that? It's a Shifter thing."

"The mystical binding created by the Goddess found only by true mates." Rhianne turned to Ben, her eyes flickering when she realized how close he stood to her. "It isn't only a Shifter thing. Most creatures of Faerie can find it. Goblins included."

Ben hadn't heard that. "I've been out of Faerie for a thousand years, and I didn't exactly have the chance to take a mate among my own people. I've thought once or twice that it might happen for me, but no."

He recalled how he'd believed the mate bond had been forming between him and a Shifter woman, and his disappointment when he'd discovered he was mistaken. He hadn't minded all that much—Kenzie had found great happiness with her gruff mate, Bowman—but he'd concluded that perhaps goblins couldn't form it at all.

Rhianne slowly lifted her hand and placed it on his chest. Her fingertips stirred tingles in his blood, and a painful dart of longing lanced his heart.

"I believe it will happen for you, Ben." Rhianne's whisper was soft in the warm darkness. "You are a champion."

She said the last words in Tuil Erdannan, ones he knew. *Champion* for the Fae was the highest honor, a person who would sacrifice themselves without hesitation to save others from harm.

Ben supposed the word described him. He'd sacrificed his entire life, not because he was special, but because he needed to make up for the exile and death of his people that his actions had caused. He never would make up for it, he knew, and the despair of that drove him on. He also knew that if he ever gave into the despair he'd not survive.

"Champion." The word emerged from his mouth tinged with irony. "If you say so."

Rhianne touched his lips. "I do say so."

Ben sensed the mate bond that wove between Jaycee and Dimitri as they stood locked in their embrace. He could see it, the glistening threads that bound them in love.

He couldn't stop himself. Ben slid his hand under Rhianne's hair, and she moved closer to him, her breath touching his face.

Ben closed the small space between them and kissed her.

Fire ignited, the spark searing through his body. Their lips met simply, no prolonged, intense kiss, nothing like what Jaycee and Dimitri did. A light touch, the satin of Rhianne's lower lip brushing his and opening something inside him.

Ben wove his fingers into her thick hair, the silk of it heavy.

When she unbraided it, it would wrap her like a cloak. Ben could happily lie tangled in her tresses.

Rhianne was the first to end the kiss, drawing back slightly but not pulling away. She gazed at Ben with her brown eyes brushed with black, her face still, as though she strove to tuck her emotions away.

Ben tried to release her and found that he couldn't. Giving up, he tugged her to him and kissed her again.

When Rhianne made a tiny sound in her throat, Ben's heart pounded like a freight train. He wanted to take her down to the grass, open the silky blue blouse and discover her firm body inside. He only kept himself still by massive effort.

He deepened the kiss, drawing the tip of his tongue along the seam of her mouth. He wouldn't delve inside, not now, not here. But tasting her—the sweetness of powdered sugar, the bite of ale, the spice of herself—flooded even more fire inside him.

Making love to Rhianne would be the most powerful thing that ever happened to him. And it was completely impossible.

The thought knocked through him, but Ben couldn't make himself release her. Rhianne's hand rested against his chest, right over his heart. She'd implied that he, a creature of Faerie, could find the mate bond, something Ben thought would elude him forever. He wasn't certain she was correct, but he was grateful to her for believing.

Her hair tickled his fingers as Rhianne came ever closer. Her body fit to his, her soft thighs against his hard ones. Ben wanted to sink into her and never come out. His cock, plenty stiff, rested against her abdomen, its wanting obvious. She couldn't not feel that.

Rhianne drifted from their kiss, a tiny smile pulling her lips. She'd felt his cock, all right. And she smiled.

Ben smoothed her hair from her forehead. He should say something, tell her they couldn't do this, walk away.

Instead, he kissed her again, lightly this time, the incandescence of it melting him.

He felt two hard stares and glanced up to see Jaycee and Dimitri watching them with Shifter focus. Ben gently stepped away from Rhianne, who kept her chin up and stared right back at the two, daring them to say a word.

Shifters didn't like people who looked straight into their eyes. They interpreted it as a challenge, usually one involving teeth, claws, and blood.

On the other hand, Ben had a feeling few existed who could meet the gaze of a Tuil Erdannan and live.

Jaycee and Dimitri were giving it a try, but Ben could see them begin to falter under her scrutiny. Rhianne showed no fear, which was wise, with Shifters.

Ben rubbed his hands together. "We could stand here all night and have a staring contest, or we could return to the house and throw back some brews."

Dimitri recovered first, his perpetual good nature returning. "Brews sound good. Meet you there?"

"Let's go," Ben agreed.

Jaycee gave Ben and Rhianne one final sharp look then she and Dimitri strolled off together, Dimitri sliding his arm around Jaycee. His hand wandered to her butt, and Ben heard Jaycee's voice rise in admonition. Then she grabbed *his* ass, provoking Dimitri's laughter.

"I'm glad those two got together," Ben said. "Drove us all insane before they did, though."

"You really like them." Rhianne fell into step with Ben as he led her back across the square, making for his storage room.

"Jaycee and Dimitri? They're good kids."

"I mean all the Shifters." Somehow her hand was back in Ben's. "You say you're alone, but you've made friends with them, become one of them. I hear they don't easily let anyone into their packs or prides. Or clans, or whatever they call them."

"You're right, they don't let many in." Ben let out a breath, her kiss still tingling on his lips. He noticed they studiously avoided mentioning it. "When Shifters stopped being suspicious of me, they accepted me. Mostly. They're still suspicious, but that's Shifters."

"Understandably. They have to be very careful. The Fae almost destroyed them, and the humans fear them."

"Yep." Ben squeezed her hand. "*You* be careful. Shifters can be loyal to the death, but they're also deadly. They're not quite sure what to do with you yet."

"I won't stay here forever."

Rhianne spoke with confidence, but Ben remembered that same confidence when he'd first arrived in the human world. He'd assumed he would figure out how to survive here for a time, and then return home and avenge his people.

Before he'd known it, centuries had gone by. Surviving had turned to existence, which had turned to settling in. He'd lived here longer than he ever had in Faerie, and he wasn't certain now if he wanted to return to Faerie permanently.

They fetched the purchases from Ben's storage room and walked on to where Ben had parked the motorcycle. Rhianne still said nothing about the kiss, or much of anything at all.

Did she regret it? Ben sure as hell didn't. Rhianne was a beautiful woman, ready for loving. Tuil Erdannan, true. That could make for some complications, but since Ben's whole life was complicated, why should he think this would be any different?

Ben stashed their things in the saddlebags, and they mounted up. Rhianne wrapped her arms around him less hesitantly than before, leaning into him as he turned the motorcycle to head out of the city.

All the way out to the haunted house, Rhianne's warmth poured over him. Ben had tasted her, forbidden fruit, and he wanted to taste her again.

When they reached the house, Jaycee and Dimitri were already there. The two waited on the porch, lounging together on the swing where Ben had sat with Rhianne that morning.

Ben led the way inside. The house opened its door readily for him, then closed softly once they'd entered, the locks clicking into place.

Dimitri revealed that he and Jaycee had changed their minds about Ben's offer of beer. "We decided we were tired after the long trip from Texas," he said, glancing at Jaycee. "We'll head up to bed."

"Good night," Jaycee said, cutting off any chance for debate.

She marched up the stairs, and Dimitri, with a wave, took the stairs two at a time behind her. Dimitri and Jaycee had a bedroom reserved for them here, and soon the door closed behind them.

"I hope you brought earplugs," Ben said to Rhianne, resting his arm on the newel post. "When they start in, they rattle the walls."

Rhianne's brows rose. "Are they going to couple?"

Ben huffed a laugh. "Of course they are. They're mate bonded. They like sex. They were probably so horny by the time they got here they didn't want to do anything else."

"Then we should leave them to it." Rhianne wandered down the hall to the veranda's door at the end.

Ben followed her out into soft darkness, the scent of roses lingering. Moonlight streamed over the trees behind the house, lighting the path below.

Ben thought Rhianne would linger on the veranda, but she stepped down its stairs and started around the house, Ben behind her.

"Where ya going?" he asked lightly.

"To the garden Tiger showed me. It was beautiful. A fine place to look at the stars."

Ben agreed that the rose garden, old and venerable, was a lovely thing. He got ahead of her on the path, preferring to lead in case of danger.

They entered the garden, moonlight like a pool of silver, the Big Dipper stark in the sky, planets hanging out on the ecliptic. The rose bushes were dark in the night, late roses rendered a stark white.

"Some of these bushes are more than a hundred years old." Ben gestured at the climbing roses on the wall, feeling the need to babble something. "One or two even more than that."

"They must have seen many things," Rhianne observed quietly.

"Without a doubt. This house could tell a lot of tales. Sometimes it does."

Rhianne turned to him, her face in shadow as she slid her arms around his waist.

"Do you think we could do what Dimitri and Jaycee are doing?" Rhianne whispered.

Before Ben could answer that startling question, Rhianne pulled him close and kissed him.

CHAPTER NINE

B en jumped slightly under her lips, then he gathered
Rhianne to him in powerful arms and sank into the kiss.

His mouth was strong, skilled, opening things inside her she didn't know existed. His solid hands cupped her hips, pulling her close.

In the park in New Orleans, he'd touched her mouth with his tongue but hadn't opened to her. Now he parted her lips and tasted her deeply. Rhianne tightened her embrace, her tongue tangling his, this intimacy heady and new.

Hot spice, the taste of strength. Rhianne imbibed Ben as though his power could sustain her. Fire ran through her veins, one she hadn't experienced before.

Her rescuer was the opposite of every man she'd ever known, of all Tuil Erdannan, in fact. They demanded, with arrogance. Ben gave, with simplicity.

Rhianne didn't know why she'd nearly begged for him to take her, only that a loneliness and longing had welled up inside her until she'd wanted to break.

Ben touched the corner of her mouth as he eased from the kiss. "Shifter mating frenzy."

"What?" Rhianne's voice shook.

"It's catching. Shifters go into mating frenzy, and everyone around them wants sex. Immediate, hard, satisfying sex."

"I—" Was that the only explanation? The pheromones flying between Dimitri and Jaycee had touched her and made her needy? Her heart sank even as her body craved Ben. She wanted what was between them in this moment to be more than simple reaction.

Ben drew her close again, cutting off any questions. Rhianne surrendered to him, surrounding herself with his warmth. Whatever the reason, she'd be happy to feast on him and not let go.

She slid her hands across his back, down to his hips, pulling him closer. She felt the rigidness of his cock, had in New Orleans as well. He wanted her as much as she wanted him.

The men she'd kissed in her life had been tall. Cloud-scrapers she'd called them, and they'd mocked her for being undersized for a Tuil Erdannan.

Ben was just the right height. She didn't have to crane to kiss him, having the joy of the kiss dimmed by a crick in her neck. She could stand before him and kiss, kiss, kiss, all she wanted.

Ben's hand found her waist, then rose to softly cup her breast, stoking her fires to incandescence. He knew how to touch her, to draw forth every need.

The night was warm, without a chill in the air. They could make love here, surrounded by the fragrance of roses, with the many stars in this place overhead. She could have Ben under new constellations smiling down at her.

A rustling under the roses against the wall almost distracted her, but Rhianne didn't want to stop kissing Ben. The rustling sounded again and Ben drew his mouth from hers.

His breath was rapid as he came alert, scanning the garden for danger.

"A rabbit?" Rhianne whispered. "Lily promised we'd have no danger tonight."

Faintly, in the distance, a church bell began to toll. Rhianne counted twelve strokes, then the sound faded into the quiet air. The hour of midnight, which, if Rhianne remembered what Ben had explained about time correctly, technically made this the next day.

The ground erupted even as her thought formed. Bright moonlight and the companion light of bright stars showed Rhianne exactly what was pouring out of the earth. She screamed.

Snakes. Dozens of them. No, more than that. Huge, black, gaping-mawed, unnatural snakes. With teeth.

"*Shit.*" Ben shoved Rhianne behind him, but they were surrounded. "Safe at the haunted house, sure. But we have to be *inside* the house."

"Can we get there?"

A snake touched her. Rhianne kicked out, and the snake wrapped itself around her leg. If it bit her, would the poison kill her instantly? She had no doubt these hellspawn things would be poisonous.

She reached for a place inside herself, drawing up the magic that had been simmering since she'd broken her chains in the dungeon. It bubbled to the surface, still not full strength, but restored enough to help.

"*Shantar!*" she yelled.

The snake around her leg suddenly glowed white hot and fell away.

"Damn," Ben said in admiration. "Can you get rid of all of them?"

"No," she had to tell him regretfully. "Takes a while to recharge."

"Like a taser. Too bad we don't have one of those."

The earth boiled, black loam emitting these creatures from

hell. Ben had said the house was on a ley line. Had Rhianne's father tapped into that, sending ensorcelled snakes to either fetch her home or kill her?

"What's a taser?" she shouted.

"Never mind." Ben glanced over his shoulder at her. "Hang on to me, no matter what."

Rhianne wound her arms around him from behind, and she wasn't about to let go. Another snake snagged her ankle while others rose up, higher and higher, surrounding them like a serpent forest.

Ben's body changed. His shirt dissolved and vanished as his shoulders widened and his chest broadened. He grew, the mid-sized, affable Ben becoming the tall, thick bodied monster she'd seen in the dungeon.

Rhianne clutched him as his skin hardened into an almost wood-like texture. She rose three feet off the ground as she gripped Ben tight.

The snake that had wrapped her ankle came up with them, pried from the ground with a sucking sound. The snake didn't like being in the air, though, and started to flail. Rhianne kicked and kicked until it finally dislodged.

Ben turned, ponderously, his tattered jeans falling away. He battled the snakes by the simple feat of crushing them. Rhianne hung on as he headed for the garden gate and the house beyond.

Something darted past them, snarling and spitting. Behind it, only a little slower, raced a large russet-colored wolf, the earth rumbling with his growls. Ben turned from the gate, wading back into the fray.

The first animal was a leopard, its spots flashing in the moonlight. The leopard leapt and pounced with consummate grace, knocking snakes aside, tearing them apart with a single blow of a paw.

The snakes never touched the leopard. Whenever they

struck, they hit empty air, the leopard sailing straight upward with honed cat instincts. The snakes hissed their fury, the hisses cut off as the wolf cut them in half with his claws.

Ben joined the wolf, the two of them decapitating and splitting open the snakes that the leopard batted to them. Rhianne could only hold on to Ben and pray to the Goddess she wouldn't fall.

A trickle of mysterious energy sparked inside her, bolstering her spirits. Perhaps she'd be able to use the word of power again more quickly than she'd thought.

This magic felt different, though, unlike the tingle that built in her fingers and throat when she gathered strength to use the words. Her heart skipped and throbbed, and her limbs twitched. The magic built, hammering at her as though desperate to get out.

Rhianne forced herself to calm. If she fell, those snakes would be on her faster than Ben and the others could stop them. She held on to Ben tighter, but magic jumped up and down inside her like a mystical case of hiccups.

The leopard continued to battle, light on her feet, springing with impossible speed whenever a snake lunged for her. The wolf used brute strength instead of speed, and together they made a perfect team. Ben came along behind them to destroy whatever tried to escape.

Slowly the three with Rhianne edged toward the garden gate. The garden, so peaceful and beautiful under the moonlight a short time ago now roiled like a cauldron of evil.

The rose vines shuddered. Rhianne braced herself for the next horror to spring out of the ground, but the vines themselves seemed to come to life. Were Rhianne and the others about to be attacked by the vegetation?

The vines began to flow across the garden—no, their roots did, Rhianne realized. They swarmed around the snakes, entwining the creatures, and then began to squeeze.

"They're helping," Rhianne yelled in surprise.

"Yeah, they are." Ben's response was jubilant. "Jaycee, Dimitri, get out of there."

The wolf swerved and ran with all speed toward the gate, Ben behind him, his size decreasing to that of his human guise as he went. The leopard lingered, batting and swatting at the snakes, playing with them with the focused intensity of a house cat with a mouse toy.

The red wolf turned and ran back into the garden, howling in despair as the snakes converged on the leopard.

Rhianne thumped to her feet on solid ground outside the gate, free of snakes and roots. The tingling rush in her body swelled. She turned back, raised her hands, and shouted the word of power once more. "*Shantar!*"

Light burst over the garden, glowing on the snakes and roots alike. Snakes shriveled into ash under it, and the vines pulled back.

The leopard shot upward from all four paws, twisted in the air, and came down squarely on the wolf's back. The wolf stumbled with the sudden impact, then he regained his balance and sprinted for the gate.

"To the house," Ben yelled as the wolf slowed.

The leopard tumbled off the wolf's back, landing on her feet, and loped gracefully toward the house. The red wolf dashed behind Ben and Rhianne, guarding the rear while Ben and Rhianne dashed, hand in hand, to the veranda.

All three climbed the steps at the same time to collapse on the porch floor, where the leopard waited. The house shook once, then let out a sigh as though in relief.

The wolf's face crumpled and bent, emerging as Dimitri's handsome one, his wolf's pelt receding to become Dimitri's red hair. The rest of the body flowed into that of a tall, well-muscled, naked man.

The leopard flopped down at Dimitri's side and began to carefully lick her paw.

Dimitri dragged in several long breaths. "So, Ben," he said hoarsely. "When did you become the Incredible Hulk?"

———

DIMITRI DECIDED THAT WINNING A BATTLE AGAINST EVIL snakes called for drinks, and Ben agreed. The four went upstairs, Ben and Dimitri ducking into bedrooms for clothes. Jaycee, still a leopard, zipped into the room she shared with Dimitri, and emerged fully dressed in a matter of moments. Ben heard her greeting Rhianne in the kitchen.

Ben finished dressing and hurried to join them. He found the two women sitting at the table, blood-red glasses of merlot before them—Jaycee enjoyed wine. They had their heads together, one red, one blond and brown, and they were laughing.

"Ladies," Ben said.

They looked up, exchanged a glance, and went off into a gale of hilarity. Great.

"Battling creepy snakes is funny, is it?" Ben asked as he went to the refrigerator for beer. He pulled out two bottles, one for himself and one for the still-absent Dimitri.

"No, your butt is," Jaycee said. "With your shredded pants barely hanging on it."

Ben slammed the refrigerator door. "Hey, it happens when you shift in your clothes." He could vanish all his clothes when he needed to, but sometimes he was in too much of a hurry, like tonight.

"I never shift in my clothes." Jaycee took a delicate sip of wine. "I fold them carefully first. What was that you yelled, Rhianne? Saved our butts." She slid her gaze down to Ben's jeans and burst out laughing again.

"Yeah, yeah, make fun of the goblin," Ben said, though his relief that Rhianne was safe let him not mind the teasing. "Rhianne said it was like a taser."

"Your butt?" Jaycee snickered, and Rhianne laughed, a magical, silvery sound.

"No, Feline, the—"

"Why are you talking about Ben's butt?" Dimitri waltzed into the room with his usual grace. "You shouldn't be looking at his ass. You should be looking at mine."

"So full of yourself." Jaycee sent him a lofty glance, but her eyes did slide appreciatively to Dimitri's backside as he turned to grab the beer Ben had left on the counter for him. "I was asking Rhianne about the magic she did that almost set the garden on fire."

"A word of power." Rhianne shrugged. "Not a very strong one. But enough to help."

Dimitri took a seat on the bench next to Jaycee, snuggling into her. "Burning up evil snakes trying to kill me is good enough for me. So, thanks for that." He raised his bottle in salute.

"The power doesn't last long," Rhianne explained. "It does damage, but I can't prevent the snakes from rising again."

"I think the house took care of that," Ben said. "Extended its power out to the garden, via the plants. There are vines all over this house. Hard to tell where they begin and end."

Jaycee patted the nearest wall. "Whatever happened, I'm grateful."

"I believe the attack came from my father." Rhianne fingered the stem of her wine glass. "He might have been able to reach through the ley line and make trouble. Trying to frighten me home? Or kill me outright? I'm not certain."

"Have to wonder why." Ben slid into the chair next to Rhianne's. He'd love to cuddle up to Rhianne like Dimitri was doing to Jaycee, but he knew the danger of that. In the garden, he'd wanted her with powerful intensity, had been ready to take her down to the grass and have all of her. Thank the Goddess they'd been interrupted by demon snakes.

Ben was not what Rhianne needed right now—a goblin lover who wanted to consume her, She was dependent on him and under instructions from her mother, no less, to stick with him for her safety.

But, damn, that kiss had been good. Ben had tasted the need in her, a longing that matched his own. He wanted to think the longing was for *him*, but Ben sensed she was simply lonely. It couldn't be easy for her, living in the shadow of a powerful mother and evil-as-hell father, being a pawn for political marriages, having to stay far from home to find a little peace.

"Who is this guy?" Dimitri asked Rhianne. "Your dad, I mean? Ben told us a little—floored me that Lady Aisling had a husband at all—but why would he send angry reptiles after his own daughter?"

"Because he loves power more than anything else." Rhianne's voice grew sad as she explained. "My mother found that out too late, but to her credit, she sent him away instead of keeping him around, hoping he'd change. He used her to gain power, nothing else. Ivor de Erkkonen cares about no one but himself."

"He's already a big, bad dude, though, right?" Dimitri went on. "Why does he need to be bigger and badder?"

"You have to understand Tuil Erdannan," Rhianne said wearily. "To some of us there is nothing more desirable than absolute mastery—of everything. They create new species of animals, or of people, to see if they can do it, and then they abandon them. They can be so far above the rest of the world that they don't understand what they destroy."

Ben nodded. "Like I say, Tuil Erdannan do some scary shit."

You aren't *friends* with them." He glared at Jaycee who often had chats with Lady Aisling about whatever.

"But kissing them is all right." Jaycee took a casual sip of wine.

Rhianne flushed and studied her glass, not answering.

Ben cleared his throat. "Yeah, well, that was, you know, the excitement of the moment. *Your* fault." He pointed his beer bottle at Dimitri. "Mating frenzy."

"Oh, sure." Dimitri appeared affronted. "Would you believe me if I said Jaycee and I went directly to sleep tonight?"

"No."

Dimitri huffed a laugh. "Good, 'cause it would be a lie."

"We're not discussing *our* sex life." Jaycee sent Ben a pointed look. "Dimitri and I are mated. We have a cub. Don't toy with Rhianne, Ben. I like her, and you don't want to mess with me."

Rhianne's flush deepened as Ben stared at Jaycee in disbelief. "Toy with her? What is this, the Victorian age? Been there, done that. The nineteenth century was a violent time. Everyone thinks it was so quaint and refined, but I'm glad it's over."

"You're changing the subject." Jaycee scowled.

"So are you. We were talking about keeping Rhianne safe and what we're up against."

"Their love life is their business, Jace," Dimitri said gently.

Jaycee ignored him. "Just watch yourself, Ben. Mr. Here-Today, Gone-Tomorrow."

Jaycee wasn't wrong. Always peripatetic, was Ben, as he'd explained already to Rhianne. Since he'd volunteered to be caretaker of this house, he'd stayed put more, but when Jasmine decided to move back in, or sell the place—though that was unlikely—Ben would have to leave.

"What do *you* want to talk about, Rhianne?" Ben switched

his focus to her. "Figuring out what your dad is up to, or us kissing in the garden?"

"My horrible father, please." Rhianne lifted her glass. "Is this right for a toast?"

"You say 'to' something when you toast," Ben explained. "Like, 'to besting my pain-in-the-ass dad and going home without fear'."

"Can I say 'to winning the battle' instead?"

"I'll drink to that." Dimitri lifted his beer, and Jaycee joined him with wine.

The four of them clinked glasses and bottles and settled down to drink.

"We did win this battle," Ben said after a time. "Not sure about the war."

Rhianne slumped in her chair, her braid of brilliant red hair flowing over her shoulder. "I'm thinking I'll be stuck here forever. My father won't give up, whatever it is he wants. He's very determined."

Ben slid his hand along the table and covered hers with it. He couldn't help himself. "When Lady Aisling asked me to bring you here, I didn't get the sense that she was saying goodbye to you for keeps. More like she wants you here while she takes care of the problem."

"Mmm." Jaycee's face twisted as she wrinkled her nose, as though her leopard had scented a bad smell. "I talked to her too, remember? From what I gathered in our conversation, this was a quick decision to save Rhianne's life. I think we need to know exactly what happened between Lady Aisling and your dad, Rhianne. Why would he be so harsh to you? I can't imagine doing anything to harm my own cub."

A sudden longing flashed in her eyes. It couldn't have been easy leaving baby Lucas behind to help out Ben, but Jaycee and Dimitri were trackers, having to obey their leader.

Dimitri puffed up with pride. "You should see Lucas

already trying to get up and run. I bet he'll turn out to be leopard."

"Turn out to be leopard?" Rhianne asked in bafflement. "What does that mean?"

"Shifters from mixed heritage are born in human form," Jaycee answered. "They don't shift until they're a few years old, so we don't yet know if he'll be wolf or leopard. Lucas has red hair, but his eyes are like mine."

"And he can *move*," Dimitri said. "He instantly grabs whatever he puts his eye on, never misses. He's got deadly focus, like a cat. So I'm betting on leopard."

"Could be." Jaycee shrugged. "We'll find out."

She spoke casually, but Ben sensed her tension. She wanted to know, and he could tell she hoped wolf. Dimitri wanted leopard. The two of them were adorable.

Ben cut in before Rhianne could ask any more questions about the cub. Dimitri and Jaycee, like any proud parents, would go on about Lucas for hours. Ben didn't blame them. He'd met the kid in his infrequent visits to Kendrick's compound, and the little dude was cute.

"Anyway," Ben said. "The best thing we can do is sit tight until we have more intel. Jaycee, since you're so close to Lady Aisling, please try to get her to open up to you. That means tell her more," he added for Rhianne's benefit.

"Open up?" Rhianne widened her eyes. "My mother does not open up."

"Doesn't she? She talks to me a lot." Jaycee caught Rhianne's hurt glance, then added quickly, "Probably because she doesn't see me as a threat."

Ben watched Rhianne tamp down her sorrow. "My father has and always will be ambitious," Rhianne said. "He uses anyone or anything to get what he wants. I imagine my mother is waiting for him to grow bored with whatever scheme he's pursuing and turn to something else." She sipped wine, brows furrowed. "How did he find me here? I doubt my mother let that slip—she's much too careful."

Ben shrugged. "There are many Fae spies in the human world. Even some Shifters are."

"Liam or Dylan?" Rhianne asked in worry. Ben noted she didn't name Tiger.

"No," Ben answered quickly and Jaycee and Dimitri chorused the same. "Dylan loathes the Fae and he'd not give you up to a Tuil Erdannan working with one. Probably a human spy reported to his Fae master. Everyone knows me and where I hang out."

"The psychic, Lily?" Rhianne's expression told him he hoped not. "I gave her our names."

"I didn't sense treachery in her, and besides she didn't realize what or who we were. She wouldn't have been so shocked if she'd been on the lookout for us. No, I'm guessing someone who saw us in the restaurants, or the bakery, or the club, or on the street. Everyone knows me," he finished glumly. He should have kept Rhianne at the house, but her longing to see this world and not be confined had touched him. He'd understood her feelings.

"I agree with Ben that we need more information," Dimitri broke in. "I also think that we should sleep on it. Rhianne must be exhausted."

Ben thought so too, but Rhianne showed no signs of drooping. A day and a night like she'd had would have wiped out a human, and likely a Shifter too, but Rhianne stirred restlessly.

Jaycee glanced at Dimitri. "I'm too riled up from the fight to go tamely to bed."

Dimitri slid an arm around her. "I know what might calm you down."

"Don't you always? But I need a run. By myself—you know the kind where you won't be able to keep up."

"Nuh-uh. Too dangerous," Dimitri said immediately.

"The crazed magic people are not after *me*, and I won't go far. I run around here all the time. Walk out with me, Rhianne?"

Jaycee, always energetic, leapt to her feet. Rhianne rose quickly to join her. "I'd love to."

"*You* will stay on the veranda," Ben admonished Rhianne, his heart speeding in worry. "I don't know how far the house's protection extends."

"Of course I will," Rhianne said in annoyance. "I'm not a fool. My father is deadly."

"Leave her alone, Ben." Jaycee put her arm around Rhianne. "She needs to take a breath. And I seriously want a run."

Without another word, Jaycee led Rhianne out of the kitchen. Rhianne glanced back at Ben, giving him a nod that he supposed was meant to be reassuring.

Once the two ladies could be heard talking on the stairs, Dimitri quietly set down his beer. "I'm going after them. In secret, of course."

"Me too," Ben said.

Dimitri shot him a grin. They waited until the veranda door had closed downstairs, sending a draft through the house, before they noiselessly descended and slipped out through a side door.

———

RHIANNE LEANED ON THE VERANDA RAILING, FOLDING HER arms across it, and watched Jaycee dance down the steps, discarding clothes as she went. Rhianne scanned the dark distance, not trusting her father enough to descend after Jaycee into the night. She'd be as careful as she'd promised Ben she'd be.

She tilted her head to gaze at what stars shone through the

clouds, wishing she could spend all night with a telescope, becoming acquainted with the skies of this world. The stars were not as thick as in Faerie. Rhianne wondered if some of the distant suns were the same as those she saw from her observatory, or if this place was so alien it was surrounded by a different galaxy.

Watching stars always let her draw away from her emotions, and the ones Ben stirred inside her confused the hell out of her. Rhianne needed, as Jaycee had said, to draw a breath and sort out her thoughts.

Perhaps what she felt for Ben was simple infatuation for the man who'd rescued her. Correction, the *being* who'd rescued her. Ben was clearly not a man, and Rhianne knew so little about him. These longings churning inside her were the result of stress, fear, and gratitude. Weren't they?

Jaycee stretched her naked body, beautiful in the moonlight, and then began to shift. She did it gracefully, as the woman did everything—dancing, fighting, or kissing Dimitri.

The leopard and woman merged, for a moment becoming something in between. No struggle through these stages, however. The leopard side grew more and more prominent until Jaycee dropped to all fours as a big cat.

She loped off, her speed increasing rapidly until she was a streak in the night, then she was gone.

Rhianne had to smile when she saw a wolf dart from the shadows and run after the leopard.

The night touched Rhianne, the silence and the stars comforting after the horrifying battle in the garden. If her father had been trying to separate her from Ben, he'd not succeeded.

She allowed herself a momentary flare of triumph before she sobered. Perhaps Ivor was trying to do just that. If Rhianne was forced to wander this strange human world by herself, would she survive?

Ben had showed her how to find food and drink, but she could do that only if she had money in the currency of this place. In Faerie, she had status and wealth, and respect as a prominent scholar. Here, she had nothing, knew no one.

Conclusion—she needed to stick with Ben, at least for now. Tiger had told her this as well. *Whenever you are with Ben, you will be safe.*

Why did the idea of being without him wrench at her so much? The emptiness the thoughts engendered came from more than worry about survival, and from more than gratitude.

Moon- and starlight brushed the rose vines clinging to the nearby trellis. A breeze brushed the wind chimes, and the tingle Rhianne had felt in her blood during the battle resurfaced.

As she'd noted before, the feeling wasn't quite the same as when she called up her words of power. Magic, but a different sort of magic.

She straightened, fingertips touching the railing, and let herself explore the sensation. A tightening in her belly, a fire between her shoulder blades, a restlessness in her legs. Rhianne wanted to vault over the railing and run, run, run after Jaycee, to try to best the leopard in speed.

The breeze grew stronger, the chiming louder. A tremor ran under her feet, as though the house responded to the wind.

Rhianne's skin itched. More than itched, it became fiery hot. She watched her hands tug open her tunic, buttons tinkling to the slatted boards in her haste. The blouse fell, and the silk camisole went next, the sapphire necklace landing with a tinkle next to it.

Rhianne drew a long breath, letting the cool wind refresh her bare skin. But it wasn't enough. She slid off her new shoes and the stockings beneath, wriggling her toes.

Her body wasn't satisfied yet. Rhianne glanced quickly around but did not see Ben. Jaycee was racing off somewhere in the darkness, her mate after her. Rhianne was alone in the night.

She quickly unfastened the leather pants and let them fall, then pulled off the undergarment beneath them. She tossed the clothes aside, amazed at herself for not tidying them, and stretched out her arms, welcoming the breeze.

Her hair felt heavy in the braid as it brushed her back. Rhianne loosened its bond until her hair flowed without imped- iment over her bare body. Sensual and warm, it brushed her skin.

A better feeling would be Ben touching her.

Rhianne wrapped her arms around herself, wanting to relive the heat of Ben's body against hers, his kiss on her mouth, his hand lovingly cupping her breast.

For a moment, she remembered the feeling exactly. In the next, her thoughts were scattered on another peal of the wind chimes, this one louder and more insistent.

Rhianne opened her arms without realizing she did so, and she had the strongest urge to climb onto the veranda railing and perch there. *Perch?*

Before she could stop herself, she was doing it, balancing on top of the narrow railing as though such a thing was natural. She felt the house's magic through her feet, liquid fire that reached all the way to the ley line buried far beneath the earth.

A sudden pain wracked her. Rhianne's limbs twisted with it, and she cried out.

The pain vanished as suddenly as it had come. New strength took its place, along with a wild awareness that she could do anything at all she wished.

Another cry escaped her lips, this one high-pitched and inhuman. The sound pierced the darkness, floating across the night.

Rhianne leapt from the railing. The sane part of her brain,

which had become small and insignificant, tried to stop herself in terror.

The newly awakened part of her mind laughed. The tingle in her body burned with sudden fury, and from every pore in her skin sprang a swath of feathers.

Feathers?

It was the last conscious word that formed. Rhianne spread her massive wings and caught the wind as she floated toward the ground, then she rose into the night, sailing for the moonlight.

CHAPTER TEN

Holy fucking shit!

Ben sprinted from his hiding place just inside the back door. He hit the veranda railing as the giant eagle soared upward, its screech cutting the night.

What the fucking fuck?

Ben stumbled down the veranda steps, dashing along the path that led to the outbuildings and the pool. The eagle cut into a swath of moonlight, then out again, vanishing into the darkness.

"Rhianne!" Ben's shout was lost in the wind. He cupped his hands around his mouth and bellowed her name again.

Silence. From far, far away, he heard the triumphant howl of a wolf and the snarl of a wild cat.

Since when could Rhianne turn into an *eagle?* A golden one, it looked like from the flash he'd seen. Lady Aisling hadn't mentioned this. Not that she'd mentioned her daughter much to him at all.

"Rhianne. Damn it."

Get the hell back here! he wanted to yell. Right, like a Tuil

Erdannan who could turn into a bird of prey was going to listen to him.

Ben pivoted this way and that, peering through the trees that now enclosed him. He could make himself look like a tree creature, one of the several forms he could take, but little good that would do him now. Except, he thought hysterically, he might give her a branch to land on.

Shit.

A rush of wings blew a downdraft across his face. The eagle skimmed just above his head and then surged upward again.

"Not funny," Ben called. "Come down here. I need to talk to you."

If the eagle understood, she ignored him. Ben reached the edge of the trees and watched the huge bird waft higher, then soar, wings spread, grace in the night. Beautiful.

He heard the wolf howl again, this time in surprise. Another snarl from the wild cat. Then pounding paws on damp ground sounded as Jaycee and Dimitri raced toward him.

The eagle circled above them, its jubilant shriek cutting the air. Its circles tightened until, with an unnerving suddenness, the bird plummeted to the ground, wings spreading at the last instant to let it land with a gentle thump.

Jaycee darted forward, claws poised to strike, but Ben stepped between her and the eagle. "It's Rhianne."

Jaycee's paws skidded as she forced herself to halt. She rose into her half-beast state, leopard fur hugging her limbs, her eyes harshly golden. "What the hell?"

Dimitri changed, more slowly, into his fully human form. "Are you sure?"

Ben took a step toward the eagle. It cocked its head and stared at him from a brown-black eye that was all Rhianne.

Ben strode another step. The eagle fluffed out her wings, hooked beak opening in warning.

She was beautiful. Reddish feathers flowed from her head,

becoming more golden as they skimmed down her back. Wide talons gripped the earth, and lighter blond feathers dusted her breast and the tufts around her legs. She was far larger than a natural golden eagle, standing as high as Ben's chest, her wing-span massive.

"Rhianne?" Ben asked softly.

The eagle fluttered her wings once more, then settled them to her sides. Behind them, wind chimes rang on the veranda, jangling and dancing.

The air shimmered, and when it cleared Rhianne, unclothed, sat hunched in on herself in the exact spot the eagle had stood.

Jaycee started for her, but Rhianne cried out in fear, throwing up her hands as though she'd never seen Jaycee before. Dimitri put a hand on Jaycee's shoulder, holding her back.

Ben carefully approached and went down on one knee. "Rhianne, sweetheart. You all right?"

Rhianne raised her head, her hair and face damp. "Ben?"

The word was shaky, on the verge of tears. Ben reached out and carefully took her hand.

"Why didn't you tell me you were part Shifter?"

"I'm not ... I don't ... I've never ..." Rhianne gazed at him in absolute terror, then her face crumpled, and tears poured down her cheeks. "What is happening to me?"

Ben gathered her to him. Her warm hair fell around him, exactly as he'd fantasized, but now his desires were stemmed by worry and compassion. He wrapped his arms around her, holding her close, pressing a kiss to the top of her head.

Sending a warning glance to the others, Ben lifted Rhianne, cradling her against his chest, and carried her back to the waiting house.

———

"SHE CAN'T BE A SHIFTER." DIMITRI DECLARED THIS AS HE lounged in the kitchen, his hands wrapped around another beer.

Rhianne was now tucked into a bed down the hall, her red hair fanning across the pillows. Halfway to the house, Rhianne's tears had dried, and when Ben had laid her in the bed, she'd fallen into an instant and profound sleep.

Exhaustion, Ben told himself. The stress of being captured by a *hoch alfar* asshole, then hauled away from everything she knew and brought to the human world against her will. Not to mention a long night dancing and battling snakes, plus the physical exertion of shifting into an eagle and flying around in the darkness.

"Why not?" Jaycee demanded, even as she leaned into Dimitri, seeking the comfort of her mate.

"Shifters don't fly, for one thing," Dimitri answered. "We have big cat Shifters. Lupines, and Bears. That's it."

"Foxes, remember," Ben said. "Made by the Tuil Erdannan. Why couldn't one of them make raptors as well?"

"Reason number two," Dimitri went on. "Both her parents are Tuil Erdannan."

Ben nodded from where he slumped on the bench at the window, his energy gone. "I agree. She doesn't really have that Shifter look to her."

Jaycee's eyes narrowed. "What look is that?"

"Predatory," Dimitri answered before Ben could. "You know a Shifter has an animal inside who'd tear out your guts to defend his territory, even while he's smiling at you and throwing back a brew." He lifted his beer in demonstration.

"You have a point," Jaycee conceded. "Plus, there's scent. She does not smell like a Shifter at all."

No, she smelled like roses and the wildness of the night.

Ben pressed his fingers to the table. Tattoos on his right hand spelled out the word Ben, and on his left, Gil. "I have the feeling her dear father had something to do with this. Messed with her DNA or something. Experimented on his own daughter. No wonder Lady Aisling threw him out."

"You think that's what happened?" Dimitri asked.

"It's a theory. One that fits with what a shithead her dad seems to be. Dylan wants to take him down? Well, I just joined Dylan's team."

Jaycee glared at both men. "Why don't you two stop theorizing and ask her?"

"When she wakes up, we'll have a talk." Ben thought of the fear on Rhianne's face that had wrenched his heart. "But I don't believe she'll have an answer."

"Poor kid." Jaycee sent a sympathetic glance out the open doorway to the hall. "I didn't exactly have the best childhood, but then I found Kendrick and Dimitri, who did everything they could to take care of me. Rhianne's caught between two formidable parents, both with their own agendas, which can't be easy. I admire the hell out of her for being so damned calm."

"Me too," Ben trailed off and didn't continue the thought. He did more than admire her. He liked her, delighted in her, and craved her. Oh yeah. Straight-up lust.

Ben couldn't admit this to his friends, though he realized they already knew. Jaycee was growing protective of Rhianne, and if she decided Rhianne could do much better than Ben, she'd defend Rhianne with teeth and claws.

Ben wasn't Shifter. As much as Shifters welcomed him, drank with him, and trusted him, he still wasn't one of them. The Shifters who didn't know him took one whiff of his Fae-like scent and barely stopped themselves from trying to kill him.

Shifters might decide Rhianne's ability made her one of them, and try to absorb her into them. Dylan would be very interested, in any case.

Ben hauled himself off the bench. "I'll check on her."

Jaycee and Dimitri said nothing as Ben left the kitchen, but he felt their gazes on his back.

In the dim shadows of the bedroom, Ben saw that Rhianne had curled on her side, the thin sheet rising and falling with her breath. She hadn't woken when Ben laid her down, just whimpered and frowned, quieting only when he'd tucked a sheet and blanket over her and turned off the light.

The blanket was now crumpled at the bottom of the bed, and Rhianne shivered. Ben quietly closed the door behind him, crossed to her, and drew the blanket around her body once more.

He started to tiptoe away, when she cried out, a heartbreaking sound of loneliness and fear. He'd heard the same kind of noise from his own throat, for the same reasons.

Ben turned back to the bed. Rhianne began to thrash, caught in some dream. She bunched the blanket in her hand and thrust it away, as though hot, yet she trembled.

"Shh." Ben smoothed her hair, leaning down to kiss her forehead.

Rhianne quieted somewhat but cried out again when he withdrew. Ben shook her gently, trying to pull her from the nightmare.

She swam toward wakefulness, blinked without fully coming awake, and dove right back into sleep. When Ben stepped away again, however, the shivering returned and Rhianne whimpered softly.

Ben let out a long breath. He gazed out the window at the darkening grounds, the moon setting behind trees. The chandelier in the bedroom swayed, crystals tinkling.

"Yeah, I know what *you* think," Ben whispered to it.

He seated himself on a nearby chair and slipped off his boots, then his jeans and shirt. In his underwear, he climbed into the big double bed, reaching for the blanket.

Rhianne snuggled into him as he spooned up to her, but she

didn't wake. Ben covered them both with the blanket, draping his arm around her, her fragrant hair under his nose.

Rhianne never woke. She let out a long sigh, then her shivering ceased, and she slid into quiet slumber.

———

SUNLIGHT TOUCHED RHIANNE'S EYES. SHE SLOWLY WOKE, feeling wonderfully rested, the strange and troubling dreams of the night fading into a vague memory.

She was too warm. Someone had draped a blanket over her, but the most radiant source of heat lay behind her. It also snored.

Rhianne swiftly rolled over. She became aware of two things—she wore nothing under the covers, and Ben lay next to her, his arm over his eyes, a quiet snore drifting from him.

Rhianne's heart hammered. Her first instinct was to leap up, wrap the blanket around her bare body, and flee.

Instead, she settled onto her elbow and gazed at Ben. His face, relaxed in sleep, bore none of the lines of tension he wore during the day. His black hair, cut short, lay in silken strands against his head, tempting her to touch them.

His smooth lips beckoned her as she remembered how tender they'd been against hers. Yet, she'd felt the strength in him, as though he tamed himself for her. The thought made her heart race yet again.

What was he doing in here? Rhianne was pretty sure their kisses hadn't gone further, but the aftermath of the battle with the snakes was a blur. Had she and Ben succumbed to postfight euphoria and taken it to the bedroom?

If so, why couldn't she remember? Making love with Ben was something she'd never want to forget.

No—she recalled now. They'd returned to the kitchen and

had beer and wine with Jaycee and Dimitri, thanking the Goddess they were still alive. And then ...

Nothing. Rhianne assumed she'd fallen asleep in her weariness, and Ben had carried her to bed. Taken off her clothes, and his, and then he'd climbed in beside her.

Rhianne gingerly lifted the blanket and peered beneath it at Ben's body. She wasn't certain she was relieved or disappointed when she saw boxer briefs hugging his hips.

Still, it wasn't a bad view. The briefs were tight, showing her exactly how he was shaped when relaxed. Her imagination inserted what he'd look like when *not* relaxed, and sudden warmth flooded her.

Dangerous. She lay here bare-skinned, desire flushing her. Her nipples tingled, and the heat between her legs made her quiver. If Ben woke, he'd find her ready and wanting him.

Would he be aghast? Or would he touch her, pull her down to him, rid himself of the briefs, and take her fully?

Rhianne gulped. She should return to her original plan of grabbing the blanket and running.

But what if she encountered Dimitri or Jaycee in the hall? She'd be mortified. Worse, Jaycee might mention to Rhianne's mother that she'd run out of a bedroom, clad only in a blanket, where Ben lay in her bed.

Best to stay put. When Ben woke, they could discuss what to do.

Discuss. As though they were in a banquet room conducting a formal meeting.

Rhianne's need clenched her. There was something about Ben that made her forget her loneliness and throw caution to the wind. Maybe it was his laughter, the low rumbling that told her everything would be all right. Or the sparkle in his eyes when he said something deliberately ridiculous. Or the pain she read in him that told her he was as desolate as she was.

The two of them were alone, the house silent, the sun shining, no evil present. Rhianne let good sense desert her.

She leaned down and softly kissed his lips.

Ben jerked. His arm came down, his eyes opening in an instant. Rhianne made herself remain beside him, determined not to flee.

Ben stared in surprise when he saw her, and for a moment Rhianne thought he'd be the one snatching up the blanket and racing out the door.

Then desire flared in his eyes, and Ben abruptly slid his arms around her, pulling her over on top of him.

Rhianne fit nicely on him, the shape in the briefs, no longer relaxed, at the join of her legs.

He cupped her neck, hand under her hair, as he'd done in the park in New Orleans, blunt fingers caressing, and kissed her.

Rhianne's untamed hair flowed over them both. She couldn't be bothered brushing it aside as she kissed Ben's mouth. He parted his lips, drawing her in, tasting her as he had last night in the garden. He'd been gentle then. Now she felt the force of him, no longer subdued.

Her body thrummed with excitement. Ben's strength was evident in the way he held her, the way his mouth possessed hers. One hand stroked down her back, found her bare hips, and slid between her thighs to sink a finger into her liquid heat.

Rhianne gasped, breaking the kiss. Ben gazed up at her, loosening his hold, giving her the chance to spring up and run.

Rhianne moved the slightest bit on his finger and lowered herself to kiss him again. Ben's smile warmed everything inside her before she covered his mouth with hers.

Ben's fingers performed magic, and Rhianne's thoughts dissolved into pleasure and need. It had been a very long time since she'd been intimate with a man, a long time since she'd trusted any enough to do so. She'd at first been too innocent to understand that her Tuil Erdannan lovers simply wanted to get close to the daughter of Lady Aisling and Lord Ivor—either to gain power for themselves or to have a hold over the two—and had closed herself off once she'd realized this.

Why did she not feel worried with Ben? Ben was dangerous, his threat greater because he presented himself as affable and friendly.

She saw nothing of his friendliness now. Ben kissed her with command, holding her hard while he pleasured her with his fingers, faster and faster. Rhianne writhed, needing his touch, this fire.

He sped his strokes, and Rhianne clenched around him, wanting the depth, the madness. She arched, wishing it was his cock inside her, but he was very skilled, this pleasure wonderful.

Ben's iron-firm arm kept her solidly against him. His kisses held fierce desperation that matched the torment raging inside her, drowning all her senses.

Rhianne became aware only of Ben's mouth on hers, his hand bringing her to life. Her shouted words of joy met his groans, both drowned by the sudden discordant wind chimes from the veranda.

The river of madness went on, until Rhianne knew nothing but the dark hot place inside her and Ben's heat against her skin. She reached the peak of need, longing, and cried out with it, Ben encouraging her all the way.

The wave broke, Rhianne's bare hips moving against Ben's clad ones. Her voice was hoarse with her cries, Ben cradling her, stroking her hair to soothe her.

After a long, long time, the fire began to recede, Rhianne quieting as it ebbed into a restful, comfortable warmth. At the same time, the wind chimes faded into a faint jingle.

Ben held Rhianne close as she let out a long sigh, settling

against him. He withdrew his fingers, taking away the smoldering embers.

"I think you needed that," he murmured.

Rhianne snuggled against his shoulder. "Possibly."

"Yep, needed it." Ben kissed her forehead, and Rhianne brushed back her tangled hair.

"I'm a mess."

"You are the most beautiful thing I've ever seen, and I'm not exaggerating." Ben touched her cheek and gazed into her eyes. "The most beautiful."

Rhianne warmed at his flattery. If not for her father wanting to kill her, or terrify her, or manipulate her, or all three, she could be content at this moment. She lay with Ben, surrounded by the protective house, with new friends waiting down the hall. What more could she possibly want?

She closed her eyes.

And was immediately flooded by a sharp memory of standing on the porch railing, making the decision to jump from it as though it was the most natural thing in the world. Spreading her wings.

Wings?

Rhianne gasped and sat straight up, icy fear swamping her. "Goddess. That wasn't a dream ..."

"You turning into a giant bird and flying away?" Ben put a comforting hand on her cold arm, but his eyes held wariness. "No, it was real. I saw the whole thing. I think you need to tell me about it."

CHAPTER ELEVEN

T he panic in Rhianne's eyes made Ben's heart squeeze. He realized that her shape-shifting ability hadn't been a secret she'd kept from Ben—she hadn't known about it herself. Ben saw that clearly in the expression on her face.

"This has never happened before?" he asked gently.

"Never ever." Rhianne swallowed. "I don't understand. I'm not Shifter."

"Goblins can change their shape. Not that I'm saying you're a goblin," Ben added hastily. "Why shouldn't Tuil Erdannan?"

"Because we're so full of ourselves we can't imagine looking like anything else?" Rhianne's lips twisted in a wry grimace.

"Who knows what all you can do? You're the most powerful people in Faerie."

"I'm not young." Rhianne gazed down at him from the halo of her brilliant hair, bracing herself on a firm and shapely arm. "I've been around for eight hundred years."

"Yeah, well, I just passed my millennium. Happy birthday to me."

"Then you understand. When that much time has gone by, you've learned what talents you have and which you don't."

"If you were anyone else, I'd agree." Ben tucked his hand behind his head. "But the Tuil Erdannan are a mystery, even to themselves. You can do all kinds of things, including create a species of Shifter the *hoch alfar* couldn't. Some even say they created the *dokk alfar*, just for shits."

"That's a myth. *Dokk alfar* have been around longer than anyone. They are the original inhabitants of Faerie."

"You were taught that in a classroom." Ben knew damn well who the original inhabitants of Faerie truly were, and it wasn't the *dokk alfar*. Not important right now. "Trust me, sweetie, Tuil Erdannan have powers no one else understands. They do whatever they want. If you decide to turn into an eagle—why not?"

"It wasn't a conscious decision." Rhianne frowned. "My body took over, and I had to do what it commanded." She tapped the back of her head. "I was *here*, in the background, screaming at myself to stop, and I couldn't." She sent him a stricken look. "Ben, what if it happens again?"

Ben wound a strand of her fiery hair around his fingers. "When I pleasured you just now, you lost control. Your body took over, but it seems like you enjoyed it. If that was a fake O, then you're a damn good actress."

Rhianne's cheeks went flame red. "It wasn't fake."

"You see? You didn't mind your body taking over then. And I'll accept that as a hell of a compliment."

Rhianne slowly lowered herself to him. In a way, that was too bad, because the view of her breasts shadowed by her hair had been fantastic. Not that Ben minded the softness of Rhianne pressed to his side.

"I don't think I can explain how petrifying it was," she said softly.

"I'm going to comfort myself by thinking you mean the

shifting."

"Of course I do. Stop trying to make me laugh."

Ben turned his head so they were nose to nose. "It's what I do. Diffuse a tough situation with humor. You're a strong woman, Rhianne. If you weren't, what Walther did to you, not to mention being suddenly thrown into this whacky human world, would have broken you." Instead, she'd yelled invective at her captors and taken her first motorcycle ride into New Orleans with Ben and had a blast.

"Walther is an ass," Rhianne said dismissively. "And with you, I feel safe." Her little smile sent a warm throb to Ben's heart. "Suddenly turning into a bird of prey is a different matter."

"Exactly. One you need to face. Tell me everything you can remember about it."

Ben could see she didn't want to relive it, but he wasn't wrong about her strength. She nodded.

"I was watching Jaycee," Rhianne began. "Thinking how unselfconscious she is. She disrobed without shame and then she eased so gracefully into her leopard form. I remember thinking, *so that's how it's done*, and then deciding there was no reason I shouldn't."

Ben had watched Rhianne skim off her clothes, leap sinuously to the railing, and suddenly become an eagle. She'd done it effortlessly, while some Shifters always struggled with the change.

Ben brushed back a lock of her hair. "The way I figure, there are two explanations. Maybe you've had this innate ability inside you all your life, but you were never around Shifters. They have a magic about them that they will forever deny. It's not obvious like casting spells or your words of power, but their magic touches others and enhances any latent magic it senses. Like when they go into mating frenzy and make everyone else horny." He forced himself to cease touching her before he acted on that thought. "Or, you, insanely powerful Tuil Erdannan, decided to learn a new skill."

Rhianne frowned. "Just like that?"

"I bet you have wells of ability you've never tapped. Probably why the menfolk of Faerie want to grab on to you. Make you do whatever you can do for *them*."

"Which is why my mother sent me here." Rhianne sounded understanding, but the knowledge hurt her. It was hell being a thing to be used, he well knew. "But what if I can't stop the shift the next time? What if we're in a restaurant? What if I'm in bed with you?"

She could kill him without meaning to. What Ben liked most about the question, though, was the assumption that she'd be in bed with him again.

"Well, it would be a novelty," Ben said, straight-faced. "Sharing a bed with an eagle. Feathers everywhere."

Rhianne grabbed the nearest pillow and whacked him with it.

This led to a pleasant tussle, with Rhianne ending up beneath him, surrendering to Ben's kisses.

The interlude might have segued to something even better, but Jaycee's voice sounded in the hall. "Rhianne? You awake?"

Rhianne's eyes widened. She wriggled out from under Ben, and Ben yielded, rolling away from her. Just before Jaycee opened the door, he raked the covers over his head, trying to look like an innocuous blanket lump.

Jaycee paused in the doorway. "How about a shower?" she said to Rhianne.

Rhianne had pulled up the sheets to shield herself, which put her bare hip next to Ben's nose. He licked her hip, stifling a chuckle when Rhianne jumped.

"A shower?" she squeaked.

"You know, stand under a nozzle that sprays you with water. Do you have showers in Faerie?"

"We do." Rhianne slid toward the edge of the bed, still clutching the sheets.

Jaycee moved to the closet, her footfalls catlike. "I have a robe in here you can borrow."

A slither of fabric landed on the blanket right over Ben's feet. Rhianne said a grateful, "Thank you."

"Come on. I'll show you the shower."

Rhianne's legs disappeared and her weight left the bed. More silken sounds as Rhianne donned the robe and then the patter of her bare feet as she left the room.

Ben remained still, but Jaycee's voice floated back to him. "Morning, Ben."

Damn Shifters and their sense of smell. Ben's scent must have screamed itself to her loud and clear, not to mention the sight of his clothes strewn all over the floor. Jaycee was probably laughing her ass off.

Ben rolled from the bed after he heard Jaycee depart and close the door. He snatched up his jeans and shirt, stuffing himself into them as the shower went on down the hall. Jaycee's and Rhianne's laughter floated to him.

He stood still a moment, letting Rhianne's golden mirth surround him.

He jammed his feet into his motorcycle boots. What the hell was he thinking, falling for a woman like Rhianne? This could not end well.

He stomped down the hall to the kitchen. It was Ben's thing to make breakfast for guests, and he needed to get started. Dimitri was nowhere in sight—either he was sleeping in after their long night or he'd gone out for a run.

As Ben cracked eggs and shoved toast into the toaster, he pondered Rhianne's sudden shifting ability and her fear of it. Would scare the crap out of anyone, he reasoned. Walking around in human shape and suddenly becoming a critter with claws, a tail, or feathers and wings.

Rhianne worried she wouldn't be able to control the change. Shifter cubs seemed to control it instinctively, even the first time it happened, but Rhianne, as she'd said, was an adult, and adults were bad at trusting their instincts. Maybe she could be trained.

Great idea, but who to train her? Jaycee and Dimitri might be too enthusiastic for her—they'd lived by their wits a long time. Plus, the two wanted to get home to their cub, needed to be with Lucas.

Ben did not want Dylan to know Rhianne could shape shift, not yet. Dylan was a good guy at heart, but he was also ruthless. He'd already not been happy that Rhianne refused to spy for him. If he knew she could shift, what would he do to coerce her to use that ability for Shifter benefit?

So that let Liam and Sean out. The brothers didn't like to keep things from their dad.

Tiger ... he might be best. Poor guy had grown up in a cage, and he'd understand how weird it was to be a shape shifter who hadn't been raised around other shape shifters.

The problem was how to pry Tiger from Dylan's side without Dylan knowing about it. Plus, Tiger had his own mate and cubs he didn't like to be far from.

Anyone from the Austin Shiftertown answered to Liam, and therefore Dylan, so they were out too.

Of course, there were other Shiftertowns, Ben mused as he cooked. Towns full of Shifters who didn't give a rat's ass about Dylan or his dominance. Something to think about.

By the time Ben had made a ton of scrambled eggs, a mess of bacon, a pile of toast, and a large pot of coffee, Dimitri wandered in, Jaycee following closely behind him.

"Rhianne's finishing dressing," Jaycee said to Ben. She grabbed a cup, poured coffee into it, and sat down at the table. "Ben slept with Rhianne last night," she informed Dimitri.

Dimitri, who'd started pouring his own coffee, flicked his

wolf's gaze to Ben. The coffee kept streaming into his cup and then flowed over.

Dimitri jumped and slammed the pot back to the coffeemaker. "Yeah?" He shook out his hand then licked it.

"I didn't sleep with her," Ben snapped. "Okay, yeah, I did, but the operative word is *sleep*. She was having nightmares. Scared shitless. I didn't want to leave her alone."

"I notice you didn't wake *me* up." Jaycee sent him a severe glance. "I could have spent the night in her room to make sure she was okay."

Ben's face went hot. "You were with Dimitri. I didn't want to disturb you. She was shaking, Jaycee. I couldn't not help her."

Dimitri sauntered to the table, continuing to lick spilled coffee from the back of his hand. "Right, Ben. We understand."

"I don't think you do." Ben broke off as Rhianne herself glided into the room. She'd donned jeans and the New Orleans T-shirt he'd bought her yesterday, along with the new shoes.

Rhianne moved directly to the stove, inhaling the fragrance of breakfast. "That smells good. I am very hungry this morning."

Dimitri chuckled, but Jaycee kept her mouth straight. Ben loaded a plate for Rhianne, and she carried it to the table. Ben glared at the two Shifters, warning them to be cautious.

"An eagle," Dimitri said after Rhianne had seated herself. "That's cool. What's it like to fly?"

So much for caution. Fear flared in Rhianne's eyes, and Ben watched her force it away. "It was interesting." A wistful smile crossed her lips. "Glorious, actually. I was terrified, and at the same time, it was ... I can't explain. I study the stars in Faerie. It was amazing to fly under them—it was as though I could touch them. I know that's impossible, but it's how it felt."

Ben set steaming coffee by Rhianne's side. "Leave her alone about it."

"It's all right," Rhianne said quickly. "Maybe talking about shifting will make it less difficult to understand."

"I feel a lot like that when I run," Jaycee said. "Glorious, as you said. Like the world can't hold me. Nothing else matters."

"Exactly," Rhianne said.

"What do you mean, nothing else matters?" Dimitri demanded in mock indignation. "Your mate. Sitting right here."

Jaycee studied the ceiling. "My mate who *always* takes things so personally."

Rhianne laughed, her mood lightening, which Ben realized had been Dimitri's purpose. Ben saluted his thanks with a coffee mug.

They dug into breakfast, everyone hungry. Shifters were always ravenous, but their adventures last night, plus Jaycee and Dimitri relieving tension in Shifter fashion, put an extra edge on their hunger.

"So, what now?" Dimitri asked as he scraped the last of the food from his plate. The pans on the stove were empty, the stack of toast gone.

He spoke casually, but Ben sensed his tension—he and Jaycee were feeling their separation from their cub.

"You two have probably done all you can." Ben slurped his cooling coffee. "You have a life. Go back to it."

Jaycee glanced uneasily between Rhianne and Ben. "Things aren't exactly safe for you two."

"I know. But I have many more Shifters in my contacts. They can babysit us."

"Huh," Dimitri said to Jaycee. "He means Shifters who won't report to Kendrick, who often reports to Dylan."

"Something like that." Ben casually set down his mug. "I'm thinking that Kendrick, your great leader, doesn't need to know everything that has happened here."

"Like your houseguest suddenly turning into an eagle?" Dimitri asked.

"Exactly."

Jaycee said nothing, studying her plate as she drew her fork across it. Jaycee was loyal to Kendrick, more so than to anyone except Dimitri.

"Jaycee?" Ben prompted.

Jaycee flicked her gaze to Ben. "Thinking it through, I believe that right now, what Kendrick doesn't know won't hurt him."

Rhianne relaxed, shooting Ben a relieved glance.

"Kendrick could keep something like this to himself, you know," Dimitri added. "I'm saying that in case he drags it out of us. He doesn't tell Dylan absolutely everything. Kendrick likes a little space."

Kendrick, a white tiger in a Shifter world that didn't have many tigers at all, had made being secretive a science.

"Well, swear him to silence for a while, then," Ben said. "Until we know what's going on with Rhianne."

"What does Rhianne want?" Jaycee turned to her. "Males. They decide everything like we're not even in the room."

"And females talk about males like *they're* not in the room," Dimitri countered.

"I'd like to speak to my mother," Rhianne announced, cutting through their banter. "I want to ask her why I didn't know about this shifting ability."

"Makes sense." Jaycee reached into her pocket and pulled out a crystal. "Try this."

Rhianne reached for the crystal, turning it over in awe. "This is a *ghastal*."

Jaycee's brows drew down. "What does that mean?"

"It's a very precious stone. Extremely rare." Rhianne gazed at Jaycee with increased respect. "My mother wouldn't give this to just anyone."

"Yeah?" Jaycee moved uncomfortably.

"They're valued for their crystalline structure. A good

conductor of magic." Rhianne studied the stone again. "You use this to summon her?"

"To let her know I want to talk," Jaycee said. "I doubt I could *summon* her."

"Ha," Dimitri said. "They're besties, and we know it."

"Not helping, sweetie."

"My mother has always distanced herself from me. And me from her." Rhianne kept her eyes on the crystal. "I don't resent you for connecting with her, Jaycee."

Jaycee shrugged. "Probably easier for her to unload to a stranger."

Rhianne didn't answer. Jaycee remained troubled, but Rhianne seemed resigned that her mother preferred to speak at length to Jaycee rather than to her own daughter.

Rhianne rose and moved to the door that accessed a balcony over the veranda. Ben quickly followed her. Jaycee and Dimitri stood, ready for any danger, but they hung back, giving Rhianne space.

Ben stepped out into the cool morning, sun slanting through trees behind the house. The view looked across the grounds to the thick stand of live oaks that separated the old plantation from the newer industrial area beyond it.

Rhianne lifted the crystal to catch the sunlight. The crystal Lady Aisling had given Ben was similar, but Ben hadn't offered his because there was a much better chance Lady Aisling would answer a call from Jaycee than she would from Ben.

Rhianne kept her gaze on the crystal as she spoke in the little Tuil Erdannan that Ben understood. "Lady Aisling mac Aodha, heed me. Across the barrier, I call you."

Ben waited for Lady Aisling's impatient, *What is it?* That was how she responded to Ben's rare calls. On the other hand, she could call and bug *him* anytime.

Silence answered. Sunlight glittered through the stone, throwing a rainbow of spangles onto Rhianne's face.

"Lady Aisling mac Aodha, heed me."

Ben noted her avoidance of the word *Mother*, or any other endearments. A sad thing.

More silence. The wind chimes on the porch below them tinkled, as though the house tried to boost the magic, but nothing happened. Lady Aisling didn't answer.

"I guess she's busy." Rhianne lowered the crystal and quickly turned from Ben, but he saw the tears shining in her eyes.

———

DIMITRI AND JAYCEE DEPARTED. JAYCEE HAD TAKEN BACK the crystal, nodding to Rhianne's quiet *thank you*. Both Shifters knew the call had been a failure—their Shifter hearing let them easily eavesdrop.

Jaycee volunteered to call Lady Aisling for Rhianne, but she got the same response. Not unusual, Jaycee said quickly. Lady Aisling didn't always answer. Rhianne thanked her for trying.

Rhianne and Ben waved them off. When the motorcycle roars had faded into the distance, Ben slid his arm around Rhianne's waist.

"Have to make some phone calls. Will you be all right a few minutes?"

"I think so." Rhianne lifted her chin, as though determined not to break down. She had a lot of guts, and Ben silently cursed Lady Aisling for ignoring her.

"Explore the house," he suggested. "No tourists today."

Rhianne's lovely hair flowed around her, unbound, stirring in the breeze. She nodded absently and wandered back into the house, leaving Ben alone on the front porch.

Ben slid his cell phone from his pocket and scanned through his contacts. He'd been pondering who could help

Rhianne, discreetly, come to terms with her shifting ability, and had finally settled on one person.

"Kenzie," he said in hearty tones when Kenzie Dimitru O'Donnell, mate to the leader of the North Carolina Shifter-town, answered his call. "How are you, darling?"

"You want something." Kenzie's jovial voice was suffused with her deep contentment as Bowman's mate and mom to two cubs. "You never call me *darling* unless you want something."

"Guilty. What I have is an unusual situation, and I need to ask you to stay quiet about it. Don't even tell Bowman, if you think he won't keep his mouth shut."

"Good thing he's not here, or he'd have heard you. You have a loud voice, my friend."

"That's because I'm agitated. Or, as your son, Ryan, would say, freaking out a little." Ben then told Kenzie about Rhianne, who she was, why she was staying at the haunted house, and what had happened to her the night before.

When he finished, Kenzie, a wolf Shifter with deep wisdom, said nothing.

"Kenz?" Ben checked to see whether the phone was still on. "You there?"

"Yes." The word was thoughtful. "You know, Gil—or Ben, whatever you're calling yourself these days—I can think of a much better person to teach Rhianne about shifting."

"Yeah? Who? Zander, maybe? He's a bit over the top, though. I want to ease her into it without too much bullshit, which is why I thought of you."

"I'm flattered. Not Zander. Not at first."

"Tiger then?"

"Would you stop interrupting me? The best person to teach her right now ... is you."

CHAPTER TWELVE

B en shook the phone at Kenzie's pronouncement, not
certain he'd heard her correctly.

"Me?" he demanded. "Why? I'm not Shifter."

"Neither is she," Kenzie said reasonably. "But you change
shape. And vanish at will, and pretend to be a ghost, and other
weird things no Shifter would ever do."

"Huh. You haven't known all the Shifters I have. I have no
idea how to help her."

"No? Think it through. Not that I'm saying it would be a
bad thing to have her talk to a Shifter at some point." Kenzie
paused. "Maybe bring her here to our Shiftertown later. My
uncle might be a good person to consult."

Ben blinked. "Your uncle. Christian Dimitru, the Fae-
hating, ice-cold killer wolf Shifter. That uncle?"

"Uncle Christian doesn't hate *all* Fae. He's getting along
very well with the Fae woman who came here when Bowman
and I were going through all that shit a few years ago. They talk
all the time about her returning permanently to Faerie, but so
far, she hasn't gone."

"This would give him the compassion to understand Rhianne?"

"It might."

"Huh. What would your sweet mate Bowman do if he knew a Tuil Erdannan could become an eagle? Would he trap her? Make her work for him? I'm trying to avoid that. It's why I'm confiding in you and swearing you to secrecy."

"Bowman isn't so bad, Ben." Kenzie spoke with the warm conviction of a woman who loved her mate.

"Yeah? I remember when you didn't believe that."

Kenzie's merry laughter rang through the phone. "I know— I thought he was a total asshole even while I was falling in love with him. I was wrong. I admit it."

"I'll concede he's not so bad because he is madly in love with you, which means he has brains and good taste. Still, I don't trust him with anything concerning me. Right now, Rhianne concerns me."

"Which is why I say you're the best one to teach her," Kenzie said. "Sorry, I gotta go, Ben. My daughter is screaming her head off, which could mean she's hungry, bored, saw an ant, the world is ending, or she can't find her favorite toy. Just think about it." *Click.*

"Think about what?" Ben demanded, but he knew. *Everything,* she meant.

Ben tapped the silent phone to his lips. He was tempted to call Zander, in spite of the overblown devil-may-care attitude the big polar bear approached every situation with, but he had the suspicion that Kenzie was right.

Rhianne didn't necessarily need a Shifter. Rhianne and Ben were both creatures of Faerie and bound by those compulsions, no matter how hard each were trying not to be.

Ben heaved a sigh, climbed the front porch steps, and walked back into the house. The noise the fluttering rose vines made sounded exactly like a snigger.

—————

"You don't have to take care of me."

Rhianne sat on the bottom step of the main staircase in the house, folding her hands to keep them from shaking. Ben tucked his phone into his pocket and leaned on the newel post next to her.

"I like taking care of you."

"My mother asked you to bring me here. You're not obligated to babysit, as you called it."

"I'm not obligated to do anything." Ben rested his arm on top of the post, muscles pulling at his T-shirt. "Neither are you, except to sit tight and wait for your mom to give you the all-clear. But that would be boring."

Rhianne peered up at him, but as usual, Ben kept what he really felt deep down inside. He'd had to hide his true nature for centuries, she surmised, which had made him the master of camouflage.

"Why do you appear that way?" Rhianne indicated his body with a flutter of fingers. She very much enjoyed the way Ben looked, but she was curious. "I glimpsed what must be your true self when you took me out of the dungeon and then again last night when we fought the snakes. Your real form would frighten humans, I understand. But most of the human men I've seen so far are, well ... taller."

Ben's sudden grin flashed like a beam of sunshine.

"Is that all you're worried about? Well, I'll tell you." He left the newel post and sat down on the step beside her, his warmth comforting. "When I first entered this world, about a thousand years ago, humans, at least ones in the area I'd landed in, weren't very big. There were some tall men, but so few they were given nicknames like *Longshanks*. Over the centuries, people grew bigger boned—they had better nutrition in some cases, or just changed for whatever reason. But when I first arrived, I took on the average height. I couldn't afford to stand out."

"You could have made yourself taller as things changed."

Ben's cheeks reddened. "I could have, I suppose. I could be like Dimitri and tower over everyone. Shifters love to do that. But I realized that, at the height I have, I intimidate people less. A guy most other guys have to look down at isn't threatening. They think I'm harmless."

Rhianne's amusement bubbled through her worry. "Harmless? You?"

Ben spread his hands. "It's all part of the illusion. And you know? I decided at some point in my life that I'd rather have friends than enemies."

"Oh." Rhianne's voice went soft. "That's a beautiful thing to say."

He shrugged. "It probably means I've been alive too long."

"I don't have many friends." Rhianne heard the loneliness in her words. "When you're the daughter of Lady Aisling and Lord Ivor, it's difficult to know who wants to be with you because they really like you, or because they think you can curry favor for them. I have colleagues in my field that I have discussions with, and one or two good girlfriends, but I don't see those ladies much anymore. They're married now with their own families."

"And they don't have time for the third wheel?" Ben poked his finger at his chest. "That's me. The odd one out. I've helped bring a lot of Shifter couples together, and what do they say once the deed's done? *See ya, Ben. We want to shag.*"

He said it so comically Rhianne laughed. "You poor thing."

"It's all right. I like to see the lovebirds happy." Ben twined his fingers and stretched them. "Ben, the matchmaker. Ben, the dude who gets everyone out of trouble. Not that I don't get them *into* trouble in the first place ..."

"What you mean is, you're taking care of me because it's

what you do," Rhianne said. "It's why you look after this house. You're a nice guy."

Ben winced. "Ouch. Never tell a dude he's a nice guy. We all want to be serious badasses. It's an ego thing."

Rhianne regarded him with amusement. "I've watched you battle twice now. You *are* a serious badass."

He bumped her shoulder with his. "Aw, you're just saying that."

"And you speak so strangely."

"Yeah, well, you'll get used to me. I tend to pick up the idioms of whatever country and times I'm living in, so I talk a lot of shit. You should hear what I learned in prison." He paused. "No, maybe you shouldn't."

"You were imprisoned?" Rhianne asked in shock.

"Yep. These are prison tatts." He touched the web on his neck. "It teaches people not to mess with me. Or at least, that's what the tatts are supposed to do. It doesn't always work."

"Why did the humans imprison you?" Rhianne tried not to imagine Ben stuck in a dank dungeon as she'd been. Only a very magical being would be able to capture him—she'd seen how easily he'd battled a handful of Fae warriors, not to mention the snakes. "Did the *hoch alfar* lock you up?"

"No, no. Not this time. I went to prison in this world, about twenty years back. I beat up a guy, and I went down for assault and battery." He glanced at his scarred hands. "Lots of battery."

"You battled a human? Was he magical?"

"Hmm? No, not that I could tell. The guy beat the shit out of his wife, right in front of me. I didn't know him or his wife from a hole in the wall, but I decided to give him a taste of his own medicine. She got away from him, good thing—I hear she's doing very well now. But I put the husband in the hospital with his injuries. I told the judge why at the trial. Judge was a woman not fond of men who pounded women, but she had to convict me. There was a lot of evidence and a number of witnesses, and the guy's parents and friends were pretty pissed off at me. So, I did a stretch."

Rhianne listened, dumbfounded. "Why by the Goddess did you let them put you in prison for being a champion? I don't believe you couldn't have broken out of a non-magical cell, or that you couldn't have evaded being caught in the first place. You could have changed your shape, become ... what you are."

Ben chuckled. "That would *not* have gone over well. Big, ugly, scary goblin dancing in the middle of the courtroom. I'd have been full of bullet holes in no time. I come from a long-lived species, but weapons can still kill me. I'll tell you one day about the knife in my gut that nearly ended my life. Thank the Goddess for an arrogant Shifter healer who put me back together."

"You're changing the subject," Rhianne told him. "You did not have to let the humans imprison you, and you know it. Why did you?"

Ben brushed his callused palm over his close-cropped hair. "I guess because I wanted the experience. Humans fascinate me, all the weird things they come up with. They now mostly lock their criminals away instead of hanging them for stealing a handkerchief, but locking them up breeds its own problems."

"Do you regret the experience then?"

Ben considered. "Not really. It was a bad place, that prison, but I met a few decent guys. Not career criminals, just ones who screwed up and knew it, and were paying for it. We still stay in touch. Not in person of course, cause they're going to start wondering why I never age."

"You could pretend to." Rhianne gave him a little smile, already feeling better. This was Ben's magic, she decided. Putting others at their ease.

"Sure, that would be fun. Trust me, I feel my age some

days. But my hair won't stay gray. The goblin in me isn't gray-haired yet."

Rhianne wanted to laugh. "Does the goblin in you have hair?"

"Yes." Ben looked straight at her. "And no, I'm not going to show you. I like yours, though."

He brushed his finger over a stray lock of it, reminding Rhianne of the gentle and then fiery way he'd touched her this morning. Her face heated as she turned her head and kissed his palm.

"This could get dangerous." Ben's whisper brushed her cheek.

"I don't care anymore."

Ben withdrew, the absence of his touch cold. "You might care again someday." He folded his arms, shoulders moving enticingly. "You're avoiding what we really need to talk about. The elephant in the room."

Rhianne snapped around to stare down the hall. "There's an elephant ...?"

Ben's laughter rumbled around her. "Figure of speech. Wait, you know what an elephant is? It's unique to the human world."

"My mother brings home books. I learned human languages by reading them."

"Ah, clever of you. The expression means we're not talking about the thing that we very obviously *should* be. The elephant, in this case, is you shifting into an eagle."

Rhianne pressed her hand to her knotting stomach. "I think I'd rather talk about elephants."

"We can discuss them all you want later. First, we're going to figure out your shifting ability. If you're afraid that you can't control it, then you need to learn to control it."

"That easy, is it?" Rhianne asked in irritation.

"I was wracking my brains all this morning, trying to figure out who could best help you. My friend Kenzie whacked me upside the head—another figure of speech—and told me I should do it. I decided she was right."

Rhianne had heard him speaking into the phone on the porch, but he'd kept his voice too low for her to discern what he'd said. Her heart beat faster. "Because neither of us is Shifter?"

"You're sharp. Now, much as I'd love to sit here and natter with you all day ..." Ben unfolded himself and touched her cheek. "Or caress you, or kiss you, or ..."

Definitely dangerous. Rhianne laughed shakily. "Sounds more fun than me facing my demons."

"I don't know. Fighting demons can be a kick. Like those snakes last night."

Rhianne rose quickly to her feet. "No more snakes."

"Naw, I didn't like them either." Ben rose and took her hand. "Come on."

"Where are we going?"

"Scene of the crime. So to speak."

He towed her down the hall and out the end door to the veranda. It was shaded, but sunlight dazzled the trees and grass beyond, and warm air floated around them.

Ben patted the railing. "All right. You were standing here, watching Jaycee shift into her leopard."

Rhianne went to him with reluctance. Ben's matter-of-fact attitude reassured her a small amount, but her heart pounded and her mouth had gone dry. Not even the manacles locked around her wrists in Walther's dungeon had been as frightening as her experience last night.

She rested her hands on the rail and gazed across the yard to the outbuildings in back. "My skin was itching and burning, and I couldn't stand still. As I said, when I saw Jaycee, it sort of occurred to me that I could shift too, and then something in my mind just ... took over. The next thing I knew I was up on the railing."

"I saw you." Ben abruptly vaulted to the top of the rail, crouching on it with ease. "Come on, join me."

Rhianne watched him balance in his motorcycle boots, legs in jeans folded under him. "You look ridiculous."

"Probably. All right, don't join me. Nice view from up here, though." He remained on the rail as effortlessly as Rhianne had done last night.

A prickling made her scrub her hands over her arms. "Can we not do this?"

Ben pivoted toward her without losing his footing. "What happened to the woman who picked up a stray piece of pipe and started smashing *hoch alfar* with it? This after being thrown into a dungeon and then rescued by a scary-ass goblin and a pyromaniacal *dokk alfar*?"

Rhianne couldn't help the twitch of her lips, but her fear didn't fade. "That was different. That was self-defense, plus battling Walther's thugs was easy because I was so angry at him for kidnapping me. This is me admitting there's a strange beast inside me."

"There's a strange beast inside *me*, and he's not pretty, as you know. If you think about it, there's one inside us all, but we fight it so we can live in the world with everyone else. So we won't be truly alone."

Rhianne rubbed her hands against a sudden chill. "You're trying to placate me."

"Maybe, but that doesn't mean what I say isn't true."

She let out a breath. "What do you want me to do? Take off my clothes and see if I shift again?"

Ben's eyes filled with heat that seared her. "The taking off the clothes part sounds fun. But I don't think that's all there is to it."

"What if I ... I don't know." She waved her hands. "Get

stuck halfway in between? Or what if I *can* change and try to fly, and then can't figure out how to land? Tuil Erdannan are fairly indestructible, but falling a few hundred feet to the hard ground would not be good."

Ben leapt down from the rail, landing lightly on his feet. "I think that whatever your animal can do, you just do. Like Jaycee running so fast. Or Tiger being the crazed fighting force he is. Or Zander being a pain in everyone's ass."

Rhianne appreciated that he kept trying to make her laugh. "Is being a pain in everyone's ass a trait of Zander's animal?"

"Hell, yes. Polar bear. Mightiest land animal on the planet, and Zander knows it."

"I thought that was the elephant."

Ben's grin warmed her through. "I'll tell him that. Anyway, what I had in mind was to help you find that beast inside you. Help you learn about it and figure out how to work with it instead of letting it scare the crud out of you."

"How? I never knew I had this—thing—in me at all." Rhianne plucked at her shirt as though the eagle lurked beneath it.

And yet ... How many times when she'd been absorbed in her studies or while gazing at the marvel of a nebula, had she sensed another presence, one strong and wild, that seemed to be so close? Her skin would tingle, as it was doing now.

Rhianne had always pushed the sensations aside, dismissing them as imagination or exhaustion.

Ben moved to stand next to her. "Trust me, I've had to tame this thing inside me from the beginning. *Not* taming it cost me dearly. I'll never, ever let myself lose control again."

The anguish in him touched Rhianne, made her want to comfort him. She was curious about what had happened, but his body was tight with tension that warned her off.

"How are you going to teach me?" Her voice was quiet.

Ben's amusement vanished. "It won't be easy. You'll have to

trust me, to put yourself entirely in my hands. Can you do that?"

Rhianne had put herself into his hands that morning, and it had been the best moment of her life. Not what he meant, she knew.

"I don't know," she confessed.

"Good." Ben gave her a nod. "If you were certain, I'd know you were overconfident, and this training session would crash and burn. Let's start." He took a step back, a ghost of his grin returning, and pointed at her. "Strip."

CHAPTER THIRTEEN

B en waited, certain Rhianne would punch him between the eyes, turn from him in high dudgeon, and stalk away.

His breath stopped when she grasped the hem of her T-shirt and smoothly pulled it off. She wore a camisole beneath that clung to her curves, her nipples shadowed outlines on the creamy fabric.

Training, Ben reminded himself as his gaze became glued to the camisole. *This is training. She needs to figure things out, not be fondled.*

But damn, it was going to be hard to keep his hands to himself.

"Let's go down on the grass." Ben tried to make his voice brisk. *Go down.* Had that been a slip? "Easier to work there," he added hastily.

Rhianne didn't notice his gaffe, or perhaps Tuil Erdannan didn't use the phrase. She gracefully descended the steps, stretching in the sunshine, face lifted to the sun.

Ben got rid of his shirt and sat on the bottom step of the veranda to unlace and kick off his boots. He slid out of his jeans and joined Rhianne on the grass in his underwear.

He liked the quick flicker of her eyes as she gave him a once-over, not unhappy with what she saw.

"Come on," he said. "Pants too."

Rhianne removed the high-heeled sandals from her feet. Ben could not stop himself watching her fingers unbutton the jeans and slide down the zipper. The jeans eased from her hips, and Rhianne lifted her shapely legs from them one at a time.

Ben had seen some of her beauty as they'd played in bed together, but they'd been tangled in sheets and pillows, and he hadn't seen the whole of her. Now he could look his fill.

The camisole and matching panties bared sweet curves, from her full breasts to soft hips, her thick red braid snaking over her shoulder like a silken rope.

"That's enough for now." Ben moved to her, pretending complete indifference to her beautiful, sexy, beguiling, delectable ... *I need to shut up.*

"What I'm about to teach you might seem a little eccentric but go with it. It's a human thing. They've come up with amazing ways to cope with life."

"Will it involve more shrimp?" Rhianne bathed him in a smile. "Or gumbo?"

"Not at the moment. But good idea for when we're done for the day." Ben grasped Rhianne's shoulders and positioned her in front of him. "I'm going to teach you some moves that will help you control energy, whether it's inside you or coming at you. To keep it from overwhelming you."

Rhianne nodded, though Ben guessed the nod was out of courtesy, not understanding.

"First, do nothing but feel the ground beneath your feet," he began. "Take that energy up through the earth and into your core."

Rhianne closed her eyes, her chest rising with her breath. She'd been a little shaky this morning, though she'd tried to behave as though she was calmness itself, but now she stilled, her trembling easing.

Ben didn't have to close his eyes, having done this so often it was second nature. He focused on his connection to the ground, its energy steadying him as it was steadying Rhianne. He sensed the ley line running beneath the property like a river of light, the magic that made the house a living creature instead of merely bricks and wood.

Rhianne slowly opened her eyes. "There is much magic here."

"Probably one reason why whatever ability you have manifested last night. Now, we're going to do some exercises that help take that energy and flow it through you, channeling it instead of resisting it."

Ben moved to stand beside her, showing her how to balance herself and do a few basic slow tai chi moves—warding off, rolling back, pressing, pushing, striking, and the basic footwork.

"This is an ancient practice," Ben said as they went through the postures. "Well, ancient for humans, anyway. Tai chi ch'uan is a martial art. Most people nowadays think it's just an exercise routine for balance and meditation, but it's really a fighting form. One based on understanding and controlling energy, not resisting or avoiding what's coming at you. Softness instead of hardness. Learning to be slow. Fast and hard is not always better."

Fast and hard. Listen to me.

"I think I understand." Rhianne halted her movements, which were as graceful as a willow tree, and waited for more instruction.

Ben showed her the beginning sequence of the tai chi simplified form—opening the door, parting the wild horse's mane, white crane spreads its wings—then turned her to face him again.

"This next thing is called tai chi push hands, or *tuishou.* We learn to take energy and return it, feeling and controlling the other person's intent. Like this."

He grasped her arm and positioned it across her body, then he pushed his hand against hers, teaching her to turn her wrist and send the force back to him.

Rhianne wanted to resist at first, blocking his strength or shoving him away. She overbalanced, predictably, and danced a few steps back, growling in frustration as she tried to keep to her feet.

Ben repositioned her gently. "It's about patience. Awareness. If you resist my strength, you double its effect. See?" He pushed hard, and she instinctively struggled to prevent him from shoving her over. "But if you take my energy and turn it back to me ..." Ben motioned for her to push at him. As she did so—revealing her strength—he pivoted his body with her pressure, his hand turning to send her arm back to her chest.

Rhianne regarded him in surprise, then delight. "How did you do that?"

Ben barely heard her. He wanted to linger at her breasts, warm through the silk, but he made himself release her and step away. *Training. We're training.*

"Like this." Ben rested her fingers on his arm once more. "You turn your hand when I start my journey toward you, so you're catching my force on its back or on your wrist. Like so." He gently glided their hands together toward her chest.

"Oh." After a few tries, Rhianne's movements became more fluid, she relaxing under his force, but aware of it. Whenever his hand reached her chest, she turned and flowed the energy back to him. "I've done training sort of like this when I was much younger. All Tuil Erdannan receive combat instruction, women and men alike. It wasn't quite the same, but I remember how we learned to take our enemy's strength and use it against them."

"Exactly. This is slow understanding, as you feel my every move, using what I do to your advantage."

They continued the back-and-forth exchange, Ben connecting to her and she to him. Ben felt the earth through her, the ley line reaching to the magic in her before feeding itself to Ben like an electric current through a wire.

Ben sucked in a breath. The magic in Rhianne was like molten lava, slow but searing.

Her energy didn't simply come from the fact that she was Tuil Erdannan. Ben had felt Lady Aisling's power, and it wasn't the same. Lady Aisling was a bright light in a window-less room. Rhianne's magic was more subtle, a tide of strength so quietly immense the world would never withstand it. Rhianne believed she didn't have much magic, yet he felt it in her, potential untapped.

Rhianne began to smile, her focus fixed on their hands. Once she'd mastered the first move, Ben showed her more complex ones, and soon they were using both hands together.

His connection with her sang through him. What they did was like a dance, but even more intimate. An awareness crackled from her fingers to his and enveloped his body. Her smile widened as the rhythm grew smoother, each push and turn revealing more and more of her skill.

A defiant sparkle leapt into Rhianne's eyes, and she suddenly pushed Ben in an entirely different pattern. Ben should have moved with it, continuing the dance, but he stum-bled, clamping down on her and pulling her into him. She landed against his chest.

"Little shit," he said.

"Seeing if you were paying attention."

Ben hadn't been, not to the training. He'd been distracted by her beauty, her relaxed strength, her smile. As soon as she'd made an unpredictable move, his expertise had evaporated.

He gazed into her black-flecked brown eyes, understanding now that they were the eyes of an eagle, proud, fierce, deadly.

Her breath on his lips made Ben forget all about the exercise, the training, the reason he'd brought her out here in the first place. He became aware that they were both nearly naked, nothing between them but a few wisps of fabric.

Rhianne's face was misted with perspiration, her lips parted. Ben pushed back her heavy braid, traced her cheekbone with his fingertip.

Rhianne leaned forward and kissed him fully on the mouth.

A raw sound escaped Ben's throat. His arms went around her as he parted her lips, not holding himself back from tasting her deeply. It had been only a few hours since she'd lain in his arms, and he hadn't taken satisfaction for himself, leaving the bed hard and aching.

Rhianne skimmed her hands across Ben's hips. Fingers moved under his waistband to touch the bare skin of his backside.

"Damn," Ben murmured. "I've never done tai chi like this."

"I don't think it's one of the moves."

Rhianne's whisper brushed his face before she kissed him again, Ben accepting that energy and answering it with his own. Her fingers played on his buttocks, and his already hard cock gave a throb.

"What am I going to do with you?" he asked. "That is, I know what I *want* to do."

Rhianne licked his ear. "Why not? We're not inexperienced and untouched."

"Nope. Not spring chickens. Not us."

Rhianne blinked at him. "Spring ...?"

"Never mind. I mean you're right. We're not two innocent kids with no understanding of what we're getting into."

Her smile made him hot all over. "I believe I understand quite well."

Ben gently removed her hands from his backside, though it nearly killed him to do it.

"I'm a goblin. A strange being from the deep past. You're Tuil Erdannan, who can crush goblins like they were burned paper."

Rhianne shook her head. "We're Rhianne and Ben. Exiles together."

"But what happens when you aren't exiled anymore?" Ben brushed his thumb across her lower lip. "I always will be."

Her eyes held need mixed with anguish. "Does it matter?"

"It might. When you meet another Tuil Erdannan and know he'll be your mate for life, do you want a torrid affair with a *goblin* in your past?"

"Ben." Rhianne stepped against him, her breasts to his chest. "I'm not throwing myself at you because I want a torrid affair. I'm lonely, you're lonely, and no one else wants us for who we truly are." She leaned into him and nibbled his earlobe. "And, I'm going to admit it." Her whisper in his ear heated him through. "You're beautiful."

Ben cupped her waist. "I think crossing the gate has done something to your eyesight."

"Improved it." Rhianne touched his face. "You've perfected handsomeness, Ben. I bet in your true form, you looked amazing to other goblins."

He shrugged, trying for a nonchalant tone. "They didn't complain."

Rhianne's soft laughter shook her agreeably. "I'm not complaining either."

Her next kiss took his breath away. Rhianne's skin was warm from the sun and their exercise, plus she pulsed with a longing that matched Ben's. The ground was soft here, and the magic from the house throbbed beneath them.

Ben swept Rhianne into his arms and lowered her to the cool grass. He'd prefer to cushion her with a blanket, but she didn't seem in the mood to wait for him to fetch one. She wrapped one leg around his, pulling him down so his cock rested on the silken fabric between her thighs.

"Are you sure you're not Shifter?" Ben asked her hoarsely. "'Cause I could swear you're in mating frenzy."

"You mean wanting to be with you so much it's making my blood burn?" Rhianne's eyes glistened, her smile hot.

"Something like that, yeah. 'Course, I'm not Shifter, and I'm feeling the same way."

"Good."

Their mouths met, this kiss still more passionate, Ben imbibing Rhianne's frustration, need, and loneliness. He also tasted the magic of her, the incredible combination of her ancestry and whatever had been waiting to manifest. That magic poured into him, stirring to life his own, the one he hid from all others.

He freed her from the camisole, tucking it behind her to help shield her from the grass. This morning she'd stretched out on top of him, but now she appeared content to lie back and pull him down to her.

Ben held Rhianne's gaze as he slid her underwear from her and worked his way out of his own.

What was this to her? A fling to pass the time? To scratch an itch? And why was he asking questions like that? If she had an itch, he'd happily scratch it.

But Ben knew, somewhere inside himself, in the place that spoke only the truth, that this would mean everything to him.

He silenced his inner voice by sliding his hand between Rhianne's thighs, into her liquid heat. He'd touched her there this morning, bringing to life sweet joy.

Ben licked her throat as he let his fingers play. Rhianne

moaned softly, smiles deserting her, and lifted her hips, greedy for his touch.

"You like that, do you?" Ben kissed her lightly. "Want more?"

"Yes," she whispered. "Please."

Goddess, if she didn't stop looking at him in that sultry way, begging for him, he'd come without being able to stop it.

"If you're nice, maybe I'll do it some more," Ben teased.

Rhianne arched against him, her body pleading. Ben smiled his power and rubbed through the warmth, laughing when she writhed.

Hot, strong fingers closed around his cock and squeezed.

"*Shit.*" Ben grabbed her wrist, shoving her hand away. Or tried to. Rhianne moved without resisting his strength, gliding her hand around to grasp him once more. He'd taught her that —he was a dumbass.

Rhianne squeezed again, compounding his problem by sliding her fingers up his shaft.

Ben pressed his face to hers. "You need to stop that."

"Why?"

Because you're killing me.

"I want to make it last, that's why." Ben winced as the truth came out. He wanted her to think him a powerhouse who could go all night, not a wuss who couldn't hold it in front of a beautiful woman.

But he'd never been with Rhianne before.

Rhianne gazed up at him, golden flecks in her eyes starting to drown out the brown. "I don't want to wait. I want us to do this *now.*"

"I don't know. I think I should buy you flowers first."

This mystified her. "Why? There are flowers all over the place here."

"Human custom. I'll explain later."

Rhianne lifted herself to him. "We're not human."

"I think that's abundantly clear." Ben withdrew his touch from between her legs, liking that she whimpered. "Shh. We'll take it slow, all right? I don't want to hurt you."

Rhianne apparently had no worries about this. She tugged him closer, catching his cock again. She rubbed it, sending fire through him that burned away everything he'd ever thought important.

As he came down to her, wanting her mouth, Rhianne gasped. "Goddess, help me. I'm going to shift."

Ben jerked as Rhianne's skin rippled, downy feathers blossoming across her skin. They were tiny, giving her a softness that Ben suddenly found incredibly sexy.

"Don't fight." Ben pinned her with his hands on her shoulders. "Remember what I just taught you. Take the energy, turn it around. Don't resist."

"But I don't want to hurt *you*."

Ben gave her a feral smile. "Lucky you, sweetheart. I'm the most resilient thing you could ever be with."

Tears formed in Rhianne's eyes. The feathers spread, thickening. Ben wondered what he'd do if she suddenly sprouted that killer beak.

Rhianne's face remained her own. She struggled another long moment, then she took a deep breath and slowly, slowly made herself relax.

"That's it, love," Ben said. "You're stronger than you know. Strength doesn't have to force. It can give."

Rhianne drew another breath, eyes closing. Her hands came up to press Ben's chest, and he realized she was trying to do the moves of the pushing hands. Ben knelt back, meeting her wrists with his, once more falling into the flowing pattern.

The feathers receded, Rhianne's skin smoothing. She shivered, hard, then opened her eyes, silent tears flowing from their corners. Ben leaned down and kissed them away.

Rhianne embraced him. Her strength hadn't diminished,

but her desperation had calmed. Her need had not gone away, he could tell, but she rocked against him gently, caressing instead of grabbing.

Ben slowly lowered her to the grass. "You see? You can control it. But the feathers—nothing to be ashamed of there. I bet your half-beast is wicked sexy."

She gazed at him, perplexed, and Ben smothered a laugh. He had so much to teach her.

Ben leaned to her and nipped her lips, sliding his hand between her thighs to loosen her once more. Then he positioned himself and slid his cock straight into her open, welcoming heat.

CHAPTER FOURTEEN

Rhianne couldn't stop her sharp intake of breath as Ben filled her, and filled her. She'd wrapped her hand around his very large cock, but as it slid into her, she realized just *how* large it was.

His eyes went soft, the darkness of them pulling at her. There was so much in his gaze, most hidden behind walls he'd built over centuries. Rhianne wanted to reach those walls, tear them aside, and look into the heart of the being called Ben.

For now, having him inside her, both easing and increasing the hot ache of her need, was incredible. A cry escaped her, all her worries, fears, and sorrows fleeing as the joy of locking together with Ben became a reality.

He stilled himself as he studied her, letting her grow used to him. The weight of him was soothing, protective.

Ben ran his hand along her braid. "You are the most beautiful woman I've ever seen." A smile tugged at his mouth. "And I'm not just saying that to get into your pants."

Ben used the most entertaining expressions. She wanted him to teach them all to her.

He'd called it mating frenzy. Rhianne decided that was a

very good word for it. She felt frenzied as she lifted herself to him and twined herself around him, urging him to continue.

Ben laughed softly, a sound of satisfaction. He withdrew slightly then slid back in, opening Rhianne wider, eliciting another gasp.

She wanted more. Faster, harder. The words came out of her mouth, in her own language, her grasp of other tongues fleeing.

Ben's laughter died, a groan escaping him as he began thrusting into her. There was an ache inside Rhianne that needed to be eased, one that grew hotter and more acute as he loved her.

The need increased rather than abated. Ben was thick and hard, unlocking sensations she'd never experienced. The few lovers of her past—and the last was so very long ago—hadn't touched her like this, hadn't released what Ben was unleashing.

A wildness Rhianne had always sensed in herself but never acknowledged rose screaming to the surface. It wasn't the same as the shifting instinct—this was more primal, reaching back to what the Tuil Erdannan had been in the dawn of time. Fearless, untamed, unstoppable.

A bright heat flashed through her, but this one didn't come from her. Where she and Ben joined was unbearably hot, and at the same time exhilarating. Her body throbbed with it, the ferocity emerging from her as shouts of joy.

Ben glowed. Not literally—he was the same handsome midnight-eyed man who'd towed her to safety and given her warm, tasty food and new experiences. The man who'd made her laugh, dance, and forget the dangers of her life.

Somewhere inside him was the glow of what he truly was. Not the affable Ben who preferred friends to enemies, or the massive goblin who tore apart metal and stone with terrifying strength.

Beyond both of those lay what he hid, a being of incredible

potency that gentled itself for everyone and everything around him. If he brought that potential out of him, he could devastate the world.

The thought that so much power lay in her arms increased Rhianne's excitement. She laughed with it.

Take care of him, Tiger had said. *He is the last warrior.*

Perhaps she was seeing the warrior in him, the deadly fighter Ben was in truth. She wondered if he even knew the extent of his own power.

Her thoughts dissolved on a wave of pure pleasure. His weight on her, his movement, the rise of his chest with his rapid breath, ripped away the last of her constraint. Rhianne heard the screams coming from her mouth, Ben's laughter as he caught them on his lips.

"That's my love." Ben's rumbling voice found dark spaces inside her and yanked them open. "Almost there."

Rhianne reached up with one hand as though trying to grasp the stars. Crazed sensation flooded her, the amazing peak she'd reached this morning when he'd played with her becoming nothing. This peak was all, bursting from her depths, an incredible wildness she'd never before experienced.

She was laughing, screaming, groaning, crying Ben's name, crushing him to her as though seeking absolute oneness with him. *Frenzy.*

Ben groaned, fist pounding the ground. His hips moved harder and faster, hot seed spilling into her. "Coming fast. *Fuck.*"

Rhianne held him as joy crashed through her. Their mouths met in frantic kisses, Ben's hips pumping, Rhianne rocking up to him.

The deluge of passion began to recede, little by little, becoming ripples of contentment. Ben kissed Rhianne's hair, her face, his touch tender, eyes warm.

"Damn, that was good," Ben whispered, and then Rhianne

was tumbling into a dark abyss of sleep that snapped over her and ended all sound.

———

BEN SWAM TO WAKEFULNESS FROM THE DEPTHS OF profound blackness. So much for cuddling Rhianne afterward and whispering sweet nothings into her ear. He hoped he hadn't drooled on her.

Rhianne slept beneath him, her face slack in complete relaxation. Soft September air kissed her face, rustling the leaves of the live oaks, wind chimes on the veranda tinkling.

The wind chimes had awakened him, Ben realized. Their note increased as he rolled from Rhianne with reluctance, though the wind remained steady.

A warning, Ben understood as he came fully awake.

Without moving, he scanned the house and what he could see of the grounds. Had Rhianne's father come for her, or sent other beasts to retrieve her?

A voice floated to him. "The architectural style is typical of the late eighteenth century, when plantation owners strove to emulate the English villas of the Georgian era, but with a unique design to reflect the climate as well as the personality of its owner."

Ben was on his feet, shaking Rhianne. He pressed his fingers to her mouth as she woke with a start.

He quickly helped her up and gathered their underwear. "Tour guide," he whispered.

"Tour?" Rhianne grabbed the panties from him, sliding them on. "You said there were no tours today."

"They must have changed the time. Or maybe I just don't know what day it is." Ben pulled on his underwear in frantic jerks. "Hide behind those bushes. I'll try to get the rest of our clothes."

Rhianne pulled on the camisole, concealing her gorgeous breasts. Ben tiptoed to the veranda steps where shirts, jeans, and shoes lay strewn. He heard Rhianne's giggle and realized she was beside him.

"No," Ben whispered fiercely. *"Hide."*

"Faster together," she returned.

No time to argue. Ben's hand landed on the pile of jeans as the veranda door opened above them, and the chipper tones of the tour guide floated out.

"Many of the roses were planted when the house was built and survive to this day."

Ben yanked the jeans from the steps and dragged Rhianne down into the dirt, out of sight.

The tour guide, dressed in an antebellum gown with hoop skirts that swayed enough to reveal her sneakers beneath, strode onto the veranda. "From here you can see the path to the slave quarters and the kitchen, which was built far from the house so the smoke and smells wouldn't bother the family within. We'll visit those after we see the rest of the interior."

She stood aside while her flock, mostly older women clutching phones they used as cameras, oohed over the view and the many roses that covered the railings. Wind chimes rang like laughter.

The tour guide, after pausing fifteen seconds to let her brood snap photos, zipped back into the house, skirts bouncing off the doorframe. Her followers trotted after her.

A small, white-haired woman, handbag over her arm, paused to take one more photo.

Rhianne, crouched with her nose almost into the crawl space beneath the house, stifled a cough at the musty air. The woman above paused and peered over the railing.

Whether she saw the two of them huddled there or not, she said nothing, and retreated indoors, her feet pattering as she hurried to catch up with the others.

Rhianne let out a breath. "Goddess."

Ben stifled his laughter as he slid on his pants. "Get dressed, and I'll sneak us inside."

"How?" Rhianne shoved her feet into her jeans then reached up to the veranda and whipped down her T-shirt, pulling it on over the camisole.

"I have a secret way in. We can take ourselves upstairs. Or ..." His mischievous side emerged. "We can hide there and make them think the house is haunted."

Rhianne settled the straps of her shoes. "This is a sentient house. Won't they already think it's haunted?"

"The house behaves itself and doesn't scare off the tourists." Ben found and dragged on his T-shirt. "Jasmine needs the income, and she's made the house promise to leave visitors alone. But the punters like to be a *little* bit frightened."

"Punters?"

"Paying tourists. Ready?"

He grasped Rhianne's hand and led her in a low crouch around the back to a half-door set into the foundation. The entrance was hidden by vines, but Ben had loosened them to create a swinging curtain that disguised it.

Ben pulled aside the vines, unlocked the door with the keys he always kept in his pocket, and opened it, going first to make sure the way was clear.

The space under the house was too shallow to be a cellar, more a crawl space than anything else. The ley line was strong here, Ben's skin tingling with it.

He led Rhianne on hands and knees to the place he knew lay under the large drawing room. With a smooth stick he'd left here for the purpose, he tapped the underside of the floor.

Ben always tapped in a pattern so those above wouldn't think they heard only random noises by a settling, old house. Ben paused, then repeated the thumps. Rhianne watched him, hands over her mouth, eyes glimmering in the darkness.

Ben next scratched the stick over the boards. The creaking sounded like the rusty hinges of an invisible door opening to nowhere.

Voices came to them through the floorboards. "What was that?"

"What was what?"

"Did you hear? A tapping? Like someone, or some*thing*, trying to get out."

"The house is indeed haunted." The tour guide eagerly took up the cue. She began the completely fabricated story of a girl child of the house trapped beneath the floor. She'd died there, the tour guide said, and now walked the house, searching for her way out.

The event had never happened. Ben had researched the entire history of the house and hadn't found evidence of anyone dying under the floorboards, and besides, the house wouldn't have let that happen. But a tragic story booked tours.

Ben laid aside the stick—overdoing it would only bring people down here to search—and ushered Rhianne onward.

In one corner was a trap door, which Ben had reinforced, that led to a hidden room behind the staircase. He opened the door and reached for the short ladder he'd positioned in the room above.

Ben hadn't known about this room until a Shifter guest— more a fugitive really—had revealed it. He found it handy now for hiding from the tour groups or as a space to be alone. He kept records of the house there and other things he didn't want found.

He climbed the ladder then assisted Rhianne up into the hideaway.

The room was lit by a tiny window, and Ben had made it cozy, adding a bookcase to the antique desk and chair that had already been there. He'd filled the desk drawer with snacks for the days he had to stash himself in here, like this one.

Rhianne studied the bag of potato chips Ben opened for her, then reached in for one. She scrutinized the chip then tentatively put it into her mouth and crunched. "Not bad," she admitted.

"Careful of those. Addicting."

"Mmm." Rhianne took the bag from him and munched a handful. "I understand why. Like shrimp."

Ben grinned as she dug in for more. "I could get you shrimp-flavored chips."

Rhianne wrinkled her nose. "I'm not certain that would be as tasty. But more shrimp would be nice."

"We'll go to New Orleans again once we figure out what's going on and how to keep your father from finding you." Ben lounged against the edge of the desk and opened a bag of chocolate-covered pretzels. "Why is the guy so evil?"

Rhianne crunched chips thoughtfully. If her father's perfidy hurt her, she made no sign—or perhaps she was so used to his cruelty that she'd ceased being sentimental about him.

"Tuil Erdannan can do anything they wish, as you know. We don't like the *hoch alfar*, and battle them, but that doesn't make us *good*. Tuil Erdannan don't notice what goes on in the world beyond their interests. Everything else is distant." Rhianne took a final chip and gave the empty bag a disappointed glance. "Most Tuil Erdannan keep to themselves, like my mother, who focuses on her garden, her circle of friends, her own life. Even I don't always figure into her world."

"I understand that," Ben said in sympathy. "I don't know Lady Aisling as well as you do, but it's like she's remote and sharp at the same time."

"Exactly. She knows precisely what goes on around her, but she chooses whether to put her attention on it or not. Ivor is somewhat the same. The difference is that he enjoys mastering others. He wants power for its own sake." Rhianne shook her head. "Don't worry. I got over him a long time ago. When I was little, I thought that if my father came to know me, he'd like me and take me under his wing, but I learned I was wrong. Another thing about Tuil Erdannan is we don't lose ourselves to love. If love is there, fine. If it's not, we're not going to pine away and long for it. I came to terms with what my father was long ago."

Had she? Ben read resoluteness in her, but did he see behind her lifted chin the child devastated because her father had rejected her?

"Goblins are totally different." Ben fished in the drawer for another bag of potato chips, pulled it open with a satisfying crinkle, and handed it to Rhianne. "We love absolutely. Gut-wrenching, soul-churning, pining-away passion. We love with everything we've got."

Rhianne took the bag, her rich brown eyes on Ben. "That must be hard for you."

"It's absolute hell. On the other hand, it's sublime. Drowning in love is happiness you can't imagine. It can also bring with it a world of hurt—but only if you make that love needy. When you turn it around, and love hard without being dependent on it in return, it's the most magnificent thing in the world."

Ben stopped, out of breath, wondering why he was yammering on about love while lost in her eyes.

Rhianne touched his lips. Her fingers were salty from the chips, and Ben licked her fingertip.

"I've never met anyone like you," she said softly.

Ben swallowed, her touch, her words, going straight to his heart. "I'm the last of my kind. Unique."

"That is not what I meant."

Ben wanted to answer with a joke, but he could think of nothing. As she gazed at him, Ben moved her fingers from his mouth and kissed her.

He tasted the saltiness of the chips on top of the fieriness all her own as she returned the kiss, the chip bag crumpling between them.

If Ben ever allowed himself to lose his heart to a woman—which he could not afford to do—she would be the one.

Rhianne ran her fingers through his hair and down his neck, pulling him closer. She enjoyed kissing, and Ben obliged. His lips, still tender from their wild lovemaking, gentled the kiss, caressing her in softness.

A dry cough made them jump. Rhianne's teeth banged against Ben's before they broke apart and swung around. Ben's hand went to the nunchaku he kept in the desk's drawer under all the snacks.

The white-haired woman who'd paused on the veranda gazed at them from clear blue eyes behind a thick set of glasses. Her face bore few lines but the weight of her life's experience was palpable.

"Ghosts, my eye," she said in a firm voice. She pointed at Rhianne. "*You* are Fae. Say your prayers."

She lunged at Rhianne in a swift and sudden attack.

CHAPTER FIFTEEN

Ben was in front of Rhianne like a lightning strike, the wind of his passing brushing Rhianne's face.

He closed his hands on the woman. Instead of crying out like a feeble, elderly lady, she snarled. Her body thickened, the guise of the genteel tourist dissolving into a massive creature with a wizened face and giant hands.

Ben froze in shock. The woman-thing wrenched herself from his grip and struck Ben, who slammed backward into the desk. His face was wan, eyes wide.

The creature rushed at him again. Rhianne shoved her hand into the drawer and yanked out the strange weapon she'd seen there—double sticks attached at the top. The sticks flailed, and Rhianne immediately whacked herself on the arm, but she advanced, everything in her wanting to bash at the woman and defend Ben.

Ben raised both hands. He growled something in an unfamiliar language, and the woman-creature halted abruptly. The grotesque form melted back into the white-haired woman, her clothes still neat, her handbag intact. She pushed up her glasses and peered at Ben with narrowed eyes.

"How do you speak the language of my people?" she asked in English. "It is a lost tongue. Gone, forgotten."

"Not by me." Ben carefully took the weapon from Rhianne and held a rod in one hand, tucking the second rod under his arm. "I've been speaking it my whole life. Who the hell are you?"

"I am called Millie." Her thin finger moved to Rhianne. "*She* is Fae. The hated enemy of my people."

"She is Tuil Erdannan," Ben said calmly.

Millie lowered her glasses and peered at Rhianne over them. Her eyes widened.

"Oh, my stars. Look at that. A Tuil Erdannan." She resumed her glasses and her scrutiny. "Are you certain? She doesn't seem quite right."

"I understand English, and yes I am," Rhianne broke in. "A Tuil Erdannan. Are you a goblin? Like Ben?"

"Ben." Millie rolled the word around her tongue, then her gaze filled with rage. "Wait a minute. Do you mean you're Gilbenarteoighiamh?"

"Yes ..." Ben said cautiously.

Millie screamed and went for him, hands curved into claws. Rhianne rushed between them and caught her, startled by the woman's strength. Rhianne began to summon the energy for a word of power, though she'd rather not use it in this closed space.

"Who is ... whoever you said?" Rhianne demanded.

Millie abruptly ceased struggling and tried to push her hair from her eyes with a shaky hand. "Only the one who destroyed us. Who made the Fae kill us all."

Ben's face was gray. "I was framed."

"What do you mean, Ben made the Fae kill you all?" Rhianne asked.

Millie sent Ben a furious stare through her thick glasses. "If you hadn't been making the *karmsyern* for the *dokk alfar*, they never would have come after us."

Ben tightened his grip on the weapon he held. "You know the goblins were making trouble for the Fae a long time before that. There was an uprising, remember? And so many battles, so many dead. When I said I would help the *dokk alfar,* the *hoch alfar* used it as an excuse to crush us. How could I anticipate they would massacre us and throw us out? I've spent a thousand years regretting my choice." A muscle moved in his jaw. "But at the same time, I was only one goblin. I didn't act alone."

Rhianne's heart beat rapidly as she listened. It hurt to imagine Ben watching while his people were slaughtered, knowing that he couldn't stop it, that he might have caused it. And then finding himself in a world he didn't understand.

Millie sagged in Rhianne's grasp. "I know. But we had to have someone to blame. It was easier—it helped me survive."

Ben wiped his eyes. "How *did* you survive? For centuries I searched for others and found no one. What happened to you?"

"I expect the same thing that happened to you." Millie tried to resume her crisp tones as Rhianne cautiously released her. "I made sure to lie low. I look like this ..." She waved to her neat blouse, leggings that ended below her knees, and sensible walking shoes. "So that humans don't pay attention to me. They think I'm cute. Funny. Harmless."

Ben nodded slowly. He'd said almost those exact words to Rhianne when she'd asked him why he'd taken the guise he wore.

"I worked as a nurse or governess for various families through the years," Millie went on. "I knew how to take care of people—it's what I did in Faerie. I like looking after children and after those who can't fend for themselves. In doing so, I found that humans weren't so different from us after all. Of course, I couldn't let them see me in true form. So, I stayed in the shadows and moved around, and now here I am. Millie Gainer. I like to shop and knit and bake cookies for children."

Ben remained silent as she spoke. It was difficult to see what he was thinking behind his eyes, so dark, so shuttered to Rhianne even now.

She turned to Millie. "What are you doing here at the house?"

Millie shrugged. "It's part of my disguise. I take tours of old houses. Attend improving lectures." Her primly pursed lips softened. "The truth is, I heard this house was on a ley line. That there were odd things about it. Possibly haunted. I decided to see for myself. Call me curious."

Ben gazed at her sorrowfully. "I'm sorry to tell you this, but none of our people are left. I went back to Faerie some months ago, and have been back and forth since. As far as I know there's only me. And now you."

Millie listened with a bleak expression, though Rhianne could see that she wasn't quite convinced.

The chirpy tones of the tour guide came to them through the walls. "Seven, eight, nine, ten ... Oh dear, we're missing one. Has anyone seen Millie? Where's Millie?"

A gaggle of voices took up the cry. *Millie, where are you? Millie?*

Millie rolled her eyes. "That's my cue." She pointed at Ben. "You and me, we need to talk."

Ben nodded. "Agreed. Where can I find you?"

Millie's gaze held impatience. "Don't you have a cell phone?"

"Well, yeah," Ben said, abashed.

"Then text me your number. Hurry."

Ben, nonplussed, pulled out his phone. Millie was no longer in attack mode as she removed a smartphone from her bag and shoved it in front of his face. Ben poked at the keys on his phone, and hers dinged.

"Got it," Millie said. "And now you have my number."

Ben nodded, closing his flip phone.

"You know, you really should keep up with technology." Millie resumed her superior tone. "It's easier to fit in that way. Truth to tell, I pretend to be a teensy bit slow, because people my age—the age I appear to be—are supposed to be confused by all this newfangled stuff, which is very silly. Most humans this age are quite intelligent. They've lived a long time and have gained much experience. If they don't like the phones, it's just because they don't like them. Anyway, I'll text you with a meeting spot."

With that, Millie turned on her heel and walked out of the secret room. The panel closed behind her, shutting in Rhianne and Ben. The energy seemed to depart the room with her, leaving Rhianne and Ben in stunned silence.

Rhianne blew out a breath. "She is very interesting."

"Huh. An understatement."

They exchanged a glance. "Can we trust her?" Rhianne asked.

"Who knows?" Ben's face softened. "But it's been so long since I've seen any of my own people. Can you imagine? I found one." He sank into the chair behind the desk, as though his legs could no longer support him. "I actually found one."

─────

Once the tourists had gone, Ben and Rhianne departed the secret room for the main house. The sliding panel opened into a tiny corridor which in turn led to the central hall.

Ben had a hell of a lot to think about. A goblin, here in this world, alive all this time.

Where had she been for ten centuries, and why the hell hadn't she tried to find him? Or at least tried harder, even if she had wanted to kill him?

Rhianne was watching him, gauging his reaction. "Be careful, Ben," she said in a gentle voice.

Ben knew she was right. What were the odds of Millie turning up out of the blue? The only goblin he'd seen in the past thousand years?

She must be up to something—that was the only explanation. Ben would simply have to find out what.

Meanwhile, his ongoing task was to keep Rhianne safe.

"We never did finish your Shifter training." Ben glanced toward the veranda.

The house was very quiet. It creaked a little, as though settling itself after having so many feet tramping through it.

Rhianne's gaze held heat. "I know. Because something else happened to interrupt the session."

Her smile stoked the fires inside him. Ben recalled the graceful way they'd practiced push hands, the dance that they'd created with it, and how it had led into an even greater dance.

"True. But you know, we should keep training."

Rhianne's eyes lit with amusement. "What am I going to do with you?"

Ben pretended to think about this. "I have a few ideas."

Rhianne laughed. As Ben began to pull her to him, his phone buzzed. Stifling impatience, he flipped it open.

"Damn. Millie's texting me already."

Rhianne gathered close. The text message blurred as Ben's blood seared with her nearness.

Being inside Rhianne had been incredible. Ben wanted to go there again and never come out. Mating frenzy, he figured. It was catching, and Ben was happy to succumb.

"She wants to meet," Ben announced. "Says she has some important information for me."

"Oh." Rhianne's breath wafted on his cheek.

"At City Park. Interesting choice—it's very public. I can go see what she means while you sit tight."

Rhianne's brows drew down. "If *sit tight* means I stay here and you go alone, I say no. The first thing she tried to do was kill you."

Ben closed his phone and slid it into his pocket then turned to press a kiss to her cheek. "No, sweetheart. She first tried to attack *you*. She didn't realize who I was."

"Uh huh." Rhiannon didn't soften. "As soon as she *did* realize who you were, she tried to kill you. And you want to go meet her by yourself? Why not take along someone who has a word of power at her disposal, who might perhaps be able to turn into an eagle and assist you? Or, let me go instead of you. I can find out what she really wants before I let her near you again."

Her protectiveness warmed spaces inside Ben that had been cold a long time. He'd never let her go alone, but it was sweet that she offered.

"I want you here, safe, where the house can protect you."

Rhianne assumed a stubborn expression. "Tiger told me that whenever I was with *you*, I'd be safe. No matter where you happened to be. Also that I was supposed to look after you."

"Tiger says a lot of indecipherable things."

Her eyes hardened. "His words seemed very clear to me."

Ben scowled as he pondered his choices. He really did want to know what Millie had to say. Even though he didn't trust her an inch, he *wanted* to trust her. And that was even worse, because then he couldn't trust himself.

He also did not want to leave Rhianne behind. What if she went outside the house's boundaries, unaware of exactly where those were? Or what if Ivor succeeded in breeching the house? What kind of damage could he do to Rhianne before the house stopped him, if it could? Ivor had already been strong enough to reach through the ley lines and attack them.

"Tell you what," he said. "We'll both go. We'll stand like twenty feet from Millie and hear her out. But we need to be careful, because goblins can be tricky." He huffed a laugh. "Trust me. I know this. After that, we can go see Lily again and find out if she has any deets about the danger she sees and what we can do about it."

They argued further, but it felt good to argue with Rhianne. Like they were intimate enough to *have* arguments.

In the end, they left the house together and Ben guided Rhianne out the back door to the shed where he'd left his motorcycle.

Ben liked the feeling of Rhianne wrapped around him as they rode into the city. He was soon weaving through the familiar streets of New Orleans to City Park, on the north side of town near Lake Pontchartrain for the meeting.

Millie was already there. She waited for them under a tall, ancient live oak—an innocuous woman in her blouse and pedal pushers, her glasses firmly perched on her nose, her handbag clutched in two hands.

Other inhabitants of the park looked askance at Ben with his tattoos and scruffy jeans hurrying toward this woman. When they saw that Millie waited calmly, without fear, the walkers strolled on.

Ben halted within shouting distance from her, Rhianne at his side. "Okay, we're here," he called to Millie. "What do you want to talk about?"

"I know who you are."

"Yeah, I know. We discussed this. I'm the one you blame for destroying our people. You tried to attack me. Not something I would forget."

"Not only that," Millie said. "I did some research after I left you and I know who you *will* be." She pointed at Rhianne. "*You* are more confusing."

Ben started toward Millie. He couldn't stop himself, despite his own admonitions about caution. "You need to explain. Everything."

Millie didn't move. Ben heard Rhianne behind him, her growl of annoyance that he wasn't being more careful.

Ben halted in mid-stride, every danger signal in him flaring to life. Under his boot, the earth trembled.

"What the hell are you doing?" Ben demanded

At the same moment, a fissure abruptly split between him and Millie, one about five feet wide and who the hell knew how deep, like a mouth that wanted to swallow Ben whole.

Ben flailed as his feet slipped and slithered on the edge. "Shit, shit, shit."

Rhianne's strong hands closed around him. "Stop it," she shouted at Millie.

Millie, clutching her bag tighter, backed away from the abyss. "This isn't my doing."

The crevice in the earth widened as though annoyed it hadn't seized Ben in its first gulp.

The ground broke away under his feet. Rhianne's grip on Ben slipped, and she screamed as gravity wrenched Ben from her, and he slid into the yawning gap.

———

RHIANNE'S SCREAMS MADE HER THROAT RAW. BEN'S HANDS caught the edge of the hole, fingers clawing at the grass. He let his hands and arms change to those of the goblin, but even then he couldn't pull himself out.

Rhianne caught his arms, holding on as hard as she could. A quick glance up showed Rhianne that Millie had turned and was running away.

"Wait," Rhianne yelled. "Help me."

Millie never turned back. She continued to run far faster than her appearance would suggest she could, faded under the trees, and was gone.

The sudden abyss was mystical, Rhianne knew, but it was

also very real. A stink of evil wafted from the chasm as though many dead things were trying to escape from the earth.

Ben's large fingers made furrows in the grass. Rhianne clung tighter, but when she started sliding toward the hole herself, Ben pried her hands away.

"No," he said in a hoarse voice. "Run."

"I won't leave you," Rhianne yelled.

"If you don't we'll both go down. Get out of here." Mud and roots poured into the hole, battering at him, trying to take him with them.

Passersby in the park gathered, some frozen in fascinated horror, others yelling for people to keep away or find some rope. Someone shouted at Rhianne to get back.

She sprang to her feet, not to obey, but because her skin was burning. Her heart pounded scalding blood through her body, and her limbs ached and throbbed.

She couldn't control what was happening to her, and this time, she didn't want to.

Rhianne yanked off her T-shirt and then her jeans and underwear, her shoes toppling somewhere in the grass. She felt the wild thing inside her call, and realized the screeching cry came from her own throat.

There were plenty of people staring at her, but Rhianne couldn't worry about them or halt the change. Her arms spread of their own accord as feathers burst across them, her fingers segueing into primary feathers. Her vision changed, becoming blurred around the edges but sharply focused in the center.

A rush of wind buoyed her, and with it came the lift of freedom. She wanted to catch the updraft and glide away, soaring higher and higher, far from the troubles of her life.

Her terror for Ben kept her grounded. Onlookers were trying to reach him, but the crumbling earth wouldn't let them near.

Rhianne leapt, and her wings caught her. She wafted

upward, high into the humid air. Clouds seemed to part for the wind, and she danced on it.

She became aware of nothing but herself and the sky, Ben barely visible now in the gap of the earth.

Rhianne didn't know how to fly, but the eagle did, as Ben had said it would. Her wings took over, and she glided on a thermal, pivoting back to the very spot in which Ben struggled. Then she dove.

Ben was shouting but she couldn't understand the words. The hole was closing on him, Ben being dragged slowly down, down into the devouring ground.

Rhianne righted herself, wings unfurling to their maximum to slow her descent. She spread her talons just as the earth began to pile around Ben's head, filling his open mouth.

She closed her claws on Ben's shoulders and yanked him from the belly of the earth.

Ben coughed then yelled as Rhianne lifted him into the air. She tried to keep her grip gentle, aware that her talons could dig right through him.

Ben's curses in several languages assured her he was alive. Rhianne's trajectory took her from the park and across the lake, blue and vast.

Beneath her came Ben's voice. "Fuck, fuck, fuck. If you drop me now, I can't swim. *Fuck!*"

Rhianne circled and headed landward, feeling a call to the place from which she'd departed. They flew over the dark blue waters that reflected the clouds and the endless sky and toward the green of the park beyond.

The park and its trees flashed beneath them. The fissure in the earth had filled in as though, deprived of its meal, it had decided to close its mouth and sulk.

Rhianne spied her clothes scattered across the grass, and the tree under which Millie had stood, though Millie was long gone.

She also saw plenty of people watching, gaping as she brought Ben to the ground. She released him when his feet touched down, then she furled her wings and landed beside him with a gentle bump.

The watchers held up phones like Millie's, peering at them as though they held the wisdom of the universe.

Ben, shaking, brushed himself off. His shirt was shredded, and blood streaked his skin, but by their scent, Rhianne could tell the wounds weren't deep.

Ben took in the gawkers and all the phones pointed toward him and Rhianne.

"Shit," he muttered. "Now we're going to have Shifter Bureau on us."

CHAPTER SIXTEEN

B en was amazed how quickly Shifter Bureau responded. Not two minutes after Rhianne had finished rescuing him from the hungry earth, sirens sounded.

It wasn't unusual to hear sirens in this city, but police vehicles hurtling straight into the park as far as the paved roads let them was rarer. When they could approach no closer, at least two dozen patrolmen slammed out of cars and SUVs and headed for Ben and Rhianne.

Any other time Ben would have been amused at the number of New Orleans residents who suddenly turned and melted into the shadows at the sight of the cops. Under the circumstances, Ben wanted to join them, but he doubted he'd evade the police while rushing off with a giant eagle.

Rhianne fluffed out her feathers, indifferent to the mob flowing toward them. She rubbed her beak against one wing as though polishing off the dirt she'd acquired as she'd rescued Ben.

"Better change back," Ben said to her.

Rhianne cocked her head, beautiful golden red feathers

ruffling in the breeze, and fixed a very intelligent, brown-black eye on him.

"Seriously," Ben said. "They'll have tranqs."

Rhianne only gazed at him, then she studied the sky as though contemplating launching herself into it and getting the hell out of here. Ben wouldn't blame her if she did.

The police surrounded them, guns drawn.

Ben, no stranger to this routine, lifted his hands. "Take it easy. Don't scare her." He deliberately stepped in front of Rhianne.

He wasn't sure what good his gallant gesture would do, because any bullet would go right through him and into her.

The police didn't move. Ben and Rhianne didn't move. Ben wondered how long they could keep this up. A few minutes? Half an hour? Maybe a day before somebody decided they were bored and started to shoot?

One of the men, of course, brought up a tranq gun.

"There's no need for that," Ben said. "She's perfectly tame."

Rhianne bent her head to Ben, her lethal beak open. Ben sensed Rhianne somewhere behind her dark eyes, the beautiful woman he was falling in love with. Mostly what he saw was the wildness of a creature containing itself so it wouldn't hurt him.

"Change back," he whispered.

Rhianne scrutinized him a moment as though trying to figure out where she knew him from.

Ben thought he wasn't getting through, but then the air seemed to glisten. The eagle's feathers shrank, its arms came down, and the bird vanished, leaving Rhianne standing in its place.

Her glorious hair flowed around her, covering her body from the lurid stares of the watchers and the police.

A black van had joined the police vehicles. Four men in suits emerged from it, two carrying tranq rifles.

"Get ready," Ben said. "Here they come."

"Who comes?" Rhianne's voice was a touch hoarse as though she had trouble transitioning from the eagle's cries to human speech.

"Shifter Bureau. They're a big network that regulates Shifters in this country and all over the world."

"Regulates?" Rhianne repeated.

"You know, oppresses them, keeps them under lock and key so they don't hurt anybody."

"I wasn't going to hurt anybody," Rhianne said, puzzled.

"Yeah, well, they usually don't believe that. Plus, you're not wearing a Collar. Crap. I should have asked Dimitri to send me a fake one on the QT."

"But I'm not Shifter," Rhianne pointed out.

"I know that. You know that. But I don't think Shifter Bureau is gonna buy it. You change into an animal—ergo, you're a Shifter."

Rhianne watched the cautiously approaching men in bewilderment. "What do they want?"

Ben shrugged. "To lock you away, interrogate you, try to figure you out. At least these days, they don't immediately dissect you and see what you're made of."

Rhianne gaped at him. "They do that?"

"Used to," Ben answered hurriedly. "Like I said. These are civilized times. I think you'd better put your clothes on, though, while you have the chance. Once they reach us they might just try to chain you up and take you away without giving you the dignity of getting dressed."

Rhianne listened in disbelief. "I thought *hoch alfar* were bad."

"Yeah, Shifter Bureau could give the *hoch alfar* lessons about being sons of bitches."

Rhianne stooped to gather up her clothes and quickly slipped them on.

The Shifter Bureau agents positioned themselves one on each compass point around Rhianne and Ben, tranq rifles at the ready.

"Name?" one of them said.

The agent looked at Ben, not Rhianne. He obviously assumed Ben was human, which to him meant superior to a Shifter, the only one of the pair worth addressing.

"Ben Gardner." That was the name Ben was using, anyway. "Why don't you call Danielson, your Shifter liaison?"

"He's the Texas liaison," the man, who apparently was the Bureau officer in charge, said. "This is Louisiana."

"Yeah, but he can vouch. This is Rhianne. Just ask him."

Ben was taking a gamble here. Walker Danielson possibly knew nothing at all about Rhianne's shifting ability. But Jaycee, who was loyalty itself to Kendrick, might have examined her conscience and decided to confide what happened with Rhianne to him. Kendrick wasn't in Dylan's pocket, but he could have mentioned it to trusted people, like Walker, who was mated with a Shifter and a military liaison to Shifter Bureau.

Even if Walker didn't yet know about Rhianne, he'd probably received an alert about an unknown eagle Shifter in New Orleans, and he'd know, via Dylan, that Ben was hosting Rhianne at the haunted house. Dylan worked closely with Walker and wired him in on most of his schemes.

Walker was also smart and could think on his feet. He trusted Ben … more or less. Ben had to risk it.

"Just call him," he told the Bureau man.

Rhianne folded her arms and gave the four closing in on them an imperious stare worthy of her mother. "What do you want?"

"We need you to come with us, ma'am," the leader said.

"Come with you where? And why? Who are you?"

The lofty commands of a Tuil Erdannan made the four

men hesitate, but only for a moment. They were used to dealing with arrogant Shifters.

"We're just going to talk to you, ma'am," the leader said. He likely thought he sounded reasonable. "I'm asking you to please come with us without argument. We'd hate to have to tranq you, but we will. My men are very good shots."

"I see." Rhianne continued to regard them with a haughty stare. "Very well. I assume my advocate may accompany me."

The leader switched his gaze to Ben, surprised at the reference. Ben looked exactly like what he was—an ex-con who'd just been rolling around in the dirt.

"Sure," the leader said. His sneer told them what kind of "advocate" he considered Ben to be.

Idiot. These guys had no idea who they were messing with.

The Bureau men loaded Ben and Rhianne into a luxurious SUV with plush seats, cool air conditioning, and a rack for bottles of water. Not that the Bureau guys offered any water to their captives. *At least they didn't bring out the cages,* Ben thought.

"Are you Shifter?" one of the men in the back asked Ben.

Before Ben could answer, the leader turned around from the front passenger seat. "I know about him. Ben Gardner. He's a friend to Shifters, but he's not a Shifter himself. Which means, no, we can't trust him."

Ben contrived a hurt expression. "Gee, and here I've been trying to be good for so long."

"Yeah, well," the leader answered. "It's what happens when you hang out with Shifters."

"What is wrong with Shifters?" Rhianne asked. "They seem to be quite civilized."

The men stared at her as though she'd gone completely mad.

"Civilized," the guy in the back said. "Shifters kill people with teeth and claws, and they hump anyone they can find. How is that civilized?"

Rhianne's gaze didn't soften. "You are very rude."

Ben couldn't help chuckling. They really, truly, did not know.

———

THE SUV DRIVER TURNED INTO A COMPOUND NOT FAR from the park. A huge iron fence surrounded the place and an electronic gate slid open as the SUV approached. A guard in a gate house waved them through, then the gate rolled closed again. The quiet click as the electronic lock reengaged was ominous.

Ben did *not* want to be separated from Rhianne, but Bureau men marched them to different cells. Rhianne, surrounded by guards, strode on without looking back, her head high.

The interrogation room Ben was taken to wasn't bad as far as interrogation rooms went—a small space with a bullet-proof glass window, a few chairs, a table, and a bottle of water. He hoped Rhianne had the same or better accommodations. If they put her into a cage, he'd have to kill someone.

They'd taken Ben's cell phone, but they hadn't searched him, so Lady Aisling's crystal still reposed deep in his pocket. She couldn't do much to help from her side of Faerie, but she might be able to contact Jaycee who could alert Kendrick, who could put plans in motion to get them out of there.

Ben would resort to the crystal if he had to, though he'd rather not betray that he had means of communication. The not-so-discreet cameras around the room told him he was being watched.

He was thirsty but decided not to drink the water. It was in a sealed bottle, but Ben wouldn't put it past Shifter Bureau to inject a drug into it to make him pliant and communicative.

They kept Ben in the room long enough for him to be worried, then bored, then resigned. He'd probably be stuck here overnight, and hoped the house would understand.

Ben was toying with ideas of how to lure the Shifter Bureau goons out to the house and let his unpredictable abode deal with them, when the door opened, and the leader of the pack entered, half a dozen guards covering him from the hall.

"Well, you got your wish," he said. "Danielson's here."

"Oh goody," Ben said. "Did you put out the tea and fancy cakes for him? He likes that."

"Shut up," the man growled. "Come on."

"You mean he's not coming into my parlor?"

"Just get out here."

As soon as Ben stepped outside the room, the six guards surrounded him. They all had guns of some sort. Ben wasn't an expert on guns, but basically these were black, shiny, had triggers, and probably spit bullets pretty fast.

The guards ushered Ben down the hall, which was lit with overhead fluorescent lights. One of the lights flickered and couldn't quite stay on. Places like this always had that one bad fluorescent bulb that sputtered and hummed. The Bureau dudes must deliberately change a good bulb for a bad to maintain the effect.

They took Ben into a larger room at the end of the hall that looked the same as the one he'd been in except there was space for more guys.

Walker Danielson, a tall human man with very pale hair and light blue eyes, stood behind a table. Danielson's skin was darkened by the sun and lined with white creases from his military tours in far-off lands. His hard face had taken on a gentleness and a sort of wonder ever since he'd moved in with a large bear Shifter who was the love of his life.

Next to him, to Ben's immense relief, stood the giant form of Tiger.

———

RHIANNE'S CELL WAS AN IMPROVEMENT OVER THE ONE Walther had dropped her into—it had clean walls, a window, a table and chair, and no chains or old bones—but regardless, her body itched with her confinement. She sensed the impatience of the eagle inside her—its need to roam without fetters.

Her magic had recharged overnight, and training with Ben, not to mention the explosive sex afterward, had definitely helped restore her. She could blast out the window with one word of power, spring into the corridor, and hunt for Ben. If they'd dared put hands on her mate ...

The only thing that kept her in place was fear of what would happen to Ben if she caused problems. Would they kill him for her disobedience? For all she knew, those pristine-clothed men might even now be torturing him in a dank cell.

Ben could turn into a goblin and break out if he wanted to —perhaps he was worried about what the Bureau men were doing to *her*.

Then again, maybe these humans had found a way to subdue him. They'd seemed to know Ben. What kind of magic did they have, or would they resort to their deadly projectiles? Ben wasn't indestructible. He'd mentioned being stabbed and nearly dying.

Rhianne stilled as the word that had formed unthinkingly in her head struck her.

Mate.

The thought pounded at her, and she gripped the table for support.

Shifters took mates. They bonded, as had Jaycee and Dimitri. Rhianne had seen the bond settled on Liam and Tiger when she'd spoken to them, though Dylan had been more diffi-cult to read.

Tuil Erdannan did not form the bond. They married, they loved, they bore children, but they did not refer to their spouses as mates. She'd told Ben that most creatures of Faerie could experience the mate bond, which meant everyone but Tuil Erdannan.

Her people were too self-centered to be joined to another wholly, in true surrender. Rhianne had always thought the mate bond a beautiful idea, but Tuil Erdannan refused to contemplate it.

As Rhianne stood in the tiny human cell that smelled of old coffee, sweat, and fear, the certainty grew inside her that Ben was her mate. The one she would sacrifice all for, in order to find the shining, magical threads that bound them together.

Tuil Erdannan did not form the mate bond. She wasn't wrong about that.

But Shifters did.

Rhianne's heart thudded until it blotted out all other sound. She grew lightheaded, her eyes unfocused, her breath short. She gasped, trying to breathe, and coughed.

The door banged open. A Shifter Bureau man she hadn't seen before stood outside, a tranq rifle aimed at her. He wore baggy black pants tucked into boots and a black shirt, his dark eyes cold over the gun's barrel.

If he shot her, Rhianne doubted she'd feel it among the sensations pouring through her.

"Come with me," the man said.

Rhianne walked around the table, but she had no conscious idea of directing her legs and feet to move. She barely glanced at the man as she stalked out of the cell, he backing away so she'd not pass within striking distance.

Rhianne knew without understanding how that she could take him down before the gun could go off. She'd be that fast.

Once again, the only thing that stopped her was the worry about what they'd do to Ben if she threatened any of these people.

"This way." The man motioned with the rifle down the hall.

Rhianne walked slowly and obediently, outwardly calm. Inwardly, she was seething turmoil. She'd been a mess since she'd watched Ben fall into the abyss of mud and roots, the wild thing inside her knowing exactly what she must do to rescue him.

To rescue Ben. Her mate.

The inside of her mouth tasted like ash. The only way she could think these thoughts about Ben ... No, she didn't *think* them. Rhianne *knew* them with exact certainty.

The only explanation was that her entire life to this point had been a lie.

The guard guided her with an abrupt command around another bend in the corridor. This building was bizarre, with sharp angles and maze-like hallways, designed to keep prisoners confused.

Foolish if they wanted to confine Shifters. Shifters would know instinctively where they were at all times and the location of all the exits. As Rhianne did now.

Rhianne nearly collapsed in relief when she saw Ben through the window of the room at the end of the hall. Standing upright, alive, unhurt. His dark eyes held warning, but Rhianne didn't care about anything except seeing him again.

She barely noted the others as she and the guard entered the room, until a knocking at her brain registered them. One was a blond human man she hadn't seen before, possibly another Bureau agent.

The other was Tiger. He turned his golden eyes on her, and though he said not a word, Rhianne understood that he *knew*.

CHAPTER SEVENTEEN

R hianne couldn't speak, could barely breathe. Tiger kept his gaze on her then slowly moved it to Ben. He nodded imperceptibly.

The Shifter Bureau men were deep in conversation with the blond man, who answered in short sentences, Ben occasionally interjecting. Rhianne could barely hear them over the rushing in her ears, couldn't focus enough to understand.

Tiger flicked his gaze to her. *You are frightened.*

Rhianne jumped. Had he just put the words into her head —was he a telepath? Was she?

After a moment, Rhianne realized she hadn't heard Tiger's thoughts but had read his body language. Animals didn't have to communicate with words or even sounds. The twitch of a tail, the tilt of a head, or the snap of an ear could convey a message or an emotion. She'd read that as a child in the tomes written by learned Tuil Erdannan.

Shifters had honed this silent language to perfection.

Rhianne didn't know the technique for responding to him, so she brought to mind what she wanted to answer and hoped her posture would convey it.

Of course I'm frightened. I'm not Shifter! ... Am I?

We will speak later. Tiger turned away but the line of his back was somehow reassuring.

Ben scowled at the Bureau agent who'd brought them in, his words coming to her more clearly now. "How many times does he have to explain? She's registered. Legit. Here on a legal pass."

The blond man with the quiet eyes broke in. "I saw the paperwork myself."

Rhianne had no idea what paper they were talking about but she kept silent.

"Well, *I* haven't seen it," the lead agent snapped. "No request for transfer has come through my inbox, and I monitor these things daily."

"You handle all requests personally?" the blond man asked mildly. "At my agency, there are five clerks who do the paperwork, and I get a report."

"That's what I mean. I never saw that report."

"Sometimes the clerks get sloppy." The blond man nodded at the agent in confidence. "Check your database—I know it's there."

The agent regarded the blond man with suspicion, but the blond man returned a bland stare and offered nothing more. Ben had his arms folded across his chest, his fists tightly balled, barely containing himself.

Rhianne had seen Ben's might. He could break every human in this room in half without trying, and she could use her magic to crash them out to freedom.

Excitement built inside her at these thoughts. She and Ben could devastate the place, run away laughing, and collapse somewhere private and make crazy love. Rhianne wanted it with her whole being.

What had Ben called it? *Mating frenzy.* She closed her

eyes, enjoying the waves of heat and need pulsing through her body.

When she opened her eyes again, she saw Tiger watching her. She flushed, knowing she must be broadcasting her private thoughts to him.

Patience, little one. Better to placate than destroy. A corner of Tiger's lip twitched. *I had to learn this.*

Rhianne had no interest in placating the men who'd surrounded them, pointed weapons at them, and hustled her and Ben into the large black vehicle, separating them when they arrived. She had no interest in being patient with the agent who'd dared to touch her *mate.*

Peace.

Tiger's message was like a cool whisper in a lake of fire. Rhianne curled her fingers into her palms and willed herself to breathe.

How many times in her life had she had to leave a room—or an entire district—to find calm in solitude? She'd attributed her restlessness to her unfortunate birth into a prominent Tuil Erdannan family and having an evil bastard for a father. She'd grown impatient with her mother's many gatherings both important and frivolous, grown unhappy with the threat of her deadly father always in the background, and sought solitude. Her interest in astronomy, where she could sit long nights in peaceful darkness, had helped, but not entirely.

Had there been more to it than that? Perhaps the Shifter in her had wanted space to wander, without the scrutiny of her family?

How the hell had she become a Shifter?

The answer was obvious, and Rhianne shied away from it, hard.

"We're equipped to return her to the Austin Shiftertown," the blond man was saying when Rhianne focused again. "She'll be contained there."

"The eyewitnesses say she turned into some kind of bird." The lead agent glared at Ben then the blond man. "I've never heard of any bird Shifters in the Austin Shiftertown."

The blond man didn't blink. "It's a new program. There are very few of the raptor Shifters, and our agency is rounding them up to study them. So far we only have the one."

"I'll have to verify this," the lead agent snarled then trailed off into a mutter. "Always weird stuff going on in Austin."

"It's the city's motto," Ben grunted. "More or less."

The lead agent didn't like Ben talking. "I'll check the database," he said in a hard voice.

"By all means," the blond man answered. "The information will be there."

Rhianne could hear, if she strained, a tinny voice somewhere in the room, as though speaking from far away. She cocked her head, trying to listen, and saw as she did that the blond man had something tucked inside his ear. From this the voice came to her.

Walker, lad, what are you doing to me?

The voice sounded like Liam's but slightly different. Perhaps from the same family, Rhianne concluded.

Hush, Tiger warned her.

Rhianne acknowledged him. Someone was communicating secretly with the blond man, Walker, and she couldn't draw attention to that fact. Rhianne had caught the voice because Shifters had fantastic hearing.

Her day was becoming more and more disconcerting.

The leader barked orders to his underlings, who scurried from the room. Two of the agents stood on either side of Rhianne, too close for her liking.

It cheered her that she could very quickly knock them aside, no matter that they had weapons. She could break those. She wanted to laugh.

She felt Tiger's gaze on her again, and she folded her lips to avoid a smile.

Ben would not look at her. Rhianne wanted him to, needed him to. But he kept his head turned, his gaze studiously on Walker and the lead agent.

Rhianne understood why. Ben did not want to betray, by expression or any of his body language, that she and he were lovers. Mates.

A lackey trotted back into the room after a time with a square device with a screen similar to the cell phones, only larger. The lead agent stabbed the lit screen with a finger as his lackey held it up to him, his eyes moving as he read.

"I see." The lead agent sounded disappointed. "Fine. I'm authorizing her transportation to Austin." He zipped his finger over the screen and then tapped it so hard that the lackey flinched. The lead agent swept his gaze to Walker. "Be sure you keep her there."

Walker nodded once, as though he couldn't be bothered to answer.

"You brought your own transport?" the agent snapped at him.

"Of course."

"Then get her out of my sight. Him too." He sent a glare to Ben, whose mouth tightened.

None of the agents looked at Tiger, Rhianne noticed. They'd fix on Ben or Walker or Rhianne, but all avoided gazing directly at Tiger.

Ben had used the phrase *the elephant in the room* meaning evading discussion of something obvious and important. Rhianne reflected that the phrase should be *the Tiger in the room*. She suppressed a laugh with difficulty.

Walker flicked his pale blue eyes to Rhianne. "If you'll come with me."

Ben gave Rhianne a nod. *Trust him,* his body language told her. Rhianne started for Walker, pleased she could read Ben so well.

Tiger fell into step behind Rhianne, and several agents brought up the rear. Rhianne passed Ben, but instead of joining her, he stood still and watched her go. She looked back at him, trying not to be frantic, but she lost sight of him as too many people surrounded her.

The agents escorted her through the maze of pale corridors with their buzzing lights and out into the daylight. The sky had become overcast, and as Rhianne stepped from the stone building to the smoothly paved courtyard, rain pattered down.

Walker made for a black vehicle similar to the one that had brought her and Ben here, except this one was mud-splattered, as though it had been driven a long way. Tiger swept past Rhianne and opened the back door for her before Walker could.

"Wait." Rhianne swung around, searching for Ben, but he'd disappeared. "Where's Ben? Isn't he coming with us?"

"Probably not," Walker answered in a low voice. "Ben goes his own way."

Tiger crowded behind Rhianne, expecting her to climb into the vehicle. "No," she cried. "We can't go without Ben."

Walker stepped to her, pitching his voice so he wouldn't be overheard. "Best get in before the sergeant changes his mind and confines you until he verifies all the bullshit I just told him."

Shite, Walker, came the voice in Walker's ear. *Drive now. Argue later. I'm patching everything together as it is.*

Rhianne agreed with the wisdom of the unknown speaker, but panic surged over her.

"I can't. Not without Ben. Ben!"

She couldn't see him in the crowd. Rhianne darted

forward, needing to find him, a pull that wouldn't let her leave him behind.

There was a click and a whine, loud to her newly sensitive hearing. Tiger grabbed her with intense strength and half threw her into the vehicle, leaping in behind her.

Tiger's foot caught on the step, and he fell onto the seat beside her. Walker shoved Tiger's booted foot inside, slammed the door, and leapt into the front. He started the motor and the vehicle leapt forward. The gate rolled back for him, and he pulled quickly out of the complex.

Tears trickled down Rhianne's face. "What happened?" she asked Tiger, who was half-sprawled across the back seat.

"Tranq gun," Walker said from the front. "One of the agents fired."

Tiger pulled a dart out of his thigh. "Single dose," he grunted.

Rhianne studied him in astonishment. "Doesn't a tranquilizer knock a person out? Or am I translating wrong?"

"They do," Walker said. "But one shot won't take down Tiger. That tranq was meant for average everyday Shifters."

Which Tiger was not—Rhianne had realized that the moment she'd met him. He'd jumped between her and the dart, taking it for her.

She wiped her eyes. "Thank you, Tiger."

Tiger shrugged and tossed the tranq dart to the floor, crushing it with his boot.

"I can't leave Ben," Rhianne said. "We have to go back." When Walker didn't deviate from his course, Rhianne caught the seat back and pulled herself forward to him. "You don't understand. He's my *mate*."

The stoic Walker glanced at her in amazement then quickly turned his gaze back to the street. The voice in Walker's ear blurted, *What the fuck did she just say?*

"Who *is* that?" Rhianne asked.

Another startled glance from Walker, then he slowed the vehicle and made an abrupt turn onto a road that took them behind the compound. A spiked iron fence with coils of wire wound along its top flashed past.

Walker halted at a small gap in that fence, and a hand wrenched open the back door. Rhianne's panic changed to relief and gladness as Ben launched himself into the seat beside her and slammed the door.

"Hit it, Jeeves," he said to Walker and slid his arms around Rhianne. "Hey, baby, don't cry. You didn't think I'd abandon you to these two losers, did you?"

———

BEN COULDN'T LOOSEN HIS HOLD ON RHIANNE, NO MATTER how fast Walker drove them away from the compound.

"I didn't want those goons to think you were important to me," he explained as he soothed her. "I'm not Shifter, so they can't really hold me, but I'm a font of information, so they might have kept me if I'd let on that I cared about you. I bugged out and found a weak spot in the fence."

"A weak spot," Walker repeated. "In solid iron bars."

"It's weak *now*." Ben snuggled closer to Rhianne. With Tiger taking up most of the seat, he had to sit tight against her, not that he minded. "Where are we going?"

Walker glanced at him through the rearview mirror. "Where I said I was taking you. Austin Shiftertown."

"Into Dylan's lair."

"He's the best protection she can have while we figure this shit out."

Ben scowled. "Unless he keeps trying to recruit her to do his dirty work."

"He does that to all of us," Walker observed. "What makes you special?"

"He will not recruit her," Tiger said in his low rumble. "I have explained to him."

Ben glanced at him over Rhianne's head. "Are you sure, big guy?"

"Yes."

Ben relaxed a fraction. If Tiger ran interference with Dylan, Dylan wouldn't insist. Much.

"Rhianne mentioned you told her that if she stuck with me, she'd be safe," Ben said, fixing Tiger with a stern look. "Then the earth tried to swallow me, and Shifter Bureau nabbed us."

Tiger regarded him steadily. "And we were alerted, and now she is safe."

"Huh. Nice, convenient answer."

Tiger remained impassive. "Not convenient. True."

"If you say so." He returned his attention to Rhianne, kissing her warm hair. "You all right, sweetheart? I could sense you barely controlling yourself in there."

Rhianne stroked his chest, her touch drawing fire. "I didn't want them hurting you."

"No one was going to hurt me, love. I was being ... diplomatic. Letting them think they were superior. It's a tactic."

Rhianne continued to skim her hand over his chest, fingers catching his shirt's hem so she could stroke his bare skin beneath. "I couldn't let them hurt you, because ..." She swallowed and fell silent.

"She's Shifter," Tiger said beside her. "And she's chosen you as mate."

Ben blinked. "No, she's not. She's Tuil Erdannan. They have magic we don't understand."

Rhianne nestled into Ben's shoulder and licked his neck. The fire crawled down Ben's spine and found their way to his cock.

Tiger shook his head. "Shifter. I could not scent it when I first met her, because the Tuil Erdannan side of her blocked it very well. It is obvious now. Maybe because she's found her mate."

"I'll have to take your word for it." Ben didn't have the olfactory senses of a Shifter, but if Tiger scented the truth of Rhianne, Ben believed him. Tiger's nose never failed him. "But if you're Shifter, sweetheart, that means ... *Shit.*"

Rhianne raised her head. "It means my father is not my father. It means my mother, sometime in her life, had a relationship with a Shifter."

"Yeah." Ben sat stunned, and Walker and Tiger were quiet.

A voice that had been whispering through an earpiece to Walker came clearly through the silence. "*Shite.*"

"Tell Sean hi," Ben said to Walker, then he gathered Rhianne close and held her as comfortingly as he could.

Tiger's announcement that Rhianne had decided he was her mate spun through Ben's head, not really sinking in. He had a lot to process, but the miles between here and Austin were many. He settled in to think, his stunned brain whirling.

———

In spite of the five-hundred mile drive, Ben still had no clear answers by the time they reached the Austin Shifter-town in the early hours of the morning. Ben helped Rhianne out of the SUV in front of Liam Morrissey's bungalow to hear crickets and a cool breeze ruffling the leaves of the tall trees.

At four in the morning, Shiftertown should be dark and quiet, all the little Shifters curled up peacefully together, but no. Lights were on in most houses, and there was plenty of movement in the darkness between them. Many Shifters were nocturnal, and *all* were nosy as hell.

Dylan leaned on the railing of the porch next door to Liam's home, with his sort-of mate, Glory, a crazed Lupine, next to him. She was almost calmly dressed in skin-tight jeans and a leopard print T-shirt. Sean Morrissey's mate, Andrea, rested a hip on the railing next to Glory and held her young son in her arms. No sign of Sean.

The front porch of Liam's house was likewise crowded. *Yep, the gang's all here.* Liam, his nephew Connor, the rangy young woman who was Tiger's long-lost cub, Liam's mate, Kim, and Tiger's mate, Carly. And the cubs, who were the only ones not silent.

"Who's that?" Young Katriona, Liam's offspring, pointed at Rhianne from the safety of her mother's arms.

"A guest." Kim Fraser-Morrissey spoke firmly. She left the porch and made her way to where Tiger and Walker surrounded Ben and Rhianne. "Welcome, Rhianne. How about we take a load off inside with some wine, while the Shifters argue?"

"Nothing to argue about," Ben said. "Rhianne's Shifter. She didn't know. Blame her parents, not her. No need to interrogate her."

"Exactly." Kim was a smallish woman with curly dark hair and a skewering gaze. She was in courtroom mode, which meant she used her cute smile and steely voice to drive home a point. "That's why she's a *guest*, not an inmate."

Rhianne, who had calmed during the long ride from New Orleans and even slept on Ben's shoulder, unwound herself from Ben. "Actually, I would enjoy wine."

She sounded more like her usual self, less panicked and more assured. Ben kissed the hand she'd kept twined through his and released her.

Kim threaded an arm through Rhianne's, adjusting Katriona on her other side.

Carly, who greeted Rhianne with a wide Texas smile, paused as the two women went into the house. Tiger broke from Ben and Walker, his mission over, and went straight to her.

Ben watched Tiger take his son from Carly, lifting the little guy in gentle hands. He settled the cub, Seth, in the crook of his arm, then reached over and touched the cheek of Tiger-girl. His daughter relaxed a long way, sending her father a happy smile.

Tiger handed Seth to her—Tiger-girl cuddled her brother close, a look of love on her face—then Tiger bent and kissed Carly. And kissed her. A long time went by.

Walker flashed a rare grin, chuckled, and leapt back into the SUV. He had a mate to get home to, a giant Kodiak bear Shifter who was a sassy, take-no-shit woman.

Ben was left alone to face the Morrisseys.

"She didn't know," Ben repeated. "*I* didn't know. The Tuil Erdannan side of her masked it."

"Ah well." Liam rested his arms on the porch railing. "Now Shifter Bureau knows it. Sean was typing his ass off after Walker called him."

"I'll bet."

Sean, a Guardian, one of those frightening people with big swords who sent Shifter souls to the afterlife, had access to the Guardian Network, a database of Shifter intel that was part magical. Guardians were champion hackers and could put whatever information about Shifters they wanted into human computer systems.

Ben figured Sean had been busy making it look as though Rhianne had been part of the Austin Shiftertown all along, instead of a rogue, undocumented Shifter who could be detained, interrogated, drugged, and possibly terminated if she was perceived to be a threat.

Walker had been communicating what was needed through the discreet earpiece he wore while talking to the Shifter Bureau agents—the advantage of having a sympathetic liaison Shifter Bureau trusted. Walker got things done for

Shifters while placating the assholes at Shifter Bureau. He deserved a medal—on top of all the others he'd received while being incredibly brave in an army A-Team, whatever the hell that was, exactly.

"You could have called, you know." Liam kept his voice gentle, but Ben sensed his displeasure. Liam not knowing what was going on might endanger the Shifters in his demesne, and Ben understood that. Even so ...

"It's not the same thing," Ben said. "Rhianne doesn't belong here. She has her own world, her own life. Nothing to do with the Austin Shifters."

"Everything has to do with everything, lad." Liam remained patient. "Though I understand why you didn't want to expose her. But people taking videos of her in a park kind of threw the shite onto the fire."

Connor broke in, his young voice full of glee. "Video was uploaded and viral in like ten minutes. So cool."

Liam rubbed his chin with one finger. "You'll have to explain to us what you were doing being swallowed by the ground, but I suppose there'll be time for that later."

"Mind if I go inside?" Ben gestured to the house. "Standing out here, I feel like a prisoner being interrogated in an arena." Being surrounded by six-foot-plus Shifters did that to him.

Dylan hadn't said a word. The hand Glory had on his arm and the presence of his daughter-in-law and grandson might have something to do with that.

Shifters were out in force, though, from all over Shifter-town. They kept their distance, but Shifter hearing was good enough that they'd be able to repeat this entire conversation to any who'd missed it.

Liam shrugged, opening his hands to indicate Ben could do what he liked.

As Ben started up the steps, his pocket chimed. He halted halfway up and dug frantically for the crystal as the chiming increased, to the amusement of Connor and Tiger-girl.

Ben finally yanked it out and gazed into the glowing crystal. "Yeah? That you, Lady A.?"

"It is." The answer was crisp. "I wish to speak to my daughter. To tell her that it's safe to return home."

CHAPTER EIGHTEEN

Rhianne glanced up from the glass of deep red wine Kim had handed her. Kim had poured herself a glass of water, smiling warmly as she explained she had another cub on the way.

Rhianne had scented that as soon as Kim had laced arms with her, and was startled how easily the Shifter in her recognized it. It was as though realizing she was Shifter had triggered all kinds of abilities she'd unknowingly kept dormant, but now they were happily flaring to life.

The large kitchen was bright and warm, cozy even in the wee hours of the morning. Tiger's mate, Carly, also held a glass of wine. Tiger had taken the tiny Seth upstairs to put him to bed.

"Sweetie, you're exhausted." Carly had a softly accented voice and kind eyes. "Shifter Bureau is a pain in the ass, as I well know. You deserve a day at a spa."

"It has been a long time since I indulged in a spa town," Rhianne agreed.

Kim looked puzzled but said nothing. Carly raised her

glass, and Rhianne, remembering her lessons on toasting, clicked hers against Carly's.

"To spas," Rhianne said.

"Amen." Kim joined in the glass clinking.

"Word," Carly added. "How long do you think they'll be out there?"

Kim sighed. "However long it takes Liam to explain, in his oh so friendly way, that he's in charge and Ben works for him. Could be a while."

Rhianne took a sip of wine. It wasn't bad, though little could compare to the wine grown and made around the mountains north of her home. "Ben works for no one."

Carly and Kim both sent her a startled glance, and Carly nodded. "That's true. Ben's his own goblin. But he helps out from time to time."

"He answers to too many people," Rhianne said decidedly. "Because he has a kind heart. They take advantage of him, and that should cease."

She noted Carly and Kim exchanging a look. Before either could argue, Ben himself charged through the swinging door from the living room. He held a bright white crystal in front of him as though it would burn him at any moment.

"It's your mom."

Ben thrust the crystal at Rhianne, who fumbled with her glass and nearly spilled the wine. Carly rescued the glass and set it safely on the table.

Rhianne lifted the crystal, peering into its white-hot depths. "Mother?"

There you are. Lady Aisling's voice came through clearly if faintly in Tuil Erdannan. *I'm very happy to speak to you, dear. Are you faring all right?*

Rhianne gave her mother the standard answer, which she used for all occasions. "Yes, I am well."

Good. I'm pleased to tell you that you may return home now.

The coast, as humans say, is clear. Ben shall escort you home, or at least to the sundial, and we'll have a nice celebratory slice of Great-Aunt Freya's plum pie. Tell Ben thank you for all he's done.

Rhianne's heart beat thickly. "I'm not certain I'm ready to return yet. Things have happened. I can't explain." She wet her lips at the understatement. She wanted to shout questions at her mother, such as, *Why didn't you tell me my father was a Shifter? Who was he? What was he to you? Did you love him? Or were you simply taking refuge from Ivor?*

Rhianne cleared her throat, suppressing the urge. "You and I need to have a talk. A very long talk."

Of course, dear. We can as soon as you are home, I promise. The human world can be entertaining, I know, but you belong here, Rhianne. I'll see you when you arrive.

The crystal dinged, and the light died. Rhianne had drawn a breath for more argument and then let it out in anger as the crystal went dark.

"What did she say?" Ben asked. He reached for the crystal and Rhianne dropped it into his palm. "My Tuil Erdannan isn't that great."

"She wants me to return home." Rhianne's anger tasted bitter. "Rush back to her, like a good child. As though my entire life hasn't been turned upside down. She wants you to take me to the sundial. Doesn't bother to ask you if you have the time, oh no. Just assumes you'll drop everything and do as she pleases."

"She always assumes that," Ben said calmly. "It's no problem. Time I was back in Faerie anyway, to finish up the *karmsyern*. Now that Shifter Bureau is breathing down our necks, it's probably a good thing that we go."

Rhianne stared at him in disbelief. "Just like that? After all that's happened? I go home as though nothing has changed?"

"I didn't say that."

Rhianne was aware of Kim and Carly taking up their glasses of wine and slipping out to leave Rhianne and Ben in privacy.

"What are you saying then?" Rhianne demanded.

"I'm saying that if everything's good at home, it will be safer for you there than here. I know you have to deal with your whole being Shifter thing, and yep, your mom has a lot of explaining to do. Here, you have to deal with Liam and his family, plus the other Shifters, plus continue to evade Shifter Bureau. You don't need that. You don't need *me*."

Rhianne's mouth hung open. She didn't need him? But he was her mate ...

She realized with a rush of pain she'd never experienced that while *she* felt the pull to *him* as mate, that didn't mean Ben reciprocated. He wasn't Shifter, nor was he human, like Carly, Kim, and Walker, who'd fallen in love with their Shifter mates. While Rhianne hadn't been wrong when she'd said that all beings of Faerie experienced the mate bond, that did not necessarily mean that Ben was forming it for her.

"I do need—" Rhianne broke off, her throat swelling.

Ben stepped to her, looking straight into her eyes. "You need what?" he asked quietly.

Rhianne opened and closed her mouth, trying to find words to explain.

Then something her mother had said in their short conversation struck her sharply.

"Great-Aunt Freya's plum pie."

Ben blinked. "You need pie?"

"No." Rhianne shook her head in exasperation. "My mother loathes Great-Aunt Freya's pie. Aunt Freya styles herself a fabulous baker but most of what she makes is inedible. I thought Mother was joking, but—"

"But maybe she said it on purpose?" Ben's brows furrowed. "Like a code."

"A warning." Rhianne released him, seeking her glass of wine.

"As in, it's *not* safe to go home." Ben regarded her in disquiet. "In other words, someone told her to summon you back. Three guesses as to who."

Rhianne's heart beat faster. "Only one person could challenge Mother for power." She took a fortifying drink of the wine. "What do I do? Obviously, my fath— Ivor is with her, making her contact me. I speculate that is why she did not answer when I tried to call through the crystal before. She must have been battling him or trying to keep him from me ..."

"Fuck."

"Indeed," Rhianne said breathlessly. "I must aid her."

Ben gently took the glass from her, set it down, and held her hands in a warm clasp. "It's a bad idea for you to rush home and defend her. Your mother is pretty tough."

"So is Ivor." Rhianne spat the name. "I don't know which is stronger, my anger at my mother for not telling me the truth about who my father really is, or relief that Ivor de Erkkonen isn't him." She swallowed. "But if anyone can best my mother, it's Ivor. I can't not help her."

"Me, I'd be throwing a party to celebrate not having that bastard for a dad. But I wasn't thinking about leaving Lady Aisling to his mercy. I was thinking I'd gather some Shifters, like Tiger and Dylan, maybe add a few bears for a really big throw-down, and go help her out."

"You mean without me." Rhianne glared at him. "Remember that Lily in New Orleans said the danger was greatest to you. That you need to be kept alive at all costs."

"I don't know if you noticed, but I'm pretty kick-ass," Ben stated. "Your ex-father needs to be stopped. The *hoch alfar* are bad enough, but if he's helping them—for his own benefit of course—things will be a whole lot worse. Let me go in there with Tiger and other badasses and take care of him. I'll ask

Zander to come with us. He's a healer as well as a giant polar bear, so he can fix us if we get hurt."

"Ben, you can't."

Ben's determination became tinged with bafflement. "Why the hell not? We get rid of this asshole, and that's a lot of problems solved. You hang out here with Liam and company, and once Ivor is out of the picture, you can go home and interrogate your mum about your real dad, have some terrible pie, and relax."

"If you go to Faerie, I have to as well."

"Because a psychic and Tiger told you I had to stay alive? Tiger will be with me. He'll make certain of it."

"No." Rhianne closed her eyes and decided to toss the dice. "Because I'm forming the mate bond for you."

Silence coated the room. It blanketed Rhianne, stretching between her and Ben, distancing them, though he hadn't moved.

After a long moment, Rhianne cracked open her eyes to see Ben studying her with an unreadable expression. "How can you be?" His question was tense and quiet.

"I don't know." Rhianne clung to his hands so tightly she had to be crushing them, but he never flinched. "I didn't even know I was Shifter. But I feel it when I look at you. It's there. I'm not dreaming it."

Ben's swallow traced down his throat. "Baby, I'm not Shifter."

"I know that." Rhianne's voice rose in agitation. "I had no idea *I* truly was, until I was locked in the room at the Shifter Bureau place. All I wanted to do was break out and find you. I *needed* you. I just knew, in that moment, that you were my mate. I didn't even have to think about it. That's what convinced me, in spite of everything I argued to myself, that I was Shifter in truth."

Ben continued to watch her, his face a careful blank.

Was he pleased? Dismayed? Hopeful? Disgusted? Rhianne's Shifter senses weren't yet honed enough for her to read his body language. Tiger had been easy. Ben was an enigma.

Perhaps that was a trait of goblins, to be able to hide their emotions away. Or perhaps a trait of Ben personally, learned after so many years of being by himself.

"You don't have to be alone anymore, Ben," Rhianne said softly. "I'm your mate."

He shook his head slowly. "It's not the same for my people."

"I told you—remember? All creatures of Faerie form the mate bond, except the Tuil Erdannan. That's what made me realize."

"Rhianne." Ben tugged her closer. His eyes remained still, unfathomable. "Remember what I told *you*. The *hoch alfar* want me dead. They killed everyone I ever loved, everyone I knew, and thousands who were strangers to me. What would they do if they realized you think you feel the mate bond for me?"

Rhianne jerked her hands from his. "What do you mean I *think* I feel it?"

"Seriously not my point."

"Do you think I'm delusional?" Rhianne stared at him in disbelief. "That I don't know what is going on inside me?" She banged her hands to her chest. "I know about the *hoch alfar*. I know that's why you want to go to Faerie without me, but I won't let you. We'll face them down together, or hide from them together—whatever works."

"Rhianne—"

"Do *not* tell me you will charge to Faerie and leave me behind. That is what this argument is really about, remember? We can yell at each other about the mate bond another time. Which I do feel, by the way. I'm not an idiot."

"No, but you're new to this." Ben's voice rose. "Don't you

think I *want* you to form the bond for me? What if you discover that it's not true after all? That you're forming it for someone else but don't realize because I happened to be standing in front of you? Can you imagine that torture for me?"

Rhianne rarely let her anger fully surge—she'd seen the devastation her people could cause when they lost their famous tempers—but now fury flashed out of her. As when she'd been locked in the Bureau's cell, she wanted to blast out the windows, grab Ben, and haul him away.

"*Happened to be standing in front of me?* Who the hell else would I be forming it *for*? Every Shifter I've met so far is already mated or a child. I feel the bonds, Ben. I see them." Rhianne snatched at the threads in the air.

"I usually can see them too," Ben said. "This time I don't."

"Maybe because you can't see your own?"

"Oh, sure, a reasonable explanation. I believe you are feeling it, Rhianne, but I think it's cruel of you to get my hopes up."

"Cruel?" The Shifter in her began to snarl. "I'm being cruel to *you*?"

Rhianne felt her wings unfurl, her arms stretching out to become them.

"Um." The hesitant syllable from the kitchen doorway snapped Rhianne's attention from the growing inferno inside her. She lowered her arms, the wings receding.

Liam's nephew, Connor, who was a younger version of his uncle Liam, had entered the kitchen.

With him, standing close, was the young woman Carly said was Tiger's cub. She'd pulled her orange and black hair into a ponytail, but it was the only thing about her that was subdued. Her eyes, so like Tiger's, darted between Ben and Rhianne. Rhianne sensed the wildness in her, one that could tear apart this place faster than any of them could, even if they combined their efforts.

Connor cleared his throat. "If you need a place to be private, and it sounds like you do, come with me."

He crossed to the back door past a silent and nonplussed Ben. Tiger-girl followed, her gaze moving to Rhianne and staying there.

Rhianne saw intelligence in the tall young woman, raw, but there. She was no fool. Tiger-girl swept her gaze over Rhianne from head to toe, craning to see behind her back as though looking for her wings. Rhianne shrugged, giving her a small smile. Tiger-girl grinned then hurried out after Connor, not letting him out of her sight.

Ben caught Rhianne's hand. She didn't jerk away this time but allowed him to tow her along after Connor and Tiger-girl.

Conner went down the porch steps into the common area behind the houses. Dawn had broken, the gray sky flushed with pink light. Rhianne and Ben followed Connor and Tiger-girl around the house to a large built-on lean-to, possibly at one time meant to be a garden shed.

"Hey, Connor." A young woman jogging on the common waved to Connor. The young woman, who looked to be in her very early twenties, wore shorts, tank top, and sneakers, good for running. And for Shifting, Rhianne realized. Easy clothes to take on and off.

The young woman halted and beamed at Connor, paying no attention to the rest of them. Connor glanced around at her. "Oh, hey lass. How are you?"

The words were casual, what Connor might say to anyone who happened by. The young woman brightened. "I'm doing just fine. Missed you at the party last night."

"Busy." Connor turned from her to fit a key into the padlock of the shed. "Shifter stuff with my uncle. You know."

"I do." The young woman sidled closer, completely ignoring Ben, Rhianne, and Tiger-girl. "You'll be doing his job one day. I bet you'll be awesome."

"Shew, I hope it's not too soon." Connor jiggled the key in the lock. "A good many years from now. I want to enjoy myself first."

The young woman giggled. Tiger-girl, who'd been watching with narrowing eyes, abruptly stepped between the Shifter woman and Connor. Hands on hips Tiger-girl sent forth a growl that rippled the still air. The message was clear.

Stay away.

The young woman paused, studied Tiger-girl, and took a few steps back. "Anyway. See ya, Connor." She pivoted and jogged to the green, continuing her run.

"See you." Connor, his attention on the lock for the whole conversation, hadn't noticed a thing.

The lock clicked and Connor swung open a door. "Here you go."

He stood aside and let Ben and Rhianne enter, Ben going first, as a Shifter male would. Rhianne found herself in a surprisingly large space, with two couches on either end of an empty wooden floor. A television had been mounted on one wall, and beneath it sat a bookshelf strewn with books and magazines.

"Tiger-girl and I come here a lot," Connor said as Ben and Rhianne halted awkwardly in the middle of the room. "We spar. Or catch up on vids between bouts."

Rhianne glanced at Tiger-girl, who hovered behind Connor's shoulder. She was almost as tall as Connor and shared his restless athleticism.

"Sparring?" Rhianne asked, brows rising.

"Yeah." Connor returned her questioning gaze, his innocence unfeigned. "Tiger-girl's good at natural fighting, but we're both learning to fine-tune our skills. She's going through her Transition, and it helps her to spar. She's also learning how not to kill me." He sent a fond grin behind him.

Tiger-girl's joy at his attention went beyond fondness. If

Rhianne hadn't had to worry about her own problems, she would love to stay in this Shiftertown and watch their relationship progress.

The thought that she truly would love to stay here jolted Rhianne. She squeezed Ben's hand uncertainly.

"You two could use some sparring time yourself," Connor said. "Enjoy it. I'll let you out when you have everything resolved."

He and Tiger-girl quickly ducked outside, and Connor slammed the door. Ben dropped Rhianne's hand and rushed to the exit, but before he reached it, they heard the click of the padlock snapping into place.

Laughter, both male and female, floated to them, and then receded. Ben turned and faced Rhianne, the two of them left alone with their demons.

CHAPTER NINETEEN

Ben studied Rhianne across the space of the room. She was so beautiful, with her red hair falling out of a sloppy braid, her face both animated and creased with exhaustion, her body tense.

Her words about the mate bond had filled Ben with delirious hope, one he feared to hold on to, couldn't allow himself to consider real.

Shifters found the mate bond right and left, or so it seemed, but never with Ben. He was alone, had been for a thousand years. His solitude had left an imprint on him, a deep furrow in his psyche that he couldn't shake.

"I suppose we have to hash this out," he said, throat tight.

Rhianne glanced at the door. "You know we can easily escape this room. You thought nothing of tearing metal bars out of solid stone."

True, a flimsy door wouldn't stop Ben if he wanted to flee. "I know that. You know that. Connor probably knows that too. But we should talk."

Rhianne folded her arms, which pushed up her chest under

the loose shirt. "There's nothing to talk about. We were not talking, in any case. We were shouting."

"Figure of speech."

"I wish you spoke Tuil Erdannan better. I could explain. This English is flimsy for conveying what I mean."

"Goblin would be better too. But it would take us a while. Our words get long. We add endings to words every time we want to tack on an explanation. They can become massively multisyllabic."

Ben hoped to make her smile, but she only watched him, grim-faced.

"Shall we shout more?" she asked. "You cannot go to Faerie alone."

Ben's frustration mounted. "Not alone. With Dylan, Tiger, and Zander. They'll make sure I come out alive."

"While I wait here? Tiger himself told me to take care of you. He called you the last warrior."

"I know he did. I wish I knew what the hell that meant."

"As do I." Rhianne threw out her hands. "He didn't exactly explain."

"Tiger never does." Ben tried to calm himself and think. "He could mean that I'm the last goblin warrior alive, but then we met Millie, who I'm sure could hold her own in battle. In fact, I'd like to shake some answers out of her. Is she for us or against us?" He broke off. "Not important right now. Tiger could also mean I'll be the last one standing in the next Shifter Fae war. Goddess, I hope not."

Ben ran a hand through his hair, fear forming like ice in his veins. He didn't want to be a last warrior at all. That would mean that everyone he knew and loved had died around him. It had happened to him once. He'd never bear it if it happened again.

Triumph abruptly entered Rhianne's eyes, which made

Ben nervous. "I know, I'll tell Tiger not to leave me behind." She lifted her chin. "That will do it."

"Depends on Tiger, doesn't it?" Ben returned. "He might decide it's best that you stay here."

"Somehow, I don't think so." Rhianne's mouth twitched, making Ben want to kiss it. "Very well, we'll let Tiger settle the matter."

"Sure thing." He trusted Tiger's judgement, though if Tiger chose against *Ben's* judgement, he'd dispute that long and hard. "Are we done arguing then? Want me to yell for Connor?"

"Then there's the issue of the mate bond." Rhianne's tiny amount of amusement deserted her. She issued him an arrogant Tuil Erdannan glare, which made her even more beautiful. "The one you believe I don't understand."

"Because it's complicated." Ben let his usual stoicism fly to the wind, releasing the words jammed inside him. "You dangle this mate bond in front of me, and at the same time imply I'm going to be the last man standing. Meaning I lose you. I can't lose you, Rhianne. I've just found you. It will kill me to lose you. Mate bond or no mate bond—it will devastate me. Rip me to shreds. Might as well let the *hoch alfar* do that for me, or your dear father."

"You don't have a choice." Rhianne grabbed at her T-shirt, right over her heart, and yanked at it as though trying to tear what she felt out of her. "*I* don't have a choice. I realized I had the mate bond when those Bureau men separated us. I needed to charge out of there and find you. Because I couldn't be without you. When I saw you, I saw the magic between you and me. Maybe you don't feel it, maybe you never will. I don't know how this works. All I know is I can't be without you ..."

Her face crumpled, and she broke off.

"Love." Ben was across the room, gathering her into his arms. "I'm not trying to hurt you. I never want to hurt you." He stroked her hair, held her trembling body. "I'm so scared of losing you, of the mate bond winding me up in it and not letting me go. I've seen what happens to others when the bond is broken."

"It's too late for me." Rhianne's words were muffled in his shoulder. "I never even knew you before you lifted me out of that cell. Now I can't be without you."

"I *am* pretty irresistible," Ben quipped.

Rhianne raised her head, her brown eyes swimming with tears. "You always make fun of yourself."

"Keeps me from breaking down." Ben's smile faded. "Keeps me alive."

Rhianne kissed him, her soft lips meeting the grim line of his. Ben gave up trying to hold on to the shards of his sanity and kissed her fully.

His heart gave a sudden dark throb and squeezed hard, as though breaking down a barrier to force the mate bond through. He feared the bond as much as he longed for it, but for this moment, the longing overwhelmed his self-preservation.

Ben brought his hands up under Rhianne's heavy braid of hair, stroking her as he sought her mouth. She grew frantic under his touch, fingers sinking into his shoulders as though she never wanted to let him go.

Mating frenzy. She had it all right.

Goblins had a sort of mating frenzy themselves. Not the ferocious one of Shifters, the Goddess's way of making certain they had more little Shifters, but a need that delved into his soul. Beings that lived for many centuries knew how to love fiercely.

Rhianne made a noise in her throat as Ben's kiss turned bruising. She melted under his touch, but her surrender was brushed with wild glee.

Connor had locked them in here to give them privacy for more than arguing, Ben realized. There were the sofas at either end of the room. Wide, long sofas to give comfort to large-bodied Shifters, no matter what they decided to do on them.

Ben hooked his fingers under Rhianne's shirt and tugged it off her. Rhianne's smile of joy took his breath away. Beneath, the white camisole clung to her full breasts.

Before he could slide that away from her, she grabbed his shirt and nearly tore it from him. Ben chuckled as his flesh was exposed to the room's cool air.

"Careful, sweetheart. I need to be in one piece for this."

Rhianne answered by yanking open his belt and popping the button of his jeans. She proved she'd become good at zippers by pulling his down and pushing at his jeans until they pooled around his ankles.

"Now this is getting embarrassing." Ben had to lean down and untie his boots before he could get them off and not trip on his pants.

Rhianne's expression showed she didn't care. Embarrassment would be for later. For now, this was delight, elation, desire.

Ben stood up in nothing but his underwear. "Not fair. I can't be the only one almost bare-assed. Let's get these off you."

He unbuttoned and unzipped as Rhianne had, sliding the jeans down her legs. When she started to take off her shoes, Ben stopped her. "No. Leave those on."

Rhianne's expression told him she didn't understand why, and her innocence stirred his blood. His cock gave a needy pulse.

Ben helped her get the pants all the way off, and soon Rhianne faced him in only her underwear and the high-heeled strappy shoes. A moment later the camisole was floating to the floor.

Ben's breath caught. "By the Goddess, Rhianne. You are the most beautiful woman I've ever laid eyes on."

She flushed to match her hair. "Why would you lay your eyes ...?"

"Never mind. I bet the couches are comfortable."

When Rhianne glanced at one, Ben swept her up and carried her there. She nuzzled his neck, running fingertips along his arms as though amazed at his strength.

The sofa was wide enough to take them both. Good choice.

They lay on their sides, face to face. Rhianne ran her foot along Ben's leg, the heel of her shoe sending all kinds of erotic flashes through his body.

"We're still wearing too many clothes," he said.

Rhianne's smile stoked his fires to scalding. "For this kind of arguing, yes."

Ben helped her wriggle from her underwear and she did the same for him. He decided not to let her take off the shoes.

"You are seriously hot," he said as they snuggled down again.

Rhianne touched his face. "Your skin too is warm."

He bit back laughter. "I mean sexy. Gorgeous. I want to lick you all over."

"I could enjoy licking." She ran her tongue up the side of his neck, right over the spiderweb tatt.

Ben groaned. "You're going to kill me, baby. Next time, I'll tell Connor to leave a bottle of chocolate syrup. Then we'll never come out of here."

Rhianne nibbled where she'd licked and then nipped her way to his chest. "I have always feared being confined. But right now, I rather like it."

Because she knew either of them could throw down that door without a problem, Ben with his inhuman strength, she with a word of power. Plus this thing they had going on right now blotted out all other problems.

Ben bent to her throat and licked and kissed. He took his

mouth down to her breasts, spending attention on them while she wound her arms around him and held him to her.

As wide as the sofa was, lovemaking would be awkward, but that added excitement. Ben finished enjoying her nipples—velvet soft, filling his mouth—and cupped her face to imbibe her beauty.

Rhianne lay against the couch's cushioned back. A velour throw beneath them added extra softness. Shifters liked their comfort, and Ben was glad of it.

He wrapped his hand around Rhianne's thigh and positioned it over his, bringing his cock straight to her opening.

Everything stopped. Ben wanted the world to go away until there was nothing but himself and Rhianne, the cushions beneath them, and the mate bond that was trying to infuse his body.

Ben silently said a few choice words about the Goddess and her need to bind her creations in a thing so beautiful it was painful.

Then the world surged forward again, time starting. Ben ceased worrying about his future and thrust inside the beautiful woman in his arms.

The scratch of her heel on his thigh made him wild. Ben groaned as they rocked together. In this position, they couldn't move much, but he was deep inside her, she surrounding him completely, which was enough.

Rhianne whispered his name, ending in a little sigh that became a moan of pleasure.

In the next heartbeat, Ben realized she'd said his true name, not the truncated *Ben* humans and Shifters called him because they couldn't wrap their mouths around the many syllables his parents had bestowed on him.

Rhianne had said the full thing, *Gilbenarteoighiamh*, never stumbling, the entire name flowing out sweetly.

The sound fanned his desire into high flame. He managed

to roll her under him, coming up on his fists to drive hard into her. Rhianne's face softened as she arched to him, her eyes starry.

No passive lover, Rhianne clung to him and met his thrusts, her hair, loosened from its braid, wrapping around Ben as it had in his fantasies. The silken touch of it warm on his skin sent him into spirals of madness.

He pumped faster, she crying out as she welcomed him inside her. Ben pounded one fist on the sofa, his hand sinking into the cushion.

"Need you," he growled. "Need you, want you, lov— Oh, *fuck*."

This coming was intense, Ben closing his eyes and drowning in her. Rhianne's shouts met his, her silvery voice mingling with his grating one, fusing into a soothing harmony.

Ben and Rhianne continued to move together, the couch cradling them. Ben vaguely wondered if the noise they were making disturbed anyone inside the house then immediately ceased to care. They must be used to it. Shifters lived to mate.

After a long time, their rhythm slowed into something calm, a languid back and forth as Ben and Rhianne basked in each other. Eventually, they stilled, Ben kissing Rhianne in relaxed afterglow.

She traced his lip with a gentle finger. "Need you too, Ben."

Ben thought of the L- word that had nearly slipped out. He'd swallowed it in a blaze of passion and also to keep from confusing her.

But she knew. Rhianne gazed up at him in serenity, understanding.

Ben licked her finger, then bowed his head into her shoulder, wondering what would become of him.

———

Rhianne watched Ben as they slid on their clothes a while later. His T-shirt was torn, and Rhianne flushed as she remembered how fervently she'd wanted it off him.

To cover her embarrassment, she focused on settling her own clothes. "Tiger's cub, the young woman. What is her name?"

Ben shrugged. "No one knows. Not even her." He smoothed the T-shirt, spreading the torn part and then dropping it in resignation. "They're calling her Tiger-girl for now. She'll choose her own name, so says Connor."

"Is sparring *really* what those two are doing in here?" Rhianne asked in amusement. "The couches are quite convenient."

Ben nodded, serious. "They are. Tiger-girl is going through her Transition, which is the Shifter coming of age. Shifters remain cubs a long time, until the late twenties as humans calculate years. Before the Transition, sex is the noisy and annoying activity adults are too fond of. During and right after the Transition, however, it's nothing but crazed mating frenzy."

"Then Tiger-girl is going through that?"

"She is, but Connor isn't. Yet. He's still technically a cub. During the Transition fighting—anything, anyone, anytime—helps a Shifter deal with the raging hormones. Thus, sparring. Tiger-girl will be horny as hell soon though, if she isn't already. She'll have to look to another Shifter then, as Connor's not ready."

"I don't know." Rhianne gathered her hair in an awkward attempt to braid it. "She seems quite taken with Connor. Not letting him far out of her sight. She certainly warned off that other Shifter girl."

"Connor was there when Tiger and Carly found her locked in an underground compound out in Arizona. Shifter Bureau had her and didn't know what to do with her. Poor kid. Carly says she didn't calm down until Connor talked to her."

"Uh huh." Rhianne fumbled with the braid. "Being rescued from a cell is a pretty powerful stimulus. A girl doesn't forget that."

"Is that so?" Ben came to her and turned her around, taking her hair in competent hands. "If you're Shifter, you must have gone through a Transition. Even half Shifters do."

Rhianne thought back through her life, dredging up memories from the dust of her past.

"There was a time," she said slowly. "I suddenly couldn't stand being in my mother's house, puttering in the garden, waiting for the cook to make his next fantastic meal. I wanted to be out, roaming the mountains and the ocean's shores. Being home drove me crazy. I didn't know why, because I'd always loved puttering in the garden and pestering the cook."

She remembered how her skin had burned, how she'd been peevish and snarling with everyone.

"My mother and I had been so fond of each other," Rhianne went on. "We took care of each other once she threw my father out. But I suddenly couldn't stand the sight of her. She understood, I think. She gave me my head and sent me off."

"Sounds Transition-y to me." Ben finished the braid, secured it with a strand of her hair, and turned her around. "What happened after you left home?"

"I had a blast hiking through the mountains and down to the coast on my own. I could run or walk as far as I wanted every day. I'd brought my telescope with me, and I'd set it up in the evening, spending the whole night gazing at the stars. People fed me and gave me a place to nap along the way—sometimes they were other Tuil Erdannan, or *hoch alfar*, sometimes *dokk alfar* if I stumbled across them. They were all hospitable to me."

"Of course they were. They figured Lady Aisling would blast them into dust if they refused you shelter. Or you would."

She shook her head. "Tuil Erdannan believe everyone gives

them awe and reverence, but I think the others are simply terrified. I did have the urge to fight anyone who crossed me, but I made myself leave them alone. I'd witnessed the damage my father did to those who opposed them, and I vowed not to be like him. I wasn't always successful. There was one incident ..."

Rhianne trailed off. She'd tried to forget it, but every once in a while it rose to haunt her.

"Tell me," Ben said, his tone gentle but firm.

Rhianne swallowed. "A *hoch alfar* tried to seduce me, in exchange for his assistance. He'd allowed me his tent—he was a soldier out on a training exercise. I asked for a meal, which he gave me, and a place to sleep. Then he came at me, telling me exactly what he wanted to do to me. I broke most of his bones. He screamed. A lot."

"I can't say I have a ton of sympathy for the guy." Ben scowled. "One of the bones I'd have broken was his neck. Did you kill him?"

"No." Rhianne cringed inwardly at the memory. "But it scared me how strong I was. How I could have done that to another living being. I was so afraid it was my father in me. I ran off, but I told another group of *hoch alfar* that their colleague had been hurt and they needed to tend him. I never learned his fate."

"Hmm." Ben put soothing hands on her shoulders. "I think the lady Shifter in you was to blame, rather than the Tuil Erdannan. Men mess with female Shifters at their peril."

"Is there a difference?"

"Hell, yes. Your dad—let's call him your stepdad—breaks people for the fun of it, or to teach them obedience to him. A female Shifter fights in self-defense. You didn't want this *hoch alfar's* slimy hands on you, and in your Transition state, you didn't have a lot of control. So you struck." A smile flickered over his mouth. "Damn, I wish I'd seen that."

"No, you don't. It was horrible."

"Is this why you didn't reduce Walther's thugs to dust when they groped at you? Scared you'd go all bone-crusher again?"

Rhianne hadn't thought it through consciously, but now she nodded. "Ever since that night, I fought my temper and my own strength. I didn't want to become like my father."

Tears pricked her eyes, and she blinked them away. She was finished with crying.

"Good news." Ben rubbed her arms. "You don't have to worry about being like Ivor the Terrible anymore. You have to worry about being like your *true* father, I guess, but if he's anything like you, he's a real peach."

"Peach?" Human expressions were so strange.

"A good dude. Awesome Shifter. He'd be someone I'd want at my side."

"The question remains—who is he?" Rhianne's anger seeped in. "And why did my mother hide him from me all these years?"

"I have the feeling she didn't so much hide him from *you* as from your stepfather. What would Ivor have done if he'd known you weren't his? What would he have done with the Shifter who'd had a liaison with your mom?"

Rhianne shuddered. "Taken him apart. And probably me too." She let out a breath. "I wonder if he did find out. Recently, I mean. It would explain why he was willing to let his own daughter be captured and forced into a marriage with a *hoch alfar* lord. If I'm not his offspring, why should he care what happens to me? Why not use me for his own purpose?"

"Makes sense." Ben massaged her shoulders once more and released her. "The question is, does he know that you're part Shifter, or only that you're not his?"

"He doubtless knows now if he is holding my mother hostage."

"Not necessarily. Your mother is a redoubtable woman. She threw him out before, remember?"

"That must have been hard for her," Rhianne said with sudden compassion. "I know she loved him once."

"She'd have to have been madly in love with him to be blind to his true nature," Ben said. "Love does make us stupid."

Rhianne met his gaze. "I agree."

Ben flushed. "It makes me a complete idiot who will do completely idiotic things. Goddess help us."

Rhianne curled her fingers at her sides. She'd heard him begin to say *Love you,* and then stop himself abruptly. Why? Would he ever say it again?

"What do we do now?" Rhianne asked softly.

"You and me? I don't know. I liked what we were doing on the sofa. Maybe some more of that while we work through all these emotions?"

Rhianne had to smile. "I meant about going to Faerie and rescuing my mother. She *is* my mother, and you can't stop me going home and kicking my stepdad's ass."

"If we share the mate bond, that means I'm your mate, and in Shifter terms, yes I can." Ben's grin was victorious as he closed on her. "Females in the past were sequestered so they'd be safe to have cubs away from other males with designs on them."

"Sequestered." Rhianne's brows went up, and the Tuil Erdannan side of her reemerged. "You would try that?"

"Nope." Ben chuckled. "Shifters don't do it anymore either, but the males still believe they can order their mates to do what they want."

Rhianne thought of Jaycee and her scorn whenever Dimitri tried to exert his dominance. "Do the Shifter females obey?"

"Nope." More laughter. "You're catching on."

Rhianne also recalled how Dimitri hadn't really expected

Jaycee to obey him, betraying his pleasure when she defied him. They knew each other well.

The padlock clicked, and a moment later, Connor swung open the door. He had his eyes closed. Tiger-girl stood behind him, but she stared at them in avid curiosity.

"Are you decent?" Connor asked.

"We're dressed," Ben answered. "We wrecked the couch a little, though."

Connor's eyes popped open, but he didn't appear to be at all embarrassed. "No worries. Uncle Liam and Aunt Kim wreck it plenty. Liam sent me to fetch you. There's a woman here, and she has a couple of weird-looking guys with her. Says her name is Millie."

CHAPTER TWENTY

B en was out the door, past a startled Tiger-girl, and sprinting to the house as soon as Connor finished the sentence. He heard Rhianne right behind him and realized he could sense her too. The bond tugged at him.

How Millie had found him here, and what she would do, Ben couldn't say, but alarm pulsed through him. Goblins weren't the cute, harmless things they pretended to be.

"Where is she?" Ben charged through the house, following the sound of voices to the front porch. He banged out of the screen door just as Millie, white-haired and plump-cheeked, leaned over Carly, who had Seth in her arms.

"No!" he yelled.

Carly blinked up at him. Seth, who was learning to talk with amazing rapidity, said, "What wrong, Ben?"

"She's dangerous." Ben paused to catch his breath. "Dangerous like me."

Millie beamed a smile, peering at Ben through her thick lenses. "Nonsense. I am here to make sure all is well with you." She gazed down at Seth. "*This* one. He's—"

She broke off and swung around as Tiger materialized

behind her. For something so big, Tiger could move with amazing stealth.

"He's my son." Menace and pride blended in the growl.

"Oh, my." Millie took a step back. "And you are the strangest being I've ever seen."

"He's fine the way he is," Carly said at once. She always sprang to Tiger's defense.

"I mean strange in a good way." Millie adjusted her spectacles, taking in Tiger's tall form, his intense eyes, his orange-and-black striped hair. "Are you Ben's friend? Or foe?"

"Friend," Tiger said without hesitation.

"Whew." Ben wiped his brow. "I am glad to hear that, big guy. I do *not* want you for an enemy. This is Millie. She's a goblin. Last time I saw her, the earth opened up and tried to eat me."

"Like I said, that wasn't my doing." Millie faced him in indignation, both hands closing on her handbag. "I saw what happened. Saw *you*." She jerked her chin at Rhianne. "You rescued him. Then Shifter Bureau took you away. I called my sons, and they tracked you to Shifter Bureau. They watched Mr. Danielson and this large man drive off with you." She nodded at Tiger. "I did some research and realized they were coming here. I came because I worried about you, Ben dear."

Ben had to stop and process everything she'd said. Rhianne, with her quicker mind, grasped the essential point.

"Sons?" she asked.

Millie waved a hand to the front yard. "Yes, my sons. Darren and Cyril. They're right over ... Now where have they got to?"

Ben scanned the street and saw that they'd gone as far down as Spike's house. Spike, tall and tattooed, stood in his yard, hands on hips, gazing down at two men in jeans and leather jackets. Spike's cub, Jordan, in his jaguar form, scampered between his father and the goblins.

If Spike was letting his cub run around them, he must believe the two goblins were harmless.

Ben started for them, Rhianne behind him. Tiger remained on the porch, close to his cub and to Millie, though Ben felt his watchfulness.

The two goblins in human form were a bit taller than Ben, but had similar dark skin, deep brown eyes, and black hair they both wore trimmed in a military-like cut. No tatts. Under the leather jackets they wore T-shirts, one with a heavy metal band's name on it, the other bearing a picture of three full glasses of beer: one dark, one amber, one light.

"Hey," the beer-shirted one said. "You Ben?" His gaze went to Rhianne, and his expression said he liked what he saw.

Ben sent him a warning scowl. "How'd you guess?"

"Millie told us what you look like," heavy-metal shirt guy said. "Plus you stand out from all the Shifters around here."

Ben folded his arms. "Explain to me how I never knew about you two. Or your mother."

Beer guy shrugged. "We keep a low profile? So do you, or we'd have found you before this. I'm Darren. This is Cyril." He pointed to his brother in the heavy-metal shirt.

"Hey," Cyril said.

"You could pick any human names in the universe, and those are what you decided to call yourselves?" Ben asked. Spike huffed a laugh.

"Back when we were born, those were respected human names," Darren said. "Now, they're not taken as seriously. Which is good, right? Better to not pose a threat."

Rhianne, who had given heavily tattooed Spike a thorough and curious scrutiny, turned her radiant eyes to the two goblins. "Were you born in this world? Or in Faerie?"

"Here," Cyril answered. "Mum was preggers with us when we were kicked out. We're twins, by the way." The brothers resembled each other greatly, but they weren't identical. "She went through hell."

The glint in Cyril's eyes said that he partly blamed Ben for that.

"We all did." Ben spoke firmly. "I'm sorry. Why are you here? Now?"

"Because Millie thinks we need to keep you safe," Darren said. "We're the last of our kind, and apparently, you're some kind of special powers guy who might be our salvation." He shook his head. "She gets ideas. We go with them."

Jordan, who'd circled the group a few times in energetic jaguar lopes, halted suddenly in front of Rhianne. He changed from jaguar cub to half human, half Shifter, his small body covered with fur. His half-beast would be ferocious when he was fully grown, but for now, he was adorably cute.

"Dad says you can fly," he said to Rhianne. "Can you fly?"

Rhianne's throat moved, a flicker of fear in her eyes. When she bent to Jordan, though, she was gentleness itself. "I can. It's a little scary, but yes."

"I wish I could fly," Jordan said. "Will you take me up? I could ride in your claws."

Spike rumbled. He didn't have to speak a word. Jordan deflated. "Dad doesn't want me to."

"Your dad just wants you to be safe," Rhianne said. "You wouldn't want me to drop you."

"You wouldn't drop me," Jordan said with confidence.

Rhianne scratched the top of Jordan's head, right between his furry ears. "Maybe not, but it's up to your dad. How about we let him think about it?"

Jordan butted his head up to her hand. He hadn't yet grown out of wanting to be petted. "Well, okay. But when we go, I want you to fly real high."

Rhianne met Ben's gaze. Her eyes had softened as she melted for Jordan. She hadn't been around cubs much, Ben realized. Or children of any being. Her mother hadn't given her any brothers or sisters, which was probably a good thing, considering who Lady Aisling had married.

Rhianne's own cubs would be beautiful. And eagles. Downy feathers, big eyes. In his sudden vision, one of the little eagle chicks had black eyes with a Ben-like glint in them.

He banished the vision with effort. "Your mom is looking for you," he told the goblin brothers.

"She's always looking for us," Darren said without worry.

"Trying to keep you out of trouble?" Ben asked.

"Hell, no. We have to keep *her* out of trouble. No one notices a middle-aged woman, she says. She thinks that means she can do whatever the hell she wants."

Ben raised his brows. "Like rush to Shiftertown after another goblin?"

"Goblin?" Cyril scrunched up his face. "Is that what you're calling yourself?"

Ben fought down irritation. "What do you tell people you are?"

"Party animals," Darren said. He and his brother laughed. "Seriously, dude. We don't tell them anything. We let them assume we're human."

"That's because you don't hang out with Shifters who smell Faerie on you," Ben said. "I had to give them a word for what I was to keep them from gutting me. Goblin is the closest human equivalent. I tried gnome, but they kept thinking of cute little bearded guys with pointed hats."

Cyril snorted a laugh. "Okay, we'll go with goblin. Better than troll."

"Yeah, too many bad connotations with troll," Darren agreed.

"Are you done?" Spike's growl increased. "You all didn't come here just to shoot the breeze."

Ben shrugged. "No, but it makes a break from the constant

danger and excitement." Rhianne continued to scratch Jordan's ears. He returned to full jaguar cub form and leaned against her legs.

"You two up for a trip to Faerie?" Ben asked the goblins. "To kick some Fae ass?"

"That would be cool," Darren said immediately.

Rhianne snapped her head up. "No."

Darren and Cyril regarded her in surprise. "It wouldn't be cool to kick Fae ass?" Cyril asked.

"It wouldn't be Fae you fought, but a Tuil Erdannan. One of the most powerful. Ben, you can't ask them to go."

Ben rocked on his heels. "Rhianne has this wild idea that she can go to Faerie, destroy a vicious Tuil Erdannan on her own, and waltz home in time for tea."

"No, I don't." Rhianne's mouth firmed. "But nor do I believe a small army of Shifters and goblins can defeat him. You'll just get everyone killed. Including *you*." Her glare cut to Ben.

"The alternative, having you go and confront your stepdad, even with your mother there, is nuts. If we have you, Lady Aisling, *and* a Shifter-goblin army that contains Tiger and an obnoxious polar bear healer, we might have a chance."

Rhianne stared at Ben a long moment before Ben realized his slip. "You are saying I will go with you."

"Not something I want," Ben said quickly. "But I have to admit, you're not feeble, you know Ivor well, and you'd understand his weaknesses."

"He doesn't have any weaknesses," Rhianne answered.

Darren raised his hands. "Hold on, hold on. You're saying you're recruiting a force to go to Faerie and face *one* dude?"

"Yes," Ben and Rhianne replied at the same time. Ben added, "One *Tuil Erdannan*. There's a difference."

"Never met a Tuil Erdannan," Darren said. "That tough, are they?"

"Rhianne is one. Or half one. She could kick all your asses with her hand tied behind her back."

Rhianne flushed, but she seemed pleased. "I doubt that."

"Believe it." Ben gave Darren and Cyril a pointed nod. "Don't mess with my girl."

Darren poked his brother in the arm. "Ooh, they're an item. A *ghallareknoiksnlealous* and a Shifter-Tuil Erdannan. Match made in ... a blender?"

"Watch your mouth," Ben growled. "Nothing wrong with a blender. They make hella good frozen cocktails."

Spike shook his head and turned his back on them. "Come on, Jordan."

Jordan nuzzled Rhianne one last time and scampered after his father, changing into his Shifter half-beast as he went. "Will you let her take me flying, Dad? Please?"

"Did we piss him off?" Cyril watched Spike lead Jordan into the house. "He doesn't seem like a guy we should piss off."

"Spike is good." Ben found himself drifting toward Rhianne, as though he couldn't keep away from her. "He'll pass the word on that we need help. He doesn't say much, but he's a terrific tracker. A tracker is a Shifter who can scout, report, and kick serious butt."

"What now?" Rhianne asked. "My mother is used to handling my father—my stepfather—but I don't want to leave her to his mercy too long."

"We also have to deal with the time difference," Ben reminded her. "Time doesn't move at the same pace in Faerie as it does in the human world. Kind of ebbs and flows. But there's a ley line here with a Fae warrior inside it who keeps us posted about what's going on in Faerie."

"Is there?" Rhianne asked, just as Darren and Cyril opened their mouths to do the same. "Do you trust him?"

"I wouldn't say *trust* exactly, but he's Sean's mate's father.

He likes to keep an eye on Andrea and his grandson. He won't betray her."

"Would he help against my stepfather?"

"I can ask him, but I wouldn't count on it. Fionn's a good fighter, but he is a *hoch alfar*. He probably wouldn't risk going against a Tuil Erdannan."

"Count us in," Darren said eagerly. "We try not to get into too many fights, so no one figures out what we really are. I'd love to truly let loose on a Fae who needs to learn a lesson."

"Please, don't," Rhianne said. "You'll get yourselves killed."

"Nothing better to do." Cyril shrugged. "You live a thousand or so years in exile, hiding your true nature, and see how bored *you* get. A good fight to the death is just what we need."

They were goblins, all right. Ben wanted to break down and cry, and at the same time dance around and laugh. It had been so long since he'd listened to goblins banter—pretending to care nothing for their own safety, itching to fight anything that needed an ass-kicking.

Goblins could glam, and could easily outsmart humans or Fae, or even Shifters, even these two. They acted slightly dimwitted, but Ben saw in their eyes they were anything but. They camouflaged their true nature, as Ben had been doing all his life.

He slid his arm around Rhianne. "We'll talk about it, love. Why don't we go back to Liam's and have a council of war? We'll have Fionn do some recon inside Faerie, and then we'll charge in there and save Lady Aisling. Maybe in her gratitude, she'll shower us with riches. 'Cause I need a new blender."

The brothers laughed—goblins always ready to have fun. Fight until they died, yes, but have a good time until then. Ben was so happy to hear the familiar bullshit of his own people that he was ready to turn cartwheels.

Rhianne wasn't convinced. Ben knew that the brothers were aware of the danger, as was he. Even with all of their resources Ivor would be tough to beat. The alternative was to allow Lady Aisling and Rhianne to be at Ivor's mercy. Ben vowed to do whatever was needed to prevent that.

They walked toward Liam's house. Ben felt a whisper on the wind he didn't like, sensed a tingle on his flesh. He glanced around uneasily but heard nothing except the rustle of leaves in the dawn breeze, the voices of cubs playing on the green, and the quiet laughter of the goblin brothers as they followed.

———

When they reached Liam's house, Rhianne saw that the porch had filled with Shifters. Liam and his mate, Dylan and Glory, Connor and Tiger-girl, Andrea the half-Fae Shifter, and with her the man who must be Sean Morrissey, the Guardian.

Sean resembled his brother, Liam, so much that Rhianne at first couldn't tell the two apart. She saw as she studied them that Sean had a different demeanor, somehow both more tense and more relaxed than Liam. The sword that dispatched Shifter souls and rendered their bodies dust was slung over his back.

With him stood another Shifter also carrying a sword. Rhianne couldn't place him, but Ben jumped when he saw him.

"That's Pierce Daniels. Guardian of the North Carolina Shiftertown. What's he doing so far off his patch?"

Pierce had reddish brown hair and watchful eyes. The Shifter in Rhianne identified him as Feline, but she wasn't certain what breed of cat.

The only Shifter missing was Tiger. Carly was there, lounging on a porch swing next to Connor, holding Seth and keeping an eye on Katriona, who wandered from her mother to

Carly and back, pausing to stare quizzically up at Millie, who stood a little apart from the others.

The mystery of the absent Tiger was solved when he barreled around from the back of the house, shifting as he ran. His half-Shifter, half-human beast was gigantic and ferocious.

"Here!" he roared and then sprinted, fully tiger to the rear of the house and the common ground there.

The Shifters glanced at each other in perplexity, then they began pouring off the porch in pursuit.

Ben followed Tiger at a run, Rhianne immediately behind him, the goblin brothers after her.

CHAPTER TWENTY-ONE

Rhianne panted after Ben as he sprinted behind Tiger. Tiger charged down the green, the huge Bengal scattering cubs before him. Not to hurt them, Rhianne realized, but to herd them from the middle of the common area, a long strip of grass dotted with live oaks.

Tiger gave a great barking growl, and the cubs, understanding his warning, ran toward the houses. The other Shifters, taking Tiger's cue, began to snatch up cubs and carry them away from the green.

What Rhianne didn't understand was why. She saw no danger in the middle of Shiftertown, saw nothing at all except trees moving in the morning sunshine, green grass just starting to brown for autumn.

Almost as soon as her bewildered thoughts formed, a shiver began deep inside her. A wrongness oozed over the middle of Shiftertown. It was invisible, soundless, scentless, but the sensation was there.

The Shifters felt it, voices sharp as they rushed cubs indoors. Tiger sent the last cub back toward Liam with a nudge of his paw, then charged to the center of the green, heading for a circle of trees.

"The ley line," Ben yelled to Rhianne over his shoulder. "Crap!"

Ripples of nothing spread from the center of the trees, shimmering in the air.

Ben slammed to a halt and Rhianne barely stopped herself from crashing into him. Around them chaos reigned as Shifters ran and dodged, grabbed cubs to shove them inside houses or threw off clothes and shifted. A gray wolf began an ear-piercing howl. Calling other wolves, Rhianne realized.

The ripples hit Tiger, terrible snarls tearing from his throat. He slowed, as though he'd rushed into thick glue, his limbs paddling but his body grinding to a full stop.

Then came a flash so bright Rhianne had to slam her eyes closed and turn away. Shifters screamed around her as the light seared the air.

She pried her eyes open again and saw the mucus-like ripples envelop Tiger like a cocoon. Then Tiger vanished.

"Fuck!" Ben yelled.

Rhianne couldn't speak, her throat going dry. Tiger, the indestructible, the wise, the one who'd understood Rhianne almost instantly. *Gone.*

A keening rent the air. Tiger-girl raced toward the circle of trees, desperately pursued by Connor. Carly came after them, Seth screeching in her arms.

"No!" Tiger-girl's wail cut over the growling, snarling, and howling of the other Shifters. She threw off her shirt, the rest of her clothes falling from her as she shifted into a Bengal tiger nearly the size of her father.

"Shit, shit, shit," Connor snarled. He loped after her, shifting as he ran into a black-maned lion, his mane not fully grown. Connor sprinted on powerful limbs, trying to catch up to Tiger-girl. She outran him, leaping toward the ripples where Tiger had disappeared.

Ben caught Carly before she could run after them. "No," he said sternly.

"Let me go." Carly writhed in Ben's strong grip. Her son kicked and squirmed, Carly barely able to hold him. "He's my mate. He's my *mate*."

"Your mate who'd kick my ass if anything happened to you," Ben growled. "Stay. Let Shifters mess with this."

"Whatever the hell *this* is," Carly shouted back at him.

"My father," Rhianne said quietly. "He's come for me."

Ben sent her a grim look. "Your *step*father. He didn't sire you. So I don't have to feel guilty when I rip his heart out."

"What are you talking about?" Carly demanded. "How could anyone get through the gate? Fionn is there holding it, isn't he?"

Rhianne's body flooded with coldness. "This Fionn is only a *hoch alfar* lord. Ivor de Erkkonen could cut him down without trying."

Andrea, Fionn's daughter, must have understood this, because she was racing toward the clearing herself, Sean in hot pursuit. The other Guardian, Pierce, sprinted after them.

Dylan Morrissey was the only one not rushing around or shifting or shouting. He had halted a few feet from Ben and Rhianne, hands on hips, watching the confusion with emotionless eyes.

"Dylan, honey." Carly wrenched herself from Ben and marched to him. "You'd better be thinking of a way to rescue my mate."

Dylan glanced at her, not in rage but understanding.

His own mate, Glory, slid clothes from her tall and beautifully curved body, dropped into wolf form, and moved off to join the other wolves gathering on the opposite side of the green. The wolf pack parted to let her in, welcoming her.

Dylan turned to Rhianne. "Ivor?" he asked.

Rhianne's lips were stiff. "It's me he wants. If I return to Faerie with him, your Shifters will be safe."

Ben's furious, "The fuck!" was joined by a chorus of "No way in hell," and other negations from Carly, the goblin brothers, and Kim who'd tensely joined them.

"Rhianne, love, if you go to him, he'll squelch you," Ben snapped. "Or imprison you, and then I'll have to rescue you again. It was no cake walk the first time."

"Cake walk?" Even in the midst of terror, Ben could befuddle her.

"I mean it wasn't easy. A shitload of trouble. Not doing it again, because you're not going anywhere. You're *my* mate, remember?"

Rhianne stilled as joy eased through her cold and fear. Ben's denial of what was between them had evaporated.

She smiled widely. "I remember."

Ben's face went scarlet as he realized what he'd said. "We can argue about that later. *This* argument is an extension of the first one. You are not going anywhere near that asshole Ivor. He'll either kill you or use you, and you know it."

"And if I don't go?" Rhianne planted her hands on her hips. "You'll let him destroy good Shifters like Tiger? What about all the cubs sitting here, vulnerable? What about Tiger-girl and Connor?"

Both Tiger-girl and Connor had been stopped outside the circle of trees by Liam, who'd become a giant lion, his black mane full. Between himself, Sean, and Pierce, the two older cubs and Andrea were not getting through.

"I didn't say I'd let the dickhead wreak havoc," Ben said. "I'm going to go all goblin on his ass."

"Sweet!" Darren shouted, and Cyril high-fived him. "We're with you. Millie? You in?"

"Of course I am." Millie opened her handbag. She carefully

took off her glasses, folded them, tucked them into a glasses case, and set the glasses case back into her purse. "I will happily join you boys in kicking Fae butt."

"Tuil Erdannan," Rhianne said. "Never forget that."

"You are Tuil Erdannan too, dear," Millie said.

Darren and Cyril high-fived each other again and laughed.

"Meanwhile, my mate is the Goddess knows where." Carly bounced on her toes, barely containing herself. Rhianne had to admire her self-restraint. "Dylan?"

"Working on it, lass." Dylan had his cell phone in hand and started punching in numbers. He lifted it to his ear as someone on the other end answered. "Kendrick? You busy? Good. We have ourselves a little situation."

———

ONCE UPON A TIME, BEN HAD BEEN DRAGGED FROM HIS workshop by Fae soldiers using spells, ropes, bronze chains, shackles, and anything else the *hoch alfar* bastards could put their hands on in order to capture Ben. They'd taken him to a hill and tied him to a post, hoisting him up to hang from the chains and observe their savagery.

The *hoch alfar* had proceeded to put to death hundreds of goblin warriors, using explosives and magic. The goblins had fought valiantly to the last, but they'd not been able to save themselves.

The *hoch alfar* had then rounded up the survivors— women, children, and men too feeble to have joined the battle, and marched them through a ley line gate to the human world.

As the procession had faded through the tear in the sky, the *hoch alfar* had taken Ben from the pole and sent him through the gap, the last of his kind to go. All others were dead.

"This is what being friend to the *dokk alfar* has gained

you," the *hoch alfar* general had sneered, and then he'd shut the gate behind Ben forever.

The *hoch alfar* sorcerers had cast spells on the gates and the ley lines, barring Ben from ever entering Faerie again.

The small group of goblins in this world that he'd found and joined hadn't castigated him, though they, like Millie, blamed him. At the time, they were too busy trying to stay alive to do much arguing.

Monsters, the humans who saw the goblin refugees in their true forms called them. Devils from hell, come to devour their children. Goblins were hunted and slain.

Ben and the others soon learned to change their appearance, but even this was not enough. Most human communities at the time were small and close-knit, everyone knowing everyone. Strangers were unwelcome unless affiliated with someone familiar.

So, the goblins scattered, searching for larger cities where they might fade into the crowd.

Ben had become a master of dissembling, inventing connections and plausible stories about where he came from to relax the humans frightened of the unknown. They had reason to fear, as a thousand years ago, bandits and raiders cut swaths across countrysides, killing indiscriminately. Humans had been very much like the *hoch alfar* in that respect.

Ben had soon lost track of all other goblins. He'd done his best to hide and fit in, laughing with humans over their ale and weeping in desolation alone at night.

Later, he'd met Shifters, beings who also lived in hiding. Some trusted Ben, some didn't, but things had grown easier after he'd come to know them. The Shifters had won their freedom from the Fae, but they'd been forced to retreat to the human world, and like Ben, learn to survive there.

Shifters weren't as long-lived as Ben, and he'd mourned the passing of very good friends. He'd moved from country to country, town to town, never staying long enough for people to realize he didn't age. He couldn't afford to make ties or put down roots.

Throughout his life in the human world, Ben had never entered a long-term relationship with a woman. He'd had plenty of sex, yes. Coupling had been a way to forget his troubles for a time, but the ladies were never permanent partners. They shared his bed to escape their own loneliness, and then they moved on. Ben had fancied himself in love a time or two, but he'd always believed he'd never start a real family.

And then he'd met Rhianne.

Ben now watched Rhianne draw herself up, fear and determination warring in her eyes. Her stepfather had come for her, would kill to get to her. Rhianne couldn't let that happen. She was telling herself that she needed to sacrifice herself so that the Shifters, and Ben, wouldn't be hurt.

Ben couldn't lose her. Not after the years and years of emptiness, of searching for something he could never have.

He did not want the Shifters, his friends, people who'd aided and supported him, to be casualties of this personal war. But nor would he sacrifice Rhianne to save them.

He had to save them all instead.

There was only one thing to do. One thing that Shifters would understand, and would instinctively champion.

"Rhianne." Ben raised his voice to be heard over the maelstrom that was beginning. "Rhianne mac Aodha, before the Goddess and in front of witnesses, *I claim you as mate!*"

CHAPTER TWENTY-TWO

R hianne jolted as Ben's words fell around her. At the same time, she felt something inside her *click,* as though two parts of her that had always been asunder at last joined.

"I don't ..." Rhianne coughed, found her voice. Her heart skipped and thumped, her chest tight. "I don't know what I'm supposed to do."

Ben said nothing, only held her with his gaze. His dark eyes, usually so unfathomable, now showed her triumph as well as hope and a little bit of trepidation.

Dylan, the phone to his ear, glanced over at her. "You don't have to do anything." He snarled into the phone, "Where is that damned polar bear?"

"That damned polar bear is right here," boomed a large voice.

A huge man in a long duster strode toward them from Liam's yard. Two thin braids of white hair strung with beads hung to his shoulders, the hair on his head cut short and white-blond. In contrast, his trim beard was black, and so were his eyes.

At his side was a young woman with very dark hair, intense gray eyes, and a Sword of the Guardian slung across her back.

The big man halted a few feet from Rhianne. Ben had fallen silent, waiting, body quiet.

"You can answer one of two ways," the tall man said to Rhianne. "You can agree to accept the mate claim, or you can tell him to go to hell." He swung to Ben. "How are you, old friend? I catch you at an awkward moment?"

"Zander," Ben said tightly.

The young woman addressed Rhianne in a melodious voice. "You're not obligated to accept the mate claim, and you don't have to say anything yet. But the tentative claim keeps all other males from being able to take you for themselves. I think Ben just wants the ability to tell you what to do." She smiled at Rhianne. "Ben's not Shifter, but he's picked up a lot of their habits."

"This is *my* mate, Rae," Zander said. "Like she lets me tell *her* what to do." He peered at Rhianne. "Who are you, by the way?"

"Lady Aisling's daughter," Ben said, while Rhianne stood tongue-tied.

"Yeah?" Zander's black eyes opened wide. Ancient wisdom lurked in that gaze, but Zander strove to hide it under his banter. "Cool. Hey, Dylan, why are you still on the phone?"

"Reinforcements." Dylan had punched in another number. "Tiger's missing. Sucked into something near the ley line."

Zander's eyes widened in true alarm. "Seriously? No shit. Then why are you standing around? Rae, sword time."

"I'm not standing around," Dylan growled. "I'm rounding up my army, and then we'll go take down a Tuil Erdannan who's made the mistake of becoming a pain in my ass."

"Sounds like fun. You round up and I'll go check out what happened to Tiger."

"No." Rhianne quickly put herself in front of Zander. Ben joined her, his warmth at her side bolstering.

"Agreed," Ben told Zander. "If you rush after Tiger, we'll lose you too, and we need you. You'll have to be rearguard."

Zander's dark brows snapped together, but Rae touched his shoulder before he could speak.

"They're right, sweetie. A healer and a Guardian have to be held in reserve."

Even Carly, hovering on the edge of the conversation, anguish in her eyes, nodded. "When we find Tiger, he might need healing. Please, Zander."

Rhianne noted that Carly said *when*, not *if*.

Zander glared mutinously but finally heaved a sigh. "Gotcha. Good advice—don't run to the spot where the most formidable Shifter ever created disappeared without a trace and see if it happens to me too. But we can scout." He brightened. "Scouting with stealth. Coming Ben? Rhianne? You're something different, aren't you?" He looked Rhianne up and down. "I have the feeling I missed a staff meeting about you, but I haven't been checking my messages."

"We were in Alaska," Rae explained. "Fishing."

"Yep. My old friend Piotr looks after my boat, but I like to take it out once in a while. Have alone time on the water with my mate." Zander winked.

How he'd known to transport himself from Alaska to Austin and so quickly, Rhianne didn't understand, but she didn't ask. Zander had called her something different, but she sensed he was too.

Ben's hand found Rhianne's. He squeezed her fingers, the new bond between them weaving around Rhianne's heart.

"I'll show you where he disappeared," Ben said. "We'll find him, Carly. I promise you."

"Find him, haul his ass home, make him good as new,"

Zander said, pointing his forefingers at her. "You sit tight, sweetheart."

Carly nodded tearfully. Seth, in her arms, wore a scowl on his baby face, his eyes the gold of his father's. Rhianne wondered how much he understood—Shifter cubs seemed at the same time both younger than their human and Fae counterparts and more astute.

As they approached the green, Rhianne's sense of forbidding grew. The ripples had ceased, but the center of the common was deathly still. Wind ruffled Rhianne's hair as they walked, but no leaf stirred within the circle of oaks.

Just outside the ring of trees, Sean had his arms around Andrea, as though keeping his mate from darting into the circle. "Father!" Andrea cried in desperation. "Where are you?"

The only answer was silence.

"This is bad," Ben murmured to Rhianne. "They rely on Fionn to be a bastion between this world and Faerie. *Hoch alfar* have come through before to be their usual bastard selves."

Rhianne drew Ben apart from the others. "If Ivor is doing this, then no one here is safe. Tell the Shifters to get out. If Dylan brings in reinforcements, those are just more Shifters who will die."

Ben scowled at her. "Don't start telling me again that you should run through the gate in the ley line and sacrifice yourself for the rest of us. I'm not going to lose you, Rhianne. I don't care if Shiftertown is razed to dust—you're not giving yourself up."

"There are children here. Cubs. Ivor will care nothing for them."

"I agree the cubs need to be protected." Ben raised his voice. "Sean, we should get all the cubs indoors on the far edges of Shiftertown."

"Just what I was thinking," Sean answered. "Andrea, love,

you can see to that, can't you? We'll do everything we can for
Fionn."

Andrea nodded, wiping away tears. "If Fionn is ..." She
gulped. "... compromised, then we have to save the cubs."

"Connor and Tiger's daughter included," Ben said.

That pair were currently prowling outside the ring of trees,
wisely keeping their distance from where Tiger had disappeared. Rhianne had heard the frantic note in Tiger-girl's voice
when Tiger had vanished, as though she'd watched her world
collapse. It spoke much of Connor that he managed to keep her
from simply following Tiger and vanishing with him.

What exactly had happened? Rhianne scented no air of
Faerie, did not feel its magic. She sensed the gate itself between
the trees, but it was closed.

Andrea broke from Sean and headed for Connor. Sean, his
face bleak, turned and made for the houses.

"Sean and Andrea will look after the cubs," Ben told
Rhianne in a low voice. "They all will." He took her hand
again. "I'd love to tell you to evacuate too."

"It won't matter." Rhianne knew this in her heart. "Ivor will
find me wherever I am. I'm not certain why he wants me so
much, but I know he'll hunt me down." She turned to Ben. "If
you stay with me, he'll take you too."

Ben shrugged. "Then he takes me too. Good thing I have a
few tricks up my sleeve." He wriggled his hand, his arm bared
by his T-shirt.

"Ben, do *not* go up against one of the strongest Tuil
Erdannan alive. My own mother couldn't best him."

Ben sobered. "I know. But you're my mate. It means I
defend you, no matter what. Do you expect me to say, *Okay
sweetie, you go face the badass, and I'll be over here downing a
brew. Let me know how it goes?*"

"Not what I mean."

Zander, passing them, shook his head. "It's the mate's

dilemma, Rhianne. I lose my mate or I lose my life. We all have to choose that sooner or later." He paused. "So this bad guy is your stepdad? Wow. I really did miss a staff meeting."

He strode on, Rae at his side, to examine the trees and the stillness within.

Andrea had finally convinced Connor and Tiger-girl to follow her toward the houses, Andrea's face grim.

"Warrior." Millie's sensible voice called. She approached them, followed by Darren and Cyril, and addressed Ben. "You'll not have to face the Tuil Erdannan alone. We've talked about it, and we're pledging ourselves to you."

Ben gave them a puzzled look. "Pledging? I thought you blamed me for everything bad that's happened to you."

"We blame you for giving the *hoch alfar* a target," Millie said primly. "But that was then. This is now. You are the warrior, and we will fight with you."

Millie, glasses restored, every hair in place, did not seem like a woman who should be in a fight of any kind. She should retreat home and roll bandages for the wounded instead, perhaps bake them a pie.

But Rhianne had seen Ben's true form, and Millie's as well, when she'd begun to attack Ben at the haunted house. Neither were weak.

"Yeah," Darren put in. "You'll need some goblins on your side. The badass-est of the badasses."

Cyril nodded. "So, we're pledging. It's what our people did in the old days, so says our mum. She was there. She's very old."

Millie sent him a severe look. "My son is a smartass, but he is correct. I am even older than Ben. In the bygone days, we'd pledge our loyalty to the warrior who could lead us. Which right now is you, Ben. One for all and all for one." She adjusted her glasses. "I stole that from *The Three Musketeers*, but the sentiment is the same."

Ben's expression was a study of longing and alarm. Rhianne

sensed that he wanted to accept Millie's pledge, that it was important to him.

He also worried he wouldn't live up to the pledge, but he was wrong about that. Rhianne had come to realize that Ben had more strength than anyone understood, perhaps more even than Tiger. He'd be formidable in battle, underestimated by all, until it was too late.

Even Ivor, Rhianne thought smugly, would be surprised by him.

"Better accept," Darren said. "Our mother is one determined lady. She usually gets what she wants."

"I don't want to lead you if it's to your deaths," Ben said quickly.

"Young man." Millie drew herself up. "You let us decide that for ourselves. We've been in this world a long time. A very long time. If we meet our ends following you in a just cause, so be it. I believe slaying a Tuil Erdannan too big for his britches is a just cause. No offense, dear," she added to Rhianne.

Rhianne nodded absently, riveted on the dynamic between Ben and the three goblins.

She saw the moment Ben decided to embrace their loyalty. Something relaxed in him, a barrier softening that had been held in place too long.

"All right." Ben sighed as though resigned. "I guess I can't really stop you."

"Excellent. Please hold this, dear." Millie handed Rhianne her handbag. It was far heavier than the small bag appeared, and Rhianne made herself not peek inside in curiosity.

The four goblins drew together. Millie stretched out her right hand and her sons laid their right hands on hers. Ben, slowly, placed his on the top of the pile.

The hands changed from human to the gnarled, brutally strong ones of goblins. The rest of their bodies remained the same, but their hands became massive and powerful.

Millie began a chant, and the brothers joined in. Rhianne didn't understand the goblin language, but the words held force. The very air seemed to darken. Even Rhianne, an outsider, could feel the strength of the phrases.

Ben entered the chant, his rumbling baritone melding with the voices of the other three. The words rose, flowing around each other, knotting together in a bond of allegiance.

When the chant ended, all four hands returned to their human form. The four released each other, assuming casual poses as though nothing very significant had occurred.

"Okay then," Ben said. "Welcome to the team." As Darren and Cyril did a little victory dance, Ben pointed a blunt finger at them. "Before you get all hot to destroy our enemies, keep in mind, he neutralized *Tiger* right away." Ben broke off and gazed pensively at the circle of trees. "I sure hope the big guy is all right."

———

TIGER WATCHED. AND WAITED ...

CHAPTER TWENTY-THREE

Tiger couldn't move, couldn't speak, couldn't call out to Carly or his cubs to tell them he was all right.

But he could observe.

He'd been caught while shifting from tiger to his between-beast—or maybe the fabric of null-time-space had forced him to shift to it. Tiger wasn't quite certain. Somewhere in the back of his mind, he was puzzling that out.

He liked his half-beast, which was massive and deadly unless he decided to gentle it for his cubs. Seth liked to cuddle against his fur, and Tiger-girl seemed calmer when he touched her with his paw-hand.

"They don't know." A tall man with hair bright as flame and dark eyes like holes to nothing stood next to Tiger. The man could move and speak, all the things Tiger could not. "They have no idea what's to come."

The two of them gazed through the ripples of not-time the Fae had caused. It was like peering through thick glass, similar to the blocks used to build decorative walls but without as much distortion.

Tiger could clearly see his mate and Seth across the green

next to Dylan. Good. Dylan could protect Carly and his cub. He also saw Tiger-girl loping away with Connor and Andrea. Again good.

None could see him, though, and they were afraid.

"You will help me," the Tuil Erdannan said. Tiger knew he was Tuil Erdannan and not *hoch alfar* because of his scent. He even smelled arrogant. "They trust you. I will have the spawn of my treacherous wife under my thumb and use her to destroy all who oppose me."

Tiger did not answer, unable to move his mouth or work his larynx to push air across it.

"I need soldiers like you. Like you were meant to be." The Tuil Erdannan didn't bother speaking English, but Tiger understood him. When he'd been in Faerie to help Dimitri and Jaycee, he'd heard Tuil Erdannan words that his brain had stored and learned, which was how he'd been able to speak to Rhianne fluently in that language.

Tiger had been created to be a warrior to best all warriors. His original purpose, a noble one, had been to seek and rescue the stranded, but that purpose had been taken and perverted by ambitious men.

"You will help me." The man's air of disdain was sliced with the callousness of one who did not care whom he hurt. "You have no choice."

In his silence, Tiger couldn't growl, not in his throat. His mind, however, began a deep rumble, that of a tiger who was becoming very annoyed.

The Tuil Erdannan was wrong. Tiger had a choice. His creators had tried to breed him to be obedient. They'd stuck chips laced with magic into his brain that would make him so.

When Tiger had been abandoned, left alone for years, the chips had corrupted, and Tiger had broken the programming, replacing it with his own.

What everyone except Carly, and maybe Connor, did not

understand, was that everything Tiger did and had done since he'd been freed, was and had been his choice.

He could do nothing at the moment, imprisoned by this thick miasma, but Tiger had learned patience living through cold and lonely years in a cage. Patience was one of his strengths.

He could wait.

———

BEN JOINED THE RANKS DYLAN FORMED AROUND HIMSELF. Kim had persuaded Carly to return to the house with Seth, but the two ladies remained on the porch, not about to hide when their mates were in danger.

"What about the humans of this city?" Rhianne asked Ben in a low voice. "Shifter Bureau, and so forth. Won't they notice Shifters gearing up for battle?"

"They might," Ben said. "Unless your father has taken care of that. I notice no one has left Shiftertown since the ley line started acting up."

The sky overhead was a pale blue, a fine Texas autumn morning. At the edge of the horizon, however, clouds were forming, a dark ring encircling the blue, though they were a long way away. Storms blew up here quickly, or passed by altogether—it could go either way. Ben wondered if Ivor could manipulate the weather in this world and didn't like the implications if that were true.

Kendrick and his reinforcements had arrived. They'd shown up singly or in pairs to not draw the attention of human law enforcement. Kendrick's people, who'd started life as Shifters who'd escaped the roundup twenty-five years ago, lived in secret out in the empty lands west of here, and didn't wear real Collars.

Kendrick was a white tiger, a rare beast. He'd found himself a mate in the cute Addison, who'd come with him and joined Kim and Carly. Other human mates of Shifters migrated to Kim and Liam's house as well.

Dimitri and Jaycee, Kendrick's top trackers, along with a lion called Seamus, waved to Ben and Rhianne but stuck with Kendrick, listening to his orders.

Walker Danielson, in black fatigues, arrived with Rebecca, a Kodiak bear Shifter. All the bear Shifters of that household were present—Ronan, their leader; Scott, who'd just passed his Transition; and Francesca, who moved back and forth from this Shiftertown to Kendrick's compound. So was Olaf, an orphaned polar bear cub who apparently couldn't be persuaded to stay home.

"I want to fight too," Olaf declared. He had white hair and the same dark, soulful eyes as Zander.

"Olaf, honey," Carly called to him. "Why don't you come here and help me take care of Seth?"

Olaf debated as he gazed from Dylan lining up Shifters, to Ben and Rhianne, and then to Carly.

"Okay." Olaf trotted to the porch and bounded up the steps.

He was getting bigger every year, Ben reflected. In time, he'd be as huge as Zander. Wouldn't that be fun?

"Rhianne," Ben began.

Rhianne swung on him. "Don't you dare tell me to stay behind while you strike out in this hopeless battle. I'm the only one here who knows how to fight a Tuil Erdannan. The method is, don't fight them."

Ben lifted his hands. "I was going to say, *let's stick together, kid.* Or *two is better than one.*"

"Oh."

Ben closed the space between them and caressed her flushed cheek. "You're cute when you're embarrassed." He turned the touch into a caress and then a kiss. "But I really mean, let's stick *together*. No flying off on your own, trying to take down your stepdad by yourself. I want you next to me, where I can protect you."

"That's where I want to be. To protect *you*." Rhianne raised his hand to her lips. "After ... If there is an after ..."

"We can talk about it when after happens, if there's anything to talk about." He shook his head. "I know that people like us don't always get happily ever after. Sometimes all we can hope for is happy-for-now."

"I *am* happy now." Rhianne's voice went soft. "Or I would be if my stepfather hadn't decided to interfere." Her expression changed to that of an annoyed Tuil Erdannan. "I'm growing a little tired of that."

Ben grinned at her. "All right then. Let's kick his ass."

Rhianne's answering smile held Shifter ferocity. "Let's."

"And then go out for ice cream."

Rhianne considered this. "How about shrimp?" she asked, a roguish twinkle in her eyes.

She was adorable. "We'll argue about that when the time comes," Ben assured her. "Dylan? Where do you want us?"

———

Dylan formed the Shifters into a big circle around the ring of trees. They'd attack from all sides, he instructed. Shifter species were intermixed within squads, so that the strengths of each type of Shifter could be used to greatest advantage and the weaknesses of each guarded. Felines were swift, wolves savage and determined, and bears were just fucking big.

"I want everyone in Shifter or half-Shifter form." Dylan gave his orders in a voice that could be heard through the crowd. "Whichever way helps you fight your best. You won't have time for shifting once we start."

Clothes fluttered from the Shifters who were still in human form, and soon the common filled with lions, leopards, wolves, bears, and the jaguar that was Spike.

The Guardians were held in the rear. If there were Shifter casualties, Guardians would be needed to quickly dispatch Shifter souls to the Summerland, the afterlife. Sobering thought.

Dylan also asked Andrea, who had some healing ability, and Zander, to remain behind.

Zander rumbled. "You need another bear, Dylan. They're your strongest fighters, and sparse in this Shiftertown."

"You're the only one who can heal serious wounds," Dylan reminded him. "If you're taken out, who's going to save me when I have my stomach ripped open?"

"We can't risk you either, old timer," Zander said.

Dylan sent him a deadpan stare but didn't respond. "You have your orders," he called to the others. "Form up."

Shifters dispersed to take their positions.

"The Mongols did this," Ben observed as he moved with Rhianne to the north point, where they'd been assigned. "Surrounded their target with strength and struck without remorse."

"Who are the Mongols?" Rhianne began to unbutton her jeans to prepare to shift, which distracted Ben all to hell. "Do you think they could come to our aid?"

"This was more than eight hundred years ago," Ben said in amusement. "But I have to say, the Mongols would be handy right now. The *hoch alfar* could take archery lessons from them. The problem is, the Mongols would then turn around and take over *here*. They perfected pillaging and plundering and not in a good way. I should know. I was there when they sacked Samarkand. Things I wish I'd never seen." He grimaced, swiftly blocking out the memories.

Rhianne skimmed off her jeans then her T-shirt, and Ben forgot about the past, the present, and some of the future.

"Ivor will know we're coming, if we can even get to him," Rhianne said. "He's probably watching now, sizing up the Shifters and deciding how to destroy them with the least amount of effort."

"Most like." Ben studied the center of the clearing, where the ley line came to a point at the gate. A similar point happened in the haunted house, but the house decided when it opened and shut.

Rhianne, clad only in camisole and panties, glanced about shyly. The Shifters around her ignored her, either already animal, or in various stages of undress, preparing to shift.

"You can hide behind me to take off the rest of it," Ben told her. "Not that Shifters care." He shuddered. "Geez, I hope I'm not around when they all shift back. Shifters forget about clothes after a while. A nerve-wracking sight, dozens of male Shifters walking around with their ding-a-lings out, pretending everything is normal."

Rhianne shook with nervous laughter. "Their whats?"

"Their pride-and-joys," Ben amended. "But use me as a tree if you're bashful."

Rhianne stepped behind Ben, who promised himself he'd not glance over his shoulder while she stripped out of her underwear.

Ben broke the promise almost immediately and admired Rhianne's graceful body as she slid off the final pieces. The curve of her waist came into view, then the firmness of her breasts tipped with dark nipples.

Rhianne caught him looking, but she only flushed and didn't admonish him.

"I'm not sure I can do it," she whispered.

"Not sure you can do what?" Ben's voice was hoarse.

"Shift. Without going insane, or forgetting I'm me. How do they do it so easily?"

She glanced at Broderick McNaughton and his brother

Mason as they kicked off jeans and melted into the form of gray wolves.

"Practice." Ben faced her. "You did it easily at the park in New Orleans."

"Because all I could think about was saving you. I don't know how to shift when it's not instinctive."

"Remember what I showed you at the house?" Ben took her hands. "Concentrate on each move, find every part of yourself. Flow with it."

He placed himself in front of her, forcing himself not to look at her bare body. Her red lips parted, and Ben wanted nothing more than to kiss her, touch her, and take her down to the ground, to hell with the battle.

Ben held on to his self-control with difficulty and began the tai chi rhythm he'd taught her. Their hands went back and forth, Ben transferring energy to Rhianne, who then returned it to him. The connection between them filled his body with vitality.

Rhianne began to relax, to smile. Her eyes lost focus as she trained them on Ben, and her movements became more graceful.

What was a Tuil Erdannan deep down inside? Ben saw the truth in Rhianne's eyes, a being of light, of pure energy, formed long ago into a shape that would make them slightly less terrifying. The shape caused others to underestimate them, to the others' peril.

Mixed with the Tuil Erdannan effervescence was the more solid, earthy energy of the Shifter. Strength plus unimaginable magic.

The combination was deadly.

Ben realized that this combination was why Ivor wanted his hands on Rhianne. Ivor doubtless had discovered that Rhianne was half-Shifter, and he'd see in her a weapon he'd want to bring under his control.

If Ivor had Rhianne in his arsenal, he could be even more powerful than he already was.

This was why Ivor had helped Walther le Madhug kidnap Rhianne and try to force her into marriage. To breed more part-Shifter, part-Fae, part-Tuil Erdannan warriors.

The fury that thought unleashed had no equal. Ben growled, the terrifying beast inside *him* pushing to get out.

He held Rhianne's gaze. "Let's go end that bastard."

Rhianne nodded once, then her head went back, and the beautiful eagle poured over her frame. Rhianne didn't change like most Shifters, whose limbs and faces gradually morphed, ears and tails emerging. Instead, her body shimmered, feathers sprang forth, and the form of the eagle suddenly inhabited the space where she'd been.

She turned her head, studying Ben with her brown-black eyes, the flicker of Rhianne's humor somewhere inside them.

The Shifters in the vicinity turned and stared. They'd never seen a raptor Shifter, and they were understandably curious.

Ben had to wonder about Rhianne's true father. Had he been a raptor as well, an unknown Shifter species? Or had the Tuil Erdannan inside her bent her DNA and decided her Shifter shape?

Dylan barked an order, and the Shifters moved into formation. Inexact formation, it was true, because Shifters didn't fight like ordinary soldiers. They remained in loose alignments, the better to fight the way each were best able.

Ben, the goblins, and Rhianne were in a group of their own. Ben had joked to Dylan that they didn't have to pair up with Shifters to balance out strengths and weaknesses, because goblins had no weaknesses. Well, except for enormous egos, but they'd have to live with that. Dylan hadn't laughed.

Dylan gave the final order to advance before tossing off the last of his clothes and shifting into a black-maned lion. Dylan as human showed signs of his age with graying hair and a few lines on his face, but the lion appeared as formidable and vigorous as his sons.

Dylan's nearly three hundred years of existence could be seen in his eyes, however, the wisdom and experience he'd gained—as well as the pain—from leading his family through every tragedy and triumph of his long life.

Ben and the goblins remained in human form. They'd discussed things and decided not to change until the last minute, keeping their true abilities under wraps. Ben had also strapped to his arm a pad made of wadded up T-shirts Carly had brought him.

Rhianne fluttered upward and settled gently on Ben's outstretched arm. She was about double the size of a wild golden eagle, and heavy, but she carefully gripped his arm in such a way that her talons wouldn't gouge him.

"These are Tiger's T-shirts," Carly told Ben cheerfully before she withdrew.

"Great," Ben answered. Rhianne had already torn through a few layers. "Which of us gets to explain this to him?"

Ben would be happy to see the big guy at all. Carly's eyes had held strain when she'd spoken, but she hadn't given up, Ben knew. She and Tiger had the mate bond, and she'd know if that had been broken.

Ben studied Rhianne. Would today's battle sever the mate bond that had begun between them?

As the Shifters closed in on the ring of trees, Ben wondered what Dylan had in mind. They were preparing for an attack, but an attack of what? The ground inside the circle remained empty.

The Shifters milled uneasily as they advanced, holding to their groups, but growling their impatience. They liked to strike, shred, and get back to sleeping in the sun or having sex with their mates, not do a prolonged stalk.

Rhianne was silent, occasionally ruffling her feathers or stretching out her wings to keep her balance.

Dylan gave the great barking growl of a lion, and the Shifters halted, quieting.

Dylan shifted back to his human form. Andrea darted forward and handed him something, then retreated to stand with Sean and the other Guardians, who were still in human form, and Zander, who'd shifted to polar bear. Sean held his sword loosely in front of him, and Pierce and Rae had drawn theirs.

Ben understood what Dylan was doing. Someone needed to open the gate in the ley line, and Dylan had volunteered himself. Andrea must have handed him a Fae talisman, since something Fae had to be used to open the gate. Strong Shifters —Ronan, Spike, Liam, Ellison—surrounded Dylan to protect him from whatever waited for them on the other side.

Dylan's task was more dangerous than that of any other Shifter today, and by the tension in his shoulders, he was fully aware. But there was no other way. They had to find Tiger and stop the threat before it fully manifested.

It spoke much of Dylan that he did not command another Shifter to do this. Glory hovered near the edge of the trees, her gray wolf's eyes riveted on him. She'd be next to him, Ben knew, but Dylan had likely ordered her to stay back.

Dylan moved the piece of silver in his hand to the place where the gate should be.

"Knock knock," Ben heard Sean mutter. "Anyone home?"

A high-pitched whine sprang to life, growing louder and more piercing by the second. Shifters, with their superior hearing, cringed and snarled, shaking heads and trying not to flee from the noise. Dylan held his ground but snapped at the Shifters around him to get back.

Once the whine passed beyond human hearing range, but not Shifters', the ripple of magic that had swallowed Tiger blasted from the point, enveloping all Shifters, including the Guardians and Zander, within it.

They slowed, and stopped, suspended in mid-leap, shake, or howl. Silence dropped like a switch had been thrown.

Ben, Rhianne, and the goblin family, in the rear, backpedaled from the ripples, which ceased a foot away from them.

Carly and friends cried out from the porch, as did other mates and cubs who'd been watching from a safe distance. Rhianne added her eagle's screech to their screams.

Ben's heart pounded as he scanned the circle. The Shifters faded with each pulse of the ripple, as though thick glass layered itself over them.

"Son of a *bitch*," Darren muttered.

The ripples parted. Out of them strode a tall man, his long red hair glowing like fire, a circlet of silver on his head.

"Daughter." His voice boomed across the green. He walked past the unmoving, dimming Shifters, ignoring them utterly. He halted a few yards from where Ben held Rhianne, the goblins hovering behind them.

"That word tastes foul in my mouth," Ivor de Erkkonen sneered. "I've known your secret for some time now, Rhianne. You will come with me at once, or all of these creatures ..." He waved disdainfully at the Shifters. "They will die. So will the goblin." He fixed eyes blacker than night on the eagle.

"*Choose.*"

CHAPTER TWENTY-FOUR

Rhianne launched herself skyward, the shriek of her eagle rending the air as rage boiled inside her.

How *dare* Ivor threaten her mate? How dare he threaten all the friends she'd made in her stay here, and all *their* mates and cubs. How dare he terrorize and threaten her *mother*.

She brought a word of power to mind. Could she use it in this form, when she couldn't speak?

As Ben might say, worth a shot.

Rhianne felt the force of the word welling up inside her. When the piercing cry came out of her mouth she realized that the syllables of it didn't matter. It was the intent, the will, that contained the magic.

The power flew straight at Ivor, who watched it speed toward him without concern.

This word had shriveled the snakes Ivor had sent, rendering them ash. Ivor, on the other hand, calmly batted it aside with a word of his own.

The wave of power split and crashed into the thick, suspended ripples of nothing. Bits of the magic that contained the Shifters splintered off, and the magic of the words died.

Rhianne blinked. She'd known Ivor was strong, but he'd countered her without breaking a sweat.

A cold smile spread over Ivor's face, and he shouted another word of power back to her.

Rhianne rent the air with her wings, flying frantically out of the way. The light from Ivor's magic flashed past her, singeing the tips of her feathers. Rhianne lost her balance but thrust out her wings, catching the wind to soar high. The power the word unleashed struck a large rock that was instantly pulverized.

Rhianne looked down as she flew, her eagle vision sharply focusing on one thing at a time. Ivor, gloating. Ben, roaring his fury, charging him. And a *hoch alfar* who stepped out of the rift that led to Faerie, an arrow knocked to his bow.

The *hoch alfar* took aim at Rhianne, and shot.

Hoch alfar were famous for their archery. Walther le Madhug was a legend even other *hoch alfar* admired. He'd won many honors with his ability, and he'd boasted to Rhianne about the number of animals he'd slaughtered with his skill.

Rhianne dove as soon as she spotted Walther, and so wasn't where his arrow had been aimed, but her feathers ruffled in the breeze of its passing.

Her rage honed to one thought, as sharp as her eagle's vision. Walther, who'd kidnapped her from her mostly peaceful existence and thrust her in a dungeon to await his evil intentions—Walther, she could kill.

She streaked toward him, turning at the last minute to drive her talons at his face. Walther smacked at her in panic with his bow, and in the next instant, Ivor blasted Rhianne with another word of power.

Rhianne dodged but the power dealt her a glancing blow. She tumbled end over end down the green, only saving herself from crashing as a mess of bones and feathers by hurriedly thrusting out her wings and gliding to the ground. She wished she'd had more time for flying lessons before this.

Thunder rumbled in the distance, a roll that went on for some time. The clouds on the horizon had drawn closer, the sky blue-black in all directions.

Rhianne righted herself. She'd been flung a long way from the ring of trees, almost to the end of the houses that lined the common. One of the houses bore a picture window, through which she spied the white-haired boy, Olaf, watching her with wide black eyes.

As Rhianne shook out her wings and regained her equilibrium, Olaf waved.

Behind him was Tiger-girl, her wildness barely contained, her golden gaze meeting Rhianne's.

Find him.

Rhianne understood the growl that she couldn't truly hear. Another rumble of thunder sounded, as though Tiger-girl's demand had triggered it.

Rhianne acknowledged them both with her eagle's cry, then shot into the air with renewed strength, winging back to the battle.

———

FEAR AND FURY ROSE IN BEN AS HE WATCHED IVOR'S MAGIC hurl Rhianne away. His heart beat again when he saw her catch herself and land without mishap, and his anger roiled anew.

Fuck this crap. It was time a Tuil Erdannan found out what happened when he enraged a goblin.

Ben didn't bother, like Shifters, to undress. When Ben took on a new form, he didn't actually shift, he simply became it.

One of his forms resembled a redoubtable ancient tree. The other was a monster from hell.

Ben's clothes simply vanished. His body changed in an

instant from that of the affable Ben with cool ink to a giant, massively muscled, hard-faced, hard-skinned, hideous nightmare.

Goblins were creatures of the forests, rising from the bones of the earth and the roots of trees. *Dokk alfar* often claimed they were the oldest race in Faerie, but goblins had been there to watch *dokk alfar*—the dark Fae, the iron workers, the thorn in the *hoch alfar's* flesh—emerge from their caves.

Goblins were born of the earth itself, creatures from the dawn of time, guardians of the forests. They'd grown into immensely magical beings who lived for centuries and hid their true natures.

They'd become complacent, Ben had witnessed, certain they were too strong for the *hoch alfar* to throw down.

Ben himself had been flattered when the *dokk alfar* had asked him to create the *karmsyern*, which he, drawing on the magics of rocks and trees, plus the iron flowing in a molten river far beneath the surface, could easily create. Why not build a talisman that could stop the *hoch alfar* from destroying the *dokk alfar*? Why not enjoy being a total pain in the *hoch alfar's* ass?

The humans had a saying: *Pride goeth before a fall.* And fall the goblins had done.

Not entirely, though. Ben had survived. As had Millie, and with her, her sons.

Millie had removed her glasses once more and set down her purse. Darren and Cyril were already changing.

Ben didn't wait for them. He sprinted for Ivor, liking the surprise on the Tuil Erdannan's face to see a wall of dark-muscled fury barreling straight at him.

Ivor tried another word of power. Ben broke the flash of it with his fist.

A roll of thunder boomed across the land. Maybe they'd get lucky and Ivor would be struck by lightning.

Ben immediately thought of a way to make the annoying

Tuil Erdannan a lightning rod. It would hurt Ben too, but what the hell?

Conditions had to be right, though. For now, Ben would settle for simply beating the shit out of the guy.

Ivor shouted as Ben neared him. Not a word of power, but a bellow of rage. He drew a slender sword that glowed with magic.

Next to him, Walther le Idiot shot arrows rapidly at Ben. Each glanced off Ben's hard body. Moron.

You can shoot at an ancient tree or a rock all you want. We don't care.

Ben yelled his own war cry and slammed himself into Ivor. Ivor, a seasoned warrior, kept to his feet, spun from Ben, and struck him with his sword. The magic in it cut and bruised Ben's hide, and damn it, that *hurt*.

Ben bashed at Ivor with his fists, a boxer fighting a swordsman. He'd have laughed any other time.

Ivor had grown larger. He now matched Ben in height, wielding his sword in expert strokes. Ben would have to break the sticker before he could take Ivor down.

Walther had given up trying to help Ivor with Ben and started shooting at the other three goblins. Darren and Cyril laughed, and from the corner of his eye, Ben saw the two catching arrows and breaking them. Millie caught them too but set them neatly aside. Walther was probably about to pee his pants.

Rhianne, with the cry of her wild eagle, soared toward them. She passed overhead, ducking within the ring of trees, and plunged her talons toward Ivor.

Walther swung around, rapidly fitting his bow with another arrow, and Rhianne had to swerve out of his way.

Ivor slapped the bow down. "Leave her alive."

Walther dropped the bow, but a cunning look crossed his

face. He reached up and abruptly grabbed at Rhianne, trying to catch her bodily.

He got scratched with talons for his troubles. Walther stumbled back with a curse, blood on his arms, then he snatched up his bow to beat her away from him.

"Keep them off me," Ivor yelled at him.

Walther wiped away the streaming blood and resumed shooting arrows at the other goblins as Ben went for Ivor.

"Enough!" Ivor grew still taller, the might of the Tuil Erdannan flowing from him.

He roared another word of power, and Ben's entire body suddenly burst into flame.

Rhianne shrieked. She hurled herself between Ivor and Ben, the impact knocking Ben aside. Ivor reached for her, but Rhianne repulsed him with her talons and flapped hard skyward.

Ben had no choice but to get the hell away from the trees, drop to the ground, and roll around like a fool. He let his body shrink back to his human form—less surface area to burn.

His tough skin had deflected the fire so that when he rolled in the damp dirt, he came away with only a few minor singes. They stung like hell though.

"Asshole," Ben snarled as he gained his feet. "You trying to take me out a millimeter at a time?"

That could be exactly what Ivor wanted to do, Ben realized. Ivor couldn't strike down the tough goblin, but he could dismantle him a chink here and a chink there.

Rhianne circled high above, her cries full of anger and anguish. The goblins were busy dodging arrows from the maniacal *hoch alfar*. Ivor had returned to the circle of trees. Ben needed to get back there and stop whatever evil Ivor was planning.

Thunder rumbled.

Chime.

The clear tone of Lady Aisling's crystal vibrated the air.

"Shit." Ben started to reach for his pocket and remembered he wasn't wearing any clothes. He called them back from the ether, the sudden feel of denim and cotton heavy on his skin.

Chime!

Ben dug the crystal from his pocket, where it still resided. "Lady A.?" he yelled.

"Yes, it is I. Where is my daughter?"

Ben gazed up at the speck in the sky that was Rhianne. "I'd say about a thousand feet up. Maybe fifteen hundred. Hard to tell. Are you okay?"

"I am well, now that my unlamented husband has departed. I managed to throw him out, with the help of my staff."

"Good. We were about to charge in and rescue you."

"Which would have been quite futile. Ivor can easily obliterate you. He is keeping Rhianne alive on purpose."

"Yeah, I figured. He wants to use her to create more Tuil Erdannan Shifters."

"He does, indeed." Lady Aisling's sigh came over the crystal. "I thought by not explaining her origins, I was keeping her safe. She never showed any signs of the Shifter in her, and I believed Ivor remained ignorant. But it seems I was wrong."

"What happened to Rhianne's real father?"

"Happened?" Lady Aisling's tone turned perplexed. "Nothing happened to him. He's alive and well, in France. We meet from time to time."

Explained all her shopping trips to Paris, then. "Are you really all right? Dickhead—I mean, Ivor—didn't hurt you?"

"He did hurt me, but I weathered it. Am weathering it. What I need for you to do is keep my daughter safe. It is what I have charged you with." Her voice turned steely. "Don't fail me, Ben."

"I want her safe more than you understand. Any hints on how to fight your ex?"

"With magic. Lots and lots of magic. Your Tiger man should be able to help."

"Tiger man is down. Or at least, trapped in some sort of warped air, or space, or whatever."

"Is he?" Lady Aisling's tone became thoughtful. "Or is he?"

"I don't know. Can't see anything. What kind of magic can we use? Does Rhianne have it?"

"She has more than she believes. It is why Ivor wants to trap and use her."

"Noted. Any way you can cross over to this world and help us bring him down?"

"That would be a mistake," Lady Aisling said decidedly. "If he and I began to battle there, it might destroy half the human world. I rather like that world the way it is."

"Yeah, me too," Ben said.

"Then we understand each other. Do take—"

She broke off as a male voice cut over hers, growling words in Tuil Erdannan Ben didn't understand.

"Who the hell is that?" Ben demanded.

Lady Aisling returned. "My gardener, Akseli. He is being very solicitous of me. Insists I cease speaking to you and rest. My housekeeper is glaring daggers, so I will go. Bring my daughter to me in one piece."

With that admonition, the crystal in Ben's hand went silent. Ben held it up to the light, studying it a moment, before he heaved a sigh and tucked it once more into his pocket.

When he turned to the ring of trees, he found Ivor watching him, having heard the entire conversation. Ben saw a spark of—was it fear?—in his eyes.

Was he afraid of Lady Aisling? Any sane man would be. Or her instructions? Or the crystal itself? Something to think about.

Ben vanished his clothes and burst back into his goblin form. His stretching skin hurt where it had burned, splintering Ben's already shredded temper.

Ivor's energy was building—Ben could feel it in the earth, in the tingle of the ley line.

Shit, the ley line. Ivor, the bastard, was going to tap the magic of the ley line, part of a magical net that encircled the world. Who the hell knew what would happen if he did that?

Best never to find out.

Ben charged at the circle, batting aside the arrows fired at him. Walther really needed to get a new hobby.

Ivor had to know the arrows wouldn't penetrate Ben's flesh, but a good archer could slow Ben down and give Ivor time to do what he wished. Ben couldn't turn aside and whack Walther back to his ancestry without losing the chance to stop Ivor.

He heard Rhianne bellow a shrill cry, saw her turn to skim herself at Walther. Walther let loose arrow after arrow, and Rhianne spun and dodged. She was drawing his fire, Ben realized, so the other goblins and Ben could get to Ivor.

Ben dashed into the circle of trees. At the same time the sky seared with lightning. Thunder crashed, once more shaking the ground.

Ivor turned, sword in hand. "Give her up. You can't win."

"It's not up to me," Ben said. "Rhianne makes her own decisions."

"You know little about Tuil Erdannan women. Or Shifter women, for that matter. Without their mates, they are nothing."

"Oh?" Ben steadied himself while looking for a chance to rip Ivor's head off. "How'd that work out for you and Lady Aisling?"

The rage in Ivor's eyes told Ben he'd scored a point. Lady Aisling was home and safe, while Ivor puttered around the human world trying to kidnap his own daughter.

"What'cha doing in here?" Ben asked him casually. "Cracking open the ley line?"

"Drawing its power into me." Ivor lowered his sword point to the ground. "I will use it to flatten your Shiftertown and this human city, if Rhianne does not come to me."

"Yeah?" Ben hid a qualm. Ivor could do it, he had no doubt. "How about I bounce you on your face instead?"

"Goblins. Always so violent. If you like the earth as much as you say—enjoy it."

Ivor swiped the sword across the grass. A fissure opened in the dirt, widening and lengthening on its own, the ley line shimmering the air.

Ben scrambled backward to keep from falling into the abyss. Ivor had done this exact thing at the park in New Orleans, he realized. He must have been there on the other side of the gate, waiting for Ben to be swallowed so he could grab Rhianne. Except Rhianne had saved Ben, and then Shifter Bureau had slid in, blocking Ivor's way.

Ben never thought he'd be grateful to those assholes, but in this case they'd probably saved his and Rhianne's lives.

Dirt and grass spilled into the crack as Ben readied himself to leap it. He would grab Ivor and throw *him* into the hole, end of problem.

Before he could, a roar behind him made him swing around. Beyond the goblins, who were laughing as they caught Walther's many arrows and threw them back at him, a horde of Shifters headed for them in a full-on attack.

Not adult Shifters, Ben realized as he stared. The cubs.

A lion whose black mane hadn't fully grown led them, along with a fleet Bengal tiger who darted from the lion to their troops and back again. Next to Connor came a half-grown polar bear, his roars occasionally deepening into those of the massive beast he'd become.

Following them were all the cubs of Shiftertown—Jordan as

jaguar, the bears from Ronan's household, lean-legged wolves, and more wild cats. Every cub who'd progressed above baby-hood through those who'd reached their Transition rushed across the green, intent on the enemy.

Ben felt a surge of glee and pride followed swiftly by terror. "No!" he yelled at Connor and Tiger-girl.

Ivor watched the approaching horde with contempt. "Why warn them? They can do nothing against me."

He turned away, swirling his sword to continue his work on the ley line.

The Shifter cubs raced toward them, bounding, roaring, ready to fight. Ivor could obliterate them in an instant, but he seemed in no hurry to do so.

He didn't consider them a threat, Ben realized. Ivor under-estimated them, just as he underestimated Rhianne, and Ben, and everyone else he'd ever encountered.

Ben turned for the cubs. "To me!" he yelled. He'd gather them and lead them the hell away from Ivor and Walther's deadly arrows. "To me, little ones!"

Their yowls of fury and triumph increased. Olaf bellowed the roar of a polar bear who could tear apart his prey with one swipe of his paw.

Thunder answered their shouts, and the crack in the earth widened.

INSIDE THE SILENT STASIS OF THE GLASSLIKE RIPPLES, Tiger heard the voice of the young Bengal, his cub. His body was tight with energy drawn from Ivor's magic, the earth, and the lightning that stalked the skies.

The waiting was over.

Now! Tiger roared and broke his bonds.

CHAPTER TWENTY-FIVE

R hianne, from her swirling height above Shiftertown, watched the thick ripples splinter like glass. Tiger sprang from them in his between-beast form, his roar drowning out the thunder.

The cubs shrieked with delight and rushed for Tiger. Ivor swung around, but his amazement at Tiger's escape did not halt him for long. He gathered his power, the immensity of it touching Rhianne high above him.

No! she shrieked.

Her thoughts flashed to a scene from her childhood, one of the rare times she could recall her mother and Ivor together. They'd been traveling from somewhere Rhianne couldn't remember to her mother's home and had come upon a trade caravan of *hoch alfar* on the road, the slow-moving conveyances blocking their path.

The *hoch alfar* hadn't been warriors or lords or haughty Fae princes, but merchants returning from a market fair, laden with goods.

Ivor, impatient, had risen in his stirrups, called down terrible magic, and obliterated the entire caravan. Men, women, children, horses, dogs, livestock. Dead in an instant, and then they'd shriveled to dust from another blast of his magic.

Rhianne, a child, hadn't been able to banish the horrifying images from her head for decades, and they'd never truly gone.

After that she hadn't seen Ivor much anymore. She'd not witnessed her mother turning him out, but he'd vanished from their lives.

Ivor could kill all the Shifters emerging from the stasis, down to the last cub. He'd imprisoned the Shifters inside the ripples not from any compassion but to save himself having to expend the energy on killing them. He'd come here to take Rhianne—everything else had been unimportant.

The thick stasis field continued to shatter as more and more Shifters returned to view, shaking themselves free.

No! She wanted to scream at Tiger. *Put them back. Keep them safe.*

The Shifters quickly took in the situation—Walther, Ivor, the cubs, Tiger. As one they sprinted toward the advancing cubs, their first instinct to protect the offspring.

Dylan roared for them to halt. Shifters snarled, skidding in the grass, turning back. Dylan's air of command was enough to make them remember their purpose, to defeat the enemy. Only then would the cubs be safe.

Under his barking roars, the Shifters formed up into columns, putting the cubs behind them, and then they struck.

Rhianne screeched her eagle's cry. She sensed Ivor reaching for the deep, nasty magic that would destroy the Shifters. It was difficult magic, but the Shifters were leaving him no choice, in Ivor's opinion. It was him or them.

The cubs didn't stay put. They raced along with the Shifters, their smaller bodies rushing under those of the adults. Tiger-girl, darting ahead, bound in one swift leap over the gap in the earth, landing paws-first on Ivor.

Ivor stumbled back, fighting her with his bare hands. Olaf also jumped the gap and began biting Ivor's boots.

The scene would be comical if it weren't so terrifying. Rhianne dove, wings coming out to slow her as she neared the earth. She righted herself, latched her talons into Olaf's thick fur, and rose with him, carrying him out of harm's way.

Olaf kicked and squirmed, growling his displeasure. Rhianne felt the waves of his irritation rolling to her.

Why'd you do that? I was kicking butt. Put me down!

Rhianne rasped her admonishment. *Cease flailing or I might drop you.*

Olaf at least quieted long enough for Rhianne to circle to the rear of the Shifters and deposit Olaf in front of the giant polar bear Zander, who'd risen to his hind legs to watch them come.

Olaf hopped up to his back legs as soon as Rhianne let him go. *Did you see me, Zander? Did you see me? I kicked butt. And then I was flying.*

Thanks for that, Zander's body language said to Rhianne. He gave her a salute with his giant paw before he turned to round up more of the cubs.

Rhianne winged once more to the front of the fight. She couldn't fly all the Shifters to safety, she knew. She had to kill Ivor instead.

Ivor had managed to get Tiger-girl off him. He must have used magic, because she limped along the far side of the trees, snarling her fury, with Connor circling her, protecting her.

Walther was laughing. His hands moved in a blur as he shot arrow after arrow at the Shifters, happy to have targets he could hit. More than one Shifter went down with arrows in their hides, even as others strove to reach him.

An arrow flew straight toward Sean's mate, Andrea. Sean, who'd sprinted from the circle of trees as soon as he'd been freed, shoved her hard, both of them going down in a spurt of dust as the arrow flew harmlessly past them. Sean lost hold of his sword, which tumbled away from him and imbedded itself, point-downward, in the grass.

A bright light rent the space between the trees, and a tear in the fabric of the air opened. From it stepped another Fae, this one in bronze chain mail and a cloak, long white braids swinging.

He rapidly positioned himself behind Walther and grabbed him by the throat.

"That was my daughter you were aiming at," he declared in *hoch alfar*.

Walther elbowed the Fae but struck the hard links of the mail shirt. The warrior positioned his hands on either side of Walther's head and unceremoniously snapped his neck.

Walther's face went still, and he dropped. Dead.

The warrior dusted off his hands. "I never liked him. Dylan!" he shouted in English. "Come help me clear out the rubbish."

Ivor glared at the warrior—Rhianne assumed he was Fionn, who guarded the Fae gate from the other side. Ivor's expression turned to annoyance, and he pointed a finger at Fionn.

The Fae warrior screamed as electricity suddenly wound through his mail shirt. Andrea, who'd squirmed out from under Sean, shifted to wolf and ran for Fionn. She dragged him from the clearing, using her teeth and claws to rip the mail from his body.

The warrior lay limp, Andrea whining and nuzzling him, Sean bending to tend him.

Ivor stepped back, alone once more.

Lightning struck not far away, the crash of thunder obliterating all other sound. Tiger was roaring, summoning the cubs to him and leading them at a lope away from Ivor. Even Tiger-girl and Connor abandoned the fight, Tiger-girl stumbling eagerly toward Tiger.

Ivor drew magic from the ley line, from the earth, from the air, from the gate, from the storm. He was about to lay waste to the Shifters, and Rhianne had no idea how to stop him.

————

BEN DID HAVE AN IDEA OF WHAT TO DO, BUT HE DIDN'T like it. Rhianne floated over the cubs while Tiger led them to safety. Olaf ran around beneath Rhianne, joyfully growling up at her.

Dylan had the Shifters in formation once more, somehow keeping discipline among independent Shifters who hated to obey anyone.

Ben felt the change in Ivor—he was ready to end this. He wanted Rhianne, and he'd do what he had to in order to capture her.

In spite of Tiger's efforts, Ben knew he couldn't get the cubs away before Ivor struck. The three goblins had joined the Shifters gathering for battle, Darren and Cyril making all kinds of smartass remarks about how they'd torture Ivor. The Shifters, smartasses themselves, growled their agreement.

Rhianne circled back toward Ben, anguish in her cries. She knew what Ivor was capable of better than the rest, and she feared it.

Ben didn't know exactly what the guy could do, but he was plenty worried himself.

Ivor floated a few inches above the surface of the earth. He pointed into the fissure that had stabilized, no longer growing. From it flowed a darkness, thick like mucus, that moved swiftly toward the Shifters.

When it touched paws, the Shifters screamed, jumping and scrambling as though it burned. Darren, unafraid, stepped right into the black ooze, then he too shouted and leapt away.

"It's like acid," he yelled at Ben. "Everyone back."

The Shifters retreated, but Ivor wasn't finished. He drew power into his hands, terrible power that held the stench of death. If he threw *that,* whatever it was, the Shifters would die, and their bodies would be eaten by the dark slime that continued its slow flow toward them. End of Ivor's Shifter troubles.

Ben watched the sky, smelling the ions that bounced around, waiting to bang into each other and ignite into the hottest fire possible. Right about ... *now.*

"Clear a path," Ben shouted.

He sprinted past the Shifters who were in full retreat, leapt over the crack in the ground, and landed on Ivor. The strength of the Tuil Erdannan kept Ivor from going down under Ben's assault, but Ben hadn't intended to knock him over.

Ben grabbed Ivor's arm and thrust the hand that still held the Fae sword straight upward toward the sky.

Lighting flashed down. It burst through the sword, into Ivor, and into Ben, who held the man in his iron hard embrace. Ivor shuddered and screamed, the power he'd held vanishing into dust.

Oh, man, that seriously hurt. Ben slid from Ivor, barely aware of landing facedown on the damp grass.

"Love you, Rhianne," he whispered, and then his world went dark.

CHAPTER TWENTY-SIX

"No!" Rhianne screamed from on high and shot like an arrow across the green.

Ivor climbed shakily to his feet, the black magma that had tried to envelop the Shifters vanishing. Ben had stopped it, but Ben was on the ground, unmoving.

Rhianne felt the mate bond between her and Ben dissolving. That never happened, she'd been told, unless ...

She flapped her wings to move faster. She followed her own shadow on the ground, haloed by the bright sun behind the clouds. A double shadow, she noticed, like a trick of the light. Except the second shadow moved differently from the first.

Rhianne was too grief-stricken to puzzle that through. Wind from the storm buffeted her, threatening to send her straight into the trees as she approached the circle.

Millie reached up with large goblin hands and caught Rhianne before she could get snagged in the branches, setting her gently on the ground.

Rhianne shifted to her Tuil Erdannan form and ran, breath ragged, to Ben's side.

His body shrank, the goblin retreating to Ben the man, his limbs askew, his flesh gray. Rhianne dropped to her knees beside him, but Ben didn't move.

"Come with me." The rasp from Ivor made Rhianne jerk her head up.

Ivor reached a shaking hand to Rhianne. His power was spent for now, but he was still alive, and would regain his strength. While Ben ...

"I can restore him," Ivor said. "Come with me to Faerie, and I will bring him back to life."

"You will keep your filthy hands off him." Rhianne climbed to her feet. "You killed my *mate*, you fucking bastard."

"Your mother never taught you manners. If you stay here, he's dead. You bring him, he can be restored."

Rhianne wavered. She didn't trust Ivor, but he was correct that there were magics in Faerie that could work miracles. Ben was a being of Faerie—perhaps taking him to his native land and laying him on the earth where he'd been born would help him.

But then Ivor would have her, not to mention Ben, at his mercy.

"Screw you," she shouted.

Rhianne attacked Ivor, never mind shifting, never mind magic. She simply went at him, punching and kicking, avenging herself, her mother, the caravan of *hoch alfar* he'd killed because they'd inconvenienced him, the Shifters he'd hurt today.

Ivor struck back. Rhianne dodged and turned, deflecting his blows to serve blows of her own. *Take the energy, redirect it to him.*

Ben had taught her a new way to think, to feel. He'd taught her so much, especially what it was to truly love.

When Ivor regained his strength he would lay waste to this Shiftertown, perhaps this entire human city, and Ben would be no more. Rhianne would not be able to take Ben through the gate in time, if that would even help him.

What to do? She could punch and kick Ivor to make herself feel better, or she could finish this.

Rhianne leapt into the air, becoming the eagle as she spread her arms. She flew the few yards from the circle to Sean's Sword of the Guardian still sticking out of the grass.

Rhianne threw off her eagle form, grabbed the sword, and ran with it to the trees. The sword tingled her palm, but it felt right nestled in it, as though she was meant to wield it.

She halted in astonishment. Inside the circle of trees, Ivor battled with a *second* eagle, who circled and struck with the ease of long practice.

Rhianne nearly dropped to her knees at the realization of who this eagle must be.

She kept to her feet, knowing she couldn't lose her determination now. She raced to Ivor, who continued battling the second eagle.

Rhianne waited for an opening, then thrust the sword at Ivor's chest. "This is for my mate," she yelled.

Ivor caught the blade in a strong hand, redirecting all his magic to keep it from penetrating his body.

The second eagle screeched and dove at his face. Ivor fought him off, but his solid grip on the sword did not move.

Rhianne reached into herself for her Tuil Erdannan magic, searching for something that would infuse the sword with the extra power it needed to finish him. She felt Ivor call up a word of power at the same time. They'd kill each other if they both invoked at this close range, and possibly take out part of Shiftertown.

A hand on hers made her yelp. Rhianne's breath stopped as she beheld Ben, wan-faced, in his man shape, drag himself to his feet, using the sword in Rhianne's firm grasp as a hand-hold.

"Let me help you there." Ben's whisper was weak,

containing the barest trace of his humor. He held up the crystal Lady Aisling had given him for communication, the quartz glittering in the stormy light. "This kinda scares him. Want to find out why?"

Ivor's eyes widened, his grip tightening in desperation. Ben sent him a ghost of a grin.

The second eagle touched to earth and rose into the body of a human male, his face hard, his red-brown hair flecked with gray. He laid a strong hand over Ben's and Rhianne's.

Ben added the crystal, and the three of them sent the Sword of the Guardian straight into Ivor's chest.

Ivor screamed as the magic of goblin, Shifter, Tuil Erdannan, and the Fae magic of the Sword found his arrogant heart and destroyed him.

Ivor writhed, which only drove the sword deeper, then his body began to smoke.

Ben's hand on hers kept Rhianne from recoiling and dropping the sword. She held it firmly on the man who'd terrorized her with his arbitrary viciousness, had driven her mother into another man's arms, who'd destroyed innocents because they annoyed him, and who'd come here to take Rhianne against her will. He'd wanted what Rhianne was so he could expand his own power and feed his ambition, and he'd been willing to kill all the Shifters, including their human mates and their cubs, to do it.

Ivor screamed once more, his skin scorching and crumpling. His clothing was consumed by fire and then his skin and hair, his face last, mouth open in a keening cry.

Rhianne, Ben, and the Shifter stepped back as one as Ivor's body collapsed into ash, which floated down to the green, the storm's calming wind stirring the ashes in silence.

The three stared at Ivor's remains, Rhianne barely aware of the Shifters drifting toward them, or the rain that began to fall.

Ben groaned. He released Rhianne's hand as he slid to the ground, all life going out of him.

"That's it for me," he whispered. "I love you, Rhianne. Always, my mate."

He lay still and ceased to breathe, his heart under Rhianne's frantic hands fluttering to a halt.

"Please try," Rhianne begged.

She clung to Ben's hand as he lay on Liam's big bed, where Tiger had carried him once the battle was over. Tiger had laid him down, pulled a sheet over Ben's bare body, and then pointed at Zander.

"Heal him," Tiger ordered.

"Not that simple, big guy." Zander, who'd resumed his human shape, beads clicking in his hair, touched Ben's lifeless face, his dark eyes filled with compassion. "I can't reach him beyond a certain point. I'm sorry, Rhianne."

Everyone in this room was grieving, Rhianne realized past the haze of pain that filmed her vision. Tiger, Zander, Jaycee and Dimitri, the Shifters who'd arrived from North Carolina, and a few from Las Vegas and New Orleans.

Shifters filled Liam's house and spilled out around it, all of them now in human form, including Rhianne, she having thrown on sweats Carly had handed her, Carly's eyes filled with tears.

Tiger had allowed only a few besides Rhianne and the healers into the bedroom, and those denied camped out in the hall and on the stairs.

These were all Ben's friends. From the Shifter leaders who relied on him, to the women who found him a trusted confidant and supporter, to the men who called him friend and drinking buddy, to the cubs who admired and trusted him.

Everyone loved Ben. The man who'd believed himself alone had touched hundreds of lives, and now they surrounded him to mourn.

"Please try," Rhianne begged Zander once more.

Zander's expression told Rhianne it was far too late. Andrea had put her hands on Ben outside, where he'd lain in the circle of trees, but said she could find nothing inside him that connected. Rhianne wasn't certain what she meant by that, but the look in Andrea's eyes had filled her with anguish.

Zander now laid his hands on Ben's chest and closed his eyes. His mate, Rae, holding her Guardian's Sword, put her fingertips on Zander's shoulder.

Binding with him, Rhianne saw, their magic stirring her own. Rae's Sword of the Guardian rang softly as its magic passed through Rae and into Zander.

Zander began to chant words in a Fae-like language. The Shifters in the room whispered along, except Connor, who only stared numbly at Ben. Tiger-girl stood next to Connor, subdued, her hand in his.

For a long time the chant went on. A soft breeze came through the open window, and with it the sweet sound of wind chimes.

Rhianne's thoughts flashed back to the haunted house. Ben was its caretaker. If he was moved there, would its magic help?

A long journey. Rhianne's heart sank. Could she fly him? she wondered. Did she have the strength to make it five hundred miles without dropping him or damaging him even more?

Zander's chanting trailed off, and he opened his eyes. "I'm sorry. He's already gone. I can't reach him."

Rae met Rhianne's gaze. "Do you want me to do it, Rhianne? Or Sean?"

"Do what?" Rhianne asked, her voice barely working.

Connor coughed to clear his throat. "She means send him to dust with her sword. I don't know if that works on goblins."

"He's of Faerie," Rae said gently. "It should."

"No." Rhianne laid her head on Ben's chest, willing his heart to beat. It remained still, Ben's skin cool. "Please don't," she begged Rae. "Not yet."

"The touch of a mate," Tiger rumbled.

No one explained what he meant. Zander said quietly, "Not sure that will work either."

Rhianne shut them out. She caressed Ben's tattooed arms, thinking of how powerfully they'd held her. He'd given her everything—a place to stay and a shoulder to cry on, showed her new and exciting things, taught her not to fear the beast inside her, taught her how to fall in love.

"I love you, Ben." Rhianne whispered his real name, the syllables flowing from her tongue as though they belonged there.

Millie's voice wafted through the door. "Yes, you do need to let me in, young man." Dylan's growl answered her. At any other time, Rhianne might be amused at Dylan's reaction to being called a young man, but now she could feel nothing.

Rhianne lifted herself from Ben but kept her hand on his arm. "Tiger, let her come."

Without a word, Tiger crossed the room and opened the door. Millie, carrying her handbag, marched in. Her sons peered worriedly around the doorframe, their way blocked once more when Tiger shut the door.

Millie sidled through the Shifters to the bed. "This might not work, dear," she said to Rhianne. "I do not wish to give you false hope. But he is a goblin, and Shifter magic might be useless on him."

"Please." Rhianne sent Millie a desperate look across the bed.

Millie opened her handbag and removed what appeared to

be a small iron bar. Rhianne saw as she brought it closer that it was a statue, about five inches long, in the shape of an upright man, so ancient its features had nearly been worn away.

Millie placed the statue on Ben's chest. She closed her eyes and began a chant. Unlike Zander's smooth, almost musical words, these were in the harsh, guttural language of goblins.

Rhianne felt the magic in the talisman. It was old, so very old, it must have existed long before the Tuil Erdannan. Some historians claimed that goblins were the first race of Faerie, but none knew where they'd come from or how they'd arisen. The earth itself had given birth to them, was the speculation. Goblins were powerful, strange, and connected to the earth like no others.

The jangle of wind chimes came to Rhianne, more insistent now. They sounded exactly like the chimes at the haunted house—Kim or Carly must have hung up a set of the same type.

A whisper that sounded like laughter wove among the chimes. Rhianne thought she felt the ground tremble, though that might simply be her own shaking. None of the others reacted to it.

Outside, rain fell in a gentle patter. Millie continued to chant. At long last, she fell silent and straightened up, though she left the talisman on Ben's chest.

"Old magic," she said. "It is the only relic I brought when we fled Faerie."

She'd carried it from that day to this, Rhianne thought with sudden insight, to help her and her family survive.

The last threads of the mate bond were dissolving, and Rhianne's thoughts scattered with the profound pain of that loss. A part of her had wrapped itself in Ben, and he in her.

The wind chimes became more insistent, the whisper audible in her mind. *Save him.*

I can't. The words wailed inside her. *I'm losing him.*

Rhianne clung to the final strand of the mate bond, let the

music of the wind chimes surround her, and leaned down and kissed Ben's unmoving mouth.

His lips were cold, so cold. Rhianne warmed them with hers and silently repeated the syllables of his true name once more. "Ben," she finished in a whisper. "I accept the mate claim."

Under her, Ben jerked. Rhianne popped up, about to scowl at whoever had shoved the bed, but Ben's body jerked again.

His limbs began to twitch, as though some unseen force controlled them. The thrashing increased violently, and Zander and then Tiger leapt forward to hold Ben down.

Rhianne joined them, lying across Ben's chest, kissing his neck, fearing what was happening to him.

Ben continued to convulse. The iron statue didn't move, as though it was fused to his chest. The wind chimes jangled frantically, but no heavy wind was evident to move them. The rain came down harder, beating on the roof of the porch outside the open window, a rumble of thunder booming in the distance.

Under Rhianne, Ben gasped.

She shot upward, and Tiger and Zander sprang back. Ben's chest rose with a sharp breath, and a flush infused his skin.

Ben's eyes flew open. For a moment, he saw nothing, staring without comprehending.

Then Ben blinked, glanced at those around the bed, and tried to raise his head. He crashed back down to the pillow with a groan.

"Whoa." Ben's voice was a croak. "That was weird. Hey, sweetheart. Did we get him?"

Rhianne, tears flowing, flung herself onto him. She heard the others sigh, relax, sniffle, even sob. The tension of those bracing for grief eased away to rejoicing.

"Yeah, you got him," Connor answered shakily for Rhianne. "Got him and a half."

"That's good." Ben weakly stroked Rhianne's hair. "That other eagle. Was that your dad, Rhianne?"

The man with the red-brown hair and deep brown eyes was outside the room, waiting. Eamon, he'd said his name was. Rhianne nodded at Ben.

"Well, that's something." Ben continued to caress, trying to comfort *her*. "You did it, Rhianne." A tiny note of triumph entered his whisper. "And I heard you say yes to the mate claim."

The wind chimes slowed to a soft shimmering, which matched the mate bond that wove with renewed strength around Rhianne's heart.

"I did," she answered. "I love you, Ben."

"Love *you*, Rhianne." Ben rumbled, and thunder answered him. "My *mate*."

CHAPTER TWENTY-SEVEN

Ben soaked in the sunshine on Liam's back porch, Rhianne squashed next to him on the padded porch swing. Connor sat cross-legged on the wooden deck, close enough to touch Ben and make sure he was really there. Tiger-girl perched on the railing above Connor, watching all with her assessing gaze.

The storm had broken and rolled away as swiftly as it had arrived. Blue sky arched over Shiftertown once more, tattered clouds drifting on a soft breeze. The same air moved wind chimes, which gave off a silvery note.

Funny, Ben never remembered those wind chimes being there before. Maybe Jazz had brought some here from the haunted house.

Rhianne hadn't let go of Ben since he'd woken a few hours ago, which was fine with him. He'd made all the other Shifters go away once he realized he was starkers under the sheet. Embarrassing.

He'd dressed in sweats that were too big for him, with Rhianne assisting. Okay, so they'd spent some time on the bed kissing and caressing. A little crying too, on both their parts. Ben had been too weak to do much more, darn it. He'd had to put in great effort just to reach the porch, but he hadn't wanted to stay in bed.

Millie stepped out from the house, bearing a tray filled with glasses of iced tea. Ben would have preferred something stronger, but decided that this soon after death, maybe caffeine was better than alcohol.

Millie's handbag swung from her arm, such a small thing in which to carry the elixir of life.

She set out iced tea for everyone, including Connor and Tiger-girl, then stood back, tray pressed to her abdomen as she peered at Ben.

"You appear to be on the mend," she announced.

"Hell of a lot better than I was." Ben had known only darkness, thick and strange, for a long time. He hadn't been afraid, just ... unsettled. In all this darkness, he'd seen one slender glow of light beckoning to him. He'd made his way to it, wrapped a hand around it, and held on.

Ben had realized after he woke what he'd clung to had been a thread of the mate bond. It wove around him now and stretched to Rhianne, who was satisfyingly close against his side.

"You wouldn't have died all the way," Millie told him, in a tone that was meant to be reassuring.

"Sure." Ben didn't believe her. He'd certainly felt dead. "What was that thing you put on me? It was heavy." It weighed on his chest until he'd sat up. Millie had caught it before it rolled off the bed.

"I don't know." Millie set the tray on the railing, opened her handbag, and removed the iron statue. Light played on the molded lines, which didn't tell Ben much. "I picked it up when we fled Faerie. It had been abandoned on a vendor's cart. It has always brought my family good luck, sped our healing, things like that. I figured it couldn't hurt to try it on you."

Ben studied the statue, its long shape rounded at one end. He winced. "I hope it's not a ... you know. A personal pleasuring device."

Millie lifted the statue and scanned it in all seriousness while Connor went off into gales of laughter.

"No." Millie dropped the statue back into her purse. "Those are quite different."

Connor's laughter trailed down to chortles, while Tiger-girl watched him in puzzlement.

"Why do you say he wouldn't have died all the way?" Rhianne asked. "Because of the mate bond?"

Millie shook her head. "The mate bond helped, of course, to keep him from drifting too far. But I knew he'd come back. He's the last warrior."

"So everyone keeps telling me," Ben said impatiently. "What does that mean, exactly?"

"It means that you will not perish until the last battle." Millie folded her hands. "Until you've saved your people or lost them entirely."

Whatever the hell *that* meant.

"That's cheerful," Ben said, rubbing his hand over his hair. "Something to look forward to."

Rhianne lifted her head from Ben's shoulder. "How do you know that, Millie? When we first met you, you wanted to kill him."

Millie's lips pinched. "I have apologized for that already. After I went home, I looked you up, Ben, and realized who you truly were. That is why I wanted to meet with you again."

"Looked me up where?" Ben asked in suspicion. "The Goblin Encyclopedia?"

Millie didn't laugh. "The Shifter Guardians have a database they call the Guardian Network. The goblins have a similar one. Except *I* created it. Once we were exiled, I knew goblins would be forgotten, so I gathered every bit of knowledge about our people I had saved and searched for hidden bits of it in this world. When we left Faerie, others grabbed money or family heirlooms. I took manuscripts. Once computers came along, I input all the data for faster retrieval."

"Very resourceful," Ben said with new respect.

"My sons did not think so. They can be ignorant louts."

"But brave fighters." Ben gave her a nod. "Please thank them for having our backs." The goblin boys had gone out to make friends with the Shifters once they'd made sure Ben was truly all right.

"You are welcome." Millie lifted the tray from the railing. "Enjoy the tea." She vanished into the house.

"She is so weird," Ben murmured.

"I think she's wonderful." Rhianne snuggled into Ben's shoulder. "She gave you back to me."

Ben knew that Rhianne and the mate bond had done that, though Millie's talisman had given them a boost.

He kissed Rhianne's hair and held her close, aware of Tiger-girl watching with avid intensity. The wind chimes tinkled, a sound of satisfaction.

———

MANY PEOPLE CAME TO VISIT BEN THAT AFTERNOON AND on into the night. Rhianne kept near him, not wanting to leave him for a moment.

Shifters did what Ben said they always did when disaster had been averted. They brought out music, lights, drinks, and started to party.

Ben, with goblin resilience, felt better quickly, and soon was wandering among the Shifters, beer in hand, Rhianne at his side. Sean had fired up a grill and cooked charred meat he called burgers.

Everyone wanted to pay respects to Ben, greeting him and hugging him, males and females alike. Shifters liked to embrace, Rhianne saw. Which was fine—she liked it too.

The Shifters hugged her as well, congratulating her on the mate bond. "Sun and Moon soon," Connor had said jubilantly. "I love the mating ceremonies."

"He means the little get-togethers Shifters have to make the mating official," Ben explained to Rhianne. "One in full sunlight, the other under the full moon. And then more dancing, drinking, and ... ah ... mating."

Rhianne laughed. "I've heard of the ceremonies." She had a bottle of cold beer in her hand, enjoying the bubbly concoction just as she had in New Orleans. "Are you saying we'll have this mating ceremony?"

"If you want it." Ben stopped her under a tall tree, moonlight dappling his face through the leaves. Beyond them, Shifters milled about the green in human or animal form, chasing each other, dancing, or pairing up and sneaking off into shadows. "Do you want that, Rhianne?"

His eyes held wariness.

Rhianne took his hand in hers. "After all we went through, you have to ask me? Are you afraid I'll want to run back to Faerie, return to the life of a Tuil Erdannan?"

"A goblin in exile can't compete with the glamor of that." Ben kept his voice light, but his trepidation rang through.

She shook her head. "I am not leaving much behind. The astronomy work I did I can do here—I'm eager to see the stars of this world and learn all about them. I can return from time to time to visit my mother and tutor the children I like to help, otherwise ..." She let out a breath. "I took the post in a remote part of Faerie because I was searching for ... I didn't know what. Trying to figure out who I was. You helped me find out who I am in truth, and then helped me deal with it. I never want to go back to that life, that uncertainty. I want to stay here. With you."

Ben stepped closer, his voice quiet. "You mean a happily ever after? Not just happy for now?"

"Happily ever after." Rhianne erased the last bit of space between them. "I want that, yes. More than anything."

While Ben stared at her, stunned, Rhianne leaned to him and kissed him. She took her time, tracing his lips, tasting them, before licking inside his mouth.

Ben started, then he slid his arms around her, strong hands molding her back as the kiss deepened. He'd certainly recovered swiftly.

"I can take happily ever after," Ben said softly when they eased apart. "Can you take it in a house that makes decisions for you?"

"I think we have to." Rhianne glanced at Liam's porch, now lit up in the darkness, the strand of silver wind chimes hanging from it. "Kim says she never bought any wind chimes, and Carly said she didn't know where they came from. I met Jasmine, and she said she didn't bring them either. I think the house helped you."

Ben's brows twitched. "The haunted house that's five hundred miles away?"

"Five hundred miles on a ley line. You've traveled the lines, you said. Distance on them is nothing."

"True ..."

"So why couldn't the house reach its magic to blend with Millie's talisman and the mate bond?" Rhianne traced Ben's lower lip. "I think the house loves you too."

"Aw." Ben feigned amusement, but moonlight glittered on the moisture in his eyes. "It's such a sentimental pile of bricks."

"Everyone here loves you. They've come from Shiftertowns all over the country to make sure you're all right."

"Dylan called them for backup," Ben said as though he believed that.

"He did *before* the fight. Once the fight was over, they stayed, or they kept coming. He didn't call the Las Vegas Shifters. Or the New Orleans ones. Or the North Carolina ones. They arrived to make sure you were okay."

A gruff wolf called Graham, and his sweet mate, Misty, had been waiting outside the house when Ben first emerged. Misty had flung herself into Ben's arms, and Graham had blustered, then pulled Ben into a tight hug. The Lupine had been wiping his eyes when they finally parted.

Then a tall Lupine woman called Kenzie had likewise embraced him fervently, her mate thumping Ben on the back so hard he almost knocked him over.

After that, a young Shifter woman with bright red hair had bounded to Ben, giving him a similarly enthusiastic embrace. When she'd straightened up, she'd bumped Rhianne's shoulder with hers.

"Tell your mom Tamsin said hi."

"I will," Rhianne answered, bemused.

Tamsin had laughed and told Rhianne an exciting tale of how Lady Aisling had helped her defeat bad Shifters and Shifter Bureau and discover her own happily ever after.

"It makes us sort of sisters," Tamsin declared. She'd turned and embraced Rhianne, holding her tightly until her mate, a large Lupine with gray eyes, had pried her away.

Dimitri and Jaycee had come by next with more hugs and congratulations. They'd gone home to retrieve their cub, Lucas, a red-haired, sweet little boy with big brown eyes. Dimitri had held him with incredible gentleness.

Lucas had clasped Rhianne's finger, hard, and given her a wise Shifter look. Rhianne had been instantly smitten, to proud Jaycee and Dimitri's delight.

"You see?" Rhianne told Ben now. "They all love you,"

"Stop it. You're choking me up." Ben sent her a thoughtful glance. "They're pretty happy with you too."

"Yes, because I saved you."

"Not only that." Ben pulled her close again. "You saved all of them from a perilous threat."

Rhianne grimaced. "That I caused. Ivor wouldn't have come here if I hadn't."

"Shifter Bureau sent you here, and anyway, danger always lurks around Shifters. Instead of letting them be slaughtered, you walked in and solved the problem."

"With your help," Rhianne reminded him.

"Yeah, we're heroes." He brushed back a loose strand of her hair. "I love you, Rhianne."

The words were a whisper, but an impassioned one.

"I love you too." Rhianne touched her forehead to his, her heart in her words.

They stood near the ring of trees, which were quiet now, where Ivor had met his end. Inside the ring, the white-braided Fae was speaking with Dylan, a glass of ale in his hand.

"You'll have to burn this ground." Fionn's words wafted to Rhianne. "Any dust from this Tuil Erdannan getting into the soil won't be a good thing. And you don't want any of his followers seeking it as a shrine."

"We'll burn it, then," Dylan said in his low rumble. "Will that mess with the gate?"

"It should not," Fionn answered. "Ivor de Erkkonen was a very evil being, trust me. I tried to stop him when he came to the gate, but he put me into the stasis on my side, as he did to your Shifters. When Tiger broke you free, I was freed as well."

"With a timely intervention." Dylan's voice held respect. "I thank you for your help. Again."

"You take care of my daughter and grandson every day." Fionn lifted his glass. "I think we're even."

Their voices drifted into indistinct rumbles, and Rhianne's

focus moved to two young women, arms linked, who headed their way.

One was Jasmine, the other Lily, the psychic from New Orleans. Rhianne almost didn't recognize Lily, who wore a trim white skirt and a flower-print blouse, a far cry from the flowing, colorful garments she'd sported in the woo-woo shop.

"You remember Lily," Jasmine said with a smile. Jasmine had short dark hair and very blue eyes, her belly softly rounded with the cub she carried.

"Of course they do." Lily unlinked herself from Jasmine and pulled Rhianne into a warm hug. "My cards and crystals told me about some very bad shit going down along this ley line," she said as she released Rhianne. "I called Jazz, she told me what was happening, and I couldn't sit still. I had to come and make sure you were all right." She turned and embraced Ben with as much enthusiasm as she had Rhianne, then stood back and studied him. "You look good for a man who stepped beyond the veil."

"Thank you." Ben saluted her with his beer bottle. "I'm glad to be back."

"What did you see?" Lily asked in frank curiosity.

"Not a lot. I saw the mate bond, and that was pretty much it. I climbed that bond back to the land of the living."

Ben spoke in his usual jovial tone, but Rhianne saw the flash of darkness in his eyes. She slid her hand in his and squeezed it.

"Was that the danger you divined?" Rhianne asked Lily. "The one you warned us about?"

"Hmm?" Lily studied her in puzzlement, then waved an elegant hand. "Oh, no, there's much more danger to come. I'd say what you did here, killing that evil guy, is the beginning."

Rhianne's heart beat faster as she and Ben exchanged a worried glance. Ben was the first to speak. "Can't the big, bad universe give me a day alone with my mate?"

Lily laughed and slid her arm through Jasmine's, who listened with interest. "Of course you can. Sorry, I didn't mean to scare you. I've been doing some research, poking at many things. This danger is coming, but some time from now. You'll have a nice stretch to kick back and enjoy life. And it looks like it will encompass more than just you. I'd say all Shifters will be involved."

Jasmine regarded her friend with raised brows. "We need to talk about this."

"Yeah, we do." She patted Jasmine's arm. "We'll pull out some crystals and have a chat."

Ben relaxed. "Shifters live and breathe danger. Business as usual then?"

"Looks like. For now." Lily's smile warmed her face. "So good to see you two together." Her smiled widened. "I *knew* you were a couple."

Jasmine laughed, and the two moved off, their laughter floating back to them.

"Well, that was interesting," Ben began, but he stopped, his gaze going to the tall, red-haired man who strode toward them, having waited until Lily and Jasmine moved off.

Eamon halted a few feet from them. He studied Rhianne, not in an awkward way, but as though learning her.

"My daughter," he said.

Rhianne swallowed the lump in her throat. She had so many things she wanted to ask him, so many things she wanted to say. The words clogged inside her and wouldn't emerge.

"There will be time," Eamon said, as though guessing her dilemma. His voice was rich, with just the hint of a Scottish accent. "For both of us."

"Since when are there eagle Shifters?" Ben blurted one of the questions in Rhianne's mind.

A smiled tugged Eamon's mouth. He had much quietness about him, the patience of a bird of prey.

"My father was the only one I knew. His father the only *he* knew. The story I was told was that the emperor of the *hoch alfar* wished for a raptor Shifter. One was bred for him. But the other Fae were afraid of what havoc a flying Shifter might wreak, so the project was abandoned. My ancestor apparently escaped with his mate to the human world, to live in secret, and so has passed down the eagle from father to son. And now to daughter."

Rhianne still couldn't speak, so she did the one thing she knew another Shifter would understand. She stepped to Eamon and enfolded him in an embrace.

Eamon stilled a moment before he wrapped his arms around Rhianne, holding her tightly, his arms bearing the strength of his wings. Rhianne felt the love in him, the love of a true father, the one thing that had been missing in her life.

"I couldn't tell you, dear." Lady Aisling came out of the darkness in her gardening clothes and sensible boots, her long hair in braids looped on her head. "I wanted to—so many times —but it was far too dangerous for you with Ivor always hovering in the background. It was all I could do to guard you all your life, encouraging you to go far from home, out of his demesne. You were strong, with my magic in you,.."

Rhianne went to her, her throat tight. Again, many questions swam at her, and she finally focused on one. "How did you and Eamon meet?"

Lady Aisling rested her hands on Rhianne's shoulders, her face holding sorrow and the weight of keeping too many secrets. "I often visited the human world to think. I wanted to leave Ivor, but I was afraid of him—I was so very young still. I met Eamon while I was wandering among the Highlands in summer, and he saw me."

"I was in eagle form," Eamon put in. "I followed her. I'd never seen such beauty."

Lady Aisling's cheeks reddened. "He has always been very

flattering. He revealed that he was an eagle Shifter, and I was intrigued. We had—a passionate fling." She cleared her throat. "When I returned home, I discovered I was pregnant with you. If Ivor had believed the child not his, he would have killed you. And possibly me."

Rhianne nodded. "He would have." She hesitated, glancing at Eamon. "Did you know about me?" she asked him.

Lady Aisling answered. "I told him right away, but Eamon agreed we should not let on about your true parentage unless it became absolutely necessary. He gave me the courage to send Ivor away. That terrible journey in which Ivor destroyed the *hoch alfar* caravan—we were traveling to my home. I hadn't told Ivor of course, but I'd planned to dismiss him once I was on my own territory, where I'd be strong enough to fight him, and I did just that. Ivor had given me plenty of reason, even before that horrible day on the road. My marriage with Ivor had been empty—he'd married me to use me and my magic, he fully admitted. He'd conducted plenty of affairs of his own, so I had no shame about falling in love with Eamon. And Eamon gave me you, the greatest gift I've ever known."

She let out a breath, her arrogance and self-assurance falling away. "I am so sorry, my darling," Lady Aisling said softly to Rhianne. "For all of it."

She drew Rhianne into her embrace. Rhianne held the mother she'd often found so distant, tears springing to her eyes as the pieces of her life fell into place.

The times her mother had seemed to push Rhianne away, she realized now, had been to protect her from Ivor, to not let on to Ivor how much Lady Aisling cherished her daughter, and to prevent him from seeing any hint of the Shifter in her.

Her mother had been keeping Rhianne out of Ivor's focus, to prevent exactly what had happened now—Ivor pursuing Rhianne to use her for his own machinations.

Lady Aisling had been in a tough position—let Rhianne

and Eamon have a loving relationship and risk their very existence, or keep them apart and alive and well.

"Ivor did find out about me," Rhianne said as she released her mother. "He tried to give me to Walther to breed more like me." She swallowed on her revulsion.

"Yes, Ivor had me followed on a trip to Paris not long ago. I visited Eamon there, and Ivor must have put two and two together. I did not know this until he'd helped Walther kidnap you. I was most displeased," Lady Aisling finished with a hint of her usual haughtiness.

"He was there when you didn't answer when I called you with Jaycee's crystal," Rhianne said with conviction. She remembered how angry she'd been, anger she regretted now.

"He was indeed. I was fighting him, and at first, he bested me. Then he forced me to call you, to coax you to come home." Lady Aisling smiled shakily. "I see you understood my code."

"You'd never eat Aunt Freya's pie if you could help it." Rhianne grinned, then sobered. "I wanted to come home anyway, to save you."

"I am very glad you did not." Lady Aisling's crispness began to return. "He might have killed you, and that I could not have borne. I knew that in this world, the Shifters would help you, and Ben would be your greatest protector." A twinkle entered her eye. "I knew that the moment I met him."

Ben listened in surprise. "Is that what you meant when we were out at that trailer in Shreveport?" he asked. "And you said *Perhaps* ..."

"Indeed," Lady Aisling returned. "I knew you'd suit Rhianne. But that was not the time to discuss it."

"Shit," Ben said softly.

"I do thank you for keeping her safe, Ben dear," Lady Aisling said.

"Sure." Ben appeared shaken. "Any time. My pleasure. I mean that with all my heart."

Rhianne's own heart warmed. She pulled her mother close again, giving her a soft kiss on her cheek. "Ivor's gone," she said quietly. "May we be a family now?"

Lady Aisling's eyes filled with tears. "I'd like that."

Rhianne reached out and took Eamon's hand. "I'm glad my mother kept you safe."

Eamon's voice went soft. "It was hard not to be with you, Rhianne. Your mother told me everything about you, everything you did, every honor you took in your studies. She brought me drawings of you and then photographs. I knew all about you, but I never realized how beautiful you would be."

Rhianne gave up on dignity and threw her arms around Eamon. "I want to know everything about *you*. Thank you for coming to help us."

Eamon held her hard, and the Shifter in Rhianne relaxed. This was right. This was family.

When Rhianne and Eamon parted, Lady Aisling slipped her arm through Eamon's, and he clasped her hand lovingly.

"Rhianne is right," Lady Aisling said. "Now that Ivor is no longer a threat, it is time to be a family. There is ample room around my house for you both to fly." She sent Eamon a fond look. "Though I will miss sneaking off to meet you in Paris. There is something about that city ..."

"We can keep the *pied à terre*," Eamon offered. "Will be a nice place for a vacation. You can shop to your heart's content. You as well, Rhianne."

"Aren't you sweet?" Lady Aisling tugged him closer. "You will love it there, Rhianne."

"I'm going to live here," Rhianne announced. "Not *here*, but in New Orleans. With Ben."

Lady Aisling's wise eyes softened. "Well, of course you are, dear. I plan to be at the Sun and Moon ceremonies. And the house will be a convenient respite for when we attend Mardi Gras."

Rhianne burst out laughing, Ben rumbling beside her. It felt good to laugh.

Rhianne still had many questions, but Eamon was right. There would be time. They'd sit on the porch of the New Orleans house, or in her mother's garden in Faerie, and talk about all the things they needed to.

For now ...

Rhianne laced her fingers through Ben's. "Thank you for sending me here, Mother. And for asking Ben to guide me. You were right. I belong here."

Lady Aisling smiled warmly. "You are very welcome, dear. Ah, I see that the Shifters have gathered for dancing." She gestured to the howling, laughing, yowling Shifters who were forming a circle under the moonlight. "I say we join them. I do love to dance."

Lady Aisling embraced Rhianne one more time, her tight arms around her daughter saying more than words could. Eamon, after embracing Rhianne again himself and giving a squeeze to Ben's shoulder, led Lady Aisling away, the two clasping hands.

Ben tugged Rhianne back to him. "You and your crazy family. We're going to have a fine time." He nuzzled her cheek. "I love you, my mate."

"I love you too, Ben." Rhianne's voice dipped shyly. "Mate of my heart. Thank you."

"Hey, it's what I do. Make people happy. This time, I get to make me happy too."

Ben kissed her, the intensity of it strengthened by the mate bond that wound around them. When they eased apart, Ben studied her, his eyes like pieces of midnight, his love clear.

"Now," he said. "Let's go join the knees-up."

Ben started across the green, towing Rhianne behind him, his hand the warm lifeline it had been the first time she'd touched it.

They headed for where Connor cavorted in a series of gravity-defying moves inside the ring of happy Shifters, to Tigergirl's obvious delight.

Rhianne laughed as they ran, her heart soaring as freely as the eagle inside her.

The wind chimes on the porch stirred and jangled, echoing their laughter in the night.

EPILOGUE

Moonlight glowed on the walls of the bedroom in the haunted house, the shadows of rose vines dancing like Shifters at a rave.

Ben was buried inside Rhianne, the mate of his heart, her face soft with pleasure as she lifted herself into his thrusts.

Ben couldn't get enough of her. He closed his eyes and drove on, blocking out all sensation but Rhianne squeezing him, her hands on his hips coaxing him in, her strength exciting.

Ben opened his eyes again, needing to gaze upon her beautiful face, her black-brown eyes, the mass of her red hair spread around them.

"Love you," he whispered. "Love you. *Love* you."

"Love *you*." Rhianne's answer was a groan, and Ben gave up every thought to simply be with her in that moment.

Rhianne tightened around him as she reached her peak, scalding him with her liquid heat. Ben's thrusts grew more frantic as he built toward the same height.

"*Goddess.*" The word tore out of him as Ben came and came.

He continued his thrusts until first Rhianne quieted, then he did. They crashed together to the sheets, kissing and touching, murmuring, nipping. The house let out a little sigh.

The full moon ceremony had occurred last night in the Austin Shiftertown, and Rhianne and Ben had left for New Orleans this morning while the Shifters were still recovering from their all-night party.

The moon, one night past the full, shone down on the house and into the bedroom, surrounding them with Goddess light.

"I love you, Ben." Rhianne traced his cheek, her fingertips light.

Ben's heart overflowed. Rhianne had come into his life so unexpectedly and transformed it just by being her.

"Love you too, sweetheart," he whispered, truth in every word.

He hated to unlock from her but thought he should give her a chance to breathe. Ben rolled onto his back, musing that lying naked with Rhianne was almost as enjoyable as sex with her. Almost.

He laced his hands behind his head. "Now that we're mates, what do you want to do first?"

Rhianne considered. "I don't know. How about finding some shrimp?"

"Is that all you can think about? New Orleans cuisine?"

She propped herself on her side, her fingers lightly caressing his chest. "It was a long trip from Austin. I'm hungry. And that restaurant was excellent."

Ben grinned, everything worth laughing about right now. "Tell you what. We'll clean up, head into town, find some gumbo, and then a club, where we can dance the night away. We can call Jaycee and Dimitri to join us. They're always up for some fun."

"Sounds good." Rhianne's eyes lit with excitement. "Can we do one more thing first, my mate?"

"What's that?"

Rhianne growled and rolled on top of him. She slid herself over his already hard cock and settled down on it. "This," she said.

"I think I can go for that." Ben's words died as the joy of being inside Rhianne took over.

It was a long time before they finished. Rhianne wrapped herself around Ben as they loved each other, her arms strong like her wings. They basked in the moonlight after that, kissing in afterglow, whispering love.

Later they rose, showered, and dressed, mounting Ben's motorcycle as they had that day weeks ago, when Ben had led Rhianne into his strange world. Dimitri had readily told Ben, when Ben had called him, that he and Jaycee would be on their way, and would meet them at the club after Ben and Rhianne had supper.

Ben started the bike, picked up his feet, and roared off into the night. Rhianne, hanging on to him on the back, whooped and punched the air, as Connor had taught her.

Behind them, the haunted house creaked, the wind chimes ringing. It settled down to wait for their return, knowing that Ben and Rhianne would fill its rooms with happiness for a long time to come.

Iron Master

The Last Warrior

Tiger's Daughter

Shifter Made ("Prequel" short story)

ABOUT THE AUTHOR

New York Times bestselling and award-winning author Jennifer Ashley has more than 100 published novels and novellas in romance, urban fantasy, mystery, and historical fiction under the names Jennifer Ashley, Allyson James, and Ashley Gardner. Jennifer's books have been translated into more than a dozen languages and have earned starred reviews in *Publisher's Weekly* and *Booklist*. When she isn't writing, Jennifer enjoys playing music (guitar, piano, flute), reading, hiking, and building dollhouse miniatures.

More about Jennifer's books can be found at
http://www.jenniferashley.com

To keep up to date on her new releases, join her newsletter here:

http://eepurl.com/47kLL

Made in the USA
Monee, IL
24 December 2021

87117871R00177